DETERMINING

POSSESSION

Book #3 of the Connecticut Kings series

Christina C Jones

To God be the Glory...

Thank you so much to everyone who made this book what it is. To Love Belvin for believing in me enough to do this again (and the first time). To the friends and peers who have encouraged me along the way. To my amazing betas who gave feedback that kept me pushing forward. To my family, who dealt with me isolating myself to get this done, and kept me fed and loved on in the meantime.
And, as always, to the readers. Your excitement and support for this project have provided much-needed energy through this whole process (and my whole career) and I can't thank you enough.
Enjoy. ☺

One

Wil

April 2017

    "She ain't sorry – or at least, that was sports news sweetheart Wil Cunningham's attitude just last night when she was captured on video giving the middle finger and plenty of "boy byes" to her – apparently – former fiancé at a popular local club. Beyonce's "Sorry" was the backing track for the dramatic scene, that a witness tells us was sparked by actor Darius Hayward's attempt to pull his estranged fiancé down from dancing on a table. Three days ago, we broke the story of Darius' steamy affair with his "Boardroom" costar, actress Jessica Leigh.

    An anonymous source reached out to us with videos, pictures, and screenshots that collectively, served as irrefutable evidence that Darius – recently honored by Sugar&Spice magazine as their annual sexiest man – is no angel. The news came just two days before the couple, often revered as hashtag, relationship goals, was due to get married. Our source from this video claims that Wil was out with friends and family who had come to New York for the wedding, in an attempt to mitigate her heartbreak over her fiance's dramatic betrayal with drinking and dancing. Someone spilled the beans on where the anti-bachelorette party was taking place, and Darius decided to pop up in attempt to communicate with Wil, who has reportedly not been speaking to him.

7

Her limited response to his attempt was an emphatic declaration that she wasn't thinking about him, and advice that he would be better served by "finding Becky". Sounds like Darius might want to get used to the bitter taste of sour lemonade."

I rolled my eyes at that corny last line and then tapped the screen of my phone to close the browser window where the video had been playing. Of course I knew better than to watch gossip news, but my cousin had sent me the clip, so I couldn't help it. Hell, watching a cheesy video about that particular drama was preferable to living it.

Here I was, doing both.

I navigated my phone back to my music app, where I cranked up the brand-new playlist I'd created during a bout of sleeplessness two nights ago. Once it started up, pounding through the Bluetooth surround system Darius had been *so* adamant about needing, I picked up his golf club again.

Ciara and Nicki Minaj serenaded my angry soul with "*I'm Out*" as I positioned a tiny, frosted vellum box of chocolates inscribed with "*Wil & Darius get hitched*" in the perfect spot on the floor. Cici was just reminding me that I was better than the new chick my "King" was on when I swung, sending the offending chocolates soaring through the air. The package – like the fifty or so before it, broke open, causing the chocolates to land haphazardly among the lighted shelves that contained Darius' prized sneaker collection. A whole damn room full of shoes he valued and cared for and treated like the babies we'd planned to have.

Once I finished my game, I would crank the heat for this room straight to hell.

The thought made me smile.

"Wil! Wil! Girl, I've been looking all over this house for you! What is all this mess?!"

I grinned a bit more at the sound of my mother's voice, looking up from a freshly positioned box of chocolates as she appeared at the door. There was clear concern etched into features that mirrored my own. Enviably thick brows that required weekly trips for grooming to avoid looking werewolf-ish, thick lashes that made the thick brows not seem quite so bad. The kind of lips that been declared "soup coolers" – and worse – on the playground, and that cute nose we shared? Wrinkled.

"What in the world are you doing?" she asked, big brown eyes growing even bigger as she surveyed the room from her place in the door.

I smirked, then swung the golf club, causing her to let out a little shriek as chocolates flew in the air. Picking up another box, I put it into position before I answered. "Working out my aggression."

She snorted as Jhene Aiko began with *Lyin' King*, singing about a man who essentially lied and broke hearts for the fun of it. "Is that what you're calling this?"

"Yes."

"So that flower massacre I passed in dining room... should I assume that was part of your self-prescribed anger management as well?"

I swung again, muttering *"yes"!* as the chocolates from that particular box landed perfectly against a pair of white on white on white suede sneakers Darius had paid a particularly exorbitant amount for. "Yes," I said again, a little louder, this time answering my mother's question. "And you *know* how I feel about flowers."

"I do," she nodded. "Those looked like peonies, so you must have been particularly upset," she mused, stepping fully into the room and brushing aside a few random chocolates to take a seat on the bench Darius used to change his shoes – another reason I should have known better than to agree to marrying his ass.

I shrugged. "I think anger right now is pretty valid, don't you? I mean, you would think he would get the message – leave me alone. But no, he has sorry ass apology flowers with a sorry ass apology note delivered on what should have been our wedding day. So maybe I did shred four dozen peonies by hand, who hasn't?"

Instead of replying, my mother sighed, looking around the room for another few moments before she spoke. "Well... you haven't been speaking to him, or letting him back in the house, so I suppose he's trying to get through to you any way he can. And *before* you say I'm defending him, I most certainly am *not*. Simply stating facts."

"I'm not keeping him from anything," I contended, even though we both understood the shaky veracity of *that* claim. "Just because I changed the code for the gate and called and had his name removed as an authorized person with the security company doesn't really mean *that* much. If he was really about that action, he would figure it out."

She raised a single eyebrow. "But the security guards know the code, and know *him* - yet no one is letting him in. You have nothing to do with *that* either?"

"If they took sides, that's not my fault. They love me. Everybody that matters does… except, apparently… the man I almost married."

A harsh sigh burst from my lips after that and I shook my head, grabbing another box of chocolates from the plastic bin they were stored in. I was barely halfway through, and my shoulders were starting to ache from swinging the golf club.

Maybe I should just dump the rest and call it a day.

Feeling my mother's gaze against my back, I turned to find her staring at me, and lifted an eyebrow. "What?" I asked, and she straightened a little, resting clasped hands atop crossed legs in that uniquely Carla Ann Cunningham way that always made me question my manners.

But there was no scolding, only a slight raise of her shoulders as she leveled me with a steady, kindly gaze. "Nothing, I guess. I think I assumed your statement about Darius was going to be followed by tears. I was just waiting."

I laughed at that. A deep, hearty laugh that turned the kindness in my mother's eyes to concern for my sanity as I straightened up, clutching my stomach. Looking her right in the face, I shook my head. "No. Absolutely not. I *refuse* to cry over him. Haven't shed a single tear yet, and don't plan to. *Ever.*"

My mother's deep, knowing sigh set my teeth on edge. That universal sound of *oh, just you keep living* was all too familiar, and as usual, ill-timed. Three days ago, my world had been turned upside down. I wanted to stay firmly rooted in my anger, strong in my conviction that this man, this situation, would not break me, wouldn't bring any tears from my eyes.

Of course, if they did… I would've been justified.

Three days ago, I was happy.

I was just days away from being Mrs. Darius Hayward, and we were going to celebrate after in the most major turn up possible. Aunts, uncles, great-grands and cousins were starting to filter into town, with my mother's home serving as central station. My phone was blowing up with delivery and vendor confirmations, and the working out of last minute details.

10

I was over the moon.

We were taking one of the last moments of quiet we would have together until after the wedding. My man liked fried chicken, macaroni and cheese, yams, and collards, so that's what I was cooking for him. He didn't stay in the kitchen to keep me company while I cooked, but I didn't mind that. I had the TV blasting some trashy gossip news while he was upstairs in his ManCave™, or maybe smelling the leather in his sneaker room, which was right beside it.

I laughed when his name came from the TV. Rumors and fake scandals came with the territory, and I wasn't the slightest bit concerned. The lies about he and Jessica were nothing new, and they were ridiculous. The woman had hugged me, told me she watched the show, gushed over my engagement ring. Shaking my head, I'd gone to the wall and pressed the intercom button for upstairs. "Hey babe," I giggled, knowing my voice was echoing through the whole second floor of the home we'd shared for nearly two years, to my mother's chagrin. "They're talking about you again. Apparently, they have "undeniable evidence" about you and Jessica now," I laughed.

They didn't have anything. She was his coworker, nothing more.

I took my finger off the button and turned to look at the screen.

His coworker that he'd supposedly been sexting.

They showed the screenshots, like those couldn't be faked.

His coworker he'd supposedly been sending pictures of his dick, with downright filthy captions. They showed those, with the naughtiest parts blurred out, like it couldn't have been pictures of *anybody.*

His coworker he'd supposedly been screwing long enough to have a whole playlist worth of clandestinely shot sex tapes with. They couldn't really show any of those, but assured the audience that it was her, and it was him.

I took my eyes away from the TV screen long enough to look up at where Darius had come down the stairs, and was staring at the screen too. There was tension in his shoulders, anger in his curled fists, and when he turned to look at me, fear in his eyes. Fear, and… guilt.

The stick of butter I'd been holding – I didn't skimp on the butter in *my man's* yams – fell from my hands and hit the floor with a wet thump.

It *was* him.

He didn't even bother denying it. After years of denying that anything was going on with the woman... this time he didn't. This point, three days before I was set to devote my life to him, *that's* when he decided there had been enough lying.

Only because he couldn't anymore, when there was video, and pictures.

So, no.

There would be no tears.

"You know he had the nerve to have special temperature controls installed for the room? *Just* this one." I tossed down the golf club and grabbed handfuls of chocolate boxes, opening and spreading them throughout the shoes to make sure they *all* had their own special treat. "To protect the leather, he said." Once I was done, I turned back to my mother, who'd been silently watching.

"You know he's going to sue you about these shoes, right?" she asked, a question that made me shrug.

"If he does, his judgement can come out of whatever I'm awarded in my countersuit for emotional pain and suffering."

I walked up to the temperature control pad and cranked the green numbers as high as it would let me, then motioned for my mother to follow me out. She shook her head about it as I used my phone to turn the music off, then closed the door behind us.

"I feel *so* much better now." I told her as I headed down the hall. Her hand on my wrist stopped me, and she gave me a little tug intended to make me turn around. But I didn't want to. She tugged me again and I turned around anyway.

"Do you *really*?" she asked, looking me right in the eyes. "What are you doing, Wil? Trying to hurt him because he hurt you?"

I swallowed the lie that I wasn't hurting, and averted my gaze. "Maybe."

"Don't." Her reprimand was firm, but not unkind. "Let this be the last move you make that's intended to hurt him back, because I promise you baby girl – there is *only* more pain down that path."

I pulled in a deep breath through my nose, letting it filter back out before I shook my head. "He humiliated me, Mama. I'm out here with my face splashed across gossip blogs and entertainment news looking like a fool because I trusted him!"

"And the *best* thing you can do for yourself now is to not let him see you sweat. You want to hurt, scream, curse, cry, baby girl *do*

12

it. But when he, or a camera sees you? Your head had damn well *better* be high. No more of these video clips, or destroying his property. You need an outlet, you get yourself to a track or a boxing ring. You understand me?"

I scoffed. "So he just gets let off the hook, and that's okay with you? He gets to betray and embarrass me with no repercussions while I pretend to be the bigger person?"

"No repercussions?" My mother laughed, and shook her head before she raised her hands to cup my face. "Sweetheart... you were always the best thing that happened to that man. Anyone would have been lucky to be able to claim you as theirs, and now he has lost that opportunity. Trust me, my love. He will see you whole and happy without him, and it will tear him up inside."

I chewed at the inside of my lip, trying my best not to give in to the heat building in my cheeks, and the tears pricking the corners of my eyes. It wasn't until I felt them subside that I shook my head. "If I was so good to him, good *for* him... why?"

My mother's expression softened to a wistful smile. "Sweetheart... he probably can't even answer that for himself. But I can tell you this – it's about *him.* Not *you.*"

She was my mother. That was what she *had* to say, to attempt soothing her daughter's broken heart. Instead of arguing, I just nodded, knowing I really didn't have the energy for anything else.

"Have you eaten?" she asked. "Or slept?"

I shrugged. "I'm fine, mama."

She let out a shoulder-heaving sort of sigh that made it clear she knew the real answer – no. But I didn't have the heart to say I hadn't eaten because the intense betrayal I felt made my stomach queasy, or that because I hadn't been able to help myself, and had found the sex tapes online, now I couldn't close my eyes without seeing Darius screwing another woman.

"Get yourself cleaned up," she told me. "And pack a bag. I'm taking you home, and you can stay with me and dad until you find a new place, okay?"

Again, I just nodded.

It hurt like hell to think about it, but the truth was, I didn't really want to be here. Yes, this had been home for me and Darius, the house we bought together, the house I thought we'd eventually raise kids in.

13

Now, being here made my skin crawl.

Every inch of this house was permeated with him.

So he can have it.

Keep your head held high.

That was a lesson my mother had drilled into me from a very early age. Through middle-school track meets and beyond, win or lose, no matter what, I was never supposed to "let my crown slip", not in public.

It was a lesson I took to heart.

So much so that that it was something I became lauded for – professionalism and grace, being a good sport. Even when I was privately seething, I could put on a warm smile and tell a joke, shake hands with a conniving opponent, keep my cool in tough interviews. This was no different – or at least, I was trying my very best to convince myself of that as I walked onto the set of *"From the Sidelines"*, the sports talk show that held one of WAWG's prized timeslots.

The greetings were warm from everyone I passed – cameramen, producers, crew. They acknowledged me just like usual, and I greeted them back in the same way, as if nothing had happened. But I could see the sympathy in their eyes, feel the *"I'm so sorry"* and *"I can't believe he did that to you"* and *"well, it's his loss"* just dying to spring from their mouths. There were other sentiments though, ones no one would express out loud to me.

She must not be good in bed.

Maybe she can't cook.

I wonder what she did to make him cheat on her.

And hell… honestly, I wondered too. But I still managed to keep a smile on my face and kind words on my tongue. I was at work. This was my job. Even though the only thing I really felt like doing was taking the last of Darius' golf clubs to the windows of his matte

14

black on black Tahoe, my usually sunny disposition was where my *"America's Sweetheart"* reputation had come from.

I'd already lost my pride to him – I wasn't losing *anything* else.

"Wil, what on earth are you doing here?"

I stopped on my way into the green room for a cup of coffee to see Connie, one of WAWG's execs, hurrying my way. She was followed in close succession by Sarita – the bad cop of their duo. Together, they were the HBIC around here, even though they weren't "supposed" work directly on *From the Sidelines*. I wasn't surprised to find them prowling around though – instead of delegating and sitting back like other execs, they were always putting their noses in something, and honestly becoming harder and harder to work with.

"I'm here to work," I said brightly, in a tone that gave the impression I had no idea why that was in question. All present parties knew I did.

Sarita cleared her throat. "You don't think you might need... a little time? You had a rather eventful weekend, and you were initially supposed to have this week off. For your honeymoon."

"That's very true," I responded, squaring my shoulders. "But, since I am obviously *not* in Bali right now, I felt it would be wise of me to continue my life as normal, instead of wallowing. Any other Monday, I would be here. Besides, it's draft week. I shouldn't leave my cohost to handle it by himself anyway."

She snorted. "After you compared the combine to the slave trade, I'm sure he was probably relieved by the idea of covering the draft alone."

I ran my tongue over my teeth, taking a second to choose more careful words than I wanted to. "Ah," I smirked. "But isn't that why our ratings are what they are? Hard-hitting analysis, delivered with a smile?"

"Is that what you think it is?" Sarita asked with a sneer, but before I could respond, Connie cut in.

"Of course it is," she said, with a dismissive wave. "If you're sure you're up to it, we're glad to have you, but please don't feel like you have to. Your emotional health is important to us, but if you need more time..."

I smiled. What she was *really* saying was, *"Men don't watch our show to see you crying on air, so if we put you on, you better be ready to talk sports like a man, and smile and show a little cleavage while you do it."*

"I'm up to it, I promise," I told her, adding a reassuring nod for good measure. "Aren't I always?"

Neither of the women seemed that convinced, but it wasn't as if they could really tell one of the stars of the show "no" about going on, not without it turning into a thing.

Connie and Sarita hated *things.*

"Fine," Sarita said finally. "But we'll be watching."

With that "warning", they left me alone, and I shook my head as I continued about my business. Coffee, and then to my dressing room for wardrobe, makeup, and hair, where my stylist fussed over the fact that instead of my usual press, my hair was in its natural state.

That had been a *screw you* to Darius, who preferred it to be sleek, and straight. Not that I'd ever given his opinion on my hair too much weight, but for the audience that our show pulled, the network preferred the straight hair as well.

So maybe my natural coils were a *screw you* to them as well. I wasn't really in the mood for complaints.

As soon as he pulled out a flat iron, I nixed the idea, insisting that I wouldn't wear it straight. He mumbled under his breath about it the whole time, but I wasn't concerned about that. When he finished with it, my goddess braid updo was on point, and that was all that mattered.

The wardrobe stylist put me in a chic, slim-fitting pantsuit that made me feel like a badass, and by the time the makeup artist was done with me, I actually felt halfway human – a stark difference to the preceding days.

A knock sounded at the door, and a moment later one of the production assistants, Ellie, stuck her head in the door. "We're ready for you on set Wil," she told me, her normally perky voice holding a distinct note of pity. "Live in twenty."

I nodded. "I'm on my way."

Two minutes later, I was taking a seat in my chair, and makeup and hair were all over me again, making last minute adjustments to what the camera, and America, would see. A few minutes later, my costar ambled onto the set, and my first real smile in days blossomed on my face.

16

"What are you doing here?" he asked, dropping his heavy hands onto my shoulders for a squeeze before he moved to his own chair, which barely accommodated his solid frame.

"Why do people keep asking me that as if I'm not the cohost of this show? And a little birdie implied you may be disappointed that I'm here today. What's up with that?"

One of Ramsey's eyebrows shifted up, and then he frowned as a makeup artist went after him. He'd always hated their insistence on it, and always fought them off.

"Not a damn thing. Who told you that lie?"

"You know who."

He grunted. "Yeah. Anyway – I like the hair. That's fly."

"Thank you. So is your suit."

But that was no surprise. Ramsey was habitually fly, and today was no exception. The rich, dark navy of his suit popped against his caramel skin, and teal and lime accents added modern flair without making it "flashy". Unlike me, Ramsey dressed himself for the show, and still managed to be better dressed than I ever felt.

"Thank you," he said, running a hand over the thick, well-nourished hairs of his beard. "But seriously…" He leaned in, looking me in the eyes as production assistants and the like cleared the set. "What are you doing here? I expected you to need some time or something." Under the desk, out of the view of the cameras, he put his hand on my knee, and squeezed.

I covered his hand with mine and squeezed back. "No. What I need is to *work*."

"Alright everybody," Tyrell, our technical director called out. "In your places. We're going live in ten, nine, eight—"

I released my hold on Ramsey's hand and scooted away from him to line my chair up on my mark, and put a bright smile on my face.

"four, three, two—"

"Hello everyone," I started our standard show greeting. "As always, thank you for tuning in. I'm Wil Cunningham, and over there is my handsome cohost, the ever-stylish Ramsey Bishop, and we're here to give you what you didn't know you missed *From the Sidelines*."

Beside me, Ramsey chuckled. "What they didn't know they missed, really?"

I shrugged. "Sometimes I have to put a little ad-lib on it, you know? Shake things up a bit, make it more swaggy."

"I'm always on board with added swag, so I'm not complaining, but you forgot something in my greeting."

A smirk spread over my lips. "I already reminded the people you were fashionable, and I was *sure* to give them your name."

"Ah, but it's been a minute since we reminded them that I rushed for twenty-six hundred yards my last season in the NFL, breaking a record that had been held since 1984, and hasn't been topped since," he said, popping his collar as he grinned at the camera.

"Okay, okay," I nodded. "But if we're talking about record breaking, we'll have to get into the ones I *smashed* in the 100 and 200 meters for Olympic Gold, and I don't think y'all are ready for that, sorry. I just don't. You're not."

Ramsey grinned. "Are you stunting right now?"

"Just a little," I said, raising a hand to show the camera my pinched fingers, and he laughed.

"You're right, we're not ready. But you know what we *are* ready for?"

"I'm going to guess it's the highlights from last night's game four between the Celtics and Bulls," I mused, and playing along, Ramsey nodded.

"You would be right."

"So let's get into it."

For the next forty minutes, we went through various highlights and analytics, sprinkled as always with plenty of laughs as we played off of each other. Peace was a feeling that had been hard to come by since the day of that gossip report, but here on this soundstage, bantering back and forth with Ramsey about sports... this was blissful.

"It's one of my favorite times of the show," Ramsey said, relaxing back into his chair. Somehow, he didn't look slouchy, just comfortable.

"That's because you're a sucker for any type of feel-good story. You can't help it," I teased, and he grinned in response.

"I'm not even going to try to deny that, I'm just going to take us right into "*Off the Clock*", where we talk to you about the good things happening in the sports world – after the final whistle."

"Okay, so what's up first? Tell me something good."

"Well, as you know, the second installment of Trent Bailey's football camp wrapped up last week in New Jersey. Trent is the head quarterback for the Connecticut Kings, who, due to a shake up in the team roster, made his comeback last season after having been away from the game because of trouble with the law. He and wide-receiver Jordan Johnson brought the Kings back from a season that started out looking like an impending disaster, taking them all the way to the Super Bowl. Now, Trent has been giving back to high-schoolers in both Connecticut and New Jersey, helping them focus their energy into something productive – football."

"I'm really, really glad to see that, especially from someone like Trent, who could have allowed an irresponsible, costly mistake to turn him into a "what not to do" story for these kids with dreams of being in the NFL. Instead, he's not allowing what could have destroyed him to take up residence in his legacy. Yes, the jail time will be there, as part of his biography, but I have a feeling it's going to be outweighed by what he did *after*. It really is a helluva comeback story."

"Yes, it is," Ramsey answered, in a distinctly wistful tone that I made a note to ask him about later, once we were off the air. "And I was honored to have our request for access approved, so that I could see it with my own eyes. Trent – and Jordan, too – you can tell that they absolutely believed in those kids. This wasn't just some "good PR tour" thing, they genuinely cared about giving those kids an outlet other than running the streets."

"Which is exactly the type of heart that actually does good in the world. When can we see it?"

Ramsey grinned. "After draft week."

"How did I know you were going to say that?" I laughed. "In any case, it sounds amazing, and we're excited to see what you've put together." My eyes found the teleprompter, searching out the next item. This segment was constantly evolving, down to the minute sometimes if news broke while we were on the air.

"Our next item is pushing the boundaries of "sports" news a little bit," I read from the on-screen script, grateful that I didn't have to make anything up. Beside me, I felt a change in energy from Ramsey, but couldn't look up to see what the problem was. "But the producers, crew, and entire staff here at WAWG and *From the Sidelines* want to offer a warm congratulations to our very own—"

Ramsey nudged my foot under the table at the same time I realized what I was reading. Behind the teleprompter, people were scrambling, trying to figure out what was happening. My eyes skipped ahead, silently absorbing the rest of the message.

...want to offer a warm congratulations to our very own Wil Cunningham on her recent nuptials to network television's hottest young CEO, Darius Hayward, star of "The Boardroom" which makes him part of the WAWG family as well. We wish you all the best.

The screen blinked, and something else came up. Ramsey – Thank God – had enough presence of mind to take over, while I plastered a smile on my face and pretended to pay attention.

What the hell was that?!

I mean… I knew what it was, but still. I knew the prep work for each episode sometimes happened days and days in advance, with items being put in as placeholders, so… I was answering my own question.

Someone had forgotten to take it out.

I wasn't even supposed to be here today – that script was something they'd put in for Ramsey, even though he probably would have ad-libbed. It was sweet, that they'd wanted to be sure to acknowledge me, but… damn.

In the middle of my first moment of peace, where I wasn't thinking about the troubles of personal life was really, *really* bad timing for an inadvertent reminder.

Somehow, I made it through the rest of the show. I managed to brush it off enough to – hopefully – not be painfully awkward, but as soon as we were clear, I practically snatched off my mic, and rushed back to my dressing room.

The staff was to intuitive enough not to mention it.

They had to know I was bothered, because of my lack of my usual demeanor. The talking, laughing, joking I usually did as they helped rid me of the makeup and clothes and hairpins was nowhere to be found. Thirty minutes later, I was back in my yoga pants and jacket, with my hair wild and face scrubbed clean.

I should be on my honeymoon right now.

That thought kept playing in my head, even after the door had closed behind the last person, leaving me in the room alone. Wondering what I would be doing right now if Darius hadn't cheated was a given – I would be happily married to him. But… what if I'd simply never found out? What if she'd waited a month, a year, before she decided to spill the beans?

Would he ever have told me on his own? If I'd gotten pregnant with our first child, would the guilt have eaten him up so much that he couldn't hold on to it any longer?

Would I have been less unsuspecting? Once I was his *wife*, not his girlfriend, his fiancé, would the ring and the title have given me better insight? Would I suddenly know better than to believe him when he looked in my eyes and said, *"Babe, come on. I know you don't believe that shit. They lie about everybody fucking everybody. It's just part of this life."*

Had he always given such roundabout answers? Did he ever blatantly, specifically say, *No, I'm not screwing Jessica"* or was it always, *"man, these tabloids are always lying"?* I shook my head, not wanting to allow my thoughts to travel down that path, but they were already barreling away from me, at high speed.

How stupid could I be?

There were always signs. *Always* signs that something was up, that something had changed. Maybe I ignored them, maybe I missed them, or maybe... maybe it had just been naïve of me.

Like he said... it was part of this life.

A knock at the door startled me so badly I clutched my chest. After a deep breath, I stood to go answer it, ignoring the continued buzzing of my phone – concerned friends and family who'd probably seen the live broadcast of the show.

I opened the door to find Ramsey draped in my doorframe. He'd changed too, and was in a dark gray Henley and jeans instead of his suit, but somehow looking just as well-dressed. He didn't wait for an invitation before he ambled inside, and I closed the door behind him. I turned to face him as he pushed his hands into the front pockets of his jeans.

"That was... fucked up." I nodded. I didn't have to ask to know he was referring to me almost reading the wedding announcement. "I'm sorry."

"You didn't write it. You didn't forget to remove it. It's not your fault."

"Still. If it makes it *any* better, there was supposed to be a picture of you and him on the big screen behind us. That wasn't there, and the announcement wasn't on the ticker either. It just… somehow didn't make it out of the script," he shrugged.

"That does make me feel slightly better, actually. Thank you for that."

One of his hands came out of his pocket to stroke his beard. "Not a problem. How are you holding up?"

"I'm managing."

"You never responded to my text."

For about half a second, I frowned, but then I remember the text in question, and smiled.

"Do you want me to kick his ass? – R. Bishop"

I'd gotten it the same night the news broke, but had been in no position to answer then. In the chaos of everything that had happened since, it slipped my mind. This was our first time talking since then.

Now that we weren't on air, where I was paid to look happy, my smile felt foreign enough to make the corners of my mouth itch. I was heartbroken, angry, embarrassed – I wasn't supposed to be *grinning*.

"So… is ol' boy keeping his teeth, or not?" Ramsey pushed, and I forgot my musings about not smiling long enough to laugh.

"Um… let's put a pin it for now."

Ramsey shrugged. "Okay. Will do." Neither of us said anything for several moments, but then he came closer, enough to grab my hand, threading his fingers through mine. "I…" he met my eyes, and I could tell he was struggling with what to say. His Adam's apple bobbed as he swallowed. "I'm sorry he hurt you like this, Champ."

"So am I," I replied, because… I didn't know what else to say. His grip on my hand tightened for a second, a gesture of comfort, or reassurance, or *something*… but I shook my head. "I… I just want to understand. Was it something I did, or didn't—"

My words died on my lips, muffled by his body as Ramsey pulled me into an embrace. "Don't do that shit," his voice rumbled in my ear as his solid arms closed around me. I buried my face in the space between his neck and shoulder, hoping the pressure would help me fight off what I'd been trying to avoid.

It didn't.

Hot tears started pouring from my eyes, and Ramsey didn't even flinch. I tried to grab onto the anger that had been sustaining me for the last several days, but I couldn't. The sorrow I'd been holding off consumed me abruptly, like an eclipse. Ramsey's hold around my waist simply grew more firm, supporting me as I released deep, energy-draining sobs onto his shoulder.

"I'm sorry," I said, sniffling as I pulled back, after several long minutes had passed. "I'm soaking your shirt, and getting you all snotty."

He laughed, and shook his head before he wrapped me in another quick hug before he released his hold, taking a half-step back. "You're good, Champ. Seemed like you needed to let it out."

"Yeah," I nodded. "Probably so."

"You gonna take that break now? Or you're going to be hard-headed, and come in tomorrow?"

I sucked my teeth as I wiped my face with the backs of my hands. "You already know the answer to that. Actually… I need my morning session."

His eyebrow shot up. "You sure about that?"

"Another question you already…"

"Right. I'll see you tomorrow."

"Sure will."

Shaking his head, Ramsey laughed at me again, then reached out, grabbing my shoulders. "Hey… seriously though. If you need anything…"

"I know."

He nodded, and dropped his hands. "Okay. Well… I'm headed out. Gonna drive up to Bridgeport and kick it with the fam, but I'll be back in time to pick you up in the morning. You're at your parents place?"

"Yeah, until I find something."

"Cool. See you at six."

"Okay. And… " I pushed out a deep breath. "Thank you for…"

"I've got you."

He gave a salute type of gesture as he headed out, closing the door behind himself. I sat down for a moment, then immediately got back up, gathering my phone and purse.

Now that I'd let *those* tears out, more were sure to follow.

I needed my mother.

two

RAMSEY

The drive was tedious, but necessary.

Maybe I'd grown too used to walking, to car services, whatever. Ways to get around where I could distract myself with whatever was happening on my phone. The drive from New York City to Bridgeport provided no such thing.

With my own hands on the wheel, for that hour and a half, I was forced to… think. Not that there was anything inherently wrong with thinking, of course, but thinking led to memories, and memories led… to a place I wasn't really ready to be.

Not now.

Not… yet.

For now, distraction was much easier.

I was passing New Rochelle when blessedly the phone rang. My left thumb tapped the button on the steering wheel that would pick the call up through the car's Bluetooth, not even bothering to glance at the display to see who it was. I'd take a call from pretty much anybody to get myself out of my head.

"Bishop," I answered, and was immediately met with a familiar laugh that made me shake my head.

"Whaddup bwoi?" Jordan asked, in a fake accent so terrible I wasn't even sure what he was trying to emulate.

"Not shit. Headed up to kick it with the fam."

"On a Monday?"

There was obvious surprise in his tone, and I got it. I lived in New York, worked in New York. Even though the trip was short, it was still out of state, and something normally reserved for the weekends I was otherwise unoccupied. A late trip on a Monday just to turn around and be back early Tuesday wasn't exactly the most sensible thing.

But…

"Yeah," I told him, easily maneuvering my truck around the slow-moving car in front of me. "My aunt, Phylicia… my mom's sister. She called and asked me to come up. *Insisted,* actually, so… you know what it is."

Jordan chuckled. "Yeah, I do. Gotta keep the women happy. You good with all of that though? I know *I* would still be fucked if—"

"I'm good bruh, yeah," I said, cutting him off. "What's up with you, did you need something?"

"Not really. Just hitting you up to let you know I talked to Nicki about the special you wanted to do for your show, showed her the film you sent from Trent's minicamp. She's into it, but you know what she wanted to know, right?"

"Why was I pitching it to the Kings."

"Smart man," Jordan answered, and I nodded.

It wasn't an unreasonable question, since the entirety of my career in the NFL had been spent with the team I was drafted into. I'd spent some of the best years of my life there, remaining until personal circumstances forced my hand.

But it wasn't home.

Connecticut was.

The Kings had always been my hometown team, and as such, even after particularly ugly games against each other, I consistently got nothing but love. When they lost, I *felt* that shit, even when my team was the one delivering defeat. That Super Bowl last year?

Whew.

I'd been so fucking proud.

I wanted to do a special about the Kings for the simplest of reasons – I was a die-hard fan.

"I already explained it all to her though," Jordan continued. "She's going to put a bug in Eli's ear about it. I'll let you know when I have anything else."

"Appreciate it man."

"No problem – aye, you'll be at the wedding, right?"

"TB and his girl? Yeah, I'll be there. Gotta find a plus-one."

On the other end of the line, Jordan made a disbelieving sound. "Nigga *please*, go on and pull out that pussy rolodex and pick one out, stop playing."

"Relax," I chuckled. "You know that's not even my style… anymore."

"Yeah, I'm fucking around," he conceded. "You bringing Lena though, right? Nicki was telling me something a few months ago about y'all being out together, so I figured…"

I pushed out a sigh through my nose, and shook my head. "Nah. That's done."

"Oh. Well… anyway, I asked because Eli will be there himself, and I can make an introduction for you."

"That's what's up. I would appreciate that man."

We spent a few more minutes on the phone before we hung up, and silence blanketed the car again. Common sense provided that I could've turned my music back on, but for some reason I couldn't make myself do it.

My mind was too focused on the mention of Lena.

Dodged a goddamn bullet with that.

There had been a moment, a few months back, when I thought things could maybe be… different. Thought *she* could be different.

I was wrong – very wrong.

Lena was the same damn girl she'd always been, but our story wasn't meant to be a Jordan Johnson – Nicole Richardson fairy-tale rekindling. Lena McBride thought she was doing the hood a favor by dating me back in college, and my dumb ass had believed it too.

I didn't suffer from that same delusion now.

Shaking my head, I went ahead and turned my sound up in the car, blasting mind-numbing music mind-numbingly loud until I pulled into Bridgeport.

Home.

This was where I was born and bred, in a part of the city that was often named as an area to avoid. I'd learned to navigate though.

27

Kept my head down, stayed away from the gangs, focusing on what would keep me from being absorbed by my surroundings – school.

That other shit? My mother wasn't playing that.

Call it a cliché, but I was determined to pull myself out of the hood. I did okay in school, but there were never delusions about me becoming an engineer, or a doctor. That just wasn't my lot in life. I was good at basketball, but I wasn't tall, and my solid frame was better suited to something else - Football.

I gave my high school the best running back they'd ever seen. That paved the way for being scouted onto a college team that had power and money behind it. And it didn't hurt that Blakewood State University was historically Black. That meant something to my mother, and her influence taught it to mean something to me.

Her influence taught me… everything.

People called both of us stupid for not going into the draft as soon as I could. *What if you get hurt? What if a better player comes along?* Blah, blah, blah.

I wanted my damn degree.

So I got it.

And still went first in the draft.

Running backs weren't getting twenty-million dollar contracts left and right like wide receivers or quarterbacks – *especially* not on the first contract. But it was enough to do what I'd set out to do – get my mother someplace safe, where she didn't have to worry about getting her windows shot out, and I made that same thing happen for a few other select relatives too.

The flipside of that was the misconception that I was BOR – Bank of Ramsey. All of a sudden, my father's side of the family wanted to pop up with their sudden pride and regret that they hadn't done a goddamn thing to assist my mother in the conspicuous absence of my father.

I shut that down.

For better or worse, even though I lived in New York now, Bridgeport was home. Driving through the familiar intersections, passing familiar sites – I used to live for the moments when I had the time and energy to make this trip.

Now, it was all bittersweet.

I pulled up at my aunt's house and climbed out of the car, tossing a hand up at her neighbor across the street. The sun was

28

setting, and taking the last of the light with it, but the woman was apparently determined to finish working on the yard before it was completely gone.

The door swung open as I was raising my hand to knock, revealing my Aunt Phylicia on the other side. She propped a fist on her hip, and her lips twisted into a frown that she wouldn't have been able to hold if she tried.

"Took you long enough boy," she scolded, then reached her arms out to me. "Come here."

"How you doin' P-Diddy?" I teased her as I came in for my hug. She squeezed me as I rocked her back and forth for a second, then pulled away to close the door.

"I'm *tired* is how I'm doing," she answered, motioning for me to follow her into the kitchen. "Got me up all late, waiting on you. Don't you know it's past bedtime around here?"

I laughed as I sat down at the large island that anchored her kitchen. I still remembered her crying her eyes out the day I brought her into the house and told her it was hers, if she wanted it. *"If I want it? If? Are you crazy lil' boy? Don't be talking crazy in my new house!"*

"Stop acting like an old lady," I told her, earning myself a raised eyebrow as she put a steaming mug of tea in front of me, then went back to the counter to retrieve one for herself.

"Acting like what I am, baby. Sometimes you have to recognize your limitations, take care of your body. It's the only one we get, you know?"

I answered her with a deep nod. "Yeah, Auntie. I know."

My eyes fell to the mug she'd handed me, zeroing in on the *"FCK CANCER"* printed on the inside, designed to be seen when the mug was empty. Maybe something was wrong with me though, cause it shone right through the dark color of that tea like a beacon.

I pushed the cup away.

"So if you know," she said, too preoccupied with a frantic search for something on her tablet to notice my revulsion for the tea. "Then you wouldn't be acting like you don't know why I go to bed early. And why you should have come sooner."

"I came as soon as I left work. It took time to get out of the city, and then get here."

"Mmhmm. Speaking of work, how is Wil holding up? Is she okay?"

No.

And how could she be, really? The dude she was supposed to marry had never struck me as a particularly good guy – not good enough for her, not to me – but she'd loved him, and she seemed happy. But it was Wil – she was damn near always happy, that was just who she was.

Those tears earlier... that had burned me up.

Of course she was heartbroken, and angry, and embarrassed. He'd hurt her in the worst kind of way, and it made sense completely for her to not be her bubbly self. But *tears*? I'd known Wil for almost three years now, and never seen her cry.

"She's... making it the best way she can. Probably still hasn't really processed it," I said, propping my elbows on the counter.

My aunt shook her head. "I can't believe that boy did her like that. She was such a sweet girl. I'll *never* forget when me and your mama came up to the television studio to visit you, and she took us out to lunch cause you were stuck in an interview. You remember that?"

"I do," I chuckled. My mother had already been a fan, but that simple act of grace had landed Wil permanently on her "*Ramsey, why don't you marry that girl?*" list. Nevermind that Wil had been in a long-term relationship since we met, and then engaged.

"Mmmhmm. I promise you this – he'll live to regret it. I swear these young men don't know a good thing when they have it. Your uncle Reginald? Would have *never* done me like that, no sir. And that man was handsome as they come, and you know those are the worst ones. I used to tell your mama all the time – I'm so *glad* Ramsey had him to look up to, put some sense in his head before he became a teenager. Because with that face and those wide shoulders, you would've been worse than the devil boy. And then with one of those football paychecks? Whew! You know I've got friends that don't know or *care* not a lick about sports, but they've got their TVs set to make sure they see you every day? I can't even watch TV with those horny old broads, got me sitting up somewhere ready to fight about you."

"Your whole generation is wild, Auntie," I laughed. "But hey... what was it you needed to show me? I know you didn't have me

30

drive up here to hear about your friends wanting to live out their cougar fantasies with me."

"Are you rushing me?"

I grinned. "No ma'am. Just trying to keep you on task."

"Why do I need to be on task? You're not going back home until in the morning, right? Your niece and nephews are downstairs on that damn video game, they probably want to see you."

"What are they doing out here on a Monday? They have a long weekend from school or something?"

"Mmmhmm. I've gotta get them back to Stamford in time for school in the morning," she mused as she slid the tablet across the counter to me.

I drummed my fingers on the counter. "I would say I could take them for you, but I'm heading back so early that it—"

"Did I ask you to do anything for me boy?" she scolded. "Get the tablet. Look at the video. That's all I need you to do."

I chuckled a bit as I slid the tablet in front of me, and hit the "play" button in the middle of the screen. The first thing I saw was my mother, seated in a chaise on her back patio. There was no sound playing, but the scene was loud. Our family was all over the place, mouths open to talk or laugh, plastic cups in hand. My nephews were in front of my mother, doing some silly dance to music I couldn't hear, and she loved it. She *loved* those kids so much, and it was all in her eyes, in her smile. They ran off – presumably driven by the end of the song – and a moment later, I saw myself on screen.

I was handing her a glass – one of the thick, heavy ones only *she* drank out of, one of the few things she'd brought along from the house I grew up in. I knelt in front of her, running a hand over the patterned scarf that covered her head, tied in an intricate knot Wil had taught her on a completely random, impromptu segment of the show.

She brought up the fact that she'd been on *national TV* at least once a week after that.

Her expression changed for me. Watching the video reminded me of the moment, but I don't think I could see it then like I saw it now. I was too busy wondering if she was too hot, if she was comfortable, if the music was too loud. I doubted that *then* I could see the pride in her eyes.

"Will you get on somewhere and let me be?"

I watched her mouth form those words, and my memory filled in the sound. I was hovering – doing too much, when she was just trying to enjoy herself. I did leave her alone – long enough to go turn the music down a little bit – and by the time I made it back, her boyfriend had taken a place next to her, so I stayed back, and went and found something else to do. The camera didn't know all of that though – it just remained focused as Desmond leaned in, pressing his forehead to hers as he spoke what context clues told me were gentle words.

The video ended there.

"Chloe said she stopped there because she didn't want to be "creeping"," my aunt laughed, when I still hadn't moved after the video was done. "That was a couple months before your mama's birthday, remember? My baby sister looked good, didn't she? With that scarf on, looking like a queen."

When I looked up, her eyes were glossy, which… I couldn't handle. My gaze dropped back to the tablet, then to that goddamn mug.

Shit.

Was anywhere safe?

"Chloe was trying to clear space on her phone, she said when she dropped the kids off. She told me she had the video, but she'd moved it all to the cloud or something, and she was trying to… I didn't really understand what she was telling me, but she remembered to email the video today. I thought you'd like to see that."

She was wrong, but I didn't say that.

Maybe in three months, maybe in six, but for now… nah.

"This is nice, Auntie," I told her, because it was. Future Ramsey would find value in it, but right now, the shit felt like a blade to the chest. "You good with me kicking it here for the night?"

She frowned. "Why on earth wouldn't I be? Don't play with me like that," she warned, and I laughed. "You're laughing, but I'm serious. You are *always* welcome in this house. You hungry? I made you a plate cause I knew you were coming. I can heat it up for you."

I got up, coming around the other side of the counter to wrap her in a hug that she laughed and tried to squirm out of. "You always take good care of me."

"I promised your mama I would, and I meant it."

"And it's appreciated."

A little grin climbed onto her face as she looked at me.

"I know. Now go on down there and see about those kids. Alexis has a boyfriend."

I frowned, then shook my head.

"Nah. We'll see about *that*."

"You know it didn't have to be like this, right?"

"Shut up."

"You were the one who insisted on coming out here."

"Shut up."

"I tried to give you a little break, let you get yourself together."

"Shut up."

"But *naaaaah*. "I need my morning session" – that's what you said, remember?"

"Shut up."

I grinned down at where Wil was sprawled on the ground, in a pool of sweat. As athletic as she was, Wil was the girliest of girls, so I knew she had to be desperate for a break to let even a pinch of dirt touch her skin. But still.

"Come on," I said, wiping sweat from my own eyes before I bent a little, smacking her firmly on the backside. "Get your ass up, let's go Champ."

"Ouccch," she moaned. "Be careful with those heavy paws, damnit."

I chuckled, then picked up the water bottle I'd left beside my backpack at the base of the steps. Wil had exerted just enough energy to roll from her side to her back, so she couldn't get smacked again, and I shook my head as I raised the bottle to my mouth and squeezed. Once I had a drink, I lowered the bottled... and squeezed again, spraying her with water.

"Ramsey!" she squealed, and immediately jumped up, but I was already gone, dropping the water bottle to the ground. I took the bleachers we were supposed to be running two at a time, then waited until she was three-quarters of the way up to move to the second set.

"I'm gonna kick your ass!" she shouted after me, and I grinned.

"Gotta catch me first! Come on, I thought you were fast? Thought you were Carla Ann Cunningham's daughter, but not with those slow ass legs!"

Behind me, she let out what I could only describe as a growl, and when I glanced back again, she was decidedly closer than she'd been before. Up, over, down. Over, up, Over. Down, over, up. One by one, we ran the line of bleachers, finishing out the round that would bring our workout to a close. Total exhaustion was the goal, and I'd be damned if I wasn't going to get her there.

At the top of the last set, I waited for her to reach me before heading back down. She didn't work out as often as I did and even *my* legs were burning, so I didn't tease her about how long it took to drag herself up the last three steps. I pulled my cell out of the pouch on my arm and navigated to my camera as she approached. I tapped the button that would activate the forward-facing camera and wrapped an arm around her neck, pulling her into me. I laughed at the scowl she was giving the screen, and snapped the picture, letting her go before I posted it to my Instagram with the #FromTheSidelines hashtag.

"How you feeling?" I asked her, returning my phone to my armband. She'd dropped down into one of the seats and had her head tilted back, sucking in deep breaths of air.

"Like I'm gonna puke," she managed, then closed her eyes.

I sat down on the steps beside her seat. "Good. Proof you worked your ass off."

Instead of responding, she flipped me off, which was a good sign – meant she was still mobile. I took a moment of my own to rest, closing my eyes. When I opened them again, Wil had pulled out her phone. Suddenly, there was tension in her shoulders that had nothing to do with our workout.

"What's up?" I asked, sitting up to nudge her shoulder. "Why is your face all sour?"

She shook her head, then held up her phone, showing me the screen. "*This*." All I saw on her screen was the picture I'd tagged her in and shared, which confused me. Despite her scowl, she looked good. Actually… the scowl was kinda sexy.

But then my gaze traveled lower.

I hadn't been back to the picture to look at any comments from my own phone, but from here I could see that people were already being stupid. Not that it was surprising, or new, but still... damn.

"@jamochashake43: no wonder her man went and got him a white girl, she always on Instagram hugged up with you @RB_TheSledgehammer! Gonna start calling you RB the Homewrecker!"

I shook my head. The picture already had sixty-something comments, and if I had to bet, I would say at least a third of them were along those same lines, or worse.

This was the first time I'd been called a homewrecker though.

Nothing had ever happened between me and Wil. People gossiped and made shit up, sure, but the truth was that the only romance between us existed in people's imaginations. From the time we'd met – back when she hated my guts – Wil had been seriously involved with the clown that ended up being her fiancé.

If that wasn't the case... maybe things would've been different.

But they weren't.

Nevermind that us being "always hugged up" was a blatant exaggeration, it was pretty fucked up to imply that our platonic relationship had anything to do with the clown not choosing to keep his dick in his pants.

I hope Wil doesn't internalize this bullshit.

"What if she's right though?"

Shit. Too late.

She'd tossed the phone into her lap and was looking up at the sky again.

"She's not. And neither is anybody else who lets that dumb shit come out of their mouth."

Wil pushed out a sigh. "Seriously, though."

"I'm being serious," I countered.

She opened her eyes, looking right at me when she responded. "He complained once. Last year, at the Connecticut Kings benefit ball. Me and you danced together that night, just one damn song. We were having fun, and there was *nothing* sexual about it, but he flipped out on me. Brought up us working out together, me being on your Instagram..."

"You've never said anything to me about it."

"Because it was just that once, and he never mentioned it again. I'm friends with other guys, other athletes. Y'all all do the neck hug thing, and hell – I can't count how many times Jordan Johnson has picked me up, tossed me over his shoulder, the whole nine. No complaints. But something about *that* night…" she trailed off with a faraway look that made me wonder if voices were the only things that got raised that night.

Nah.

Wil's daddy was a boxer, and I knew from experience in the ring with her that Wil had inherited his hands. She would've set him straight with no problem.

"I wonder if she'd threatened him, you know?"

The gloss in her eyes was back, and I had to look somewhere else. If I watched her cry over that dude again, I was going to rock his skull the very next time I saw him.

"Like maybe he was on edge, looking for a reason to be upset with me, to justify what he knew *he* was doing. How can a friendship between coworkers be believable to you when you're screwing *your* coworker?"

I scoffed. "Wil, his ass didn't really think you were doing anything you shouldn't. It was just like you said – him trying to pass around some blame, when it *all* rests with him. You'll drive yourself crazy trying to find logic where there isn't any."

"I just want to understand why though." She whispered that, but I could still hear the lump building in her throat. "I tried to be a good girlfriend, a good fiancé. Show him I could be a good wife, and he—"

"Stop making his shit about you." I pushed myself up from the steps to stand, then extended a hand to help her up too. "You can't make a person be faithful by doing things for them, and not doing things for them isn't gonna make them step out. There's *one* reason – because they wanted to. And that's about *them*. Not *you*."

"That's a nice sentiment, but this is real life. You're really going to tell me consistent sex, keeping your appearance up, being encouraging, blah blah blah, doesn't help a man's dick stay in his pants?"

I chuckled. "I'm saying… maybe there are things that lead people to, and away from, wanting to step outside of their relationship, sure. But ultimately… we're adults. It's time out for calling the shit "a mistake", or acting like we didn't have the option of ending shit, or talking about it with the person we committed to. He had options. He made his choice. A bad one. And now... fuck him."

"That's so much easier said than done. My feelings aren't controlled by some switch I can just flip to suddenly make everything okay."

I raised an eyebrow. "You *really* think you need to explain that to *me*, Champ? Of all people?"

Immediately, her harsh expression softened. "No. I don't. But... you should especially know – it's not that easy."

"I do. That's why you work toward that shit every day. A week from now, two weeks, a month... you feel better, handle it better, than you did today. Maybe it takes a year, or five, for the shit to be okay. I don't know, I'm still figuring it out myself. But I know I won't get there blaming myself for shit that wasn't in my control – like what a grown ass adult decided to do."

I extended my hand again, and this time she took it, using it as leverage to pull herself up.

"I don't think I'm there yet."

"You don't have to be. Hasn't even been a week."

When she looked up, there was a little bit of a smile on her face as she looked around. "I messed this up. Letting you kick my ass this morning was supposed to be an escape. A release. But... here I am, right back where I was."

I shrugged, then started down the steps. "I mean... we could hit these bleachers a few more times."

"The hell we can."

Back down at the bottom, we gathered our things, and headed to my truck. Wil had taken a car service to her parent's house in Stamford, so she was riding with me back to New York.

"You know what I need?" she asked, as she strapped her seatbelt. "A reason to get dressed up. Like, *really* dressed up, you know? Go somewhere and drink champagne in a cute dress."

I laughed. "I might have an opportunity for you, but... not sure it's the best idea in the world."

"Tell me," she insisted, as I pulled out of the parking lot of the small public stadium we'd used to work out. "Why wouldn't it be a good idea?"

I sighed. "It's a wedding. Trent Bailey's," I told her, then glanced over to see her face. "I have a plus-one, but…"

"I want to go," she said, her voice soft but determined. "I love weddings."

"But—"

"When is it?"

I peeked at her again before I pulled away from a traffic light. "A few weeks from now."

"Then I definitely want to go. A few weeks from now, I'll be completely fine."

I raised an eyebrow, but didn't say anything. Wil must've caught the change in my expression, because she shoved my arm a little and laughed.

"What kind of friend are you? This is the moment where you help me lie to myself. *Of course, Champ, you've got this,*" she said, in a deep voice that was obviously meant to mimic mine.

I chuckled. "That's what I sound like?"

"That's what you sound like," she agreed, then stuck out her tongue.

"Okay then, you don't need me to tell you shit. You've already got it covered."

She laughed, and then neither of us said anything for several moments.

"You really think I'll be okay?"

I glanced over to find her already looking at me, and held her gaze for a second before I returned my attention to the road.

"For the wedding?"

"For life. For both."

"You'll definitely be okay for *life*," I laughed. "For the wedding… it's debatable. Run that one by your homegirls first, then let me know."

"They're gonna say no."

"Well then…"

"But I want to go. I want to be okay. I want to grab this thing by the horns."

I blew out a sigh. "I'm not going to say no, but…"

"You reserve the right to say "I told you so". I know."

I grinned. "Then we're cool."

"Perfect. And if all else fails… alcohol."

38

Three

Wil

**"You do realize you could've started a fire, right? –
Cheating Bastard."**

"You do realize I wouldn't have given a damn, right?"

I typed that response, but then deleted it before I hit send,
choosing instead to drop the phone on the bed, leaving it buried under
the covers as I climbed out. I wasn't – and didn't plan to ever be – in
the mood for dealing with Darius.

There was something about finding out that you narrowly
escaped legally binding yourself to a lying cheater that drastically
lowered your bullshit threshold.

Following my mother's advice – because she'd rarely, if ever,
led me wrong – I'd allowed him back into our shared home, but only
because I wasn't there. I'd removed everything that mattered to me
already, and those boxes were in my parent's garage. It had been just
over a week since the news story broke, but there was nothing for me
to wait around for. If it was at all possible, I wanted to expedite the
process of moving on.

Hurt and betrayal sucked, and I wasn't trying to linger.

Instead of showering, I pushed in the stopper on the deep,
garden-style tub in the bathroom and turned the water on. After a

quick rustle underneath the cabinet, I grabbed a plastic canister labeled "Epsom salt" and poured half of it into the tub. My muscles were *screaming* from the workout session with Ramsey the day before.

Small price to pay for the mind-clearing effect. It was incredibly hard to be wrapped up in your emotional problems when you were legitimately concerned you were going to puke up your lungs.

I sank into the tub and closed my eyes.

Maybe I should have saved yesterday's session for today.

At this very moment, a week ago, I should have been waking up filled with the best kind of nervous butterflies. Should've been mentally preparing to marry the man I loved. My thoughts should've been consumed with last minute details, concerns about if my hair looked okay, if everybody would be able to find the venue, if my father would *really* contain himself at the reception and not do the butterfly in the middle of the dance floor.

I should've been fucking *happy*.

Instead… I was broken.

I was *still* broken, and I really, *really* could've used the distraction of yesterday's workout. I knew better than to call – Ramsey would chew me out about not letting my body rest. And besides that… I didn't have the energy for another one of his workouts anyway.

From my place in the bathtub, I could hear the buzz of my vibrating phone. I'd intended to silence it, because I didn't want to talk to anyone. Not the liar, not my friends, not my cousin, not my parents. But they were the only ones I couldn't temporarily ignore, not while I was staying in the same apartment I'd used in college. *Their* apartment, connected to *their* home.

I planned to rectify my living situation into something more suitable for an adult woman, but in the meantime, I grudgingly pulled myself out of the tub. I cursed the whole way, and cursed some more when I got to the phone and saw that none of the missed calls were from my parents, who, now that I thought about it, could have just come and knocked on the door if they were trying to reach me and I wasn't answering my phone.

Several were from Darius, whose number I was sorely tempted to block. It started ringing again while it was in my hand – him again – and instead of ignoring it like I *knew* I should… I answered.

"What the hell do you want?" I snapped. The beginning of a headache was already starting, and he hadn't even said anything yet.

"To *talk* to you, if that's not too much to ask," he responded, his tone tinged with an urgency that only served to turn my smoldering anger into a blaze. He had no right to be *urgent* with me.

"If it's not too much to ask? If it's not – Darius, you couldn't even do something so simple as keeping your genitals to yourself and you have the *nerve* to ask me if talking is too much to ask? *Anything* is too much to ask, you lying, cheating, sonofabitch."

"Eight years, Wil," he said, calm and collected as ever. "We're going to flush eight years down the drain without even talking?"

I scoffed. "Don't you *dare* put this in my lap Darius! I'm not flushing anything – *you did* when you screwed someone else and then lied to me over and over and over. You didn't respect me enough after eight years to not lie to my damn face, and put me in a position to be humiliated. So don't you dare bring up "eight years" as a reason for me to hear anything you have to say. *Fuck* those eight years, and *fuck you.*"

I snatched the phone down from my ear and ended the call, cursing the fact that our house hadn't *actually* burned down. At least that would have been a little bit of catharsis – the remaining symbol of our love destroyed in flames. Just the mental image felt so, *so* good.

He called back because of course he did, because he was never one for being denied something he wanted. I had very little issue being the person to deliver his petulant ass a firm *no.* He wanted me back. He wanted me to bend to his will, to forget that this had happened, to take his hand and move forward. On the one-week anniversary of the day we didn't get married because he - gleefully, repeatedly, and several other adverbs – stuck his dick in someone who was not me, his fiancé.

I was about to rock his world with disappointment.

I blocked his number and then went back to my bath, groaning when I stuck my fingers into lukewarm water. I drained the tub and took a shower instead, dressing in yoga pants and a tee-shirt, and pulling my hair into a ponytail.

I knew exactly where I could go for some encouragement.

"You can't turn me away. I brought ice cream," I said as soon as my cousin opened her door. I held up the bag of pints from a local shop, and a smile spread over Naima's face as she stepped back to let me in.

"I wouldn't have turned you away anyway, but that *Dreamery* bag in your hand damn sure doesn't hurt." Naima pulled me into a lingering hug, rubbing a few soothing circles into my back before she let go. "I called you earlier. Are you okay?"

I knew I didn't have to lie to Naima, so I shrugged. "I just want to eat this ice cream and talk about anything *except* Darius."

Naima nodded, and squeezed my hand. "Okay honey. Come on."

We stopped in her massive gourmet kitchen for her to grab a stack of bowls and spoons, and then she led me outside to the pool, where several other women were gathered. One of them was her girlfriend, Ashley, and the other two I'd never met, but recognized because of their notoriety in sports world.

Margo, an agent with an impressive roster of the kind of superstar athletes other agents salivated over, and Nicole Richardson. Daughter of Eli Richardson who owned the Connecticut Kings, and girlfriend of Jordan Johnson, star wide-receiver for the Connecticut Kings. And most importantly, in my opinion – well-respected member of the Kings' front-office staff.

Naima's girlfriend, Ashley, was a physical therapist on the Kings' staff, and Naima herself had just accepted a position as team chef. With Jordan Johnson being a key member of Margo's professional roster, I was the only person who *wasn't* connected to the Kings some way. It had me feeling something I didn't feel often – nervous, like the odd person out.

"I should've called first," I whispered to Naima. "I didn't realize you had company. I don't want to impose."

She sucked her teeth. "Oh please, Wil. You're welcome to join us, we aren't doing anything but kicking it. And besides – ice cream.

These bitches aren't about to turn you around. Hey ladies," she yelled, and they all looked up from their conversation. "Wil is here!"

She announced me like I was already part of their group, even though I wasn't. They all lived here in Connecticut, and though I talked to Naima often, I didn't physically visit enough to be welcomed into their fold. My other homegirls lived all over, so we couldn't congregate like I knew Naima and her girls did.

"Hey Wil!" Ashley waved, and I waved back as she stood to greet me. Cole and Margo followed suit, and Naima took the opportunity to make the introductions that hadn't formally been made before.

I scolded myself for the way my hands were shaking a little as I stood face to face with Margo and Cole, women who had the kind of respect in the sports industry that I dreamed about. They both brushed off the hand I offered, pulling me into hugs that weren't unlike the one I'd gotten from Naima. I didn't have to dig deep to surmise that those hugs were only partially "nice to meet you". The other part was "Damn, it was jacked up what that man did to you for the world to see."

"I watch your show *all* the time," Margo told me, making me blush.

"Seriously?" I asked, and she gave me one of those half-nod, half-frown expressions.

"Uh, yeah. Half the time it's the only way I know what my clients are *really* up to."

"Same here," Cole chimed in, nodding. "God knows you've kept me informed on JJ enough times."

"Jordan isn't your client anymore, remember," Naima teased. "That's yo *maaan* now."

The women erupted in laughter, and I watched, enthralled, as the Cole Richardson I was used to seeing as ultra-professional, almost stoic, erupted in laughter like a schoolgirl. I – and everyone else – had seen Kendra Fulton's "Love on the Highlight Reel" special about their fairytale love story after their unfortunate SuperBowl loss at the beginning of the year, but Cole herself had never been interviewed about the relationship.

Hearing it from her perspective would be amazing, I thought. The struggle of the professional conflict, preserving her reputation, him maintaining his focus on the game. The ratings would be phenomenal!

Stop it, Wil, I scolded myself.

She was hanging out with her friends, relaxed, happy. It was so far from appropriate for me to be thinking about her "story" that it was a little shameful. I smiled along with the rest of them, and mentally put my "journalist" hat away.

"Speaking of," Cole said, "Ashley, I really need you to get him before I kill him. He picked me up *again* yesterday, when he knows better. Can you impress upon him that if he wants to play next season, he has to heal first, and he's not going to be ready to get through training camp if he's not taking it easy. The man acts like a broken collarbone is a damn scratch."

Ashley gave her a sympathetic smile. "I can try, but… I'm not his therapist, Rebecca is. Have you tried talking to her?"

Margo laughed. "No, are you trying to get your coworker killed? Cole hates her."

"That's not true," Cole shook her head. "I don't hate her, I just recognize her for what she is, so I don't *respect* her."

"And what is she, Cole?" Naima asked, clearly amused. "Drop knowledge."

"She is exactly the kind of disrespectful, sorry excuse for a woman who thrives on getting dicked down by involved men. I don't know why it's so appealing to her, but she's screwed half the team. If she wasn't good at her job, we'd be rid of her ass, cause it's not a good look."

"Involved *black* men," Ashley amended Cole's description of the physical therapist in question as we gathered at the patio table to dish out the ice cream. "Only *ever* the black ones. It's *weird.*"

Margo chuckled. "It's not weird. Fetishization of Black sexuality goes back to the beginning of time. She's chasing down her "Black Bull" porn stereotype. Let her be. They'll learn."

"Nobody is bothering that girl," Cole argued, then took a seat with her bowl. "Like I said, as long as her job is done within the team quality standards, I have nothing to say about her employment. I just warn my players to be careful where they're putting their dicks."

"*That's* the key," Margo agreed. "Wrap it up with a condom *you* provided, make sure there's no boyfriend involved, make sure you aren't being set up, and the list goes on. I never have to give these

44

warnings to the women or the gay men. The rest of these folks though…" she let out an exasperated sigh, then shoved a big spoonful of ice cream into her mouth.

There were a million ways this conversation could be labeled "problematic", but they were clearly speaking the truth as they knew it, from their inside vantage point of this world. It may not have been politically correct or pretty, but… it was real.

So I stayed quiet and ate my ice cream, grateful that through my connection to Naima, I was privy to a conversation like this in the first place.

"So, Wil…," Cole started, and I nearly jumped out of my seat. "A little birdy told me that *From The Sidelines* is angling for exclusive access to the Kings this season."

I swallowed the ice cream in my mouth. "Oh, um… that's really Ramsey's thing, with his "Overtime" specials."

"*Mmmm,*" Margo groaned. "Ramsey Bishop. That is one *fine* little man."

"Little?!" Naima laughed. "That's so shady, that man is not *little*. He's average height for a running back, right Cole?"

She nodded. "He's actually almost *tall* for a running back. He's what, like five-nine?"

"Yeah," I added. "We're almost the same height. And Ramsey is like… solid muscle. *Thick* solid muscle."

"See?" Naima teased, nudging Margo's chair with her foot. "Always calling somebody little cause you're a damn Amazon woman."

Margo shook her head. "Ladies, let me clarify – I wasn't complaining. Y'all can have these seven and eight foot tall men – that extra height usually comes directly from their dicks, and I don't have the time."

"Margo!" Cole shrieked, then broke into laughter that infected all of us. Margo wiped tears from her eyes before she spoke again.

"Tell me I'm lying!" she challenged. "I mean, sure, there are outliers, and the guys in the lower end of the six foot range are typically working with something. But hand over my heart, anything over six and a half feet… gain an inch of height, lose an inch of dick. *Tell me I'm lying!*"

I was laughing too hard to get any words out, partially because in my brief period of sexual exploration before I started dating Darius my sophomore year of college, my experience matched what she was saying. It must have been true for Cole too, because she was wiping tears of laughter from her eyes as well.

"Come on Naima," Cole said, nearly wheezing with laughter. "I *know* you tried a few before you dove into the lady pond full time…"

With her hand over her mouth, Naima scowled at Cole and Margo for a few seconds before she couldn't hold it anymore, and burst into laughter again. "I swear I can't *stand* you Margo," she screamed, still giggling as she fell back into Ashley's lap on the oversized ottoman they were seated on.

"See?" Margo said, nodding as she pointed at each of us. "It's true. And *come on* – going back to Ramsey, the man's nickname is goddamn *Sledgehammer*! What does that tell you?"

"Oh my God," Cole yelled. "He got that name because an opponent said getting tackled by him was like getting hit with a sledgehammer. It is *not* about his dick!"

"How do *you* know?" Margo challenged, barely keeping a straight face. "I'm just saying, I don't think God would do him like that. A nickname like sledgehammer, with a small dick. That doesn't even *match*. Wil!"

My eyes went wide at the sound of my name, and I looked up from my bowl to find all four women looking at me.

"Give us the scoop girl," Margo said with a smirk. "Does the dick match the nickname?"

"I have *no* idea," I stammered immediately, truthfully, and I'm sure my face was probably bright red. I'd definitely heard rumors, even before we worked together, that his nickname was definitely bedroom appropriate, but… Ramsey was my coworker, and my *friend,* and I had a man with enough dick. I wasn't trying to think about Ramsey like that.

"So you really haven't slept with him?" Margo continued, only to be scolded straightaway by Naima. The instant shift in Margo's expression confirmed her sincerity when she told me, "Oh, shit, sorry! I'm *so* sorry, I got a little carried away. My bad."

I closed my mouth from where it had dropped open in response to her question, and nodded. "Uh, no worries. But, to answer your question, no. Nothing has ever happened between us."

46

"*Why the hell not?*" Ashley muttered, clearly louder than she intended from the way her eyes bugged out when everybody's attention shifted to her. But, she shrugged. "Sorry, but I'm just saying. If I were you, I'd definitely be exercising my temporary hoe-pass."

Cole's head tipped to the side. "Do lesbians do post-breakup hoe-passes?"

"Yep," Ashley and Naima said in unison and then Ashley added, "I was dancing on a bar at a go-go club when I met Naima. Hoe pass. But back to you," she said, turning to me again. "How are you holding up?"

"She doesn't want to talk about it," Naima sang, but I shook my head.

"No, it's fine."

Naima and Ashley were family, and Cole and Margo were cool enough that it didn't bother me to come right out and say, "I'm... not holding up. I'm pissed, and I'm lonely, and I'm hurt, and... right now, I'm just hoping that I don't snap if I see him or her in public. He had the nerve to try to pull rank with me, I guess. Talking about some goddamn "are you really going to throw away eight years?" I cursed him out and hung up."

"More than his ass deserves," Margo replied, reaching out to squeeze my hand. "I'd still be somewhere under the bed right now, so I admire the fact that you're even upright."

"Only because of Ramsey." I regretted those words as soon as they were out of my mouth, but the women didn't seem moved to tease me about it, turning it into something it wasn't. So I continued. "I mean, it was my own choice to go back to work, and my mother didn't particularly like it, but I couldn't sit around the house wallowing. So I'm trying to get back to life, as much as I can, which includes working out sometimes with Ramsey. The other day, he was like... you have to always be moving forward, working towards being okay even if it's not immediate. So... I'm trying."

"He sounds like a good friend," Cole said, and the rest of them nodded. "That's great advice."

"Yeah." I stirred the melted ice cream in my bowl for a few seconds. "He invited me to a wedding. The Bailey wedding."

Cole reared back, and then shook her head. "Okay, nope. I take it back – not a good friend. Why the hell did he invite you to a wedding, so soon after...?"

"Because I want to go," I countered. "I love weddings, and any other time, saying yes would be a no-brainer. Part of moving on has to be not avoiding things that I enjoy, things that make me happy, just because of this situation with Darius."

Naima pushed out a sigh. "You don't think it might be a little too soon for that though, Willy? Like… there's no way it's not going to be hard as hell to watch their special day when you didn't get to have yours."

"Maybe so," I agreed. "But… it could also be pretty cathartic to watch it happen for someone, even though it didn't happen for me. I gotta be honest - right now… I'm not feeling particularly optimistic about love, which isn't like me. So maybe going could be the little jolt I need to… I don't know. Put me back on track."

"So you're thinking about dating again?" Margo asked, and I shook my head.

"Hell no. No time soon. I was with Darius eight years. I spent the first few chasing and meeting my Olympic goals, and finishing college. Then, I spent time trying to nail down a career, and establish myself there. While being somebody's girlfriend and fiancé. I've pretty much always had to consider him, instead of being able to just… focus on me. So that's where I am on a personal level with that. I just don't want to be cynical."

Margo nodded. "I understand. You want to believe in love… just not ready to be *in* it."

"I guess you could put it like that, but really… I'm still in it now. You can't be with someone that long, and just turn the love off. That's why it hurts so much, you know?"

"All too well," Naima agreed. "But… like Ramsey told you: You gotta keep moving towards being okay. And, he probably knows, right?"

Right.

It hadn't even been six months since Ramsey lost his mother, and he'd been handling it with a strength I wouldn't be close to capable of. He'd been different since then – a little quieter, more… serious, sort of. I didn't really know how to explain the change, and I wouldn't call it negative at all. He was just… different. But somehow, still the same.

"Is this line of conversation blowing anyone else's ice cream high, or just mine?" Margo asked, and I shook my head.

"No, you are absolutely not alone. I'd rather talk about literally anything else."

Naima nodded. "We've got you boo. One thing these heifers aren't ever short on is a line of conversation."

"Damn right," Margo added. "As a matter of fact, let me tell you what I heard about America's lil' favorite light-skinned basketball player."

"This has to be a joke."

"It's not a joke."

"Forty-five hundred American dollars a month?"

"Forty-five hundred American dollars a month."

"For *this*?"

"For this."

"No."

"Yes."

"You've gotta be shitting me."

I managed to clamp my mouth shut after that slipped, not letting out the longer stream of curses I wanted to – not in front of the realtor. My eyes slid over to Naima, whose expression mirrored mine. We were in agreement – this was some bullshit.

Maybe I'd been spoiled – okay, I'd definitely been spoiled. My parents had a thing about paying my expenses through college, and as my years at BSU came to a close, I started getting serious about my Olympic training. They paid for my expenses through *that* too. Their investment netted four Olympic gold medals flanking my high school and college diplomas on what they affectionately referred to as the "honor wall" in their home.

From there, I'd moved in with Darius, who I'd been dating more than four years at that point. It was his place, so he insisted on paying for it, and a year later, we bought a house together.

I *had* money, that wasn't the issue. I'd just never had to spend it to live on my own. And now that it was imminent, I couldn't help thinking – *this is bullshit.*

It wasn't that anything was necessarily *wrong* with any of the apartments we'd seen. A studio in Harlem, a one bedroom in Park Slope, the one with the great hardwood floors in West Village. They were all perfectly fine. I just refused to pay so much for the spatial equivalent of a goddamn matchbox.

It was damn near as much as the mortgage on the house with Darius, which would be on the market as *soon* as I could help it. Yes, we were out in Kensington, and had to drive into the city, but at least we had room to breathe, a yard, privacy, and a kitchen that could hold more than a week's worth of food.

I pushed out a sigh, shaking my head at the tiny, beautiful Chelsea apartment we were currently viewing. Maybe I was going to have to adjust my expectations to make this happen – and *soon.* I loved my parents, but I was too damned old to be getting my covers snatched away by my mother as she declared there was *"No good reason for a grown woman to be in the bed past eight in the morning."*

As if I hadn't gotten my heart yanked out of my chest barely two weeks ago.

"Maybe we've seen enough for today?" the realtor suggested, in a tone that vaguely suggested we'd wasted enough of her time. Luckily for her potential commission, I agreed. We'd looked at nine different apartments, none of which moved me, so regrouping was probably for the best.

In my hand, my phone started buzzing, and I excused myself when I saw Ramsey's name on the screen. While Naima talked to the realtor about setting up another time to meet, I stepped into a "bedroom" that was barely bigger than my current closet to answer the phone.

"How is the apartment hunt going, Champ?" he asked, as soon as I said hello. "You got us a place to watch the game yet?"

I shook my head, as if he could actually see me. "No, unfortunately not. I swear it's like this realtor is committed to showing me the *least* bang for my buck."

"New York is just expensive as hell," he laughed. "Glad I bought my spot when I was young and impulsive and a fan favorite.

50

Signed jersey and a slice of pizza with the owner's kid knocked a hundred thousand off the asking price."

"Lucky you."

"Could be lucky *you*. I'll be a fair landlord, promise."

My eyes went wide. "Wait... so you decided? You're going for it?"

"Don't get excited," he warned, with a chuckle. "I'm still considering. Today I'm eighty-twenty. Tomorrow might be a forty-sixty day."

I shook my head. "I don't know why you keep going back and forth about this, Ram. It's heavy on your mind for a reason. I think you should go for it."

"If I do that, where does it leave *you*?"

"Don't worry about *me*," I countered. "We're talking about your *passion*, dude. Doing the show is cool and all, sure, but we both know it's in your blood."

On the other end of the line, he sighed. "Okay, Ms. Motivational. I hear you, I do. But... you know I know your reasons for pushing this are selfish, right?"

I grinned. "Maybe you could look at it like that. *Or* you could see it as me being fine either way, so there's no reason for *my* prospects to factor into your decision. This needs to be about you. *Just* you."

I glanced up in response to Naima knocking on the door, and she mouthed that we had to go, so the realtor could lock up.

"Hey," I told him. "I have to go. What are you eating tonight?"

"Whatever you're treating me to."

I rolled my eyes. "Okay. I'll call you back later to make plans."

"Bet."

After we hung up, I joined Naima, and we followed the realtor back down to the lobby, where we parted ways.

"You know that lady wanted to stab you, right?" Naima murmured to me as we headed for the front doors.

I snickered. "You know the feeling was mutual, right?"

We were still giggling as I put my hands out in front of me to push open the door. My skin had just connected with the cool metal when I heard my name, and looked up to see a familiar face standing just on the other side of the entryway.

Jessica Leigh.

My tongue felt like lead, feet cemented to the floor as she approached me with way less caution than a smarter woman would have. Her sun-streaked hair was in a disheveled topknot, red eyes only slightly obscured behind chunky eyeglasses. My eyes narrowed at her pink and gray Lululemon yoga outfit and pristine floral sneakers.

Perfectly put-together, but just the right amount of distraught for a woman who'd broken up an engagement in the most publicly possible manner.

"Wil," she said again, when she was right in front of me. She reached for my hands, and I had just enough presence of mind to draw back. "Wil, *please*."

"You really should just keep it moving, okay?" Naima told her, stepping between us. "She doesn't have anything to say to you."

Not true. I had plenty – *plenty* to say. I just valued my reputation too much to do it.

"Wil, I'm *sorry*," Jessica insisted, following behind as Naima steered me back toward the door. "I swear, I didn't mean to hurt you. You've never been anything but sweet to me, and I promise, I never meant for this to hurt—"

"You lying *bitch*!" I snapped, reeling back to face her, sidestepping Naima. My raised voice would surely attract unwanted attention, but in that moment, I didn't care. "How dare you look me in my face and tell that lie, huh?"

"Wil, we need to *go*," Naima demanded, stepping in front of me, but I shook my head.

"No, do you hear this shit?!" I asked, honestly baffled. "This *trash*, who smiled in my face and then fucked my man says she wasn't trying to hurt me. Let me tell you something, *Jessica*," I spat out her name like it was dirt on my tongue, because it basically was. "A woman who isn't trying to hurt another one doesn't knowingly fuck her man, how about that? Let's say maybe she didn't care at first, but now she wants to change her ways – *you have my phone number, bitch.* You didn't *have* to put the shit on TV, did you? So miss me with the "I wasn't trying to hurt you", because that's *exactly* what you were doing."

Jessica crossed her arms, clearly miffed that I wasn't buying her remorseful act. "Darius is the one you should be mad at. *He's* the one who made the commitment, not me."

52

"But we're not talking about him right now, are we? We're talking about *you*, and nothing you can say now makes *you* any less awful."

She dropped her arms to prop her hands on her hips. "*Darius* didn't think I was awful. I *know* you saw the videos."

I advanced on her so quickly that Naima grabbed my arm. Standing right in Jessica's face, I grinned. "See? There it is. *Not* sorry. You really thought you were doing something I bet, getting a black man to betray his black woman to fuck you. You really think you *gained* something, think you *beat me*, don't you? But guess what? If his standards have dropped so low that a used up trash bag like you was where he chose to stray… I don't even want him. Have fun with your "prize", since you're so proud of yourself."

Jessica was still sputtering, presumably trying to figure out a response when I really did let Naima drag me out of there, and force me into the car that she'd called before we left the apartment upstairs, and had probably been waiting several minutes for us to come out.

"What the hell, Wil?" Naima snapped, once she'd given the driver directions and we pulled off. "Why would you even give her the satisfaction?! You know that's probably spreading all over the internet as we speak, and you *know* what it's going to get painted to look like!"

I sucked my teeth. "I don't care what it looks like, I care what it was. She stepped out of place, and I put her ass right back in it. *Never meant to hurt me my ass*," I muttered, crossing my arms as I turned away from her to scowl out the window instead.

"No, it's going to look like an angry black woman cursing out a fragile white woman, and you know it. This is the way it goes – the way it *always* goes."

I snapped my head back. "Nevermind that she was screwing my fiancé, never mind that she approached me, she gets to be the victim because I yelled at her?"

"And called her names. You were mean. And you *know* they're going to say you're racist."

"Mean?! Racist?! Are you serious?!"

"As a heart attack, Wil," Naima said, leaning toward me. "Look – you're better than me, cause if that were reversed, I would've put Becky's head through that front door, and you'd be figuring out my bail situation right now. But I'm not *you.* You're goddamn… Wil

Cunningham. Sweet as pie, always gracious, even-keeled. *Cutting a bitch* isn't your thing!"

"Well maybe it is now!" I countered. "Maybe it *should be.* Maybe I wouldn't be in this situation now if I wasn't so *fucking* gracious! I don't want to be *amiable* and polite, and tactful. I want to drag that bitch by her hair, and I want to nail his dick to a table, and I want to get on snapchat and tell the world I had to teach him how to wipe his ass back in college because I was tired of washing skid marked drawers! I don't want to be *nice*, not right now!"

The end of my rant was punctuated by my phone ringing again. The first thing I saw, before I even looked at who was calling, was the steadily climbing number of social media notifications I had – even more than usual.

Shit.

Naima was right.

That lobby had been far from crowded, but it was silly to think that no one would whip out a camera and start recording in the age of smartphones. I should have learned that lesson from the video of me going in on Darius that night.

The phone stopped ringing and started again, and this time I actually looked at the name on the phone. I groaned when Sarita's name flashed across my screen. I'd gotten a phone call after the Darius thing too. A surprisingly sympathetic reprimand, but a reprimand nonetheless.

I had a feeling this time wouldn't be so kind.

Instead of answering, I silenced it, tossing it onto the seat beside me and closing my eyes as I pressed my head back into the headrest.

"Wil…," Naima said gently, grabbing my hand. That was all it took for tears to well behind my clenched eyelids, as a wave of hurt broke through my anger. When I didn't say anything, she squeezed. "Hey," she insisted, and I opened my eyes.

"Yeah?" I used my free hand to brush away the stray tear that broke free when I opened my eyes, rotating my head to face her.

There was glint of mischief in her eyes as she propped a knee up on the seat, turning to me and leaning in. "So… bitch, did you really have to tell him about not washing his ass properly though?"

She was barely containing a laugh as she asked, and that little bit of humor was so infectious that I couldn't help smiling too as I nodded. "Unfortunately."

"If that's what they mean when they say "loving a man's dirty draws"... girl, good luck."

I busted out laughing at that, covering my face with my hands as a few more tears slipped free. After several moments had passed, and we finally stopped laughing, I shook my head.

"I have to text the realtor," I said, and Naima's head tipped to the side.

"Why?"

I raised my hands in a "*duh*" gesture. "If *she* lives in Chelsea, guess where I won't be living?"

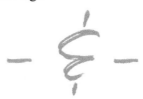

"Will you stop laughing and open the damn door?"

I propped my hands on my hips as the door swung open and Ramsey entered my sight, laughing his ass off. "What the hell are you doing girl?"

"Being inconspicuous," I told him, stepping past him into his condo, which I absolutely *adored.* Brushed oak floors, tons of windows, incredible view of Central Park during the day, and the lit skyline at night.

And *space.* Glorious, glorious *space.*

I wasn't even trying to think about how much it had to cost.

I pulled the baseball cap off my head, and the oversized sunglasses from my face before I unzipped the floral bomber jacket I was wearing.

"You realize you still look like *you*, even with all that shit on, right?" Ramsey asked, passing me to get to his kitchen.

I sighed. "Perils of being a "public figure" I guess." My empty stomach growled I followed him to the counter in the open kitchen, peeking around him to see what he was doing. "Did you *cook*?" I asked, getting my hand swatted away as I reached for the top to one of the dishes. "Is that why it smells so good in here?"

"I guess I had to, since *somebody* can't show her face in public tonight," he teased, turning to face me.

I crossed my arms. "Really bruh? That's how you're going to do me?"

"That's how I'm going to do you."

"I could have picked up a pizza. As a matter of fact, *that's* what I was expecting when you offered for us to have dinner here instead of going out."

"You know damn well you didn't want to eat pizza."

"Oh, but I do. A whole pizza, to myself. And a cake."

"A whole cake?"

I nodded. "I'm in emotional hell right now, so... yeah."

He blew out a sigh as he crossed his arms, mirroring my stance. "Damn. Well... my bad. I don't have any pizza, but we can order one. I guess these baked wings, broccoli and rice casserole, nice little green salad... I can put all of that away. Save it for another day."

"Oh my God, don't play with me," I said, bouncing toward him and trying again to peek into the dishes. "Where is my plate?"

"I thought you wanted pizza though?" he laughed, easily holding me off. "I've got some menus around here, I got you."

"Stop *plaaayyinng*," I whined, only making him laugh harder as he finally stepped aside, reaching into the cabinet to hand me a plate. He stood there teasing me as I loaded the plate with delicious smelling food from those dishes.

"*Damn*, Champ. You're seriously about to eat all of that?" He was over my shoulder, peeking down at the pile of chicken wings I'd accumulated. "I don't want to hear your mouth the next time we work out."

I laughed. "No, asshole. *I'm* not about to eat all of this, but I know *you* will. You're welcome," I told him, as I handed him the plate I'd fixed, then reached into the cabinet for one for myself.

"You didn't have to do that."

I shrugged. "You did the cooking. What do you have to drink?"

"Water. Beer. More water."

"Wow, a whole *two* different types of water?"

He frowned. "What? Only the best for my guests. Your choice of filtered – or filtered with *ice*."

"Oooh, such a hard choice," I giggled. "I think I'll take the filtered with ice."

"Good selection. That's the house special tonight."

We took our plates, drinking glasses, and a carafe of ice water to the table. The next hour was spent filling my belly and belly laughing, two things I hadn't gotten nearly enough of in the last few weeks. Naima and my mother had both been on me about not taking care of myself, but honestly, just getting out of bed some mornings felt like work. Once I was alone with my thoughts, no matter how determined I was to not be destroyed by a breakup… it was hard.

"Hey, do you remember that show we started watching, months ago?"

Our plates were empty, and the sun was down. It was probably time for me to go, but even the thought of that was a reminder of my displaced situation. Home wasn't home anymore, my mother's house wasn't my own, and I knew I could stay with Naima for a night, but she and Ashley tended to get… *loud.* The idea of going to a hotel just felt pathetic, but I knew I had to make a choice, at some point. I just didn't want to make it *now.*

"The one with the woman with those titties, and the fro, trying to find the serial killer?"

I rolled my eyes. "Those titties?"

He shrugged. "Yeah. They deserve specificity. Those weren't just *any* titties."

"I really can't stand you," I laughed, following his lead as he stood to carry dishes back to the kitchen. "*Those titties* aside, did you ever watch anymore?"

"Nah." He shook his head. "You know my TV stays on the sports networks or news. I don't really watch other stuff unless somebody is here for me to bug about it. Why?"

"Oh, I don't know. I just thought about it… you want to watch a few?"

"Fine with me," he said, taking the plate from my hands. "But you really mean to tell me Mrs. Carla isn't expecting you home before curfew?" I gave him a warning raise of my eyebrow, and he laughed. "I'll handle this, you go set it up for us."

I tried not to let my shoulders sink *too* deeply with relief, but I wondered if he knew the favor he was doing me by making it okay for me to stay. Even if it was just another hour or two.

Only because I knew it was fine with him, I curled up on one side of the couch with my feet under me and grabbed the remote to pull up the show.

There she was, Lynn Ryan, in all her afrocentric, boobalicious glory. She was an awful person, but a *great* character, the kind Black women on TV didn't often get to be. She drank too much, cursed a lot, slept with men she probably shouldn't. But she was a great... detective, or private investigator, or whatever the hell she was, and she was brown-skinned and kinky-haired and sexy as hell doing it.

"Here."

I looked up to see Ramsey standing over me, with a glass of wine in his hand. Once I took it, he plopped down a few feet away from me on the couch, then raised a beer bottle to his lips.

"What is this for?" I asked, lifting the glass of wine to my nose and inhaling. "And where the hell did you find a bottle of wine?"

"That has been in my fridge since the last time my cousins were up here. Never got opened. And you kind of seem like you need it."

I put the glass to my lips and tipped it back, moaning my approval when the sweet, peachy notes hit my tongue. "You, my friend, are correct."

"Thought so. I saw the video."

I drained half the glass before I shifted my gaze to his. "It looks that bad, huh?"

"To someone who wants it to look bad... yeah, probably so. The rest of us are amazed it didn't end with you popping ol' girl in the mouth."

"God knows I *wanted* to. Hell, maybe I should have, since I ended up getting reprimanded by the network anyway. My second "official" strike, with the first being the video of my interaction with Darius. Holding what should have been private conversations against me. You know they're talking about "we can't have you making racially charged statements"?! Like, what the *fuck* was "racially charged" about what I said to her?"

Ramsey cringed. "I mean... you kinda implied that a white woman only wanted your black man to feel like she had one-up on *you*, a black woman."

"*But was I lying on* her *though?!*" I asked, then poured the rest of my glass down my throat. "I mean, I could see if I said that was the case for *every* white woman who dates a black man, but I didn't. It's not even what I believe! Be with whoever the hell you want to be with. But for *her*? Oh yeah. That shit is definitely true."

In place of a response, Ramsey stood, walking to the kitchen to grab the rest of the bottle of wine from the counter. Wordlessly, he filled my glass, then put the bottle down in front of the couch. When he was seated again, he looked at me and said one word – *relax.*

So... I did.

So I *tried.*

I stretched out with my glass of wine as the show started up, trying to get comfortable while I ignored my body's urge to stretch out. When I finished my second glass of wine, I put the glass down beside the bottle, then attempted to pay attention to the TV. Inevitably though, I found myself watching Ramsey's face for a reaction as I inched my feet closer and close to where he was.

"Wil, I hope you don't think you're slick. I see you easing those cold ass feet over here." He said, not even looking away from the TV.

I scowled. "Joke's on you, my feet aren't even cold!"

The corner of his mouth turned up in clear skepticism. "Then why are you trying to sneak them over here?"

"No reason I guess," I said, sliding them back. "I can keep my feet to myself."

"No reason? Seriously?" He pulled his eyes from the TV to look at me. "You gonna absorb my life energy through your feet or something?"

"What?! No!"

"Then what the hell kinda reason for putting your feet on me can you not just say out loud?"

I sighed, leaning back into the pillow I'd propped on the arm of the couch to stare at the ceiling – and being careful to keep my feet on *my* side of the couch. "It's weird."

"Okay, so I'll consider myself warned. What's up?"

I swallowed hard. "I just... sometimes, to get comfortable, I just... I need..."

"Spit it out, Champ."

"I need a physical connection," I blurted out, under pressure. "Not that I need you to do anything but sit there. I just wanted to put my feet against you, but it's okay, I promise."

"Gimme your damn feet, girl."

"No, seriously, it's—"

Before I could get the "fine" out of my mouth, he'd hooked his arm around my ankles, and pulled my feet into his lap.

"You good now?" he asked, and even though I felt completely ridiculous, I nodded. "Good. Consider yourself lucky these things are cute," he teased, peering down at my toes, which I reflexively wiggled under the scrutiny. They were only in such a state because my mother had insisted on taking me to the spa a few days before.

Thank God.

His attention returned to the TV, and after a few moments, mine did too, and I was able to do what he'd initially insisted – *relax.*

For the first episode, at least.

Somehow, his hand landed on one of my feet, with his thumb absently stroking back and forth. I closed my eyes as the pressure increased – purposeful now – and tried not to moan as sensation traveled to somewhere much more personal than my feet.

"You look like you're enjoying this."

When my eyes popped open, my gaze went straight to Ramsey, zeroing in on his smirk. He brought his other hand to my foot too, kneading a spot that made me glad I had my arm draped over my breasts, conveniently hiding the fact that my nipples were hard as rocks.

"Y-you don't have to do that," I breathed, then bit down on the inside of my lip.

"You want me to stop?" I shook my head, and he shrugged. "It's not a big deal."

Oh, but it was.

My *intimate touch* levels had been sorely lacking, even before the wedding that never was. All of the coordinating and planning while trying to work had zapped my energy, and Darius had been shooting overtime for special episodes of his show. Between the two of us, we never seemed to have the energy for more than a quickie, and I wasn't… a quickie kind of girl. So that was one-sided anyway.

All of that resulted in this moment, in my friend's condo, with him rubbing my feet, in an attempt to help me relax. Only, instead of relaxing, I was trying not to notice the fact that my panties were suddenly wet, and fantasizing about him deciding my "cute" feet were "cute" enough to put my toes in his mouth.

Down girl. This ain't that type of party.

Mercifully, he moved his hands to a spot that still felt good, but was much less... orgasmic. I could actually feel the tension and stress melting out of me, and closed my eyes, listening to the show instead of watching.

"Damnit."

That was the first thing I heard after my eyes popped open, and I narrowed them, willing myself to adjust to unexpected darkness. The TV was off, and so where most of the lights. The one from the hall provided just enough illumination to see Ramsey kneeling in front of me.

"I was trying not to wake you," he said in a low voice. "You were twisted though. I was trying to fix your neck before it turned into a problem."

I tried to raise my hand to brush my hair out of my eyes, and realized then that I had a lightweight blanket draped over me, that hadn't been on the couch before. I groaned as I pushed myself up. Now that my eyes were adjusting, I noticed that Ramsey was shirtless, and a little damp, like he'd just showered. All he was wearing was basketball shorts.

"What time is it?" I asked, keeping my eyes on his face.

"Uhhh." He peeked around me, probably seeking out the glowing numbers on the stove. "One twenty-eight."

"Shit." I moved to get up, but Ramsey caught me by the arms, urging me back down.

"I know you're not trying to get back to Connecticut by yourself, at this time of night?"

I frowned. "What else am I supposed to do? I need to get home."

"What? Nah, man. Just crash here for the night, get a few hours of sleep. We have to be on set early tomorrow anyway. It's too late to make that drive."

Damn it.

He was right. I was barely keeping my eyes open now honestly, and Naima and my parents both lived in Stamford – at *best*, a forty minute drive away. And going to a hotel for just a few hours would be silly – especially when I was about to have to start paying exorbitant rent.

"Thank you," I said, quietly. I was more than a little embarrassed at my level of imposition, even though Ramsey and I were friends.

But, in typical Ramsey fashion, he shook his head. "It's not a problem. You need anything?"

"No, you've done enough," I answered. "But... do you mind if I turn on the TV? I need the noise, to fall asleep."

His eyebrow went up. "Really? You know that's not really healthy for you, right?"

"I know," I nodded. "And I never used to, but lately... I need it."

His expression softened, and a moment later, he was pressing the remote into my hands. "Do what you have to do to be okay. I'm right down that hall, the door on the left," he explained, pointing. "If you need anything... holler."

"Thank you," I said again, smiling at him as he stood. He leaned in, pressing a kiss to my temple before he walked off, leaving me alone in his living room. I waited until I heard his door close to switch the TV on.

I flipped through channels until I found *Bernie Mac Show* reruns, then snuggled in under the blanket again. Even though he was in the other room, just knowing Ramsey's presence was close by made me feel... less alone.

I focused in on the TV so I wouldn't have to review the events of earlier in the day, or the last few weeks, in my head. I didn't want to give it space, didn't want to give it power. Instead, I just wanted... to sleep.

So that's what I did.

Four

RAMSEY

May 2017

"Get on out there man. Show these rookies how it's done."

Despite the fact that I was practically aching to do just that, I shook my head at Jordan's words as he approached me on the sidelines. "Right after you, bruh. Those new receivers are out there looking a little weak around the elbows."

Jordan sucked his teeth. "Nigga, my old lady will wreck shop on *both* of us if she sees me on that field."

"You gonna be ready for training camp?" I asked, squinting against the sun to look out at the field, where newly drafted rookies, undrafted rookies, and free agents were all moving about at the annual mini-camp trying to prove their value and secure a place with the Connecticut Kings.

I was wondering why I wasn't out there myself.

I should have signed up. *Could* have signed up. When I left, I was at the end of my contract with New York anyway, so I was an unrestricted free agent with an excellent record. I just wasn't... *sure.*

"God willing," Jordan said, answering my question. He was out of the sling he'd had to wear for weeks following surgery on a broken collarbone, but I knew he was still taking it easy. He wasn't officially cleared yet, which I knew was killing him, but I *also* knew that as soon as he could, he'd be beasting through workouts and drills to get ready for the season.

Looking at the newest additions to the team... the Kings were going to need him and Trent Bailey to make a Super Bowl worthy team again, just like last season. From what I was seeing, the new recruits weren't adding much. The Kings' draft picks had been late, so they weren't picking up any superstars for their other positions, which was what they needed. Or hell – not even superstars, just solid players.

This minicamp was lacking.

"That fucked up look on your face," Jordan started, shaking his head. "You must be seeing the same thing I'm seeing."

I nodded. "Yeah. A bunch of guys giving mediocre effort, because they think that's all that's needed."

"Right. So... I'm saying, you're already in shorts, nigga. Throw on some cleats and embarrass these dudes. Give them some goddamn motivation."

"JJ, I don't know about that shit, man. You know how long it's been since I ran drills for scrutiny?"

He rolled his eyes. "You work out every damn day. You could do these drills with your eyes closed. In your sleep. What, you scared or something?"

"Nigga, you know *goddamn well*, I ain't scared of sh—" I broke off when Jordan's face spread into a laugh, over how I'd walked into that obvious ass trap.

But I got the cleats.

Jordan led me out to the exhausted-looking running back coach, who honestly seemed relieved at the interruption. We sold it as a motivational thing – before I left the NFL, I was well-known, a star player. The faces of some though – guys I'd played against, and kids fresh out of college alike – let me know there wasn't much respect for me there, not as a player.

Twenty minutes on the field changed that.

I put every single one of them to shame – speed, form, power, and honestly... heart. I hadn't been on a field with other people like this in two, almost three years, but now that I was here, it felt like I'd never left.

By the time we'd run through a round of drills, a little crowd had gathered, and one of the coaches motioned me over. "What kind of forty can you run?" he asked, and I shrugged.

"It's been a long time since I had an official number, but when I was in the league, a 4.3 was nothing."

His eyes narrowed at me for a second before he nodded. "Okay. You feel up to testing that out? Seeing what you can do now?"

I gave him another shrug. "I'm here, so... hey, why the hell not?" I was trying my best to appear nonchalant, but truthfully, I was loving this. Jordan hung close, smirking his ass off about the attention I was getting, which was probably his goal in the first place. He knew I wanted to be back on the field, so he wanted me back on the field. Problem was, this was something where I had to be not physically, but mentally ready.

That was where the uncertainty was.

A little shred of anxiety tried to take over as we got set up. It was just going to be a hand time, nothing official, but still... this felt like all those years ago, back when I was going through the combine.

"You ready?" the coach from earlier asked, and I nodded. I moved into position, and focused on the finish line, forty yards ahead. And then I took off.

It was exhilarating.

The other coach who did the actual timing didn't say anything to me once I'd finished the quick sprint and was walking back. He took the stopwatch to the first coach, where they conferred about it quietly until Jordan spoke up.

"Hey, are y'all gonna tell us how slow this nigga is, or nah?" he asked, a question that was met with laughter from the gathered crowd.

The coach smirked as he looked up, shaking his head as he looked right at me. "4.28," he said, and it felt like all the air rushed from my lungs. At my *fastest*, fresh from college, a 4.26 had been my quickest time. Obviously I knew there was a big margin of error with a hand-timed sprint, but just the fact that at 30, I was anywhere *near* a time like that was... *shit.*

Jordan clapped me on the shoulder, as outwardly hype as I internally felt, but was still frozen. "See, bruh?" he asked, leaning in. "This is what I mean. Your ass *belongs* on this field."

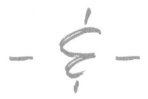

"4.28? Are you kidding me?! You've been holding out! – The Champ"

I grinned at that text, the first thing I saw when I picked up my phone after my shower. I'd been at the mini-camp the rest of the day, just observing like I'd actually come to do, but my mind was reeling.

The coaches were talking.

And apparently, I'd gone viral. I was getting a little sick of people and their damn camera phones. While my own phone was in my hand, it buzzed again with another message, and I shook my head as I read it. It was like she'd read my mind.

"At least you're going viral for a GOOD reason though. Why didn't you tell me you were going to do that??? – The Champ"

In typical Wil fashion, both texts were punctuated with emojis intended to help get her point across. The "angry" faces at the end of this particular text didn't accomplish anything but making me laugh though, as I imagined her in front of me, trying her best to hold that same expression.

She was too damned cute for it.

"I was just out there to watch. Wasn't planned. JJ talked me into it." I texted back.

"SMH. Nobody is immune to the Flash's charm. I'm proud of you though. You looked sooooo good out there, OMG. – The Champ"

I had to mentally check myself for my internal reaction to her words. Not that it was out of character for her to be encouraging like this – it was very, *very* her – but somewhere along the way, something had shifted, and sometimes... only *sometimes*... I had to remind

66

myself that we were friends. Now that The Clown was out of the picture… *sometimes* were happening a little more often.

"Appreciate it, Champ."

I kept my response simple, almost hoping she'd only texted me as a passing thought this time, and wouldn't respond, but of course that wasn't what happened.

"Anytime. Hey, you should let me treat you to dinner. I owe you one anyway, after the other night. – The Champ."

I read that, then shook my head. I still didn't really get why she thought she owed me anything, when she'd done me as much of a favor as I'd done for her. Not that she knew it, but she wasn't the only one who'd needed, as she phrased it, a human connection that night. As far as I was concerned, it had been equal exchange.

Well… almost.

Keeping my hands on *just* her feet had been a little bit of a struggle.

"And I don't want to hear that "you don't owe me anything" stuff either, okay? You and me + the soul food bar at Jacob's. SOON. – The Champ"

"Seriously?"

"Still on my comfort food kick, let me live LOL. – The Champ"

"Aiight, if you say so. Tomorrow?"

"It's a date! – The Champ"

"Thank you for hanging out with me so much lately, btw. I only need like… another week or five of being the needy friend, promise. – The Champ"

I plopped down on my bed and stretched out, holding the phone over me as I typed my response.

"You make it sound like kicking it with you is a chore – it's not. Don't forget, the wedding is next weekend… unless you changed your mind."

"Nope. I'll be there with my tissues. – The Champ"

I was interrupted from responding by a loud, booming sound that I quickly identified as somebody knocking on my door.

Knocking like they'd lost their damn minds.

I tossed on some sweats and a tee shirt to head to the door as the knocking continued, mentally preparing myself to throw hands with whoever was on the other side. There wasn't a goddamn thing important enough to be beating on my door like the police. My agitation went even higher as the knocks grew even more insistent the closer I got. I put my eye up to the peephole to see who the hell it could possibly be… and smiled.

This motherfucker.

"What the hell is your problem, fool?" I asked as soon as I opened the door, scowling at the man on the other side. He squinted at me like he was confused, then looked at the plaque beside the door like he was making sure he had the right condo.

"My bad sir. I used to have a homeboy that lived around here, but *you* look like the dude I saw in this viral video today trying out for a football team. And my homie didn't say *shit* to me about that, so you *can't* be him, nah."

I shook my head. "Here you go with this dramatic shit," I chuckled. "Get in here before one of my neighbors calls the police on your Black ass, man." I extended a hand to him, pulling him into a half-handshake, half-hug before he stepped in and I closed the door behind him.

"So when do you sign the contract?" he asked, making himself comfortable on my couch and reaching for the remote. Clayton Reed was one of very, *very* few people in this world with the privilege of treating my home like it was his.

Hell, he was the one who'd facilitated the purchase in the first place.

"Nobody is signing a damn contract," I explained, dropping into one of the chairs that flanked the sofa. "I was just out there to observe the camp, got talked into hitting the field."

His face bunched into a scowl, skepticism written clearly in his features. "Got talked into? Man, *please*. You know damn well it didn't take much talking. You were dying to get out there."

I shrugged. "Maybe a little bit."

He laughed at that. "Maybe a little bit my ass. It was all over your damn face, you were back at home out there. So… seriously, when are you signing the contract? Cause I know damn well the Kings are trying to snatch you up, or at least need to be. The only decent running back they have is Sanchez, and that dude can't stay out of drama enough to keep his head in the game. What did they say to you?"

68

"They didn't say anything. I *wasn't* there to try out, wasn't on any official roster."

"And?"

I chuckled. "Fuck you mean? It doesn't really work like that, where I just sign with a team because I want to."

"So you want to?"

"It's not that simple."

"Why not?" he challenged, not for the first time. "You keep putting the shit off, and you're gonna fuck around and watch the season go by without you."

"It's *not* that simple."

He scoffed, shaking his head. "You're making excuses and you know it. You can't even use the show as an excuse anymore, cause those three years you agreed to are about to be up. You didn't sign another contract did you?"

"Not yet," I answered, leaning into the cushion behind me. "They haven't even offered new ones yet, but the show has good ratings, so I'm expecting it."

"When does the current contract end?"

"Mid-June."

"*Nigga,*" Clayton exclaimed, sitting forward. "That's perfect timing for you. Time for you to talk to the Kings, get an answer *before* your contract is up. But we *both* know what their answer is going to be."

I shook my head. "I'm not a twenty-something anymore. Haven't touched NFL turf in three years. We don't *know* what the answer will be."

"Fuck that. What's the next excuse?"

I chuckled. "They aren't excuses man, it's just real. And everything else aside, I have to consider how it might affect Wil."

Shit.

As soon as I said her name, Clayton's eyes glazed over, and I didn't have to ask to guess the visual that had come to his mind. I distinctly remembered the 2012 Olympics, where Clayton had been insistent on stopping *everything* just to watch the women's track segments.

"*Nigga,*" he'd explained, with his voice filled with the kind of wonder and excitement you'd expect from somebody waiting to get keys to a brand-new luxury car. "*You ain't seen ass until you've seen*

69

these asses, I promise you. And the thighs—Nigga, the ass and thigh combo – nah, the waist to ass ratio… Just wait, you'll see. Goddamn works of art."

He hadn't been lying either.

I loved sports, but the Olympics had never been my thing. When they started introducing the women who were about do those sprints though, in those little ass shorts and sports bras… *damn.* Those were definitely the kinds of asses that could make a man a little emotional.

That was actually the first time I saw her. Wilhelmina Cunningham, daughter of Carla Ann Cunningham – Olympic track royalty. While the announcer was going on about the legacy she had to live up to, speculating on if she'd be faster than her mother, earn as many career gold medals, etc, she was waving at the camera and the crowd with this sweet smile on her face, as if she didn't know she was fine as hell.

Actually, Team USA was fine as hell, period, and the island women too, in every shade of black we came in. Clayton had two in particular he was all about – Wil, and one of the Bahamian competitors, a woman named Soriyah.

Five years later, he still wanted both of them.

"Speaking of your fine co-host… I might have to pop up and visit you on set tomorrow. Use that as my excuse to give her my condolences on the end of her relationship… and help her transition into a new one."

"It's barely been three weeks, man. Don't come at her with that."

He waved a hand, brushing off my words. "Three weeks is plenty of time, old boy was a clown anyway. You saw who he was fucking, right? On what planet do you trade a perfectly cooked ribeye for a Big Mac?"

"Women aren't food, so… you lost me."

"Aiight Mr. Elevated Thinking," Clayton laughed. "I forgot to put my realtor voice on, my bad. Gotta talk to you like I talk to these white folks – why on earth would that young man ruin what he had with a beautiful, successful woman like Wil in the pursuit of a shallow affair? Perish the thought."

70

"Nigga, I'm about to kick your stupid ass outta here," I chuckled. "And I don't know why that clown did what he did. I mean, Wil is…"

Shit.

Several not-exactly-"friendly"- descriptors ran through my head as I thought of all the reasons why she didn't deserve what he'd done. Many of the qualities that made a person a good friend – positive energy, willing to listen, willing to push you when you needed, being a supporter, a comforter, somebody that could make you laugh, could tell your problems, understood you, etc – were the same things that made them a good romantic partner.

The fact that she was beautiful, had an amazing body, and a warm, vivacious, comfortable sort of sex appeal that I had – mostly – mastered the art of ignoring on a day to day basis were *not* among those qualities.

"I mean, the ass alone would have been enough to keep me loyal, if we're keeping it all the way one hundred. Baby girl picked up a lil extra thickness since those Olympic days, but it went to the right places like a muhfucka. I saw those pictures a couple months ago, her and that *fine ass* Soriyah down in The Bahamas talking about some "hashtag, reunited"." He bit his fist, being full on dramatic. "There was this video, bruh. They're out in the ocean, Soriyah in a thong, ass looking like two scoops of chocolate in a dish just for me. I *know* you saw that!"

I stopped cracking up long enough to nod. "Yeah, I saw it."

"So you feel me then! Hell, you see Wil damn near every day, and I don't see how you do it."

My eyebrow lifted. "How I do what?"

"Go day to day without putting your face in her pussy, that's what."

"*Bruh!*" I laughed. "She *just* broke up with somebody she's been with since before I even knew who she was."

"Which makes her a single woman, fuck all that other stuff. I'm serious about coming up there tomorrow. If *you* aren't going to handle that, *I* will."

"Hell nah," I shook my head. "You aren't going to be handling a goddamn thing. Not with *that* one. No sir."

Clayton put a hand to his chest like he was offended. "Damn, it's like that? Blocking ain't even your position."

"Ruling on the field stands, nigga," I warned. "She's still heartbroken over the clown, and you think I'm about to let *you* line up a shot?"

He opened his mouth, then closed it again and he slumped back, sighing. "I want to act like I don't know why you wouldn't want me around her, but shit, it's been a long day. I'm too tired for the Oscar-worthy stuff today."

Clayton was my homie – one of two people I consider damn near my brothers, the other being my cousin Reggie Jr., who was my Aunt Phylicia's son. As such, we had a policy of telling each other the truth, and the damn truth about Clayton was that son was a *hoe*. I couldn't front like I hadn't had my fun too over the years, but Clayton was very much still living that life, and that wasn't an assumption. I heard the stories, saw the pictures, had made a habit of never trying to guess their names if I ran into him while he was out with somebody. I said the wrong name once, which got Clayton socked in the eye, and I hadn't made that mistake since.

"Long day? You double book your lunch dates or something? Keisha saw you out with Shawna while you were waiting for Monique?"

His eyes popped open. "Damn, did I already tell you about this?"

"You're gonna get your ass popped in the eye again," I laughed, pushing myself up from my chair. "You kicking it or not? I was about to order some wings and turn this game on."

"You already know my order," he called after me. "But uhhh… why aren't you *at* the game? Y'all aren't covering the preliminaries or something?"

"Nah, they're just giving us a break since we'll be out in Oakland Sunday for the next two in the series. Don't get back until Wednesday, and then we're in the studio every day after that, live-tweeting the other games. We get a break Saturday since we'll be at the Bailey wedding, and then right back to the grind."

Clayton snorted. "Live-tweeting? You actually get paid for that shit?"

"Part of the show. They're filming our play-by-play reactions in the studio, but even tonight, I'm supposed to be talking preliminary finals on social media. Not that it's a chore, but… still work. Builds the audience of our show."

72

"Builds the audience of somebody else's show, cause you'll be on the Kings' starting lineup for pre-season. Mark my words."

"Chill."

"Nope. I told Ms. Debbie I wasn't going to let you off the hook about that promise, so ain't no chill, nigga."

I stopped my perusal of the wing flavor options to look up. "What?"

Clayton's head turned to meet my gaze. "You heard what I said, and you know what I'm talking about."

"Yeah, I heard you, but what the fuck are you talking about?" I asked, rounding the counter to approach where he was sitting.

"You told her – *promised* her – that you would go back. She never liked that you left in the first damn place, but she accepted it because *you said* – "once you kick this thing, I'll go back, I promise." Those were your words, bruh. I listened to you say it."

I scoffed. "But she didn't kick it. It kicked *us*. I'm supposed to act like the shit didn't happen?"

"Nah, you're supposed to keep your damn promise," he shot back, shrugging as if it were really that simple. "You're making all these excuses for why not, and I was going to let you cook since I *get it,* man. I know it's still fresh, but bottom damned line – your ass promised. And if you're pissed, wanna kick me out, that's cool, but I'm gonna see you get your swole ass back on the goddamn field because *I* promised. You aren't the only one that lost her."

"I know that shit Clayton," I growled, shaking my head. I stalked back to the kitchen and snatched up my phone, trying to distract myself, but I couldn't even get my eyes to focus on the damn screen anymore. "When did you talk to her?"

The answer didn't matter. He hadn't said anything that wasn't the truth. I just wanted to… gauge the timing. I didn't have to wonder if she knew it was coming, if she'd felt that something had shifted. I'd sat at her bedside while she gave me an early goodbye I didn't want to hear, that filled me with a kind of rage I'd never, *ever* felt,

Her current round of treatment wasn't even finished, and she was fucking *giving up.* I tried to understand it, but all I could – selfishly – think about was the fact that I was losing the person who had been, from inception, my *everything*.

I made the promise because I would have promised her anything. Three years ago, I'd left the game because she was sick –

because the doctors said she was dying. I'd been on the field too many times with my head only halfway in the game because my heart was across the country with her, in a quiet room receiving chemo treatments. I played through the end of my contract and gave them nothing more – height of my career be damned.

My presence was needed somewhere exponentially more important.

She found out on TV. I was barely out of the meeting with my pissed-off agent and pissed-off coaches and pissed-off GM and pissed-off lawyers before it was all over TV, with the team releasing some fake ass statement of support. I hadn't even had a chance to breathe, let alone call anybody to say anything, but I knew what that was – getting ahead of the story, being "nice", making it seem as if they *allowed* me to do anything. That way, if I said anything negative, I would look like the bad guy.

But it was pointless – for one, my mother raised me to understand the value of silence, and secondly, I didn't have shit to say to the media about their damned club anyway. *They* were the ones who'd written the contract. Shame on them for giving me an unrestricted out in the first place.

It seemed like I was the only one who was happy though.

My mother was furious that I'd put her health before my passion for the field, but I meant it when I told her football could wait. That was when – as Clayton had reminded me – I'd made the promise to get back on the field, when she was healthy again. Maybe she already knew, or suspected back then, but I was optimistic. I honestly believed we would see that day.

But it never came.

"About a week before," Clay finally answered, and I nodded, understanding that he was referring to what was easily the worst week of my life. Lots of family, and flowers, and phone calls, none of which could distract me from what was inevitably happening. "Lena had stopped by. You were outside talking to her and Ms. Debbie was *pissed*," he chuckled. "Whew, shit, your mama couldn't stand that girl."

I couldn't help the grin that came to my face. "She was perky as hell for a good two months when I told her I'd broken off the engagement."

"Can't say I blame her. Lena was… a lot, bruh. Still don't understand your thought process on that one, but she is still bad as *fuck.* Aiight… so maybe I *do* understand your thought process."

I shook my head. "It definitely wasn't because of that."

"I know, I know. Head of the fine and bougie committee shows some interest in a dude from the hood, had you thinking she was the one. She got her hooks in you early," Clayton laughed. "She was fine *and* smart."

"Cold and calculated is more like it," I quipped back, then shook my head. "What am I putting in this wing order man?" I asked, completely changing the subject. I didn't want to talk about any of it right now, if I could help it.

Because Clay was who he was, he twisted his mouth into a smirk to make it clear he knew what I was doing, then nodded. "Spicy lemon pepper. It's been that long, you forgot?"

"Just double-checking. You know your tastes change with the weather – weather being whoever your flavor of the week is."

He laughed. "I can't even argue that."

I put the phone to my ear to place the order, and a few minutes later I was opening the fridge for beers. I hadn't yet arrived to a place where talking about my mother didn't leave me exhausted, so I was glad for the distraction of my responsibility to talk about this game.

It was much-needed.

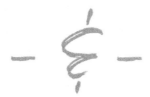

"I see you've still got that speed, boy!"

I grinned at the welcome I received from Wil's father as soon as he opened the door. His words were accompanied by a hug and handshake, with a grip strong enough to intimidate a lesser man – a lesser man being the clown Wil was going to marry. He had gleefully told me the story of leaving ol' boy with watery eyes every time they crossed paths, which had been often.

Obviously, he wasn't a fan.

But Wil was his one and only, his baby girl, and for the most part, if she was happy then so was he. This was my first time seeing him in the month since the cancelled wedding, so I wasn't surprised at all when the subject immediately changed from my viral, impromptu mini-camp video to an explanation of the violence he wanted to enact on his daughter's former fiancé. When he wanted to, Jackie Cunningham was a man that held a certain sense of... *don't fuck with me or mine* that people tended to abide by.

He hadn't earned the nickname "Jackhammer" as a professional boxer for no reason. Jackie Cunningham was known for the lightning fast speed and persuasive power of his fists – *not* a man you wanted to be on the wrong side of.

Hurting his baby girl couldn't get you *any* more wrong.

"You know he had the nerve to call my damn house?" Jack asked, speaking in a low tone. According to her last text, Wil was still upstairs with her mother, getting ready. "Talking about he wanted to apologize to us. I told him if he called here again, I was kicking that apology up his ass. You think he got the picture?"

I snickered. "Yes sir, I'm sure he probably did."

"*Fucking knucklehead,*" he muttered, shaking his head. "I welcomed that sonofabitch into my house for eight years. You think he appreciated it? *Hell no.* Because he was stupid. I mean... look at my little girl," he said, motioning to the wall by the stairs. The Cunninghams were unquestionably proud of their daughter. The opposite wall prominently featured her accomplishments – diplomas, Olympic golds, NCAA track, and other regional medals. But the wall *he* was pointing to was a gallery of framed pictures in varying sizes, with one subject in common – Wil.

He pointed to one in particular, a recent, obviously professional shot of Wil and her mother that fulfilled that whole cliché of "looking more like sisters than mother and daughter". "That is a *beautiful* girl," Jack continued. "Talented, smart, good head on her shoulders, not no damn pushover." He waved a finger at me. "But that right there, that was likely the problem. Weak man like that? Can't handle a woman like the one we raised."

I gave a noncommittal nod in response, to avoid getting him fired up, but... I strongly agreed with that. As genuinely warm and sweet-natured as Wil was, she was nobody's punk. She couldn't be, not in our business, where she regularly dealt with men who would pat her

76

cute little head and ignore her if she let them. She wasn't the type to sit back and take bullshit, and the clown seemed like the type who wanted a woman who would.

The shit just didn't match.

"Ramsey! Baby you sure can wear the hell out of a suit!"

I was smiling before I even turned around in time to see Wil's mother heading down the stairs. Well, just her feet at first because of the spiral staircase, but a few seconds later, I was able to see the woman herself.

"I peeked at you from the landing," she told me as she pulled me into a hug. "What is my husband down here fussing about?"

"I ain't fussing, I'm *telling*."

"He didn't come here for that, he came to get Wil," she scolded, shaking her head.

Me? I was just trying not to laugh at them, especially when Jack not-at-all inconspicuously pinched Carla's ass, making her yelp.

"Will you stop it?!" She half-whispered half-laughed, clearly pleased as she stepped closer to me – probably not realizing I knew what had just happened. "This gray suit is *sharp* on you, sweetheart, and these dusty rose accents in the pattern of your tie are a perfect match to Wil's dress."

I frowned. "Match? Is that why she asked for a picture of what I was wearing a few days ago?"

I really meant to ask that question in my head, but Carla nodded. "She's your date, you're supposed to coordinate a little. You two are going to look so good together. *Wil!*" she shouted, stretching out toward the stairs as if that made her louder. "Are you coming down or not?"

"Yes! Trying to buckle the shoes you said you were going to help with!" Wil yelled, and Carla's eyes went big.

"Sorry baby, Ramsey distracted me. I'm coming!"

I shook my head as Carla rushed back up the stairs, and Jack moved to stand beside me.

"You know," he started, and just those words let me know something awkward was about to happen. "I really did always think you were a better man than that Darius, especially after I met your mother when y'all did that parent's day segment on your show. Fine woman, with a beautiful spirit, and she raised you right," he said, leaning in like he was telling me a secret.

I didn't know what else to do, so I nodded. "Thank you sir."

"You're very welcome," Jack grinned. "Between you and me – I'd love to have you as a son-in-law. Think about it – Jackhammer and Sledgehammer. Wouldn't that be something? They'd probably write an article about us."

He cracked up at his own words, and before I had to figure out who "they" were, or come up with a response, I was saved by the sound of Wil and her mother coming down the stairs.

Damn.

I wasn't expecting her to look that good.

I mean, I'd always thought she was a beautiful woman, but… *damn.*

That dress was… *damn.*

It was the same pale rose color as the accents in my tie, and she was wearing these nude, strappy heels that made her legs look… *damn.*

The folded, off-shoulder style of the dress was sexy as hell on her, leaving her collarbone and plenty of golden brown skin in full view. The length – just past her knees – gave it an air of sophistication, and the fit… again, *damn.* That dress was hugging curves I'd never quite seen hugged that way.

A really, *really* good way.

Her hair was straightened, but pinned up, with loose tendrils framing her face. For some reason, she looked nervous, and her looking nervous made me *feel* nervous, something I couldn't recall ever experiencing around her.

"Do I look okay?" she asked, smoothing the fabric over her hips, and I'm pretty sure I looked at her like she was crazy.

"You look amazing," I told her, which immediately eased the tension between her eyebrows, and a little smile spread over her face.

"So do you. But I mean, we already knew that would be the case," she teased as she walked toward me, coming in for a quick hug before she turned to her parents to say goodbye.

Thank God for *quick* hugs.

Because looking like that, and smelling like that… *damn.*

This was going to be a long night.

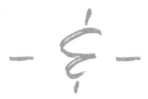

I knew this wasn't a good idea.

Wil had been either in tears, or on the edge of them, all night.

Not like she was sobbing, or even audibly crying, but throughout the vows, through the special performance as Trent and Jade entered the reception, and now as the groom performed his signature dancing for the bride, errant tears had been creating streams down her face.

This was tough for her – it *had* to be.

Only a month had passed since what was supposed to be *her* special day, that never ending up coming. Here at LaChateau, in midtown Manhattan, the Baileys had created an ultra-romantic vibe. Tiny white lights, flowers, music, the whole shebang, in an event obviously filled with love. Everybody was laughing, dancing, having a good time celebrating the newlyweds. Everybody – including Wil – seemed thrilled for them, which created a great energy.

But Wil's tears were messing me up.

On the drive from Stamford to Manhattan, she'd explained why her parents were so giddy, seeing us off like we were teenagers going to a homecoming dance.

"They're just glad I'm getting dressed up to get out of the house," she'd said. *"All I do really is go to work, and kick it with you or Naima. They think being out with celebrities tonight is going to make me feel… renewed, or something. Make me forget about Darius."*

Looking at her now… they hadn't quite predicted that right.

It wasn't as if she seemed out of place. Anybody watching her would assume that she was simply overcome with the beauty and emotion of the wedding and reception, which wasn't entirely untrue. But *I* knew – because I'd asked - she had her own failed engagement on her mind, and was trying her best to hold it together.

That's what prompted me to reach for her hand under the table, squeezing it to get her attention before I leaned in to speak into her ear.

"Are you sure you're good? We don't have to stay if you're not really feeling it."

"We can't leave yet," she whispered back, turning to face me. "We haven't even said congratulations to them."

I nodded. "Okay. After they finish up with these, I'm sure we'll get an opportunity. But after that…?"

"Yes." Her answer was too immediate for it to not have already been on her mind. "All this love in the air has me feeling sorry for myself."

She said that with a faint smile, but I didn't get the impression it was because she was kidding. When she turned away again, she picked up the glass of champagne – her second since the reception started – and knocked it back in one swig.

Guess she wasn't lying about coping through alcohol.

Once that performance section was over, we left our table to make our way through the crowd to where the bride and groom were posted at the front of the room. I grinned at the smiles on their faces. The way Trent looked at his brand new wife… *that* was how it was supposed to be.

One glance at Wil told me she was thinking the same thing, but it was obviously hitting her differently. There was a little quiver in her lip that gave it away.

Instead of saying anything about that, I chose distraction. We were waiting in a pretty slow-moving line to greet the couple anyway, so I pulled out my phone and turned to the camera, telling her to say cheese. Whatever makeup she was wearing must have been some sort of sorcery, because despite the numerous tears she'd shed throughout the wedding, she looked just as good as she had when we left her parents.

She didn't protest the appearance of the camera – in fact, she seemed relieved by it, immediately making duck lips at my screen. For the next several minutes, we played around, until we were closer to the front of the line, where I put it away. After that, it didn't take long for it to be our turn.

"Look at you bruh," I exclaimed, extending a hand to shake Trent's. "I see wifey already has you branching out, with the burgundy," I teased him, motioning at his suit jacket – which was pretty damned fly.

He shook his head as he accepted my greeting. "Nigga, I thought you were the fashionable one? This isn't basic ass burgundy – this is *wine*, and I look damn good," he laughed, then supplemented the handshake with a quick fist bump.

"Can't argue with it," I agreed. "Congratulations man."

His gaze slid to the side of me and landed on Wil, and his eyes widened a bit, like he was surprised to see her there. He stiffened a little, which Wil didn't even notice as she ignored the hand he offered to give him a hug.

"Congratulations," she gushed. "This is *such* a beautiful wedding, and your *bride*, oh my goodness." She skirted past me to get to Jade, who I hadn't spoken to yet. "You're just glowing, and your bump is adorable, and it's so… *beautiful*," she finished, her voice cracking with emotion as she hugged the bride too. Jade and Trent exchanged a look that I didn't think was just about Wil's emotional, possibly tipsy greeting.

I should have thought about it before I invited her, but when Trent was re-signed to the Kings, Wil had been a little… critical. Nothing mean-spirited, or over the top, but she'd definitely gone in, naming him in the "Out of Bounds" segment we did sometimes, for athletes who'd been into shit they shouldn't.

In fairness, Wil was a *huge* Bailey fan, had even admitted having the same harmless crush that millions of other female fans had on him. It was exactly that fandom that left her disappointed when he'd had to leave the field to serve jail time, even though that had been years ago. In the segment, she'd talked about being glad to see him back, but she was still salty about him "turning himself into a cliché".

Something I admired about her though, was her objectivity when it came to these athletes. Maybe because she'd been one herself, she was never callous with her critiques, just sharp. And when it was time for praises, she piled those on too, and had certainly had plenty for Trent as he proved himself again on the field.

But… people tended to remember it when you said things that cut and bled – fair or not.

Still, they were absolutely gracious.

"Ramsey, Wil, let me formally introduce you to my bride, Jade Bailey," Trent said, putting a hand at Jade's back. She was tiny, especially compared to Trent, who towered over her, and just as Wil had put it – glowing and beautiful in her pregnancy.

I gave her a short hug, and we exchanged a few more pleasantries before we moved along, giving the people behind us their chance to speak to the newlyweds. We'd only walked a few steps before I heard my name, and turned to see JJ and Cole Richardson, approaching.

Cole immediately went to Wil, exclaiming, "This dress? Are you kidding me? Could you possibly look more amazing?" before she hugged her, staying close to speak about something in her ear. I couldn't be too nosy though, because one second I was exchanging greetings with Jordan, and the next he was leading me off, saying someone wanted to speak to me.

I stopped moving to look at Wil, who'd found yet another glass of champagne. She waved me off, telling me to go, and Cole gave me a reassuring smile.

"I've got her," she said, looping an arm through Wil's before she led her away, giving me no real reason to protest wherever the hell Jordan was taking me – though I had an idea.

Which proved to be correct.

The group of men he led me to had a whole lot of money and a whole lot of power to go with it. Jackson Hunter, the Drake brothers, Azmir Jacobs, Kingston Whitfield, and the person Jordan was undoubtedly bringing me to speak to – Eli Richardson.

"Ramsey Bishop," he declared, stepping toward me as soon as I walked up. After quick introductions to the rest of the circle, he pulled me away and spoke again. "You created quite the stir at my mini-camp last week," he said, extending his hand.

"Not intentionally sir," I answered, firmly returning his handshake. "Got talked into it by my friend here." I motioned to Jordan, who grinned, then clapped me on the shoulder.

"Somebody had to get you on that field. Why not me? Besides – you belong out there anyway."

In front of me, Eli nodded. "After seeing that video from last week, and taking a look at your tape… I would tend to agree."

He looked at my highlights?

"Why'd you leave the game?" Azmir asked, stepping in. "Your contract was up, yes, but you were young, healthy, top of your game. Were you unhappy with the league? Dissatisfied with your team?"

Something told me they already knew the answer to that – probably knew the answers to every question I was sure they were

82

about to ask me. I swallowed hard, taking a second before I answered. "My mother was very sick. The way I was traveling for the team, I didn't feel that I was able to care for her the way I needed to. When my contract was up, I declined to re-sign. Exercised my option to leave the team, and leave the league."

Azmir nodded, and then Eli spoke up again. "And since then, you've been using the journalism degree you earned at BSU. Hosting your show with Jack and Carla Cunningham's daughter," he stated, rather than asked me. "But you haven't signed a new contract there either, have you?"

I didn't have to wonder how he knew. This group's money was long enough to know… everything.

"No," I said. "I haven't."

"Instead of just talking about football… how would you feel about playing it again?" Eli asked, his gaze piercing as he waited for me to answer.

Again, I paused, carefully considering my words before I responded. "It's what I promised her I would do," I said, remembering my conversation with Clayton last week. It wasn't that I didn't want to be on the field again, because I did. But at this point… keeping my promise was the thing that would make me take action, so I clung to it.

Azmir spoke next. "You're from Connecticut, right? Bridgeport."

"Born and raised."

Eli grinned. "See there? This is your destiny, Bishop. Think about it – playing for the home team."

I nodded. "It would be an amazing opportunity."

He and Azmir exchanged a look, and a light chuckle.

"We have your contact information," Eli said. "We'll be in touch to schedule an official workout so we can see what you can do."

My eyebrows shot up. "I…*wow*," I stammered, as what had just happened *really* hit me. "I… I look forward to hearing from you. Again, thank you for the opportunity."

"No." Eli stepped forward, putting a hand on my shoulder. "If all goes smoothly, it's not just an opportunity," he corrected. "It's your future."

The next few minutes were a blur.

I know goodbyes were exchanged and all of that, but I damn near felt like I was floating as Jordan led me to find Wil and Cole.

83

Barely, I registered Jordan telling me congratulations before he and Cole moved away, leaving me with Wil, who had a cocktail glass of something that looked fruity in her hands.

"I wanna dance," she said, after she'd gulped it down and handed the glass to a passing server, and I absently nodded my agreement.

As soon as we were out on the floor, the music switched from up-tempo to something slower, with the DJ declaring he wanted to see all the couples out on the floor. Wil stepped close to me – closer than I expected her to – and I put my hands respectfully at her waist. Even in my haze, I noted that with heels on, Wil was actually a little taller than me – perfect height for my hands to fall naturally at her ass, which was looking *perfectly* grab-able in that goddamn dress.

"Ramsey," she whispered, leaning in to catch my gaze. "What's up with you? You seem distracted."

Not so distracted I didn't hear the subtle slur in her words as she spoke, but I shook my head. "It's nothing, not really. Just… I think I got offered a job."

She frowned a little, processing my words. "Offered a job? By who?"

"Eli Richardson."

For a second, she stopped the slow sway we'd been doing to the music, and then her eyes went wide. "Eli Richardson, as in owner of the Kings?!" she whisper-yelled, and I pulled her in closer just to calm her.

"Yes," I said into her ear. "But… not quite an offer yet, not really. They want me to come to a workout."

"That's basically an offer," she whispered back, and I grinned. "Yeah… it is."

She pulled back enough to look me in the eyes. Hers were glossy again, but not for the previous reasons. "That is amazing. And it's happening because *you* are amazing," she said, then wrapped her arms around my neck in a way that pushed my face right into her breasts, surrounding me in warmth and softness and *goddamn why does she smell so good?*

I knew I should pull back, but I didn't immediately, taking a second for a deep breath in before I disconnected us.

"Thanks, Champ," I told her, and her response was to give me a silly grin.

"Thanks for what?" she asked, then giggled and I bit the inside of my jaw to keep from laughing.

That was our cue to leave.

She slept for most of the drive back to Stamford, waking up just as we were pulling into the city.

"*My throat is dry*," she complained, and I chuckled as I handed her the container of gum I kept in the console.

"That's all I have for you right now, Champ."

She gave me a mumbled "thank you" and accepted a few pieces. By the time I keyed in the code to get us through the gate for her parent's neighborhood, she was upright, which was a good sign. I considered that maybe she hadn't drunk as much as I thought, but that notion was killed as soon as I pulled around to the driveway of the attached apartment she was staying in, and opened the door for her to get out.

I had to catch her to keep her from falling on her ass, which she thought was funny as hell. Shaking my head, I helped her inside, then helped her to her bedroom, with her laughing and keeping up a steady stream of conversation the whole time. Any hope that she'd slept a bit of it off was just that – hope. Leave it to Wil to wake up still tipsy, just energized.

"Everybody looked *sooo* good tonight," she gushed, falling backwards across her bed. I wasn't "just a friend" enough to undress her or help her change, but I took the opportunity to at least get the strappy heels off of her, so she could sleep for real.

Or at least, I intended to.

Her tipsy, silly ass wouldn't keep still, giggling and declaring that it tickled every time I tried to touch her. I'd seen Wil under the influence before, so it didn't surprise me at all, but this was different. This time, she was in a sexy ass dress that was climbing higher up her legs and lower down her chest with every motion, and I was trying my best to be a gentleman.

And a friend.

A *friend.*

I needed to get my ass out of there.

I sat down on the bed and grabbed her legs – yet another move she found completely hilarious. I managed to keep her foot still with one hand and unstrap with the other, but as soon as I had the first one off, her goddamn wiggles took over again, and next thing I knew, she was straddling my lap.

Why the hell is she straddling my lap?!

"Ramsey," she stated, very seriously, as she grabbed my face in her hands.

"What's up Champ?" I asked, trying not to notice that her dress was up around her hips now, and her nipples were hard, showing plainly through the fabric.

She stared at me for a second, like she'd lost her train of thought, and then... her tongue was in my mouth. Minty and cool and very, *very* insistent, and for a couple of seconds... I didn't do anything to stop her. And then for a couple of seconds after that, I maybe, possibly, definitely kissed her back. Massaged my tongue against hers, tasted her lips, let my hands drift down to her ass and squeeze, enjoyed the sound and vibration of her moaning into my mouth.

But then, her hands weren't at my face anymore, they were between us, trying to reach for my pants, and...

What the fuck are you doing, bruh?

Shit.

I pulled away from the kiss, ignoring the confused look on her face to ease her back onto the bed. Her response was to put her legs in the air, opening wide. I quickly grabbed her ankles to close them, then unbuckled that other shoe in record time. By the time I dropped it to the ground, she was already barely keeping her eyes open, and mumbling something that sounded strangely like, *"don't judge me, it's been a long ass time."*

I shook my head as I tucked her under the covers, and glanced at the nightstand. There was a hair bonnet there, and I thought about it for a second before I carefully maneuvered it over her head, then did what I'd originally intended – got my ass out of there.

I took her key to lock the door behind me. I was staying up at my Aunt's tonight, and I doubted Wil would be in any shape to leave home before I came back through the next morning. Still, I sent a text to her phone to tell her I had her key, then climbed into my truck.

Damn.

I could still taste that kiss.

Instead of lingering on it, I turned the truck on and cranked my music, trying to clear it from my mind. She was drunk, and emotional, and… horny, if I'd interpreted her mumbled words right. It was nothing to place stock in, especially knowing her mental state.

But… still.

I couldn't shake it.

Something about liquor not creating urges, only amplifying existing ones, kept coming to mind.

Five

Wil

Mmmmm.

With my eyes still closed, I rolled over onto my stomach, putting myself in a position to reach the nightstand drawer. Tugging it open, I felt around until my hand connected with what I wanted. A little tingle of anticipation ran through me as I turned to my back again and opened my legs, positioning my current favorite sex partner in just the right spot. I bit my lip and sucked in a breath, then flipped the switch to turn it on.

Nothing happened.

My eyes popped open, as I flipped the switch off and on, off and on, willing my mechanical boyfriend not to let me down, not when I'd woken up so hot and bothered.

"Ugh!"

I snatched the bright pink vibrator from between my legs and under the covers and sent it flying across the room. It hit the wall with a dull thump and then dropped to the floor, where I almost hoped the impact would shake something back into place, giving enough juice for one last hurrah, but… nope.

Nothing.

"Stupid," I muttered, honestly not completely clear on if I was talking to the vibrator or to myself as I looked down, realizing that I was still in last night's dress. I must have gotten *well* acquainted with the open bar at Trent and Jade's wedding if I'd crawled into bed without undressing or taking a shower.

At least you took your shoes off.

I groaned as I sat up, reeling against the little bit of dizziness that hit once I was upright. My purse was on the nightstand, so I made it the first place I looked for my phone. Sure enough, it was there, and almost dead, with several missed text and calls.

The one that caught my attention was from Ramsey.

"Took your key with me so I could lock your door. I'll drop it off when I come back through in the morning – R. Bishop."

And then:

"Decided not to ring the bell or call, in case you're still sleeping last night off. Key is in an envelope that I put through your mail slot. Tried to get it as far away from the door as I could. – R. Bishop."

Sleeping last night off?

Shit, did I embarrass myself at the wedding or something? I sat back against the headboard, trying to remember, but couldn't call anything crazy to mind. I'd talked with Cole, Ramsey and I had danced, and then we left, and I fell asleep in the car.

I shrugged.

Maybe he just meant my weepiness, since I'd been an emotional mess for quite a bit of the night. But I was glad I'd gone. All that love in the air had definitely cured my concern of becoming cynical about love, generally speaking.

At this point, I was just skeptical about it for *myself.*

I went through my other calls and texts, then went to my social media accounts. I grinned when I saw the pictures I'd been tagged in throughout the night, glad that nobody – yet – had posted anything of me crying. But then I came across one that nearly made my heart stop just before I blushed, *hard.*

Really, the picture was of Ramsey, but I was in it too. He looked so, *so* good in his beautifully cut gray suit, with those broad shoulders and his fresh haircut, and his beard glistening and all that. But I'd – obviously – already known that Ramsey looked good last night. What struck me was the look on his face.

Eyes slightly narrowed, bottom lip pulled between his teeth, obviously enthralled by whatever had his attention.

Me.

We were holding hands in the picture – something I'd probably been the one to initiate, because I'd been doing it since we walked in, using him for strength. I'd stepped a little ahead of him, to speak to someone, but made sure to remain connected to him. I remembered the moment in vivid detail, squeezing his hand so he would know I was asking him to stay. Apparently, his gaze had wandered a bit before it landed on my ass, which he was looking at the same way I looked at a good piece of carrot cake.

I didn't recognize the name of the person who'd posted the picture, but it already had a ton of likes. The caption underneath was a single word.

#mood.

A fresh round of heat rushed to my face.

"Thank you, dress," I said out loud as I shook my head. I'd been a little bit nervous about it, but apparently it had been a good decision if it had Ramsey looking at me like that, when I'd always suspected he'd mentally put me in the "sister" category.

Several of my thoughts about him yesterday had been far from "brotherly" though.

In between my bouts of being the "sad chick" at the wedding had been moments like the one that woke me up. He was so damned handsome and smelled so damned good, and was so damned strong, putting those big hands at my waist to lead me around and…

I pushed out a sigh.

Girl, you need help.

I climbed out of bed and went to the bathroom, stopping when I caught a glimpse of myself in the mirror. I frowned at the bonnet on my head and then pulled it off, surprised to see that aside from being a bit flat, my little updo was still in place.

How the hell did I remember to put my bonnet on, but fell asleep in my dress?

I pondered that as I sat down to pee, and pondered it more as I washed my hands, then reached for my toothbrush. While I was brushing, I took the pins down from my hair, and tried to remember putting on that damn bonnet. When that didn't work, I tried to remember taking off my shoes…

I didn't take off my shoes.

Ramsey took off my shoes, when he helped me inside, which is why he had my key.

Duh, Wil.

I shook my head as my brain finally started filling in the fuzzy memories. Ramsey helping me from the car, helping pick out the key to get inside. Ramsey sitting on the bed with me, unbuckling my shoe, handling me with care, like always. He'd taken off his jacket and tie in the car, so sitting on my bed, he'd looked so casual – so damned *comfortable.*

I blinked, and then, I remembered climbing into his lap, and trying to put my tongue down his throat.

I damn near choked on my toothbrush as the kiss flooded my mind in blurry detail. His lips had been so, *so* good, and even in getting my drunk, horny behind off of him, he'd been tender with me.

Why couldn't I have ended up engaged to a man like that?

I spat the minty foam residue out of my mouth, then rinsed before I went back to my phone to read the two messages from him again. Nothing in either text hinted that anything untoward had happened though, so…

Maybe I'd imagined it?

I *had* woken up feeling lusty, so it easily could have been part of a fantasy from a dream. Was *probably* part of a fantasy from a dream. It had to be. Probably.

Please?

I put the phone down and headed for the shower. It was already past noon, and I still needed to eat, look through a fresh batch of apartments, and drive into the city to be at the studio for another filmed live-tweeting of the game tonight.

Which meant I would be seeing Ramsey.

The very last thing I needed was awkwardness in any of my relationships with the people who were serving as my rocks right now. I couldn't be having dirty dreams and stuff about Ramsey – not only did we work together, he was my friend. Like… a *real* friend.

I couldn't ruin that.

92

I couldn't explain the butterflies I felt when I knocked on the door to Ramsey's dressing room. Even though I heard him say, "come in", I hesitated a few seconds before I touched the knob.

Stop being a weirdo.

After a deep breath, I opened the door, only to have my breath snatched right back out of my chest. Ramsey's shirt was in his hand – *not* on his body – and though I'd seen him shirtless plenty of times before, my mental state wasn't right for it today.

"Hey…," I said, averting my eyes as he pulled the *From the Sidelines* tee shirt on. "I got my key back, thank you. And thank you for getting me in safely too. I appreciate it."

He nodded, then dropped down onto his couch. "Not a problem at all, Champ."

His dressing room was much quieter than mine tended to be. He didn't use a stylist for the show, choosing to dress himself instead, and he hated when they came after him with the stage makeup. I usually had a wardrobe stylist, makeup, and hair, all crowding me. For tonight's show, everything was understated – I was wearing a *From the Sidelines* tee as well – so there had been a lot less chaos, which was why I had time to stop by and talk to him privately before we went on set.

"Hey, so… you mentioned me "sleeping off last night," I started, nervously twisting my fingers together, even though I was trying to sound nonchalant. "I wasn't like… *too* sad, was I? Was I embarrassing?"

He scoffed. "Nah, nothing like that. That's not what I was talking about though."

My eyes went wide, and I turned away from him, playing with the assorted cuff links on the vanity so he couldn't see my face. "Oh? Cause… I can't really recall doing anything *too* crazy… is that not the case?"

"Nah," he laughed. "You just… got a little silly. Same as any time I've seen you tipsy. No big deal."

I tried not to let out too big of a sigh of relief before I turned around to find him wearing a big, mischievous smile as he stood and approached me.

"Unless you want to talk about the fact that you kissed me. I mean… I guess *that* could be considered a little crazy."

"Oh my God! So I *did* kiss you?! Oh my God," I squealed, covering my face with my hands. Ramsey – *asshole* – was cracking up laughing as he pulled me into a hug, rocking me back and forth.

"Gotta say Champ, you surprised the hell out of me," he chuckled as he pulled back. "I most definitely was not expecting that."

"I'm *so* sorry. I was drinking to try to relax, and I think I had too much, and I—"

"Wil!" He grabbed my arms, looking me right in the face, with that same impish shine in his eyes. "Nobody is looking for you to apologize. Damn, you're reacting like this to the kiss, I probably shouldn't even tell you how you tried to get my pants off."

I gasped. "*No!*"

He nodded, still grinning. "Yes. You were pretty determined too, but I guess your coordination was off a little bit."

"Oh *Goddd,*" I whined, turning away from him as I clamped my hand to my forehead.

"You know what really surprised me though?" he continued, and my eyes snapped in his direction as I turned around. "I don't think I realized you were that flexible, could do a split like that."

I frowned. "A split? What are you talking about?"

"When I pulled you off my lap, you kinda laid back, and well…opened wide."

"*Oh my God!*" I shrieked, backing away. "I… Ramsey, stop playing, I didn't… did I really…?"

"Show me the money shot? Yeah, you did."

"I think I'm gonna pass out," I said, and Ramsey immediately wrapped me in his arms again, but his ass was still laughing.

"Chill, I'm just messing with you," he said, and a tiny little bead of hope blossomed.

"Messing with me?" I asked. "So… I didn't really do that?"

He shook his head. "No, you *definitely* did it, I'm just saying… I'm teasing you. I hope you don't think I'm really bothered about it."

I punched his arm, then pulled back. "Of course you aren't! You got kissed, and got the view from the box – *literally.*"

94

Ramsey cracked up at that, and even though I was embarrassed as hell, I couldn't help laughing too.

"I didn't look, I promise," he said, as if that was supposed to make me feel better. "I closed your legs and put you under your covers, and then I left."

"After you put my bonnet on," I reminded him, and he shrugged.

"Yeah, that too."

"Which was really sweet. Thank you."

He shook his head. "Like I said… not a problem."

For some reason, my mind went back to that picture, of him looking at me like something he wanted to devour – a clear difference from right now, with his barely veiled amusement of my tipsy antics the night before. Antics that probably killed any possible desire for me.

What? Why the hell should that matter?

"Did you have one of these in your dressing room too?" he asked, stepping away to pick up a packet of papers from the vanity. The front was stamped with the WAWG logo.

"Yeah," I nodded. "Hadn't really looked at it yet, since I figure it's just their soft open, to start the conversation. They probably saw your viral video, and are trying to lock you down before it goes further."

He shook his head. "Too late for that. What *I'm* thinking is that they caught wind of my conversation yesterday with Eli Richardson."

"Conversation with Eli Richardson?!" My eyes bugged wide as I stepped up to him.

"Yes, drunky," he teased. "I told you last night… the Kings want me to come in for a workout."

I frowned for a second, trying to remember, grasping a fuzzy thread in mind that led me back to it. "*Oh, shit!* Yes, you did!" I threw my arms around his waist, pulling him into a hug. "Congratulations, again."

"Nothing to congratulate yet. The workout isn't even scheduled."

"But it will be, and you'll crush it – isn't that how you got that name? Anybody between you and your destination on the field is gonna feel like they got hit by a sledgehammer. That's how you have to look at this workout – as something to take the hammer to."

His mouth spread into a grin. "Here you go with the Ms. Motivational thing again."

"You say that like it's a bad thing."

"Absolutely not. Trust me – I consider having you in my corner a privilege."

"As you should," I said, picking up the contract he'd put down on the vanity. "As a matter of fact, *I* believe in your ass so much that…" I grabbed the stack of papers in the middle and twisted, then laughed. "I'm just playing, I'm not about to rip this."

Ramsey's eyebrow went up, and then he took the papers from my hand, copying my actions. Only… he *actually* ripped them, right down the middle, then held up the two halves.

"No guts, no glory, right?"

I grinned, big. "No guts, no glory. This means you're going for it? Like, full on?"

"Full on. I mean, if it doesn't work out, it doesn't, but at least I kept my word."

"Absolutely. And it's not like the network is going to tell you no. They *love* your ass."

He chuckled. "Nah, you're the eye candy around here."

"They don't care about that, *at all*," I laughed. "I mean, you see what they did to me starting out."

He shook his head. "Nah, Champ. Say it right. What you *mean* is, do I remember how you treated me like the enemy for the first few months we worked together? And the answer is *hell yes.* I swear, I don't think you liked me until you met my mama."

"Who, by the way, was on *my* side," I giggled. He wasn't lying on me though. From the time he first sat down beside me at that desk, I'd *hated* his ass.

From the Sidelines was my show – meaning, mine alone – originally. I'd hustled my ass off getting a meeting with somebody who could make a decision, making a point of *not* involving my parents. I couldn't change my last name obviously, couldn't do much to hide my legacy, but I certainly didn't use it as a selling point. I sold *me*. My idea, for my show, sports from my perspective as not only a woman, but a professional athlete with accolades, and a well-earned journalism degree.

I was nervous, yes, but I went in with my head held high to give my pitch and hopefully stake my claim. And… I got it. They let me shoot a pilot, and offered me a contract, but when I got to set for the first official filming… there was Ramsey Bishop. Well-dressed and charming and a superstar in his own right. I understood his appeal, understood what they felt he would bring to the show.

The show they'd promised as *mine*.

I was slow to warm up to him. *Very* slow. On air, I was the picture of professionalism, and would play along with his jokes, keep the right vibe going, all of that, but once we were off those cameras… it was all I could do to *just* pretend he didn't even exist.

I wasn't really mad at *him* though. It wasn't his fault, but in a situation where I felt powerless, taking it out on him was the only control I had. I'd signed a contract to do something I hated now, knowing the truth behind it.

They hadn't hired me for any of the reasons I thought I could make *From the Sidelines* successful. They'd hired me for exactly what I *didn't* want to be hired for.

The Cunningham name.

I got it, really.

My parents were black royalty – professional athletes in a time where racism was *much* more prevalent than now. The eighties were the height of their professional careers, but they still, separately, made time for civil rights activism during a time where past gains were being undone. They were vocal about homelessness, AIDS education and prevention, and it certainly didn't hurt that they were just attractive people.

Once they got together?

Whew.

It was like they had all of Black America collectively on their side. The wedding was televised, and people *still* talked about it now, since it was basically a gathering of everybody who was anybody in Black sports or entertainment at that time.

They were, again, Black royalty now, considered among our legends.

You couldn't turn the daughter of legends down.

Especially when they were notoriously generous with their checkbook. As soon as I saw my father's name and picture go up on the wall as a "platinum level supporter" of WAWG, I knew what it was.

Ramsey wasn't the kind of man you could hold a pointless grudge against for long though. He wasn't of the "larger than life" personality type, but he was definitely a strong presence. He always had a compliment or encouraging word, and he was funny and intelligent, and the man *knew* sports. And... before all this happened, I'd been a fan. Not just of his skill on the field, but of the no-nonsense tack he took with press. He didn't play along with their ridiculous questions, never fed into it when they tried to pull a negative spin, none of that. It had gained him a reputation of being "difficult", but nobody could deny the man on the field.

That translated into how he interacted with the athletes *we* spoke to. He treated them with the same respect he'd demanded for himself.

And I couldn't help but respect *him.*

That was only multiplied when I saw how he interacted with his mother. I never knew, until then, that I was a sucker for a man who loved his mother. I hadn't been cold to him since.

And so, professional respect evolved into genuine enjoyment of working with him. That developed into being buddies, which shifted into being for real *friends*. Going out to eat, working out together, text conversations, things like that. And now – even more since my breakup, honestly – he'd become one of my most valued friends, somebody I really, *truly*, couldn't imagine being without.

Funny how that happens.

"She was only on your side because she was trying to get some grandbabies," Ramsey said, bursting my bubble. "She thought she was going to hook us up, and then you would convince me."

My mouth dropped open. "Are you serious?"

"Serious as purple piss."

"What does that even mean?" I giggled, and he shook his head.

"I don't know, just saying shit," he admitted. "But mama was *definitely* trying to get me with somebody other than Lena."

Hmph.

I pressed my lips closed.

Ramsey had always made a point of not commenting on my love life – meaning Darius – since we'd been friends, and I'd given that same courtesy to him. It was a respect thing, really – I wouldn't want my man talking about his issues with me with a female friend who may or may not but probably did want to screw him and was just waiting on her chance. So I didn't complain about Darius to Ramsey either – at least not while we were together.

Now that it was over though, Ramsey wasn't shy about letting his disdain for Darius be known. It wasn't as if he ever spoke about him at length, or without me bringing up the subject, but the few words he gave were certainly never kind, or positive. I was pretty sure Ramsey hadn't even spoken his name, choosing instead to refer to him as "the clown", which was accurate, obviously.

If I had to call Lena anything, she'd be…. "the bitch".

And that was generous.

Lena McBride was polished and gorgeous and rich as hell and a *doctor* – the inflection she gave every time she mentioned it. I wasn't sure exactly how much time she spent practicing medicine though, when she was, so often, filmed having dinner or lunch somewhere posh, or arguing about something silly with her fake reality show friends, or fake family – they were her actual family, they were all just fake.

But then, I guess you *had* to have a certain degree of phoniness to thrive in the reality show world, and thrive they did. *McBrides on Call*, following their whole family of doctors, was on season four.

Now that I thought about it, Ramsey had experience with failed engagements. We'd never *really* talked about why he'd called it off with Lena, which I considered a small miracle. As far as I was concerned, Ramsey was too good for her and her family of quacks.

I wouldn't have been able to act sad about *that* breakup. If he'd wanted a parade though… that, I could've handled.

"Well, I'm glad your mother thought highly enough of me to consider me worthy to carry her hypothetical grandbabies," I laughed, and Ramsey gave me this wide-eyed look that immediately made me regret saying it. Did he think I was *angling* for that or something? Especially after that kiss…

This man probably thinks I've gone crazy.

But just as quickly as those thoughts crossed my mind, the look was gone, and he was shaking his head, laughing. "You know she loved you. *That girl is fast, baby, and I mean that as a compliment,*" he mimicked, his eyes and voice full of love at the memory that must have been crossing his mind. "But hey… if I'm doing that," he said, pointing to the torn contract, "What are *you* going to do?"

"I'm going to lobby for doing the show on my own – what they promised in the first place. We've made this show amazing, and I'd like to think I've proven myself enough for them to understand that I could handle it."

He nodded. "But... what if they don't?"

"Then... I guess we'll both be moving on to something new."

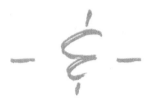

Why does this number keep calling me?

For about the tenth time in the last month, my phone lit up with a call from an international number I didn't recognize. The fact that there was never a message made me a little suspicious that it was some type of telemarketer, so I never answered.

Until today.

I *needed* a distraction while I waited to hear from Ramsey.

His workout with the Kings was today, and though I'd talked a big game about believing in him and his talent, I couldn't help being nervous. I'd just never tell *him* that. He had enough of his own concerns without me piling mine on, so when he let me know they'd called, I slipped right into the role of "Ms. Motivational" as he teasingly called me.

Really though? I was scared I was going to end up in jail for threatening to kill somebody if, for whatever reason, they didn't see what I saw in him.

So yeah, I needed the distraction.

"Good morning!" was the response I was given to my hesitantly spoken *hello.* "This is Ayu Rama, how are you?" she asked, in accented English that I couldn't quite place.

"Umm... I'm fine."

"Very good! Am I speaking with Wil-hel-mi-na Cunningham?" she inquired, carefully sounding out my name.

"You are."

"Wonderful. I am calling on behalf of the Four Seasons at Jimbaran Bay, about the stay you booked with us last year."

My breath caught in my throat. I wanted to respond, but I couldn't, feeling choked with sudden emotion.

"Are you there, Mrs. Cunningham?"

"It's Ms.," I corrected her, even though it hurt like hell. "Just Ms. The trip was supposed to be a honeymoon, but um... the wedding never happened."

"Oh." For a short moment, Ayu said nothing, but then in a brighter voice, said, "Well, I was calling to ask if you would be interested in rescheduling your trip. I understand that your wedding did not happen, so maybe a relaxing trip alone, or with a friend? You paid up front for the stay, but you never checked in, and our policy is to allow a reschedule, within ninety days."

"No refunds?"

"No, I am sorry."

I nodded. "No, no need to apologize, I understand. Um... do I have to give you an answer now?"

"Not at all. I will give you my direct line, and you can call me back. As long as your trip is before that 90 day period, your full package is valid."

"Okay. Thank you."

I got up to get a pen so that I could write the number down, and then got off the phone feeling... strange. The Balinese vacation was something I'd immensely looked forward to, but after everything fell apart with the wedding, the idea of still going hadn't crossed my mind. Now that the option was in front of me though... it felt tainted.

I was supposed to be on this trip with my husband, celebrating the fact that I'd married the man that I loved. All of the stress, the disappointments, all of it... for that week, there was supposed to be nothing except me and him, connecting in new ways and *re*connecting in others.

Yes, I could go alone... hell, reconnect with my *self*, but would the fact that he was supposed to be there with me loom like a dark cloud?

While I was still thinking through it, my phone rang again, this time with a number I recognized, but dreaded. I took a deep breath, then hit the button to answer, raising it to my ear.

"Sarita, hi!" I said, trying not to sound like she was the last person I wanted to talk to. "What can I do for you?"

"You can be in my office in an hour." Was her clipped response.

I rolled my eyes. "Sarita, I'm not in New York right now, I'm at my parent's, in Stamford."

"Well, weren't you going to need to be on set today anyway?"

"Yes, but not for several more hours."

"I guess you're coming early today. Two hours. I'll see you then."

I didn't even have a chance to respond before she ended the call, and I couldn't do anything but laugh. I'd never understood the personal issue Sarita seemed to have with me.

In any case, it had to be important for her to call me in to a meeting before the show. I hadn't signed the new contract yet, but my current one wasn't over, and I hadn't heard back from my lawyer about it yet anyway. They'd given it to me on Sunday.

Today was Wednesday.

It *couldn't* be about that.

But then again… Ramsey *had* ripped his contract in half. I knew he hadn't talked to the network yet, but that didn't mean the streets hadn't. There was a good chance they knew he was essentially at an interview with the Kings, and could easily be there until well into the afternoon. I wouldn't be shocked at all to find that they were trying to get to me before I talked to him again.

I hoped they didn't think that would work as a negotiation tactic.

In any case, I got up to go to the meeting. It wasn't as if I was doing anything other than waiting to hear from Ramsey about the workout anyway, so it was a good way to pass the time.

I arrived a little early, waited in the reception area until I was supposed to be there, and then walked into Sarita's office right on time. I was relieved to see Connie there. Not that she was some savior or something, but at the very least she gave Sarita some balance. There was another person there too, a man in a suit and glasses who I assumed was a new network lawyer, since he looked vaguely familiar.

That made me wonder if I should have called my own lawyer for this meeting.

"Wil, have a seat please," Connie asked, and I obliged. I crossed my hands in front of me on the table, waiting to hear the reason for this meeting.

102

Sarita was the one who spoke up with that. "As we're sure you already know, your co-host is in Connecticut right now, working out with their little local football club," she started, and I bit my lip to keep from smirking at her attempt at shade.

Must be a Pats fan.

"As you also probably know, were he to make the team, it would present a conflict with his ability to continue as one of our *From the Sidelines* hosts."

"I feel that it would be best to address this with him. I'm not comfortable speaking on his behalf in a matter that seems to be in reference to his employment contract."

Her jaw tightened. "Fair enough. We aren't here to discuss his contract anyway. We're here to discuss *yours*. You haven't signed it yet."

"No, I haven't. It's still with my lawyer."

She nodded, then slid a folder across the table to me. "That offer has been rescinded. This is your new one."

My eyes narrowed at the folder, but I took it, flipping to what I knew was one of the more important pages. When my gaze landed on what I was looking for, I frowned. "This number is lower than the one offered two days ago. Hell… it's lower than the *initial* contract I signed."

"Yes, we know," Sarita smirked. "You see, with Ramsey leaving, we're going to need an acceptable number to offer his replacement."

"Ramsey hasn't told you he's leaving. Second – even if he is, why does he need to be replaced? I could handle it alone, with the occasional guest host. That way, you can afford to offer me a number that isn't an insult, and the network even saves money by not employing a second full-time host."

There was quiet for a few seconds as Connie and Sarita shared a look, and then Sarita laughed. "Alone? Wil, you're a twenty-seven year old woman. You can't possibly think we're going to hand you a *sports* news show of your own."

"You wouldn't be *handing* me anything. Ramsey and I put that show on our backs and carried it to where it is. Viewers tune in for *us* as much as they tune in for the highlights and news. You shove someone in Ramsey's place, it's not going to be the same. Not the same energy, and *not* the same chemistry. Our viewers won't appreciate it."

She snorted. "But they'll appreciate you alone because of what, perky tits and a cute face?"

"And sharp analysis, quick wit, and abundant knowledge. Oh, and a fat ass too, since you seem to think my appearance is the only thing viewers tune in for."

"We *don't* think that," Connie finally spoke up, shooting a scolding glance at Sarita. "Let's take a step back, okay? While we've absolutely seen a good diversification of our audience since you and Ramsey introduced your show, our main demographic is still largely men. Our concern with having you host the show yourself is that you aren't enough to anchor the show on your own. The research shows that a male audience still, by and large, wants their news – especially sports news – delivered by men. So, we need that balance."

I shook my head. "So instead of challenging that, and taking this opportunity to stand on the promise you made when you hired me, you'd rather cut my salary to pay for a man to come on the air and say the same things I can?"

"It's not that simple," Connie urged, holding up a hand. "Yes, we need to reallocate funds, but the drop isn't significant."

I laughed. "Isn't significant? Then why take it at all? Do you not understand how offensive this is? You *promised* me."

"Girl, this is business, and we are *not* your fairy god-aunties," Sarita snipped. "Promises are made and broken every day. The terms are in front of you for you to accept. Aiden has already signed his contract."

"Aiden?"

I scowled, and then looked to where she was pointing – at the man I'd assumed was a lawyer. He was handsome, with sandy blonde hair and familiar green eyes…

"Aiden Sanders, the baseball player?"

He smiled, and perked up. "In the flesh. But – *former* player. Looking forward to hosting the show with you."

I looked at him, then over to Sarita, then to Connie, hoping this was some elaborate joke. When I realized it wasn't, I shook my head, and "*Oh* hell *no,*" was the first thing that crossed my lips. "You *cannot* be serious!" I snapped. "Is the name of this network *not* WAWG – *We all we got?*"

Connie lifted both hands this time. "Yes, of course, but we're trying to move the station beyond that, into today. We want to start embracing more diversity."

I cackled, loud. "Diversity? You want to embrace diversity? Purvi Kahn is an *amazing* sports journalist – you could have gotten her. Aiko Matsuoka. Jeremy Lopez. Kim Williams. Ali Singh. All very capable, established journalists who would probably *love* to come increase our diversity here at the network. Not to mention all the retired athletes who would have *loved* this opportunity. But you're going to sit in my damn face and tell me you hired a *blonde white man* for the sake of *diversity*?!"

"We understand how on the surface, maybe the optics look a little rough," Connie said, still using that soothing voice that was only further grating my frayed nerves, "But I really think this is a good opportunity to maybe start some important conversations."

I wrapped my hands around my armrests to force myself to stay in my seat. "Anytime I've brought up race in the last six months or so, I get a verbal swat on the hand. I get *scolded* for it. But now that you're bringing *him* on... we can have these conversations? Tell me something, what are your thoughts on the disproportionate penalization of athletes of color under current NCAA scouting rules?" I asked, turning to Aidan, who flushed bright red. Before he could answer, I shook my head. "You know, never mind that question – let me ask you something else – where did you get your journalism degree? Where did you intern? Have you done news before?"

He shifted his gaze to Connie and Sarita, then looked back at me with fire in his eyes, sputtering something about being a "fast learner" even though he didn't have his degree. *Yet*, supposedly.

I smiled, to keep from screaming.

"So, let me run this down," I said, struggling to keep my voice even, and at least *appear* calm, though I definitely wasn't. "You are cutting *my* salary by an "insignificant" thirty-thousand dollars to pay a grossly inexperienced white man to replace my cohost, so that you can increase the "diversity" of a network founded on principles of giving a platform to, and showcasing *Black* talents and excellence. Do I understand that correctly?"

Connie shook her head. "You're *simplifying* it Wil, and it's not the way it seems. We're just trying to put our best foot forward."

"Adding *him* is putting your best foot forward?" I scoffed. "I mean, no offense intended to you Aiden, but…" I turned back to Connie and Sarita. "Are you *serious* right now?"

Connie opened her mouth, but Sarita stopped her. "Wil, I'm not sure where things got mixed up, but we're under no obligation to explain anything except your contract to you. Your terms are in the folder in front of you. Review it, and get it back to us, signed, by Monday."

"I'm not signing *shit*," I snapped, before I'd even really thought about it. But honestly, there was nothing *to* think about. I'd wanted to work at WAWG because of what they stood for. I'd tried to get past the trickery they pulled with getting me to sign a contract in the first place, I'd ignored Sarita's sour face and slick mouth, but *this?*

I was done.

"Excuse me?" Sarita asked, drawing her head back.

"You heard exactly what I said." I stood up and grabbed my purse, leaving the new contract there on the table. "I've worked my ass off my entire time here, and that won't change now. I'll be back on time for tonight's show, and every other day that's necessary to fulfill my current contract. Because I'm a professional, and that is *all* I've ever been for this network. But I will *not* sign that."

Sarita sat back, crossing her arms. "Don't bother coming back for a filming tonight – we're showing a re-run. That decision was already made before you walked in here, and your cohost has been notified. But I tell you this – if you walk out of here without taking that contract with you, you will *not* be offered another one. And I promise you, nobody is going to be lining up to offer you another position. I mean… unless your father is going to write another check for you, it's a scary world out there girl."

I smirked. "That's what part of this is about, isn't it? I've seen how some of these people hop, skip, and jump around here for you, but not me. Not ever, because I'm not scared. You can levy your little veiled threats of blackballing me, try to discount my talent by saying my daddy has to pay my way around all you want to. But Sarita… I'm not afraid of you."

"If you want a career in media, maybe you should be."

I let my smirk spread into a smile. "Maybe so. But you want to know the most important investment my mother and father ever made in me? They didn't raise a coward."

I didn't wait around for Connie to try to calm me down, didn't give Sarita a chance for another snide remark. I left, with my head held high, just like my mother taught me. My chest was tight, eyes burning, head swimming with what just happened.

I pushed out a deep breath once I made it back to the safe confines of my car. Pulling my cell from my bag, I turned the screen on. The first thing I saw was a text from Ramsey.

"Just left workout. I don't feel good about it though…. I feel FAN-FUCKING-TASTIC! I really think this is happening! – R. Bishop."

I was happy as hell for him, but the reality of my own situation hit me at the same time. I'd already lost my man, lost my home as a byproduct, and now, apparently, I didn't even have a job. What the hell was I doing?

Instead of dwelling there, I shook my head. I couldn't let myself slip back into the low place I was just starting to feel that I'd made it out of.

"You killed it didn't you?" I texted Ramsey back. *"I knew you would! Dinner on me? Unless you have plans?"*

"Nah, I'm all yours. I want to tell you about it. – R. Bishop."

We went back and forth a little about the place and time, and then I started my car, anxious to get away from the building. I didn't know what was going to happen, but I knew hanging around here wasn't the best use of my time.

Not that it mattered.

Without a job, time was something I'd have plenty of.

"So you were just going to let me ramble on and on all night about a damn workout, and not tell me about this?"

Instead of answering my question, Wil averted her gaze as she took a long sip of water, trying to stall. I'd been so high on my own excitement, even when I picked her up, that it took me all the way through dinner, into dessert, to notice that she wasn't shining at her normal wattage. When I did, it took some pressure to get her to tell me.

"Don't you dare," I said, quickly reaching across the table to slide her plate of cheesecake away before she could use another mouthful as an excuse not to talk. "You're telling me they hired my replacement, without saying shit to me? And they're taking money from *your* salary to do it?"

"I'm telling you that's the impression I had. What did they say when they called to tell you we weren't filming today?"

I shook my head. "They left a message, made it seem like there were some technical issues or something. Which was bullshit, obviously."

"The whole thing is bullshit," she agreed, doing a not at all good job of sneaking her fork across the table to snag some of the cheesecake. "Sarita has always been a bitch, but this is something else going on. Something... I don't know. As pissed as I am about what happened, I really can't help but feel like we *both* dodged a bullet."

"That gut feeling is everything, Champ."

She gave me an absent nod in response, then reached for her dessert plate. All night, she'd been fully engaged in me, asking questions about the workout, getting excited. But knowing that she'd been busy celebrating *my* shit just a few hours after what sounded like the meeting from hell... I felt bad for even having her out tonight. The least I could do was give her a moment with the cheesecake she raved about every time we hit this spot.

While she ate, I observed. She was so deep in her own thoughts that she didn't notice – or didn't care – that I was staring at her like I was seeing her for the first time. She had her hair pulled back, showcasing her pretty ass face, but her expression was so somber – so unlike *her* – that it pissed me off.

"Hey," I said, reaching across the table for the hand she wasn't maneuvering her fork with. "You're going to be okay. *We're* going to be okay. Cause apparently I'm jobless too now. This is probably the last date I'll be able to get for a while. Can't impress the ladies without a job."

"Oh please," she laughed, which was exactly what I was trying to do. Her cheekbones lifted as her lips stayed spread into a smile, and that cute little gap of hers appeared.

Soft ass lips.

"You know damn well you wouldn't have a single problem getting a woman, job or not. I can probably find you a sugar mama somewhere in here."

I shook my head. "Nah. Under six feet *and* no job? I may as well hang it up."

"*Stop*," she giggled, and I squeezed her hand, which seemed to remind her I was still holding it. She looked down at our entwined fingers with this expression of... wonder, or something like that. The same look was still on her face when she lifted her eyes to mine, and staring at me in the same way I'd been staring at her a few seconds ago.

Like I was a phenomenon.

But then she dropped her gaze, and cleared her throat, gently sliding her hands back to place them in her lap. "Don't look now," she started. "But they're kinda giving us the stink eye over there."

"Who?" I asked, looking even though she'd said not to. Sure enough, we were getting the *please leave so we can clean your table and go home* look from our server and the hostess, both of whom quickly looked away when they realized I saw them. Chuckling, I brushed off my lap and stood up, fishing my wallet from my pocket. I put two hundred-dollar bills on the table – enough to cover our meal, drinks, and a generous tip – then held out a hand to help Wil up from her seat.

She accepted the hand, and then I motioned for her to lead, a move that was purely habit. I wasn't *trying* to get a peek at her ass, but she was wearing this thin little dress that was hugging and clinging and just... *good God.*

Get it together, Ram.

Our chosen dinner spot for the night was in Stamford, so it didn't take much time to get her home. Instead of talking, we'd cranked up the radio and sang along, so when I pulled around to her apartment, it went without question that I would be walking her to the door, to say goodbye.

"So what's your next step?" she asked, as we approached the door. The motion light popped on, bathing the entire porch in a golden glow that made her look damn near angelic as she put her back to the door, leaning into it.

"Next step for…?"

She rolled her eyes. "Becoming the Kings' star running back, and leading them to that Super Bowl win that slipped away last year, duh. We got interrupted by you insisting on listening to me complain."

"Okay so you can kill *that* noise," I said. "But as far as joining the team, it's really just a waiting game now. They'll call when they call. If they *want* to call."

"They *want* to call," she insisted. "They might make you sweat a little first, but they would be idiots not to call. They *need* you."

I shook my head as I stepped closer to her, off pure compulsion. "You sure do know how to pump a man's head up, Champ."

She shrugged. "All I'm doing is telling the truth. Same as you're always doing for me."

"Not the same thing."

She crossed her arms. "How so?"

"Cause you're… I don't know. You're *you*."

"And you're *you*," she shot back. "What, you don't think you're worthy or something?"

Heh.

She didn't know how accurate that was. Or rather, *used* to be, even though the shit still cropped up sometimes. Sure, I talked, dressed, lived a certain way now, but that wasn't always the case, growing up with virtually nothing no matter how hard my mother tried. For a lot of people – for a lot of *men* – the shit was hard to admit, and it certainly wasn't about to come out of my mouth, but having people look at you a certain way for so long, then have it suddenly change… you didn't always just shake that shit off.

I wasn't so far removed from having nothing that I didn't remember what it felt like. The shit was *vivid*, so much that it woke me up from my sleep sometimes. But once I signed that NFL contract, once I got that first check, I made a vow – I was *never* going back to that.

That was barely eight years ago.

Back in college, the girls… they saw it. The athletic scholarship may have taken the boy out of the hood, but the hood was *very much* still in the boy, and they didn't want shit to do with it. Lena was an exception, in a way that I didn't realize until much later wasn't healthy. She was one of the rich, bougie chicks, and she considered herself elevating me. She would bring me into her world, but wanted nothing to do with mine, never meeting halfway.

And honestly speaking... Wil was one of those chicks too. Made inaccessible by culture and class – on the surface, at least. But once I knew her, I saw different. Wil would go to the hood and talk to the mothers of budding young players– the ones watching their sons, and the ones watching their children's fathers – who congregated on raggedy metal bleachers outside in the heat of summer, to get their voice for an interview.

She never hesitated to go to the roughest of neighborhoods to get to a good chicken spots for wings. Never saw someone on the streets she wouldn't slip a few dollars to if she had it on her – something I'd had to beg her to stop doing when she was by herself. But the *point* was, Wil didn't think she was better than anybody.

There was no ulterior motive to her praise, no emotional manipulation, just... genuine admiration. I wondered if she understood how refreshing that was, in our world? How damned *sexy* her authenticity was. In that moment, I got consumed with the thought of kissing her, but then her gaze dropped as she let out a sigh.

"So..." she sighed again, before she lifted her eyes back to mine. "I've gotta say thank you."

I lifted an eyebrow. "Thank you for what?"

She shrugged. "I've been... a *lot* over the last month or so, and please don't try to make me feel better by saying *"no, no, you're not"*, because... yeah. I kinda have. My life is a complete clusterfuck right now, and I really don't know what I would do without my parents, Naima, Soriyah when I can get her ass on the phone, and really, *really* importantly... you. So just... thank you for being my friend. And not ignoring my calls so you don't have to listen to me whine, and taking me to eat whatever I want," she laughed, and then her expression shifted, and her cheeks visibly heated. "And... for not holding that kiss against me." Her nose wrinkled up as she frowned. "Not really my proudest moment, you know? Giving you the "money shot" as you called it."

I chuckled as I took a step back, *very* glad I hadn't acted on that urge to kiss her a second ago. "Why would that be something I held against you?"

"Because, you didn't want me putting my lips on you!" she answered, with such certainty that I couldn't help what came out of my mouth next, as she giggled.

"You sure about that?" The giggle died on her lips, and her eyes went wide as I stepped into her again, closer than before. "I'm gonna go ahead and get out of here," I told her, pushing my hands into my pockets. "But for the record, I could never hold that kiss against you." I leaned in a little more, speaking into her ear. "I kissed you back. Good night," I said, then placed a soft kiss against her temple and headed to the truck.

I was halfway there when I turned to see her still standing there, unmoving, and I chuckled. "Go in the house!"

Those words seemed to remind her she was outside, and she flinched, then dug her keys from her bag. Shaking my head, I climbed into the truck and sat down, watching until she tossed her hand up to wave before she closed the door and went inside.

I started the truck but didn't immediately pull off. I had a strange sense of déjà vu, from just a few days ago after the wedding. After that kiss.

Something had shifted now, and I wondered if she felt it like I did? I hadn't intended to say what I said, but it was out now.

I wasn't sure which one of us had more to think about.

Six

Wil

June 2017

Why was everything going nuts at once?

No man – because he was a cheating liar.

No house – because the cheating liar was there.

No job – apparently, since a certified letter had arrived this morning, informing me that I was essentially banned from the studio, which… whatever.

And then, on top of everything… had the man I considered one of my best friends just… shot his shot?

I think he shot his shot!

But… no.

No, that's not what that was.

Ramsey wasn't a man of… subtlety. He was a man of strong opinions, firm decisions, going after what he wanted. If he was trying to get with me romantically, he wouldn't leave me wondering, I didn't think. With a man like Ramsey, I would be very, *very* sure.

I think.

"I'm so damned *confused*," I whined, gently leaning onto Naima's shoulder as she sat at her kitchen counter, peeling apples.

"You say that like it's news."

I rolled my eyes. "Don't be mean to me Mimi, I'm serious. I need you to be a good cousin, and tell me what to *doooo*."

"Ashley already told you what to do," Naima insisted, shrugging me off of her so she could take the apples to the sink to rinse them off.

From the other side of the kitchen, perched on the counter, Ashley took a break from the selfie she was taking to nod. "I sure did."

My head made a soft *thud* sound as I dropped it onto the counter. "Screwing Ramsey is *not* the answer."

"Why the hell not?" I looked up as Cole bustled into the kitchen, a bottle of wine in both hands. "He's not your coworker anymore, so you're golden now. I say take advantage of the opportunity."

"He is my *friend*," I said, for what felt like the hundredth time, and the girls rolled their eyes for the hundred-and-first.

From the sink, Naima called, "I'm telling you – it's bound to happen anyway, sooner or later. You may as well get it over with. You need a good orgasm."

"I've *had* orgasms," I argued. "I've had *plenty* now that I'm not depending on Darius for it. I had one this morning, as a matter of fact, so *nah*."

Naima laughed. "Good for you cousin, but I'm talking about the type only another warm body can give you." She turned the water off, then faced me, resting back against the sink. "Indulge me – and yourself – for a few minutes. What do you think he's like in bed?"

I gasped. "Oh my *God*, I haven't thought about that!"

"Liar," they all said, in unison, and I folded my arms across my chest.

"I...I just... *ugh*. Okay. I've *thought* about it. Briefly. Maybe... once... or twice... or eleven times today. I don't know, am I supposed to be a machine who counts how many times I think about screwing my bestie?!"

Naima's eyebrows went up as she looked to Ashley, then Cole, then back to me. "Girl... cut the weird shit and just answer the question."

114

I huffed. "*Fine.* I… I think he would be… really… gentlemanly. He's so easy going, so laid back, you know? He would definitely make sure I came first, and he would have *no* issue giving the kitty the oral attention she deserves. And… kissing. Lots of kissing."

Once I stopped talking, it was quiet for a second, and then all three women burst out laughing.

"Bitch, *wow*," Naima giggled. "You *really have thought about this!*"

"Probably because he's been thirst-trappin' all over Instagram lately," Cole said, standing up to retrieve a corkscrew. "Is that what has you ready Wil?"

"I'm not *ready*, I'm just… she asked a question, and I answered. And what are you talking about with the thirst traps? I've been ignoring social media, for my sanity."

"Oh *wow*," Ashley said, then laughed at something on her phone. "I see what she's talking about. That thing damn near poked me in the eye through the screen."

My eyes went wide. "Wait a minute, *what*?"

Ashley hopped down from her perch on the counter and came to me, putting her phone down in front of me. She'd pulled up Ramsey's Instagram page – specifically, a video he'd posted a few hours ago.

In the video, the camera was below him as he utilized an overhead bar for pull-ups. He was shirtless, sure, but he was shirtless in a lot of his videos when he worked out. I didn't understand what was so provocative about this one, and was about to say so when Ramsey hopped down from the bar, and…

"*Oh my God!*" I yelped, clapping a hand over my mouth.

Beside me, Naima shook her head. "Uh-uh. There's no way that's his dick. He's got like… something in his pocket."

"What, a baseball bat?" Cole asked, incredulous. "Ain't nothing in that man's shorts but *dick*," she laughed. "You see how he grinned at the camera in the end? That, my friends, is expert level panty-wetting. He knows what he's doing."

Of course he did.

The posting of the video only served as a – sometimes necessary – reminder for me that although Ramsey was my friend, he was still a man. Often, when I was still with Darius, I found myself regarding him as this asexual being. I didn't really think about his intimate life, or sexuality, even though it was pretty well-known, since no one minded their business these days, that when the switch was "off" in Ramsey's on-again-off-again with Lena, he was *not* shy with the ladies.

Hell, his friendship with Jordan Johnson was born in *Arch & Point*, a high-end strip club in Connecticut, and his adoration for one in particular, a chick who called herself "Southern Comfort" was well-documented too. So it wasn't that Ramsey playing into being a heartthrob, or having a sex life, or whatever, surprised me.

I'd just never really… paid attention before.

"That's the kind of dick that *makes* you pay attention," Naima mused, as the video played again, making my eyes go wide. Was she reading my damn mind? "I don't want shit to do with a man, but… Ashley we might have to go to the store."

Ashley rolled her eyes. "Girl, the way you scream over that little medium strap back there, ain't nobody taking you anywhere," she laughed. "Wil, you aren't scared now are you?"

As I watched his dick bounce hard enough against the front of his shorts to let me know it *had* to be heavy, my answer to that question was a firm "maybe". But still.

"Why would I be scared, when I don't plan to sleep with him? Why are y'all doing this?" I laughed. "It's been a whole what, five or six weeks since I got my heart ripped out of my chest? Had to uproot myself from my home. Just got fired without *technically* getting fired. I have enough upheaval going on right now – I really don't need to add screwing my friend to that mix. I appreciate your encouragement of hoe-tivities though."

"You know we've got you girl," Naima said, giving me a quick hug before she went back to her apples, dropping slices into an already-simmering pot full of butter, cinnamon, and sugar.

Cole put a glass of wine in front of me. "I'm glad you're here tonight, actually – I wanted to ask if you've thought about what you'll be doing if you're not on the show?"

"Well, I didn't think *not* being on the show was a serious consideration, so I didn't have anything in place, but… I'm thinking about branching out on my own. People know me, I have a good social following, and a pretty decent nest egg – especially now that I don't

116

have a reason to pay New York rent prices. *That* will help a lot. I'm in a position to take a risk, you know? I'm starting over."

Taking a seat beside me with her own glass, Cole nodded. "I think you're right. You're well-known and well-respected in the sports news industry. And besides that, people really like you. Think about the fact that when this Darius and Jessica thing blew up, you never got turned on. I mean, the "mainstream" media outlets tried to make something of your verbal altercation with Jessica, but there wasn't too far they could go with that. You didn't have any old homophobic tweets to bring up, none of your nudes came out, there was no big reveal that you'd fucked a teacher or something. You are an honest-to-goodness television sweetheart, and that is… rare. And *valuable.*"

"I'm *so* not a sweetheart though."

"Oh please, you're so damn warm and fuzzy I could package and sell your personality as teddy-bears," Naima teased from the stove. "Sure, you talk shit with the rest of us, and you've got some claws under there, but you have a good heart, Willy. It's not something to act shamed about."

"Right," Cole agreed. "But, I bring all of this up for a reason. I know before all of this happened, Ramsey was trying to get access to the Kings for *From the Sidelines.* Well, that access was granted, but before I could get back to you guys about it, I heard from a little bird that there were major changes coming for WAWG, so I hesitated. Above all, my job is to act in the best interest of these players, and I was not about to have them signing anything related to their interviewing rights with a network who was in limbo."

I shook my head. "In limbo?"

"WAWG's executive board is looking for a buyer, but the only interested parties with the capitol to support it, are looking for… let's say a little more milk in their coffee," Cole said, then pretended to sip from a tea cup. "Many of their current investors aren't happy about it, but… network execs don't care."

"Is *that* why Nubia Perry ended her show there, and started NuMedia?" I asked, and Cole slid her gaze away from mine.

"You didn't hear *any* of this from me," she said, then took a long sip from her wine. "In any case, again, I have a reason for all of this. The Kings offer of access to our roster was always more about you and Ramsey than the network. Those interviews were going to be a way for us to introduce the public to our players to create a controlled personal connection. We still want to do that – with *you*."

I almost choked on the wine I'd just sipped. "With *me?* As in, just me?"

"Well, Ramsey seems to be pursuing other options, so we didn't think he would have time. But, I talked to the club's publicity team, and of course the team owner, and all parties are on board… if you're interested, that is."

"*If*?!" I put a hand to my chest in an attempt to calm my racing heart. "I… Cole, I don't know what to say! So… what is this? Would I be employed by the team, or…?"

She shook her head. "No, not exactly. There are two options here – one where you *can* be employed by the team, we would cover the expenses for sound equipment, a film crew so that the interviews could appear online, makeup and hair for you, if you wanted that. But, the Kings would have full rights to any content that you created. Or – and this is something that *I* pushed for consideration, based on having gotten to know you a little better in these last few weeks… you work for yourself. The Kings are willing to provide some funding through a sponsorship, and you'll have access to our players – *all* players. You would be responsible for your own marketing, you have to hire your own crew, take care of your own expenses. But your content would be *yours*. And not that the Kings have an expectation that you subvert your journalistic duty to make us look good, but… still. Having it be *yours* gives you freedom."

"Right," I half-whispered, as I nodded. "I… *thank you*." I reached out for a hug and she let me pull her into it, even squeezed me back.

"You're *so* welcome, and honestly –it's *nothing*. I love having the opportunity to put another Black woman on in this industry. There are so few of us that we have to look out for each other."

"So… are you gonna do it?" Naima asked, speaking up for the first time in several minutes.

I looked up at where she was standing at the stove, stirring the apples she'd be pouring into glass jars for preservation once they were done.

"I… need to think about it, but yeah, probably so." I chewed at the lip for a second. "It's a really great opportunity, but I have to think through the logistics and everything before I make a decision. That's okay, right?" I asked Cole, who looked at me like I'd lost my mind.

"Girl, *duh*. I absolutely do *not* expect you to give me an answer on the spot. We'd like an answer pretty soon, because we want to start with having you talk to our incoming rookies get some film on them, stuff like that. And we want to do that *before* their training camp starts. That's saying that we want that interview live by mid-July."

"That's definitely enough time," I told her, and smiled. "Again – thank you, so much."

She shrugged. "Like I said – pulling another sister up is *never* a problem."

"Let's toast to that," Ashley said, approaching with a freshly uncorked wine bottle. "And once Mimi finishes getting her Martha Stewart on… I say we hit a bar or something. Feels like we should be celebrating."

"Celebrating?" Naima said, holding out her glass. "Wil doesn't need a celebration, she needs a *vacay*-tion."

"Mmm! Speaking of – I forgot to tell you, the resort in Bali called. They're going to honor my reservation – as long as I go within ninety days of the scheduled time."

Naima's eyes bugged out. "Seriously?! So when are we going to Bali?!"

"I was actually thinking I would go by myself, you know? Get re-centered, purge all this negative energy, and just… *be,* for a few days."

She sucked her teeth. "Fine, don't nobody want to go on vacation with your sad ass anyway."

"Oh my God, that is *so*—"

"You know damn well I'm playing with you," she interrupted, laughing. "If less-melenated women can go on foreign adventures and shit to reclaim their lives, hell, so can you. I think going by yourself is a good idea. But… I think taking your "bestie" is an even better idea. Think about it – your very own personal on-demand dick in paradise. Tell me it doesn't sound amazing."

"It *sounds* like craziness," I insisted, shaking my head. "Ramsey is my friend, and that's that. Leave it alone, please."

I think Naima could tell I was serious, because instead of arguing, she pushed out a sigh, and changed the subject. The conversation continued around me, but my mind was buzzing with more thoughts than I could even sort through.

One kept coming to the forefront though, no matter how hard I tried to tamp it down.

I wonder what Ramsey is doing right now?

RAMSEY

I tried my best not to grin at the woman in front of me, but she was so damned cute it was hard not to. She was speaking so passionately that her accent had gotten thicker, and she kept having to brush her bangs out of her eyes. Her presentation was on point though, and I was trying to be respectful, not interrupting to pull her into a hug like I wanted.

As if she'd read my mind, she stopped mid-sentence to cross her arms, glaring at me from across the table. "Ramsey...," she warned, and my grin broke free as I held up my hands in defense.

"I didn't even do anything!"

"You're looking at me like I'm a damn four year old saying their alphabet."

"I'm just listening, I can't help my facial expression."

"The hell you can't," my kinda-ex- sister-in-law – it was complicated – Chloe snapped, glaring at me. "I'm trying to be serious here!"

"So am I, but it's *hard*," I laughed. "Damn, I already told you the job is yours if I get the position. I don't understand why you insist on doing this formal presentation shit anyway."

She pushed out a sigh. "I do this with *every* client Ramsey. Your being family doesn't make it different. I want to *earn* your business, not have it handed to me."

I tamped down the urge to tease her further, sitting up in my chair to help set the impression that I was ready to pay attention, instead of purposely getting on her nerves. "My bad Chloe. Tell me that last part again?"

"Thank you. I was saying that I had a relationship with Ase Garb clothing brand. You wear them often enough that I know you're

120

familiar – you *always* show their socks and ties on your social media when you're wearing them. I can get you paid for that, create a link where you'd never have to pay again. You wouldn't even have to do anything differently – you've been doing great free advertising for them so far."

I frowned. "So like an endorsement deal? I thought you were public relations, not an agent."

"Sometimes there can be an overlap, but no, I'm not talking about endorsements. I'm just letting you know – this is a perk. I have important relationships."

"I already knew that about you," I told her, shaking my head. "Chloe, seriously, just tell me where to sign."

She stared at me for a second, then sighed. "You promise that you aren't doing this solely because of Reginald?"

I fought a smirk. It was funny to me that even though the rest of us referred to him as Reggie, Chloe usually gave the full "Reginald", just like Aunt Phylicia did with Reginald Sr, his father.

"Why do you automatically jump to something being about him, like you aren't the only reason I have my niece and nephews? And besides that, you're one of the dopest PR reps in professional athletics, and you came *highly* recommended."

Her eyes narrowed. "By who?"

"Jordan Johnson – who *doesn't* know about Reg, by the way, just like the rest of the world. He doesn't know we have a connection."

She let out a little huff. "Like the rest of the world? Is that a jab?"

"Do I ever throw jabs at you Chloe?" I asked, raising my eyebrows. "It's just stating a fact, and I'm not mad at you for it. *Nobody* is mad at you for it. You've done what you had to do to be okay… and you know how *I* feel about that."

She pressed her lips together, staring down at the papers spread across the tiny restaurant table. We were at Afro-French fusion place she loved, and dinner had been long gone before she got down to business, which we'd been at for about twenty minutes. She stared at those papers for a long moment, and when she looked up, her eyes were glossy.

"Yes, of course," she told me. "I know. I'm sorry for getting snippy, I just…"

I nodded. "Yeah. You don't have to explain. Aunt Phylicia called me too. Early release, huh?"

She snorted. "If we can call twelve years of a fifteen year sentence "early"… then sure."

"That's a fair point," I grinned. "So… you think you two are going to try to work it out?"

"I don't know, Ramsey. We'll see."

"We'll see isn't "*hell no*", so hey, I'm excited."

Chloe shook her head. "Don't get ahead of yourself, cousin. People change."

"For the better, in this case. You know I've never been anything but real with you. I wouldn't lie about this. He misses you. Misses the *hell* outta you."

"Just because you miss someone, doesn't—"

"He loves you too. Still. You'd know that if you'd go see him, but…"

She glared at me. "Ramsey…"

"I know, I know. Married folks' shit is complicated, I get it. You'll see him once he's out though, right?"

"Of course I will, he's the father of my children."

"You know what I mean."

Finally, a hint of a smile cracked her lips. "I do. And not that it's any of your business, but since I'll know you'll relay it to At mean really, at minimum, we have children who need him, who *know* he's coming home. So we have to be able to come to some sort of… something, right?"

"Right." I was silent for a moment, considering my words before I spoke again. "You know I'm just giving you a hard time don't you? As far as I'm concerned, like I said before, you're family, and I love you like such, alright? You and Reg have your shit that isn't my business, but seriously… I want to see you two work it out. Not that what I want matters, but y'all were my favorite damn people to see together. Seeing y'all together gave the whole hood hope for love," I told her, making her laugh.

I was playing, but… I was serious.

Reg was older than me, but never treated me like I was just some little kid, getting on his nerves. As sisters, our mothers were close, and together all the time, so that naturally led to us growing up like brothers, even though "cousin" was our actual title.

122

I was ten when Chloe and her family moved into the neighborhood. Those British accents were completely foreign. In a normal chain of events, Chloe would have been a target for those chicks where we were from – and the men, for a different reason. She was beautiful, with *deep* dark skin, big curious eyes, and that accent and her imported slang made her alien. "Exotic".

If it wasn't for Reg she would have gotten torn apart, in one way or another. But at fifteen, he was already sneaking off when he could to run with a crowd he had no business fooling with, doing things he had no business doing, despite his father's attempts to reel him in. Reginald Sr. was getting older though, and was already sick with the kidney disease that would ultimately end his life. There wasn't a ton he could do. Reggie *Jr.* had street cred though. And if his wasn't enough, the people he dealt with had what it took to make up the difference.

Reggie said not to mess with her, so nobody did.

I *swear* it was love at first sight for him. Chloe, on the other hand, took some convincing, but once she was convinced… nothing was touching them. They were both smart as hell, in their own ways – Chloe with the books, Reg with the streets. She got pregnant twice, and somehow still managed to finish college in the four years she'd sworn she would when she showed me her scholarship offers. Full ride. She wanted to make something of herself – something legit.

Something that would make enough to get Reg to leave the streets alone.

I could've told her that would never happen, not without something drastic. He'd moved them out of the hood into a nice big house, put Chloe in a nice whip, all of that. Reg *lived* for her and those kids, would do anything she asked. The night before my high school graduation, he sat me down and told me he'd never, *ever* been so happy.

When the police raided his house two days later, they found enough shit he wasn't supposed to have hidden in the basement that he was sentenced to fifteen years in federal prison.

Drastic.

Across from me, Chloe shook her head, and began gathering up her documents. "That's because we've somehow glamourized this "trap queen" thing. When really, constant fear of the police kicking in your door is in no way a luxurious life. In fact, the only thing that kept it from being hell was the fact that I loved him so damned much. He loved me, and we had our babies. The house, the money… they felt like curses." Her eyes went vacant for a second, with a kind of sorrow I'd seen from her often, but them she smiled, and it was gone. "But… the *love*. That's the part the hood dreamed about, right?"

"You know it cousin."

She chuckled. "Okay. Enough about that. If you really are on board, I will have my team start working on an image strategy for you. As *soon* as the Kings call you, I need to be your very next call, okay?"

"You've got it, boss."

She rolled her eyes as we stood. "You know, you're lucky WAWG doesn't need any negative press right now. The abrupt cancellation of your show doesn't look good, and it already has a lot of ugly speculation around it. If they could, they would be dragging you and Wil through the mud."

"There's not anything to say," I laughed. "Neither of us did anything that went against our contracts, and that's verifiable. If they wanted *that* fight, I'd give it to them. And still will if any drama pops off."

Chloe smirked. "Especially with *me* on your side now. I trust you've already spoken with an agent… are you going back to your old one?"

"Hell no. Found somebody new."

"Good." She pulled her bag up on her shoulder, then gave me this long look that made me hold up my hands.

"Don't do it, Chloe, come on," I said, and she laughed.

"Okay, fine. I *won't* tell you about how Aunt Debbie, God rest her soul, was *so* proud of the man you've become, and how glad I am that you're honoring what she asked of you, and continuing your legacy."

"Seriously?"

She shrugged. "What? I didn't say anything."

"Of course not," I chuckled, wrapping an arm around her shoulder to walk her to her car. After we said our goodbyes, I finally checked my phone, and wasn't surprised at all to find a text from Wil.

"If you aren't busy tomorrow, think you could do me a favor? I have some apartments to look at, and I'd like to have some company. – The Champ"

"I'm a slacker now, remember? Yeah, I can go with you. What time?"

"First one is at 9:15, but they're all in Stamford. Is that okay? – The Champ"

I raised an eyebrow. *"Gave up on New York?"*

"Yep. ☺ I'll tell you why in person, tomorrow. – The Champ."

"Aiight. See you then."

"This place is just… beyond perfect. I can barely even stand it."

"You said that about the last four places too."

I bit back a smile as Wil shot a glare in my direction, then immediately went back to fawning over the townhouse apartment. "Hardwood floors, vaulted ceilings, big windows, granite counters, and *half* the price of living in New York," she mused, in a dreamy sort of voice as she ran her fingers along one of the custom cabinets in the large kitchen. "And *space*. Glorious, wonderful, *space*. I think I'm in love."

I laughed at her enthusiasm, but it really was a nice spot. She was so happy, so instantly comfortable, that as I watched her move around in it, it already felt like hers.

"What do you think?" she asked, bouncing up to me with this huge smile on her face, eagerly waiting for an answer.

"I think it makes you happy, and I think you deserve that, so… I think you should get it."

"Good. Cause I already texted the realtor to get started on the paperwork."

"Then what did you ask *me* for?"

"Because I care about your opinion! Come look at the bathroom," she said, then grabbed my hand, tugging me in that direction. I followed, even though she'd already shown me the master bathroom twice, and I knew she was heading right for that big, freestanding garden-style tub.

Sure enough, as soon as we were in there, she climbed in, draping her arms along the side and closing her eyes.

"This is gonna be so *gooood*," she moaned, in a sultry voice that sent blood rushing straight to my dick, so fast that I had to turn away from her.

"Damn," I said from across the room, getting really, *really* interested in the shower. "They did a really good job on this tile work."

"*Didn't they*?!" she gushed. "It's so good. Hey – I think the unit next door is available too. You should totally move in, since you'll have to be in Connecticut anyway."

"*Maybe*," I corrected. "*Maybe* I'll be in Connecticut anyway. And *hell* no to moving into a spot like this. It's perfect for you, yes, but not so much for me."

I turned just in time to see her roll her eyes. "Let me guess – you need something more "manly" right?"

"Your words, not mine."

"Whatever. Can you believe we'll be working with the same team? I'll probably have to interview you. Oooh, and I know all the right shit to ask too. All the tough questions."

I laughed. "Damn, you're pre-planning to drag my ass, huh?"

"Make you answer for every mistake on the field since 2009, baby," she teased. Well, kind of. I knew Wil well enough to understand that if I ever did sit down on the other side of an interview with her, our friendship did *not* mean she would take it easy.

As she shouldn't.

My level of confidence in Wil's ability to kill her new job role was high. She'd made me wait in suspense to tell me about her conversation with Cole, and how she'd been up all night running numbers and scenarios in her head. I was surprised she was so perky today – she'd already contacted Cole to accept the Kings' sponsorship of her new, not yet named web show, by the time I met her to look at the first apartment this morning. There was no way she'd had much sleep.

"So when is your first show?" I asked, crouching down beside the tub, almost falling backward when her silly ass pretended to scoop nonexistent bubbles from the tub and put them on my nose.

"As soon as I get my shit together," she told me, still giggling about it. "I have *so* much to do. I have a rough idea of what I want the

126

format to be, and I've already got my lawyer making sure everything is copasetic with WAWG before I start any marketing."

I frowned. "How are you gonna market when you don't have a name for it yet?"

"Ah," she held up a finger. "I *do* have a name, as of like, two seconds ago. "Wil in the Field." You get it? Like... real in the field? Get it?"

"Yes, I get it," I said, standing up straight so I could laugh.

"Why are you laughing so hard?!" she shrieked, standing up and stepping toward me. She must have forgotten she was in the tub though, because she tripped, and would have gone crashing to the floor if I hadn't caught her. Instead of being flustered about the fall, she looked up from her position in my arms to ask, "That's not *too* corny, is it?"

I shook my head. "Nah, Champ. It's perfect for you."

"Perfect... for *me*?" she asked as she straightened up.

"Don't say it like *that*." I didn't like the inflection she was putting on it. "It's not a bad thing, I'm saying it fits you. It's cute, and fun."

A little smile crept onto her face. "You... think I'm cute and fun?"

"Is that news to you?"

For some reason that made her blush. She tugged her top lip between her teeth and looked away, as suddenly interested in the fixture on the sink as I'd been on the shower tile a few moments ago.

I walked up to her from behind, keeping just enough distance not to touch her.

"Hey," I said, and she looked up, meeting my eyes in the mirror over the sink. "We should go to dinner. Not like our usual... hit up the sushi spot or whatever, but like... a *real* dinner. Me in a tie, you in heels."

Her eyes went a little wider, like she was surprised, but she nodded. "Okay. When?"

"After you finish filming with the rookies. Whatever day that is, we should celebrate it right. Nice dinner, champagne. How does that sound to you?"

She smiled.

"It sounds like a date."

Seven

Wil

It's just a house.

As ridiculous as those words sounded in my head, I repeated them several times before I unbuckled my seatbelt and climbed out of my car. My steps were hesitant as I headed up the front walk of the house that, until very recently, I'd considered a home, full of love. The place I would come back to after an amazing honeymoon, would bring babies – maybe even grandbabies, someday – home to.

Now…

It's just a house.

Nothing to get all upset about.

My key worked in the front door, which surprised me for some reason. It wasn't like I'd expected Darius to have changed the locks or anything, but it just felt… strange. When I walked into the foyer, I wasn't flooded with the sadness I'd dreaded.

There was a disconnect. It didn't feel like home anymore anyway.

The flowers I'd destroyed and left in a mess on the floor were gone now, and that wasn't the only change. Our furniture was gone –

I'd signed off on the donation to a local home for displaced minors –
and the paint colors were different. I'd agreed to everything the realtor
suggested, actually, including the staging of the house with the boring,
neutral furniture that filled it now. Anything to make it marketable,
and sell as quickly as possible.

I wanted to move on from this chapter of my life.

Our bedroom was the one room I skipped. Just the thought of
stepping into it made my stomach twist into knots. Everywhere else, I
took one last look – I had no intention of ever coming back again. The
only reason I was here now was because the realtor had insisted on me
seeing it in person before I gave my final approval. When I heard
footsteps approaching in the otherwise empty house, I assumed it was
her.

I assumed wrong.

The sight of him snatched my breath away. I'd purposely
avoided his face, afraid of what it would bring to the surface. I was
doing so well – still hurting, still angry, but I hadn't cried in weeks. I
was working on "being okay". I thought I was moving forward.

"Wil... hi."

Don't you dare break down.

"Hello Darius," was my curt response, before I turned away to
look out at the pool in the backyard, the borrowed patio furniture,
anything to keep *"What the hell are you doing here?!"* from flying off
of my tongue. I'd been clear in my request that our walkthroughs be
scheduled away from each other, so we wouldn't be here at the same
time. I was here thirty minutes early specifically so that I could have
the quiet moment I needed, alone, for closure. So *of course* he was
ruining that.

"I didn't know you'd be here. My bad," he said, from closer to
me than he should have felt comfortable being. "My appointment isn't
until this afternoon, but I wanted to grab a couple of minutes by myself
since I can't later. I planned to be in and out."

"Whatever."

I walked out of the kitchen and moved to the front room,
thinking he would take the hint and not follow me. I had no such luck.

"Wil, can I have a few minutes of your time? *Please?*"

I turned to face him, crossing my arms. I couldn't keep the
contempt from forming on my face, which... hurt. We'd had our

issues, sure, but barely two months ago, I'd looked at this man with nothing but love in my heart.

Now?

"How could you be so stupid?" Kept echoing in my head. Men this gorgeous were often not worth a damn. Men this gorgeous, with money, were even worse. Expecting faithfulness from a man this gorgeous, with money, and celebrity status?

Hmph.

What in the world had I thought my pussy was made of?

"We don't have anything to discuss, Darius," I said, ignoring the guilt that pricked me about the sweeping internal generalization I'd just made. I knew better than to throw people into boxes like that, but hell… maybe if I'd done that before I invested eight years of my life into this man, I wouldn't be in the situation I was in.

"I disagree," he said, and I let out a dry laugh.

"I am *baffled* as to why you think I care."

For a few seconds, he said nothing. I hated to admit it, but the remorse in his eyes actually seemed sincere.

"I wasn't still sleeping with her." Those words came after his silence, and raised enough interest that I didn't interrupt. "The videos, the texts, all of it – it was all from years ago, babe. I have not touched her in probably a year, I swear to you. She came to me, wanting to start up again, and I refused. Because I *love you.* She was just trying to hurt us because I wouldn't do what she wanted. Released all of that to the media because I wouldn't betray you."

"But you *did* betray me," I spat, jabbing a finger in his direction. "It doesn't matter how long ago it was – you *did it.* You don't get points for abstaining from fucking another woman for "probably a year", whatever the hell that means. Our relationship isn't a goddamn AA meeting, Darius. I'm not going to give you points for doing what the hell you were supposed to be doing in the *first* place!"

He raised his hands. "That's not what I'm saying! I promise, that's *not* what I'm saying to you. I'm just…" he pushed out a sigh, and scrubbed a hand over his face. "I'm saying that… I know I fucked up. I'm not making an excuse, not blaming you – this shit was *me. I fucked up.* But I realized it, and I stopped, and I was trying my best to do right by you."

"Doing right by me would have been keeping your dick to yourself!" I screamed. "I saw the videos – saw the difference in your haircuts, your tats. You were screwing her for *years* while I sat back and believed your lies, being oblivious and *stupid.* Are you going to deny that? Huh?"

"No," he said quietly. "I'm not going to insult you by denying it when you've already seen the proof."

I laughed. "*Finally* a sign that you have a shred of respect for me. Do you think you can string together enough of those to tell me *why?*"

"Wil…" he shook his head. "I … I don't have an answer for that."

"Sure you do. You started screwing her how long ago? When did it start?"

"You don't want to—"

"Don't fucking tell me what I want," I said, raising my voice. "Tell me when it started."

He tucked his hands behind his head. "Five years ago."

"Fine. Now tell me what the hell was happening between us, what the hell went so wrong five years ago that you had to go work out your feelings in another woman instead of talking to me."

He didn't answer.

He just stared at me, with this expectant look on his face, like he was waiting for me to catch up to something obvious.

It only took me a moment to realize what I was missing.

Too fast to try to stop them, tears pricked my eyes, and I reflexively took a step back. "You…" I whispered, then tried my best to choke back the sob that sprang up from deep in my chest. He moved toward me with his hands out, like he was about to attempt some sort of comfort, but I quickly held up a hand. "Don't you fucking touch me," I growled. "Don't you… don't you dare."

"Wil, *please.*"

"Please, *what?*" I bellowed, so loudly that it echoed through the house. "I cannot… I can't believe you. Did you at least wait until I was out of the hospital?"

"I was with you *every* day," he shot back, with the nerve to raise his voice. "Anything you needed, I was on top of it, but you still shut down, and shut me out. When it happened again, I tried to be there – you shut me out. When you hurt your ankle, you shut me out. When the network screwed you over on your show, you shut me out. *Every single time.*"

132

"Wow!" I threaded my fingers through my hair, pushing it out of my face. "Did you seriously just run down a timeline of the worst moments of my life and make them about *you*? These are mileposts, huh? Is that what you're saying? You were just going along, being the perfect boyfriend, trying so hard to keep it in your pants. But there I was, with the audacity to be having a tough time, and I just pushed you inside of her myself, huh? It was my fault?"

"Don't put words in my mouth," he said, stepping closer. "I'm *not* blaming you. I'm telling you where my weakness, where *my* failing was. I'm trying to be open, and communicate with you, putting it all on the line, hoping that maybe... maybe we can work through this." It took him another step to be right in front of me, and he grabbed my hand and squeezed. "Wil... I'm not asking you to overlook, or accept what I did. I *am* asking... can we use this as a starting point? I promise you, I can be a better man than I've been. Can we *try*?"

"You know... I maybe would've given you the chance you're asking for if you'd told me this yourself," I said, pulling my hand away from his. "If you were so interested in "doing right by me" and "being a better man", you *never* would have let me be blindsided and embarrassed on national TV like you did. And... since we're being honest? The fact that it's a white girl doesn't help your case. And besides all that... you're a *liar*. As sincere as you seem, I can't even wrap my head around the possibility that you love and care about me like you claim."

"But I *do*!"

"*How?*" I exclaimed. "How can you *possibly* say that?! We were trying to have a baby, Darius! After the two miscarriages, I was *done*. The only reason I held it together was because those pregnancies were accidents in the first place. I was *done*," I repeated, trying to hold back a fresh flood of tears. "But no... you wanted to try again. We weren't even engaged, but you wanted to try. You wanted a baby. And my stupid ass *loved* you, you trifling motherfucker, so for the last *three years*, I've been trying. Do you know how I've felt? To be told nothing is wrong, that it'll happen when it happens? Wondering if every period is actually just an earlier miscarriage than the ones before? Hating my body for not being what you needed, all while keeping up a smile, because *Wil is always fucking smiling.* Wil is always sunny!" I let out a laugh that must have sounded as crazy as it felt, from the way Darius flinched. "Is that what you were thinking? Wil looks happy, she has that big ring on her finger, this big house. She *must* be totally fine, so it's perfectly okay for me to screw this other woman while I lie to her face about it."

He shook his head. "Wil... *no,* it wasn't... I wasn't thinking—"

"Now that, I believe." I scrubbed my face with my hands, then retrieved my purse from where I'd dropped it on the decorative table beside the couch. "In case it's not clear, there won't be a reconciliation. You have hurt me beyond belief. I wasn't anywhere near ready to move past it before this conversation, and... nothing about this has made me feel any different. I was happy with you, Darius. *Loved* you. *Still* love you. But I love *myself* too much to let you drag me back into this thing."

Darius opened his mouth to respond, but the sound of keys in the front door pulled his attention away. I took that as my chance to escape, rushing to the foyer before the realtor could get the door closed behind her.

"I'm done," I told her on my way past. "Put the sign up."

I didn't look back.

I was ready to have this shit out of my life.

The house, and the man.

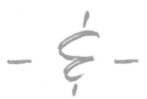

"So tell me, Steven; What will you be bringing to the field as a Connecticut King that will further their legacy – and mark the beginning of your own?"

I couldn't stop watching these interviews.

I'd been playing each one over and over for hours, taking notes to critique myself on the ways I could improve for next time. Talking to the rookies first had been a great idea – it would give me a chance to course correct before I talked to the veterans, and the star players.

I was happy though. Thrilled, actually, with the way these interviews had gone. The Kings hadn't had any early picks in the draft this time around, and the five players I talked to today didn't have the *best* stats. They had heart though, and potential. We'd pushed through shyness and jitters for five great interviews that were beautifully filmed, and would be edited and compiled into a final cut that would go live the week before training camp started.

Just thinking about it made me feel good.

A knock at my door brought my eyes away from my screen, and I frowned. As soon as my gaze landed on the time in the bottom right corner, I gasped. The knock sounded again, and I dragged myself up from my chair to answer the door.

"Ramsey, I am *so* sorry," I said, as soon as I opened the door to him looking… delicious, honestly, in a deep blue shirt, and slacks. His jacket and tie were probably waiting in the truck, where he'd put them on before we walked into whatever *really* nice place he'd surely already made reservations for. "I got caught up rewatching the interviews from today, and completely lost track of time."

Instead of the disappointed reaction I expected, he smiled as he shook his head. "I can reschedule our table for another time," he told me as I stepped aside to let him in. "It's not a big deal. I'm just glad you're excited about your interviews. You look… happy."

Yeah.

Usually, that wouldn't be notable, even since the breakup. But for whatever reason, since running into Darius at the house a few days before, I'd been in a weird headspace. I'd been able to put on a professional face, like always, to conduct those interviews, but outside of that, I'd just been… *off.*

Ramsey hadn't been happy about that.

"Not happy" was an understatement, actually. He was even more ready to rip Darius' head off than he'd been before, and I hadn't even been completely forthcoming when I recounted the story to him. Only a very, *very* select few people knew about those two lost pregnancies, both in the year after I'd won my Olympic golds. Both were first trimester, before I would have revealed anything publicly anyway.

It was before I even met Ramsey, and wasn't exactly the type of thing that just… came up in conversation, not with a man. I didn't feel like answering questions about it back then, and nothing had changed. So I simply… left it out.

The rest of it was bad enough.

"Do you want to see?" I asked, pointing at where my laptop was sitting on the counter.

"Do you really have to ask?" He countered, making me smile.

I was excited as hell to hit the "play" button, and couldn't help staring in Ramsey's face as he watched. He seemed really engaged, and interested, even talking back to the computer at some points, responding to what was being said. When that one was over, he turned to me, nodding.

"Wil… this is really, *really* good. Not the same old questions everybody asks, and you can tell that you really care about the answers, and the interview subject. And I like the way it's shot. I felt like I was in the room."

"Really?" I grinned. "You're not just trying to make me feel good about it?"

He chuckled. "So you can blame me when the internet roasts your ass? Hell no. If it sucked, I would tell you. This is the *opposite* of sucking… whatever that is."

I let out a relieved sigh, tilting my head toward the ceiling. I brought my gaze back to his when he grabbed my hand, threading his fingers through mine.

"Hey. When is the last time you ate?" he asked, and I averted my eyes. "Damn, that long huh?" he laughed. "You wanna throw something on, so we can grab a bite?"

I looked down at the faded black leggings and oversized tee shirt I'd changed into when I got home after the interviews. "You don't like my outfit?"

"The outfit is fine I guess, depending on where we're going. But I'm not taking you anywhere with those ashy ankles and elbows."

"Oh kiss my ass," I laughed, shoving his shoulder as I turned to head for my room.

"Don't tempt me."

My knees almost gave out, but I quickly righted myself and continued on, pretending I hadn't heard his response. At the door to my room, I turned to find him looking at me, which caused my mind to blank for a few seconds again.

"Um… call the restaurant back," I told him, trying my best not to stutter. "Just say we need a later reservation. I'll be ready in thirty minutes."

I shut the door behind me, then took a moment to catch my breath before I launched myself into the bathroom. I'd showered when I got home, but I took another quick one anyway, making sure to slather myself in the vanilla brown sugar body butter that always made him comment on how I smelled.

Because apparently, I cared about that now.

Out of the shower, I combed my hair down from the wrap I'd done earlier to preserve the style. I gave myself a few minutes for a quick makeup application, then went to my closet, picking out a dress that didn't need ironing.

I stood in front of my lingerie drawer for longer than I wanted to, debating what I would wear underneath my dress. I couldn't remember any time before when that had been a consideration for heading somewhere with Ramsey, but today, in the moment, I just wanted to do something different. I wanted to feel... *sexy,* while I was out with him.

And I wasn't really in the state of mind to interrogate that.

So I just did it.

To wear underneath the strappy, form-fitting black and white dress I'd chosen, I put on one of the brand-new bra and panty sets I'd purchased to replace anything I'd worn for Darius. Once it was on, I checked it in the mirror, damn near making *myself* blush over the fact that you could see my nipples clearly through the dark gray lace, and the "boy shorts" that only covered a laughable amount of my ass.

It was perfect.

Twenty-seven minutes after I told him I need thirty, I opened the door to my bedroom and stepped out. Ramsey had his cell phone up to his ear, but as soon as he looked up and saw me, he muttered, "*Goddamn.* Jordan... nigga I gotta go."

I had a smile on my face before I could help it – a direct result of his reaction to seeing me. Self-consciously, I smoothed the fabric over my hips, feeling a little déjà vu from the day he'd picked me up from the wedding. Then, I'd seen the hungry look that he immediately shuttered, purposely keeping his eyes above my neck. Today, he did no such thing. He stood up, pushing his hands into his pockets as he gave me a slow, head to toe perusal that made my cheeks – among other places – hot.

"Damn, Champ," he said, bringing his gaze to mine. "That's quite a dress to go eat fried catfish in."

I laughed, then grabbed my purse to head for the door. "Don't play with me Ramsey."

"I'm not. It's cool though. You'll definitely be the finest person in the building."

He joked with me some more as he helped me to his truck, and continued as we drove into the heart of the city. As it turned out, we were *not* going to eat catfish – he took me to an upscale, lounge-style restaurant called *Onyx*, that I'd never been to, or even heard of before.

The lights were low in the whole place, creating a vibe that was distinctly sexy. We were led to a line of booths with a great view of the stage at the front, all separated by curtains. No one was on the stage now, but slow, sensual music pumped through the air, drowning out the hum of conversation in the packed restaurant. Tall, elaborate candles encased in glass provided a little more light at the tables, but once we were seated, I couldn't shake the thought that this place was… *romantic.*

Any other time, Ramsey would have sat across from me. This time though, he slid right next to me in the semi-circle booth, leaning in to speak into my ear.

"What do you think?" he asked, his minty-cool breath tickling my skin. "Pretty nice so far, right?"

I nodded. "Yeah… and I noticed when we were walking up that *Arch & Point* is right next door… is that how you know about this place?" He smirked, but didn't answer, and I laughed. "Uh-huh, I thought so. What, are you trying to drop by after we leave here or something?"

He raised an eyebrow at me. "You know goddamn well I'm not about to walk into *that* trap," he chuckled. "Tonight, we're about to have some good food, hear some good music… have a good time." Under the table, he put a hand on my knee and squeezed. "Sound good to you?"

"Yes," I answered, in an almost-whisper, before I cleared my throat. "It sounds great."

And it *was* great. About halfway through our meal, a soul singer I absolutely *loved*, named Dani, came out to serenade the crowd. I'd purposely been avoiding her music because of the way it made me feel – extra horniness on top of the sexual frustration I'd already been having.

138

Sitting beside Ramsey, with a glass of wine in my system and his hand back on my leg made it torture.

That hand had started on my knee, then drifted up to mid-thigh, but hadn't gone further. No matter how much I shifted closer, leaning into him, trying to send a hint, he hadn't moved it up anymore. Now, Dani was leaving the stage, the check was paid, and I was staring a hole in the side of his head, on the verge of being pissed off.

Damn him for being such a gentleman.

"You ready to head out?" He asked, and I quickly plastered on a smile.

"Sure. Let's go."

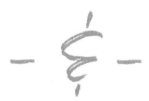

Back at my parents, he did the polite thing as always, and walked me to the door. The car ride had been unusually quiet for us, but I had so much running through my head that I wasn't really complaining about it.

"Auntie P got in my ass about it last time I went in her house all late, so I'm going to go ahead and head that way," he told me, while I was digging around to find my keys in my purse. My motion stopped for a second, and I licked my lips, trying to keep my tone neutral as I replied.

"If you're not driving back to New York, you could easily just… stay here."

The silence was deafeningly loud, only broken by the sudden trill of a cricket from what sounded like somewhere in the back yard.

"I had a rough workout this morning, Champ. The kind of rest I need requires a bed – I can't crash on your couch."

He was behind me, so I turned around, looking him right in the eyes. He was closer than I expected, so much that my breasts were a deep breath away from brushing his chest.

"Ramsey… who said anything about the couch?"

His eyes narrowed a little, but he held my gaze, like he was waiting for me to laugh, or say I was joking. When I didn't, he leaned in a little, closing that little space between us.

"So... are you opening the door or not?"

I was definitely opening the door.

As bold as I'd been about inviting him inside, once we were there, I clammed up. I mumbled something about fixing us drinks, then hurried over to the little bar I'd set up for myself next to the kitchen. My hands were shaking so bad that the corkscrew I picked up, intending to open a bottle of wine, went clattering to the floor.

I bent to pick it up, and by the time I stood up, Ramsey and his dick were right behind me. I looked straight ahead as he put his hands against the wall on either side of me, pressing close.

"Wil..." he started, leaning to speak into my ear. "You seem a little nervous all of a sudden. But we're friends here, right? All you have to do is say so, if your mind is changi—"

"No," I interrupted, looking at him over my shoulder. "Ramsey, nobody except Darius has touched me, in eight years. So... yes, I'm nervous. " I dropped my gaze, turning to face the wall again before I pressed my forehead against the firm surface. "I don't even remember what another man's touch feels like."

"Like this," he said, making me whimper as his lips connected with my shoulder. He moved one of his hands from the wall, dropping it to wrap around my waist as he pushed his body against mine. "And this." His lips brushed my neck, soft at first, then more firm, joined shortly after by his tongue.

My mouth fell open, panting as his teeth grazed my neck, and then ever-so-slightly sank in, sending a rush of sensation straight between my legs. He soothed the sharpness of the bite with a slow swipe of his tongue from the crook of my neck up to my ear, and then he bit me there too.

"Does my touch feel okay to you?" he asked, in a tone he'd never used with me before, one that made me shiver as his tongue swiped my skin again.

"Y-yes," I whispered, and my answer seemed to serve as a switch. As soon as that *yes* left my lips, the hand he'd had against my waist began to slip lower, and lower, until it was under my dress, and the only thing between his fingers and my lower lips was the soft, barely-there lace of my boy shorts.

140

Really though, it just felt like nothing.

His dick was hard against my ass, and I reflexively arched back against it as his middle finger ran over my clit. The rumble of his laughter in my ear only made me wetter as he pushed back. "Be patient. We'll get to that soon enough."

A strangled moan tumbled from my lips as he slipped the flimsy fabric of my panties aside, pushing that thick middle finger into me to wet it before he brought it back to my clit. With the base of his hand anchored against my pelvis, he moved that finger in slow, firm circles that had me panting in what felt like seconds.

With his free hand, he got my dress off, which left me in just my lingerie and heels. I was too wrapped up in what he was doing with his fingers to be self-conscious, and then his mouth was on my neck again, and I was just... gone. I didn't come back until he was picking me up, taking me off my weak knees as my juices ran down the inside of my legs.

It was pointless to be embarrassed – he certainly wasn't.

In fact, based on the smirk he was wearing when he lowered me to my bed, slid my panties off, then dropped to his knees and buried his face between my legs, he was *very, very* comfortable.

He hadn't even taken his suit jacket or tie off yet, but that didn't seem to be a deterrent. He licked me from my pelvis to the small of my back, and everything in-between, flicking his tongue in places that made me blush and scream and blush some more. Those soft, coily hairs from his beard were like a tickler against my skin – extra stimulation I didn't need, but certainly welcomed. And the sounds he was making – *Jesus.* Slurping like he was trying to suck me dry, moaning like I was the best thing he'd ever tasted... it was turning me on even more.

My fingers dug into his shoulders as he went after me with his tongue. Back and forth, back and forth, then delicious little circles that made my thighs clench around his head. I moved my hands to his head, keeping him *right there* as his mouth closed over my clit. My breath came in short pants, and then not at all as I bit down on my lip, trying not to scream myself hoarse as the orgasm rocked me. My feet pressed into the bed as I reflexively pushed myself up, but Ramsey's arms around my thighs kept me in place, forcing me to take it as he devoured me until I collapsed.

Holy shit.

Holy shit.

Holy. Shit.

That kept running through my mind as he stood up, wiping me from his beard. I couldn't have moved if I wanted to, but I watched as he took his time undressing down to his boxers, then uncovered two condoms from his wallet, tossing them onto the nightstand before he moved to stand in front of me.

He took me by the ankles, his touch reminding me that my shoes were still strapped on. "How are you doing?" he asked, lifting my feet to rest against his chest as he put his knees on the bed. He brought both hands to one of the straps, then seemed to change his mind, wrapping my legs around his waist before he leaned down, hovering over me. "Are you… enjoying the touching so far?"

"Are you teasing me?" I asked, and he grinned as he shook his head.

"Not at all."

He brought his hands to my face and neck, holding me in place while he punctuated that answer with a kiss. I moaned as he slipped his tongue into my mouth, teasing and caressing mine for a few seconds before he pulled back, peppering my nose, cheeks and chin with quick kisses that made me laugh.

That only lasted a second though, because then his tongue was on me again, and he was licking, kissing, biting my neck. My hands went to his broad shoulders, resting there as he took his talents lower, first to my collarbone, and then to the swell of my breasts.

He stopped there, and then sat back and stared at me, drinking me in.

"What's wrong?" I whispered, and he shook his head.

"Not a goddamn thing."

He slid his hands under me, unhooking my bra before he slid it down my arms. After that, he came in for another kiss, then dropped his head to my newly exposed breasts, one at a time. A long, slow lick, then a circle around my nipple before he closed his mouth over it, sucking hard. The pleasure made my back arch away from the bed, as a low whimper left my lips. He did it again, sucking even harder this time, using his hand to pinch the nipple that wasn't in his mouth. Back and forth, fast and slow, until my nipples were hard enough to cut glass and hyper-sensitive to the touch.

He kept moving lower.

Licking and biting the bottoms of my breasts, kissing his way down my stomach, until he was between my legs again. He pushed until my knees were pressed against my chest, putting his whole face in it. I was back on the edge of an orgasm two seconds after his mouth touched me, but this time, he pulled back... and took his boxers off.

I had to bite my lip to keep from gasping when he sprang free. My eyes went up to the ceiling as he reached for one of those condoms packets and ripped it open. I didn't look at him again until he climbed between my legs, lowering himself to hover on top of me again.

"You *sure* you want to do this?" he asked, looking me right in the eyes. "This isn't a bell we can unring."

I pushed out a breath as I considered his words. So far, crossing this line with him had been amazing. Just as I expected, he'd been a gentleman, very into pleasing me, had made sure my orgasm happened first – *twice.* But something about actual penetration felt like a whole other ballgame – no pun intended. Just like he said, it wasn't a bell we could unring.

"I just don't want us to not be friends after this," I whispered, and he gave me a little smile as he leaned into kiss me.

"I can't think of a single reason why we wouldn't be."

I brought my hands up, wrapping my arms over his shoulders and planting my hands at the back of his neck. "Then... yeah. I'm sure."

He nodded, and then... he was inside of me.

Immediately, my body contracted and clenched, responding to what it probably considered a breach. But he pulled back, slowly, then pushed in again, a little further this time.

"You've gotta relax," he murmured into my ear as he repeated that action, only getting a little further than before. We went like that for a little longer, with minimal progress, before I let out a sigh.

"It's too big," I told him, with more of a whine than I intended. But I was frustrated – not with him, but with my body. Eight years of extra-medium dick, and now that there was a real one available, it didn't want to cooperate.

Ugh.

Ramsey shook his head as he pulled back, then pushed in again. "It's not." He put his mouth to my ear, sucking my earlobe as a momentary distraction from the pain. "Relax, and be patient."

"But—"

"But *nothing,*" he said, with a little extra bark in his voice that sent a shiver down my spine. He brought his hand to my neck, hooking his pointer finger and thumb under my chin to make me face him. "You're not a quitter, right?"

I shook my head. "No."

"Well then…" he lowered his head to mine, gently nibbling my bottom lip before he grinned. "Take this dick like the champ you are."

He swallowed my scream with a kiss as he plunged all the way into me, so deep that his pelvis bumped against mine. Initially, pain rocked through me, but pleasure followed immediately after, as he pressed against what *had* to be the spot I'd long considered a myth. He pulled back, then buried himself in me again, and this time my body eagerly accepted him. I closed my eyes as he began to create a rhythm – slow, deep strokes that very quickly had me feeling like I was losing my mind.

"Good girl," he groaned in my ear, and *God*, why did that make me even wetter? My fingernails dug into his ass cheeks as he plunged into me, kissing and sucking my neck to the same tempo as his strokes.

It was good – it was *so* damned good – but then he sat back on his knees, hooking my legs over his arms, and suddenly it was even better. I was even wetter. And he was faster, and deeper, and harder, and just… *hell yes.* I protested when out of nowhere, he pulled away, but then my knees were against my chest again, and his face was between my legs, and… just… *hell yes.*

When he came up for air, he turned me onto my side. Still sitting up on his knees, he propped one of my legs on his shoulder and plunged in again, going so deep that I instinctively raised my hands, pressing my hands against his chest, trying in vain to move him back.

But it hurt *so damn good.*

He didn't even pull out before he turned me over to my knees, then pulled me upright with him. The only thing I could do was moan my pleasure and take it when he put that hand around my neck again, holding firm as he plunged into me from behind. His other hand moved to my clit, using his middle finger to play with it as he kissed my back.

"Ramsey *please,*" I moaned, as blissful pressure flooded my core. "I… it's too much," I whimpered, closing my eyes in response to the hot tears I felt building behind my eyelids.

144

"I'll stop when you come," he grunted against my shoulder, then returned his mouth to my neck. My heart was already racing – on the verge of exploding – when he tightened his grip, plunging deeper, sucking my neck harder, adding another layer of passion to what was already beyond intense.

"I can't – I *can't*," I managed to say, whimpering when I felt his mouth against my ear again.

"Then *come*," he demanded, pressing and holding his fingers against my clit.

A few seconds later, I stopped breathing, and there was nothing – *nothing* – but … *bliss*. No sight, no sound, just an explosion of feeling that made me burst into tears. Behind me, Ramsey slammed into me hard, arms locked around my waist, keeping me tight against him as he came. Wave after wave of pleasure kept washing over me, prolonged by the fullness of him still inside me, and every kiss he pressed to my back as he circled his arms around my shoulders, whispering soothing words in my ear.

"You're okay," he said, over and over, but… was I, really? I'd never – *never* – felt anything like that before, and even once he finally pulled out, gently lowering me to the bed, my body was still humming. At least, the parts I could actually feel, which were all below the knee and above the waist.

He left me there on the bed to dispose of the condom, and when he came back a few minutes later, it was with a warm, wet towel, true to his gentleman nature.

A gentleman who just fucked you into tears, I reminded myself, using the towel he offered to wipe my face first, then holding it between my legs – which I *still* couldn't feel.

My attention was taken away from that by Ramsey's lips, as he pulled me into a slow, perfect, lazy kiss. When our eyes opened afterward, he held my gaze for a moment before he smirked and laid back, stretching his thick frame across my bed before he hooked his hands behind my head.

"That was… *goddamn*," he muttered.

I more than agreed, but said nothing. I was too distracted by his nude body – more specifically, his dick, which was standing straight up, thick and hard and ready for action.

Again.

Already.

A thought crossed my mind, and a smiled came with it, which I quickly tried to hide.

"What you grinning about?" Ramsey asked, turning to pull me into his arms.

I shook my head. "Nothing."

At least… not anything I was about to tell *him*.

Eventually though… I would tell Margot she was right about just how much he deserved that nickname of *Sledgehammer* – on and off the football field.

Eight

RAMSEY

"So, do I start looking for your new place in Stamford or not? Or are you sticking with your roots and moving to Bridgeport?"

I chuckled at Clayton's question as I pulled up to one of the last stop signs before I arrived at my destination. Quietly, my stomach growled, and I glanced at the paper shopping bag that occupied my passenger's seat, frowning at the overpowering aroma of bacon and waffles that filled my vehicle. I was hungry as hell, but that was far from the main reason I was ready to get where I was going.

"Clay, bruh...*relax*," I laughed. "How are you more anxious than I am?"

His voiced boomed through the speakers in my truck. "I'm not anxious, I'm ready to get moving. Let's fucking *go*, son."

Shaking my head, I pulled up to the gate that would let me up to the house, and keyed in the code that would make it swing open. "Not even gonna front – I'm ready too. I'm trying to be patient though, you know? It's not a guarantee."

"Stop saying that shit."

"Why? What's wrong with me wanting to manage my expectations?" I asked, as I stopped the car and shifted into "park".

"When I know something, you'll be… somewhere in the first five people I tell, aiight?"

"First five?! Damn, who gets number one?"

"Chloe," I laughed. "She asked to be first to know so she can start… public relating as soon as possible. And I have to let my agent know too. And Aunt Phylicia. And obviously Wil."

"So that's my replacement now, huh? I see how you do, moving me out of number four so she can have it. I hope she's good to you nigga, I really do."

I was still laughing at Clay's faux jealousy when I got out the car, going around to the other side to grab the bag full of breakfast. "Whatever man, I'll talk to you later."

I got off the phone, and then took a deep breath before I moved to head into Wil's temporary housing at her parent's home. I'd taken her key with me to go get breakfast at her favorite little local spot, leaving her in a state that was miles outside of the dynamic we'd been working on for years.

Naked and exhausted.

I was getting ready to put my key in the door when it swung open. My eyes went wide at the sight of Wil's mother on the other side, but I quickly tucked the key back into my pocket and put on a smile.

"Ramsey, hi sweetie!" she greeted warmly, extending her arms for a hug that I easily gave. "You have no idea how glad I am to see you – our girl isn't feeling well this morning."

My eyebrow shot up. "Really? What's wrong with her?"

"Well, her father and I went on a little getaway yesterday, and didn't get back until this morning. I stopped in to check on her, but she wasn't answering, so I peeked in, and found her laid out in the bed, no clothes on, couldn't even get herself up!"

"That doesn't sound good at all," I shook my head. "What do you think is wrong?"

Carla glanced backward, like she was making sure Wil couldn't hear. "I'll tell you what *I* think, even though she swears it's not it – that girl is hardheaded! She's been putting herself through entirely too much. The crazy workouts, barely eating, all while she's still dealing with the Darius thing, and the career change. She probably strained a muscle or something out on the track and didn't realize it. How could she? The girl is running around pretending to be normal,

148

like she's not mentally and emotionally exhausted, but she doesn't want to hear it from her mama. So, maybe she'll listen to you."

"Listen to me?" I asked, and she nodded.

"Yes. We only came home to switch suitcases before we head to the West coast for a few days, and Mama has done all she can do. I ran her a hot bath and helped her in there, and I was going back to my house to fix her something to eat, but it looks like you have that covered. If she needs some help out of the tub, just avert your eyes," she laughed, as if I hadn't seen and tasted every inch of her daughter the night before. "I made her promise to call Mimi if she can't get around today though, okay?"

With those last words, Wil's mother breezed out the front door, closing it behind her. I put the bag of food down on the counter, then peeked out the window until I saw her round the corner to the main house before I went looking for Wil, who was indeed in the bathtub, eyes closed, submerged in a pile of bubbles.

I walked up the tub and knelt beside her, pushing a few strands of half-straight/half-curly hair behind her ear. The movement made her open her eyes, and for a few moments we said nothing as our gazes connected.

"Hi…" she said, finally, turning in my direction and planting her elbows on the side of the small tub. "I see you came back."

"Yeah. I just went to grab breakfast for us, since there was nothing in your fridge. I texted you, to say where I was."

She shrugged. "Haven't seen it. I opened my eyes to my mother in my face, asking why I was naked."

"Wow." I grinned. "Quite a wakeup call."

"It really was."

After a couple of seconds of silence, I reached forward to touch her, using my fingertips to make a line through the bubbles on her arms – a lot less than I *wanted* to do, with her barely covered and looking sexy as hell in that tiny tub.

"So…" I started. "Muscle strain had you stuck in the bed, huh?"

That question was met with a soft laugh, and a subtle shake of her head. "No. *You* had me stuck in the bed from the way you woke me up at three this morning. I was sore, and… friggin' paralyzed from the waist down. *Still.*"

"My bad, Champ."

She visibly shivered about that for some reason, then bit down on her lip as she pulled back, away from my touch. "Nothing to apologize for. I needed last night. So thank you."

I shook my head. "Nothing to be thanking me for. Last night was mutual. But why do I get the feeling that you're putting up a wall right now?"

"Not intentionally," she said, but didn't deny it. "I just… I don't really know what to do right now. I mean, you and I were friends, but then last night—"

"Doesn't have to change that, in the slightest."

"But none of my other friends have screwed my brains out, Ramsey. Let's not pretend this is just the normal course of a friendship, because it isn't. This is… something else."

I raised my shoulders. "Okay, so let's allow it to be something else. We don't have to make the shit weird."

"I'm not *trying* to make it weird, but I knew how to look at you before. I knew what category you fit into for me. *"Ramsey is my friend."* But friends don't give friends multiple orgasms. Friends don't tongue kiss. Friends don't sex friends to sleep."

"Says who?" I asked, knowing it wasn't helpful, and Wil rolled her eyes.

"Says *me.* I don't know how to define this."

"Why do you have to? We slept together *one* time, and you're bugging right now."

Her face immediately twisted into a scowl. "Okay, first of all—"

"I already know, don't tell you you're bugging."

"Thank you," she snapped. "Second – my life has too much *other* chaos happening to leave this up in the air. And third – Ramsey, do you *seriously* think it's only going to be this one night? After the way we…" she closed her eyes, and shook her head. "There's just no way."

"Too good for just once, huh?" I asked, and her eyes shot open so she could scowl at me again.

"Can you be serious please?"

I nodded. "My bad. To answer your question… no. I *don't* think it's going to just be the one night. I think that what happened last night was inevitable—"

"So you expected that? For us to sleep together? Is that what you've been thinking this whole time, while I thought we were just friends?!"

"*Hell no*," I said, squashing *that* shit immediately. "I'm not saying that, at all. I'm just… shit, look at how naturally we fell into that vibe, Wil. No awkwardness, it just felt like something that was supposed to happen. So the way I see it, maybe this was how it was always gonna be."

"So what, in your mind, we're together or something?"

I frowned. "Is that what you think I'm trying to push on you?"

"No, it's…" She let out a heavy enough sigh that it called my attention to the fact that her eyes were glossy. It felt like the whole conversation was going south, and I wasn't sure that touching her wouldn't make it worse. "I don't think you're trying to pressure me into anything Ramsey. But I can't get it out of my head."

"Can't get *what* out of your head?"

"That maybe what you're saying is right, that it was always supposed to be you and me, that maybe everything that's happened was just God lining things up the way he wanted them. And that maybe… I'm about to fuck it all up."

"Why do you think you're about to mess something up?"

"Because… I can't do this right now, Ramsey. I can't date you, or *anybody* right now, not with… everything. I know what happened between us last night – *loved* what happened between us last night. But I ended an *eight year* relationship *two months* ago. Before I'm part of an "us" again… I need some time to just be *me*."

She looked so broken up about saying those words to me that I felt bad about having to stifle a laugh. Not because what she was saying was funny, but because… "Wil… *duh*." I reached forward, cupping her chin to make her face me as I spoke. "You think I suddenly forgot everything you've been through, everything we've talked about in the last few months? I promise you, I haven't. I'm not asking you to do something you aren't ready for – I'm asking you to be open to letting our friendship shift to accommodate what happened last night, so that we don't fall into some bullshit, awkward place where it won't survive. That's all."

"You say that like it's so simple."

"Because I think it *can* be. I mean… what's *really* changed, honestly?"

She blushed a little, as a sheepish grin spread over her face. "Well... the fact that you've been inside of me now is pretty major, I think."

"I guess you have a point there. But... hey, you know what?" I tugged her toward me as I leaned forward, to speak into her ear. "It sounds to me like we just got closer. I've touched you everywhere, tasted you everywhere, been inside you... nah, we can't just call each other friends anymore. We're goddamn *besties* now."

I grinned at the way she laughed about that, using wet hands to try to shove me back. But that just made me reach into the water, slipping my hands underneath to lift her out as she squealed.

"What are you doing?!" she shrieked.

"Taking you back to your room – I saw your hands, and I can't have my bestie out here pruning up in the water."

She laughed. "Will you stop saying the word "bestie", please?"

"Why?" I asked, as I headed down the hall to the bedroom with her in my arms. "Because you're a hater, and trying to deny my status?"

"Am *not*," she giggled. "It's just not a very manly word."

"I've got enough dick not to be worried about that," I said, and she blushed about that too. "So what's the next excuse?"

In her room, I let her down onto her feet beside the bed, thinking she would sit or lay down. Instead, she stayed close to me, gripping the hem of the tee shirt I'd taken from my gym bag to wear on the breakfast run.

"I don't have any more. I'm wet and naked in front of you right now, so I guess I have to just accept it."

"Wet and naked and comfortable as hell, aren't you? Don't front," I said, grinning at her until a new smile spread over her face too. "See?" I grabbed her waist, forcing myself to keep my hands there instead of allowing them to slip lower. "This should be all the proof you need that this is just... an organic transition."

"What is an organic transition?" she asked, lifting her arms to drape over my shoulders.

I shrugged. "Whatever we say it is. You felt like putting your arms around me, so you did. I feel like grabbing your ass, so in a few seconds, I probably will. Just doing what feels... I don't know. Natural."

152

"So like this?" she asked, and then leaned in, pressing those pretty, soft ass lips to mine. I lowered my palms, grabbing handfuls of her to urge her closer as her tongue slipped into my mouth.

"Yeah," I told her, when we finally pulled back. "Just like that."

"What are the banana stickers for?"

Wil had been contentedly unloading boxes of clothes to hang in the closet of her new townhouse, not paying me any mind as I unpacked the boxes for the "office" section of her bedroom. But, as soon as that question left my lips, she came flying out of the closet and into the main area of the bedroom, snatching the thick, heavily decorated planner I'd been looking at from my hands.

"This is private!" she snapped, tucking it protectively under her arm, and I raised my hands.

"My bad, I didn't mean any harm. I've seen you post your "spreads" online before, so I didn't think it was anything you'd be mad about."

She huffed. "I post those *before* I put anything personal on them. And I'm not *mad*, I'm just… it's private."

"I've got it now," I told her, nodding. "And I didn't even read anything you wrote down. I was just skimming, and reading the quotes on your stickers. I saw the bananas were in there regularly, so I thought I'd ask what they meant. What *do* they mean?"

"I told you it was personal!"

I frowned. "Seriously? A damn banana sticker?"

"*Yes*," she insisted. "I don't want to talk about it, okay?"

"Okay."

And I really *was* prepared to let the shit go, but then I saw her face as she walked back to the closet, taking the planner with her, and it rubbed me the wrong way. After a few minutes… it started to bother the hell out of me, actually.

For the last two weeks, Wil and I had been… good. *Very* good. Since that first night of unexpected intimacy, we'd managed to get past the awkwardness and fall back into our same groove as friends… almost.

The sleepovers were a new addition to the dynamic.

But we were working with it, and we were good. This was the first time we'd had any friction, and I'd be damned if I was going see her glossy-eyed and upset over a goddamn *sticker* and just let the shit go.

"Yo," I said, as I headed to the closet to talk to her. I walked up just in time to regret announcing that I was approaching – she snapped that planner shut like it held state secrets, then shoved it onto the shelf behind her.

"What's up?" she asked, and I shook my head as I leaned against the door frame.

"I feel like that's what I should be asking you. You really just spazzed on me about a sticker, and I'm trying to understand where you're coming from."

She sucked her teeth, and crossed her arms. "It's not about the stickers, it's about the invasion of my privacy."

"Which I apologized for, because that wasn't my intention, but *then*… you snapped on me about the sticker. But you say it's not about the sticker. But if it's not, why are you tripping about telling me what it means? What, you have smoothies on those days or something?"

"I don't… have *smoothies* on those days," she snapped, then let out a heavy sigh. "Look, Ramsey, I… it *is* about the stickers, okay? And I can't tell you what that means because it's fucking embarrassing."

I frowned. "Embarrassing? What the hell is embarrassing about a sticker?"

"It's not the sticker, it's what it represents!"

My eyebrows went up. "Wil… I don't get it. But you know what? I don't *have* to get it. You said you didn't want to talk about it, so we'll just—"

"Oral sex, okay?!" she blurted, then immediately dropped her gaze to her feet. "The bananas… they're for blow jobs."

"…What?"

154

Wil didn't say anything, she just lifted her head and stared, like she was waiting for me to catch up. And after a few moments, I did, piecing together the regular placement of those particular stickers throughout her week, but then that raised a question that I honestly didn't mean to speak out loud, but couldn't seem to stop.

"Why are you scheduling head though?"

She let out a sigh that made me regret the question more than I already did. "Look, I know how ridiculous it is, okay? And I don't anymore, obviously. But... Darius and I were so busy that it got really easy to go too much time without being intimate. So, in my effort to keep the spark alive, I would... put it in my planner. Like, today, no matter what, I'm going to take this moment to make sure my man is taken care of, and nothing is going to come in the way of that. Didn't really work for keeping him faithful though, so... maybe it wasn't that great of an idea."

"I... I mean, I don't think anybody wants to feel like their intimate moments are just a to-do list item..."

Her head snapped up. "So you think it contributed to him seeking out somebody else?"

"No!" I held my hands up. "No, I'm not saying that. I'm not blaming you, or... banana stickers... for the decisions of a grown ass man. I'm just saying... I feel like if you have to schedule it, instead of doing it impromptu, maybe something else is going on, you know? I get it for people with kids and shit, but otherwise..."

"I *know that*. Which is why it's embarrassing. It should have been a red flag, you know? But instead of looking deeper, I just... put banana stickers in my planner for three days a week. And it didn't make things any better. I failed," she said, with a crack of emotion in her voice that made me feel like shit for opening the planner period, let alone asking about it. This was the type of thing that she and I didn't discuss – the kind of thing she maybe talked about with female friends.

The kind of thing that made me want to punch that clown-ass "fiancé" in his fucking face all over again.

"Hey," I told her, closing the space between us in the closet to wrap my arms around her. "You don't have anything to be embarrassed about. You tried to do something to fix your relationship. You *tried*. He didn't. And that's his bad, not yours, okay?"

When she didn't respond, I pulled back enough to grab her chin, tipping her face up to mine. With my thumbs, I brushed away the stray tears that had welled in her eyes. "You're really about to make me go roll up on this nigga on principle, Champ," I told her, and she laughed, shaking her head.

"That's not necessary. No need for my silliness to take this any further."

"It wasn't silly," I said. "It was… sweet, that you wanted to make sure you were doing your part."

She tilted her head. "So… are you saying that whenever I start using my planner again… maybe banana stickers *should* be part of my schedule?"

"*Hell no,*" I answered, with more force than intended. I immediately grabbed her shoulders, pulling her close to mitigate any damage from my response. "I'm saying… *if* you decide you want to do that… that should be the only reason. Because you want to, not on some "I have to do this" shit, okay? No goddamn banana stickers, please."

"You sure?"

"I am *positive,*" I chuckled. "There will never be a need for such a thing."

Her eyebrow lifted. "Never?"

"*Never,*" I responded, but something in the way she asked gave me pause. "Wait though – don't mistake that for me saying I *never* want… banana sticker privileges."

"So you *do* want me to use banana stickers for you?"

"No. I'm saying, I want what the banana stickers *represent.*"

"So…" her eyes narrowed. "…you want me to suck your dick, Ramsey? Is that what you're saying?"

"*No!* I mean… yea—goddamn it, why are you doing this?" I asked, suddenly feeling hot as fuck in the confined space of the closet.

"Doing *what?*" she countered, a little too innocently as her hands pressed against my stomach. "I'm just trying to get some clarity here." Her fingers drifted lower, under my tee shirt, to the waistband of the basketball shorts I'd thrown on that morning. "Do you…" I groaned a little as her fingertips brushed my stomach. "Want me…" She slipped past my boxers, cupping me with both hands as I grew harder. "To suck your dick… or *not?*"

She finished that question with her lips right against mine. Her eyes were full of mischief as she watched me through lowered lids,

156

waiting for me to respond. But she *knew* my response – my answer was hard enough to shatter glass, and right there in her hands.

"Feels like a trick question," I told her, grabbing her wrists.

She grinned, and then squeezed a little as she gave me a slow pump that made me care a little less that the closet door was wide open, and so was the door to her bedroom, and five or six friends and family members were all over her new downstairs right now, unpacking boxes.

"It's really simple… do you want my mouth on you, Ram?"

She pumped again.

"My tongue?"

And again.

"Maybe a teensy bit of teeth?"

And again.

"Do you want to know what the inside of my throat feels like around your dick?"

Goddamn, again.

I released my hold on her wrists – since I wasn't remotely interested in stopping what she was doing anyway – and cupped her face and neck instead. "You're a little naughty ass, aren't you? Where the fuck did this come from?"

She grinned, then drug her lip between her teeth. "Well, you've been encouraging me to do what comes naturally, to go with what I feel…" She let go of my dick long enough to yank down my shorts and boxers, then dropped to her knees. "And what I feel like doing is making a point."

I was still upright, looking down at her as she wrapped her hands around my dick again, while maintaining eye contact with me. Her eyes were hooded with lust, and no trace of those tears from before. Wil was dressed in leggings and a faded tee shirt, face scrubbed clear of any makeup, hair in what she referred to as a "pineapple". Completely dressed down, and so damned pretty.

"What point is that?" I managed to ask before she cupped my balls and squeezed, momentarily taking away my ability to speak.

"That "banana stickers" wouldn't only be for *your* pleasure around here."

I didn't get a chance to respond to that, because her mouth was on me. Hot, and wet, and so fucking tight it was like she was trying to suck a triple-thick milkshake through a straw.

Perfection.

And from the eye contact she was maintaining with me, she *knew* it. Knew exactly what it would do when she swirled her tongue around my head, or trailed it along those veins, or hummed her own pleasure with the act while I was still in her mouth. Knew how differently – in a good way – I would see her when she jacked me off with one hand while my balls were in her mouth. Knew how damned good it would be when she gagged a little trying to swallow all of me, how damned *sexy* she would look with her eyes watering from the effort. I buried my hands in her hair, ruining her style, and neither of us seemed to care about that, or about the fact that the voices of her friends and family were background music to what we were doing.

She'd just pulled back for air, after having me down her throat, when I felt that little tingle starting up. But I didn't want it like that – now that she'd pulled *this* out on me, I wanted to be inside of her, so I pulled her up from the floor, turned her around, snatched those leggings and panties down, and did that.

I clapped a hand over her mouth so she wouldn't scream as I drove into her. She whimpered and moaned against my palm as I stroked her as deep as I could get before I put my mouth to her ear.

"Birth control?" I asked, and she shook her head. I made a mental note to make sure to pull out, and then stopped holding back. The hand that wasn't on her mouth went to her clit, stimulating her there while I stroked until her legs went weak as she came hard, arching her back and damn near breaking my skin as she bit down on my hand.

I wasn't far behind her – she felt *too* good with nothing between us. As much as I didn't want to, I pulled out just before I came, leaving the evidence on the back of her shirt instead of inside of her.

After a few moments to catch our breath, I carefully pulled the shirt off of her, making sure to watch her hair.

"I figured since we were already in your closet, you could just grab a new one," I said, and she grinned.

"How thoughtful of you."

"I try."

Any further banter was interrupted by a loud burst of laughter from somewhere in the townhouse, reminding us that we weren't the only ones there. We quickly moved to cover up enough to get to her en-suite bathroom where we cleaned up. Afterwards, Wil went back to the closet with new pep in her step, and I went back to the boxes I'd been unpacking before.

Several minutes later, Wil poked her head out.

"Hey," she called, and I looked up.

"What's up?"

"We *are* still friends too, right?" she asked, then glanced at the bedroom door, like she was making sure no one was listening. "We've been doing a lot of adult things. Which I don't necessarily mind, obviously, I just... I still want to do other things with you too."

I put down the stack of books in my hands, and crossed my arms. "Wil...you're hungry, aren't you?"

"I... what?" she replied, frowning. "How did you know that's what I was getting at?"

"Because I know *you*," I said, pushing my hands into my pockets as I stepped forward. "Because...*friends*. All we do is kick it and eat, Champ. I knew it had to be one or the other, and considering the fact that I worked up a little appetite too..."

She rolled her eyes, but couldn't keep the smile from spreading across her face. "Okay, so maybe you got this one. But... seriously. I *deeply* enjoy being intimate with you," she said, as I closed the last of the distance between us. "But I don't want that to be *all* we do. I get it, you know? We're exploring this whole new dynamic, learning about each other in this totally different way, but I don't want to end up missing... my *friend*."

"You say that as if the words *"Do you want me to suck your dick?"* didn't come out of your mouth," I said, and she fake-gasped.

"Are you saying today is my fault?"

I nodded. "Hell yeah it's your fault," I laughed. "But also... I get what you're saying. And I agree. We'll make sure to keep it balanced, okay?"

"Okay," she said, with a little smile.

I started to – *wanted to* – kiss her then, but her father's bellowing voice carried up the stairs. "I hit up the BBQ spot! Who wants hot links?" he asked, and I cocked an eyebrow at Wil.

"I know *you* want hot links," I teased her, earning myself a swat to the arm as she eased past me.

"Just for that, I'm about to put on a show."

Coming up behind her, I smacked her ass, making her yelp before she even thought to stifle it.

"Looking forward to it… *friend.*"

"Next time I see you," Soriyah declared through the speaker of my cell phone, in her melodic Bahamian accent, "I swear to God, I am going right upside your head if you do not *stop it.*"

I sucked my teeth, and continued surveying myself in the mirror. "Right. Like you're *actually* coming to Connecticut."

"You say that as if I did not spend five hours in an aluminum can in the sky just two months ago, for a wedding that did not happen – *Thank you Jesus,* by the way – and then had to get right back on another airplane to come back. You *know* how I feel about airplanes Wilhelmina."

"Really? My full name?"

"I need you to understand how serious I am."

"You mean how seriously empty your threat is?"

"You and I will have a boxing match, and I will leave you in a state that your father is too embarrassed to call you his child. *I* will be his new child, if I hear you call yourself "fat" again. For one, "fat" is not the end of the world – that is something you Americans are obsessed with. Secondly, you aren't fat *anyway.*"

"I sure as hell ain't *skinny* anymore," I mused, poking at the layer of stomach fat I couldn't seem to get rid of. Standing in my underwear, looking at myself in the mirror, it wasn't as if I hated what I saw, or anything like that, but… damn. Everything used to be tight and right. I had guns, and buns of steel, and *abs.* I hadn't seen serious abs in a long time – not in years, since my official retirement from the track. One little funky ass knee injury had ruined my chances of competing again, and since then, my relationship with fitness had been… sporadic.

And it showed.

If some random commenter on *Wil in the Field*, which had gone live with the first episode just last night, had noticed… surely

160

Darius had too, right? He'd met me when I was super young and super fine, only for me to…

"So, like I said. My fist, your head. Consider it a date."

"Oh hush," I replied. "I gotta go, I'm supposed to be meeting Ramsey for a workout this morning, and God knows I need it."

"A workout, sure. Those "workouts" are why your hips are spreading as it is."

"Not *that* kind of workout," I told her, as I grabbed my dri-fit pants from the bed to pull them on. "We're going to the track, like usual."

"Of course, tell me anything girl. You do know you do not have to lie to *me* about your intentions with this man, when I have been encouraging you to drop that other one for years. Ramsey has powerful thighs – tells me everything I need to know about him. *This* is a man that my friend deserves, a man that is worthy of her. Not that chicken-legged man, no."

I burst out laughing as I pulled a tank top over my head. "Chicken-legged though Ri?"

"I said what I said. Now get off the phone, it is too early for this."

"Ri, you called *me!*"

"Because as soon as I saw that comment, I knew you were going to take it personal, and I was right, like I always am."

"You're *not* always right."

She sucked her teeth. "Name a time when I was not. Oh – oh – is that *silence* I hear? Yes, it is, because you cannot name one, can you? No, is the correct answer. You *cannot*. Goodbye."

I giggled as the phone went silent, and a second later, chimed to let me know Soriyah had hung up the line. As silly as she was, I really *couldn't* think of a time when she'd been wrong about anything. I was tying my shoes when my doorbell rang, and I quickly finished up to answer the door, already knowing it was Ramsey on the other side.

"You ready for me Champ?" he asked, as soon as I opened the door, immediately setting off heat between my thighs. He'd been calling me "Champ" since before we were friends, and it was a nickname I'd grown to love. Now though, ever since he'd implored me to *take his dick like a champ*, and taken to calling me that while he did *very* dirty things to me… it had a whole other connotation, and set off a different feeling than before. Now, it turned me on.

But who was I kidding?

Everything about him turned me on.

"Uhh, yeah," I said, pulling the door open for him to step in. "Let me just grab a jacket, it looks a little gross outside."

He nodded, closing the door behind him. "Yeah, we may have to skip the bleachers today. Can't have you falling on that little booty and getting hurt."

"Little? Please!" I shouted from the hall as I headed to my room to get a jacket from the closet. "A little too *much* is more like it. I'm trying to go get rid of some ass, some thighs, some stomach, all of that. The internet will *not* be roasting me, no thanks. Well… not anymore than they already have."

I zipped up my little yoga jacket as I moved back into the living room to find Ramsey standing there, arms crossed, with a strange look on his face.

"You ready?" I asked, and he scoffed a bit, then shook his head.

"Wil… you got me up at six in the damn morning to workout because of some shit some strangers on the internet said?"

I shrugged. "Yeah, what's wrong with that?"

"What's wrong with that is – that's not what I'm interested in spending my time doing. You want me to help you be stronger, be faster, be healthier for *you*, cool. We can go beast this shit any time. But I'm not trying to be part of you looking down on yourself because of some bullshit comments from people who don't even really give a fuck. They're just talking shit on the internet because they can."

"But it *is* for me. For my damn self-esteem, so I'm not getting talked about like a damn dog, and so I don't scare off another fiancé."

Ramsey's eyes went wide. "*Oh!* So this is about your bitch-ass ex too? Yeah, nah. We can do this today because I already committed to it, but after that, I can't hang. If looking a certain way for somebody else is your motivation, I gotta tap out, because I can't cosign that shit. You can holler at me when it's about *you* again."

I stared at him for a long moment, lips parted, waiting for him to crack a smile, laugh, anything to give some levity to what was surely just our normal back and forth. But when he didn't, I shook my head.

"Wait… are you *serious*?" I asked, frowning.

162

"Hell yes I'm serious," he told me, in a tone that eliminated any question about it. I watched, dumbfounded as he headed for the door, barely tossing a glance back at me. "You coming or not? Let's do this."

Any other time, he would have waited for me, but this time I got no such courtesy. He left me there while he headed to his truck, and I grabbed my keys and wristlet to hurry behind him, concerned that he really was going to leave me there.

I was… completely thrown off balance. The whole ride to the smaller track we used when the big one was occupied was completely silent, which had never, ever happened. Ramsey kept his eyes on the road, and the few times I glanced at him, there was obvious tension in his jaw.

He was mad at me.

I'd never experienced Ramsey being *mad* at me.

I didn't even know how to react to something like that, had no idea what to do or say. So I said nothing, and his silence continued all the way to our destination. Even then, he only spoke to advance the workout, and tell me what to do.

About twenty minutes in, right after he'd bossed me through running a lap at a pace I hadn't seen in years, it occurred to me that he was working me harder than usual. I didn't know if that meant he'd been taking it easy before, and he was pushing my limits now because of what I said I wanted, or if he was pushing me because he was pissed. Either way, I kept my mouth shut and worked as hard as I could, until I got sick of… whatever this was.

"Come on Wil. Five more burpees, lets get the shit out of the way," he said, once he realized I wasn't just stopping to breathe.

I crossed my arms. "That's all it is to you? Just some shit to get out of the way?"

"At this point? *Yes*. I've got better shit to do."

"Then go fucking *do it!*" I pointed to his truck. "If you're gonna be pissy, you can go do your better shit, because I'd rather not be a burden or a chore to somebody who's supposed to be helping me as a friend!"

He scowled. "That's what you think this would be, Wil? Really?! You think that feeding your insecurity is the type of thing a *friend* would do? Validating the idea that you should give a fuck what some internet trolls think, that's *friend* shit to you? I don't know what kind of friends you have, but if that's what I gotta do, then nah, I'm *not* your goddamn friend, I'm somebody who actually cares about you, unlike the motherfuckers you're trying to look good for. When you're *already bad as hell.*"

"To *you!*"

He threw his hands up. "Yes, to me! Maybe I'm wrong for thinking this, but... shit, doesn't *my* opinion hold a little more weight than some damn strangers and your cheating ex?"

"I never said it didn't!"

"But you're sure as hell acting like it! We've been working out together for damn near two years, and I've *never* heard you talk down on yourself, until some shit was said on the internet. And for you to think that grimy-ass dude left you because of your body? That's *wild*, Wil. I don't even understand that shit, can't wrap my mind around it."

He shook his head as he spoke, with such a peeved look on his face that tears started to prick my eyes as he turned away from me.

"I... I'm *sorry*," I told him, wrapping my arms around myself as a cold wind whipped past us.

My words made his head jerk back in my direction. "What?"

"I said I was sorry," I repeated. "I didn't mean to upset you, I just—"

"Wha-*no*," he interrupted, scrubbing a hand over his face. "Wil... *I'm* sorry. *Shit*," he cursed, more to himself than to me, then approached me, cupping my chin in his hands. "*I'm* sorry," he said again, looking me right in the eyes. "You don't have anything to apologize for, this is... this is my bad. I didn't mean to blow up like that, I just... if you could see you how *I* see you..." he trailed off, like he didn't know how to finish, but I didn't need him to... I got it.

It was the same way I felt when it was Naima, or Soriyah. I *hated* it when they talked down on themselves, or downplayed their talent, or saw themselves as any less amazing than I did. It actually made me angry, because I never wanted to see them letting doubt settle in, or letting negativity change how they saw themselves. Because I loved them.

And honestly, the same went for Ramsey.

But... still...

"You yelled at me," I protested, in my most pitiful voice, and his eyebrows drew together in guilty concern.

164

"I know. I'm sorry," he said, then pressed a gentle kiss to my lips, followed by one that was more firm, which immediately melted my hurt feelings away. It was crazy how he managed to do that so well, but I wasn't complaining. Not when he nibbled at my bottom lip for a second before he pulled it into his mouth, or when he slipped his tongue between my lips, tasting me. Not when his hands drifted to my waist, pulling me closer to him, or when I felt his hardness pressed against my leg.

"You see what you do to me?" he asked, then grazed my neck with his teeth. "If you want to make personal improvements, for *you*… I've got you. But just for the record, this body is *perfect* to me."

I shook my head. "It's not."

"How are you gonna argue *my* opinion with me?" he chuckled, then lowered his hands to my ass and squeezed. "I'm sorry for going in on you like that though, seriously. I don't like you beating yourself up, or letting any bullshit bring you down, but… it's not cool for me to add to that by getting upset with you about it. You forgive me?"

I smiled. "I do. Soriyah threatened to "go upside my head" for pretty much the same thing, so if I'm not mad at her… I *guess* I can't be mad at you."

"Tell me how to make it up to you."

He said that in a tone that made a tremble run up my spine, and I grinned. "Well… the other night, you did this thing with your tongue that—"

I stopped speaking as his cell phone started to ring in his gym bag a few feet away, and he groaned.

"Shit… I gotta at least see who it is. Give me a second, okay?"

"Of course."

I watched as he jogged over to his bag, quickly digging the phone out, pressing the button to answer, and pulling it up to his ear. I wasn't trying to be nosy, but the solemn expression that crossed his face as soon as he looked at the screen let me know it was important, and it didn't shift. He spoke quietly to whoever it was, doing more listening than talking, and I had to force myself not to ease closer to hear. Several minutes into the call, he nodded, and I was watching hard enough to see a "*Thank you*" form clearly on his lips. A few seconds later, it was over, and he dropped the phone into his open bag, propping his hands at his hips.

"Ramsey," I said, but he didn't move. His head was hanging, which worried me, so I went ahead and moved closer until I saw that his lips were moving. He was... *praying.*

So I shut my mouth, and I waited. When he looked up, it was with clouded eyes, and an inscrutable expression that made me feel like my chest was about to burst. And then... he smiled. He smiled so big that it cut through the gloominess of the day, completely erasing my concerns that something was wrong.

"I... I *got it,*" he said, and I froze where I was standing.

"You got it? You *got* it?! That was the call?! From the Kings?!"

"*Yes,*" he growled, then threw his arms around me, lifting me up off the ground as I laughed.

"Yes!" I screamed, grabbing his face and pressing my lips to his. "I knew it! I *knew* you would get it!"

He was holding me around the thighs, putting me in a perfect position to rain kisses all over his face as he laughed. When he put me down, it seemed like it was only because he was so wired that he couldn't keep still. I was so happy for him I could barely stand it myself, so him bumping his fists together, repeating, "*I got it. I fucking got it*" only seemed right.

"Hey," I gushed, grabbing his hands. "You know training camp is *right* around the corner? Like, a few weeks from now, right?"

He nodded. "Yeah. That's what Eli was telling me, that he wants me to start early, with the rookies, just so I can get re-acclimated."

"Exactly," I nodded. "And you know how tough it's going to be."

"Yeah..." he raised an eyebrow. "I do... but what are *you* getting at?"

I grinned. "What I'm getting at, is that... since training camp is right around the corner, and then you'll be going into what's probably going to be a really tough season... maybe you could use a little getaway first. Maybe... a little getaway with me? I'm thinking Bali."

He frowned. "What are you talking about? Let's back up – me and you, on a trip together? On your *honeymoon* trip together?"

I took a step away from him. "Oh, shit. Am I being weird? Am I freaking you out? Forget I asked, okay? It was just the heat of the moment, and I was excited, and—"

166

"Wil, *relax*. It's not that," he shook his head. "It's just… I thought you were going on that trip by yourself, to take a breather, and reconnect, all of that."

I shrugged. "Well, I *was*, but… the thought of that scares me, honestly. However, I *do* need this vacation, and with everything *you* have been through in the last year, you can't tell me that you couldn't use a break too."

He chuckled. "Yeah, I could, but… I don't want to impose on *your* trip."

"It wouldn't be an imposition. If I went on this trip by myself, I'd probably spend the whole week crying about being alone. And if I don't go, my vouchers will expire, and it'll just be money blown. You'd be doing me a favor, honestly."

"Wil…" he sighed. "I don't know."

I sidled up to him, pressing my chest to his. "What is it? You *don't* want to spend your last week of freedom in paradise with your *bestie*? That *is* what you said I was, wasn't it?"

"It is," he agreed, planting his hands right above my ass. "I just want you to be sure about this before I agree."

"*I'm sure*," I whispered against his lips. "Now… if that's settled… I've never had sex with an NFL player before."

Ramsey's response to that was to slide his hands lower and pick me up, draping me over his shoulder as easily as if I were his gym bag. He picked that up next, and started toward his truck, ignoring my half-laugh, half-screams.

"What are you doing! We weren't finished working out!"

"We are now," he said, then firmly smacked my ass. "We have other things to do."

I giggled as he put me down beside the truck and opened the door for me. "Like what?"

"Well, I need to call Chloe, my aunt, and Clayton."

My eyebrow went up. "Okay… what does that have to do with me?"

"Nothing," he grinned. "But after that… I'm giving you enough dick to pay for my half of this trip to Bali."

Nine

RAMSEY

July 2017

She needed this.

She'd made a whole big thing about me coming with her – which wasn't exactly a chore – but she needed this much more than I did, whether she would admit it or not. It was obvious as soon as we were shown into our private villa, and she let out a deep exhale. I listened for both of us as the butler gave instructions and details for everything, while Wil headed straight for the sun deck, to take in the panoramic ocean view.

I tipped the butler when he was done, then stowed our luggage in the closet before I went out to where Wil was standing, staring out at the water. I stood beside her, taking it in for myself for a long moment – the turquoise water, lush vegetation, and just an air of… *peace.*

"This really is paradise," she whispered, so low that I didn't know if she was talking to herself or talking to me. She leaned into the stone-carved railing of the deck, then turned to me, wearing a lazy smile that hit me right in the groin as she grabbed the front of my shirt and pressed herself against my chest. "Thank you for coming with me."

"Thank you for inviting me." My hands went reflexively to her waist – a location that had become their natural landing spot in the few shorts weeks since our friendship shifted into something else. "This is... bananas."

She shook her head at my word choice, then grinned as she pulled away. "I'm going to take a shower. I feel grimy from traveling."

"Okay. While you do that, I'm gonna check in with my people, let them know we made it in. And then... maybe dinner reservations? Or, no – room service, scheduled for later. But before that, we can explore a little."

She stepped back into my space to brush her lips over mine. "That sounds perfect, but you sure you wouldn't rather just join me in the shower?"

I groaned as her hand cupped my groin and squeezed, then reluctantly caught her by the wrist, stopping her. "I *would*... but I think you should enjoy this first one alone. Relax. Get yourself in the whole "paradise" mood. And then *later*... I can get back to working off my debt."

"Why must you always make such good sense?" she grumbled, but shot me another grin before she headed off to the bathroom. I was just settling into the seating area with my cell when I heard the shower come on.

There was a twelve hour time difference, so I knew my calls would be quick. Ten in the morning here in Indonesia was ten at night in Connecticut, so I kept it brief, spending a few minutes with my Aunt, and then Wil's parents, letting them know we'd arrived. After that, I shot texts to Clay and Jordan, then used the phone in the room to call the butler. For dinner, Wil and I would dine here at our villa, in the outdoor dining area on the deck. For lunch, all I did was make sure there were places in walking distance for us to choose from. Other than that, for today... we would just go with the flow.

After her shower, Wil came out of the bathroom with wet hair, wrapped in a fluffy white bathrobe. I laughed, standing up from the lounge chair as she lowered herself onto the big King-sized bed and spread out, with a low, lingering moan.

"You have to go experience that shower," she implored, with her eyes closed.

"Damn, *experience* the shower?"

She nodded at the ceiling. "Yes, *experience* it. You were so right about me going alone. I'm pretty sure I still had an orgasm."

"Well shit, let me hurry up," I chuckled, turning my phone off before I tossed it onto the coffee table. I bent to kiss her forehead before I headed to the bathroom myself, stripping off my clothes as I went. After a twelve hour flight from New York to Qatar, then another ten hour flight to get here to Bali, I felt grimy too.

There was a stone seat built into the shower, and I absolutely took advantage of it, sitting down and letting the spray of the rainfall-style shower head wash over me. By the time I was done in there, I understood what Wil meant. I wrapped myself up in the other bathrobe, then ventured back into the bedroom to find her exactly where I'd left her.

I grinned as the sound of her soft snores met my ears.

Instead of waking her, I climbed in beside her, and closed my eyes too.

Everything else could wait.

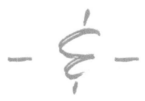

"I'm sorry, you think I'm about to do *what* exactly?"

Wil busted out laughing at the question, but the shit wasn't funny at all to me. As I stared up at the ladder I was supposed to climb up to an obscene height in the surrounding trees, my stomach flipped and twisted in knots.

"You're not... *scared*, are you Ram?" she teased, wearing a devilish grin.

I shook my head. "I didn't say I was scared, it's just... when you said you wanted to go to the adventure park, I didn't imagine... *this*."

This was a 20-meter high treetop obstacle course, that looked a little too flimsy for my liking. It was full of people screaming and having fun as they traversed the rope courses, color-coded by varying degrees of difficulty. The one Wil wanted to do, of course, was color-coded black.

Adrenaline Black Circuit.

"I just signed an NFL contract, remember that? I shouldn't be out here risking my ankles in these damn ropes."

Wil crossed her arms. "So... you're scared."

"Nah, I'm just saying..."

What I *wasn't* saying was that the idea of being up that high made me want to throw up. I could be in an airplane just fine, but being *all* the way up there, with nothing protecting me from impact with the ground... I looked up at the sky, sending up a silent prayer.

"We'll be harnessed the whole time," Wil said in a soothing voice as her hand rested on my arm. It was like she'd read my mind, and was trying to provide some comfort, but that little rope I saw attached to the harnesses on other people didn't do much.

"Looks thin as fuck."

"It will hold you, fool."

"What if it's too long? You trying to have me out here like Trevor from Fresh Prince?"

"Oh my God, *stop*," she laughed. "You have nothing to be afraid of, it's totally safe. And they'll come out and get you if you get stuck."

I rolled my eyes. "Nobody said shit about being scared, chill." I raised my shoulders. "I'm not *scared*, I'm just... being practical. If it's "totally safe" why isn't everybody on that one?"

"Because *everybody* isn't a super-athletic, strong, sexy football player like you, Ramsey," she said, easing in close to me to speak into my ear. "I don't want to do this by myself. I *need* you... please? I'll make it worth your time," she purred, then flicked her tongue along the edge of my ear. "Packed my banana stickers..."

Shaking my head, I backed away from her. "I need a refund."

She frowned. "On what?"

"On *you*," I told her. "Item not as described. You're supposed to be sweet. Warm and fuzzy. Not a damn... seductress, with your banana stickers, talking me into risking my life."

172

She grinned. "You said *talking you into* risking your life – not *trying* to talk you into it. So that means you're going to do it?"

"That's all you heard?"

"The important part, yes. Besides," she whispered, slinking up to me again. "*This* was always here. You're just now bringing it out."

Before I could give a rebuttal to that, she'd grabbed me by the hand, dragging me toward the "start" station. A few minutes later, we were both hooked into harnesses, and waiting at the base of that damn ladder.

"See you at the top!" Wil said, perky as hell, and I shook my head as she grabbed the ladder and started up. I prayed again, for both of us, since I doubted her crazy ass saw the same danger I did, then started up behind her.

The obstacle course itself wasn't the problem – it was the fact that it was up in the damn trees. Every gust of wind sent things swaying and rocking, and I was suddenly glad we'd just grabbed fruit for a snack on the way out of the hotel.

At the top of the ladder was a wood climbing wall, and I was actually impressed with how quickly Wil finished both of those. I was right behind her, close enough to see the huge smile on her face as she effortlessly moved to the next thing – flying trapezes, which were basically a line of logs tied to a rope. You held on to a rope at the top, while you essentially shimmied down this line of logs as they swayed back and forth in the air.

Craziness.

That was followed by two different sets of "monkey tracks"- grown-up monkey bars that you might die if you fell off of. After that was a tarzan jump into a net, more monkey tracks, and then another ladder taking us even higher into the trees.

Wil was having a blast.

I… was still breathing.

I made it through a zipline, a flying trapeze, and… some more shit that I just got through as quickly as I could. But by the time we made it to end, and I was still alive, successfully managing not to embarrass myself while completing the course… I actually felt good.

Wil, however, was ready to move to the next thing, dragging me right back to a cab for another destination, like we hadn't been on airplanes for the previous twenty-four hours.

"What are you in such a rush for?" I asked her, as we headed in the direction of the Telaga Waja river, according to the driver.

She grinned. "You'll see, really soon."

"Is it some more daredevil shit?" I asked, and she gave me a sly grin.

"I mean... just another *tiny* zip line," she claimed, then avoided my eyes to look out the window. "You'll be fine, just like the last one."

It was *not* a tiny zip line.

It went so far, in fact, that I couldn't even see the endpoint, traveling across rice fields and trees and all kinds of... other shit.

"*Hell no,*" I told her, shaking my head, and she grabbed me around the waist.

"Ramsey, it's just—"

"*Hell. No.* Have you lost your mind?"

"It's the only way to get to where the boats are, for our rafting tour!"

"Then I guess I'm not getting on a fucking boat today either, the hell?!"

"Ramsey!"

"What?!"

"*Please?*" she whined, holding on to my hands as she bounced up and down. I made the mistake of meeting her gaze, and as soon as I saw the pleading in those big brown eyes, I shook my head.

"*Shit,* man," I grumbled. "Why are you doing this to me? I thought we were coming here to be lowkey, and relax."

"We *are,*" she insisted. "We're just... getting the high energy stuff out of the way first. I thought you would be into this stuff!"

I shook my head. "I don't know why the *hell* you thought that! I like the ground. The water. Shit I can't fall off of and get crushed by gravity. You have something like that on your itinerary?"

"I promise, we'll relax tomorrow, if you give me today. I'm sorry you're not having a good time."

Something about that grated on me. Because... "It's not that I'm not having a good time, it's just... *shit.* I'm noticing that you really seem to enjoy pressing me."

She smiled. "Uhh... maybe just a little," she said, looking cute as hell as she held up her thumb and forefinger to emphasize her point. There it was – that adorable factor that balanced her sexiness, but also made it a lethal combination that might – *literally* – be the death of me.

A few minutes later, I was hooked in for the damn zip line.

And I had to admit… it was pretty exhilarating.

I had to go first, to prove I wasn't a punk, and those few minutes flying through the air, wind in my face, were… kinda cleansing. My adrenaline was still pumping when Wil came flying up a few minutes after I landed, with another big smile on her face. We were quickly ushered off to the river, where I soon realized that the "rafting" tour was actually *white-water* rafting, but… I couldn't even bring myself to complain. Now that I'd done that zipline, extreme rafting seemed lightweight.

It was *not*.

But, it was still cool as hell.

I got a good workout with my paddle as we passed mountains, trees, waterfalls, flowers, cliffs, and rice fields, all working together to create a peaceful natural setting that was, simply put, beautiful.

Wil was glowing. Her face and cheeks were blushed red with the effort of steering the boat, and her hair was a wild mess under her helmet, sticking out and sticking to her face, but she looked pretty as hell.

Exhausted, but pretty.

By the time the two hour rafting tour was over, I basically had to drag her to our cab back to the hotel. She fell asleep in the back seat, with her head propped on my shoulder. We made it to our room with just enough time to shower off the day before the butler arrived with his assistants to deliver our dinner.

Wil was still in the bathroom while they set up everything on the outside dining room for us. Shades up so we could see and hear the ocean as the sun set. Torches lit to provide ambiance, and later, once the sun finished setting, light.

I didn't really know what any of the food was, so I listened as the butler uncovered the dishes, explained the contents, and then covered them again while I waited for Wil. Wok-fried prawns, lemon-basil fried rice, spring rolls, vegetable curry, and a couple of different salads. Dessert was a lychee panna cotta with a mango compote, something I was sure Wil would love. Just as he was placing the cover back on the last dish, Wil appeared.

As soon as I laid eyes on her, I ushered him out.

She was wearing a thin, spaghetti-strapped dress that she couldn't have been wearing anything underneath. I could clearly see the sway of her breasts beneath the sage green fabric, and it was so short that it barely skimmed her thighs. Her hair looked damp, but all curly and fluffed out as she padded up to the table on bare feet.

"Why are you looking at me like that?" she asked, blushing under my gaze.

I approached her, making her shiver a bit as I gently tugged the hem of that itty-bitty dress. "Because... I don't want a damn thing on this table more than I want you right now." She let out a moan as my hands went under her dress to confirm my suspicion that she wasn't wearing any panties. Her lips parted, chest heaving a little as I slipped my fingertips between her thighs. Her body responded with immediate wetness as I dipped into her, first one finger, then a second.

Her eyes closed as I stroked her again, pressing my thumb to her clit as I moved. She propped her hands up on my shoulders, holding on to me I plunged deeper, faster, harder, until I had to hook an arm around her waist to keep her upright.

When the tremors from her orgasm stilled, I raised my hand to my mouth, licking her off one finger before I put the other one to her lips. Her eyes were hooded with lust as she opened her mouth, accepting the offer.

"*Good girl,*" I murmured to her as she closed her eyes and licked it clean, then brought her mouth to me for a her-flavored kiss that *really* had me ready to say "fuck dinner".

But then her stomach growled, and we were laughing too hard to keep kissing.

So we ate.

We both tried everything, some things we liked and some things we didn't, but it was cool to experience. We talked, and laughed, and I couldn't speak for her, but my mind wasn't on anything except that dinner. On her. Not on my grief, or the job change, or my concerns about the impending season, just... the moment.

Afterwards, we migrated to the lounge area next to our private plunge pool. Instead of taking separate ones, we stretched out together on the same chaise, with her practically on top of me – not that I minded. It felt like the most natural thing, laying there with her head on my chest as she drifted off to sleep with her arm hooked around my waist.

In fact, what felt strange was thinking about us ever having a different dynamic than this. Being "just friends" felt completely foreign, and her almost *marrying* somebody else? That was a distant bad dream.

I wasn't even stressed about her declaration of not being ready – or at least not ready to *define* – anything deeper than the friends with benefits thing we had going. I was comfortable here, with us doing the same damn things we'd been doing anyway, just with the added element of sex – something I hadn't realized I missed until she and I started doing it.

After my mother passed, my interest in casual flings had dissipated. Before that, after Lena, casual was the only thing I would entertain, because I wasn't willing to give another woman a chance to get her hooks in me the way Lena had. Negative aspects of the relationship aside, it had been hard to let go of. We had history, and loathe as I was to admit it, we had chemistry. Regardless of what happened between us, there was love there, and it hadn't disappeared overnight.

Which was why I was more than willing to give Wil time – I still needed it too.

Wil

This was really a great decision.

That thought kept playing in my head as I glanced beside me to Ramsey, who was holding an animated conversation with our driver as we headed back to the hotel.

We'd spent the morning at a shark conservatory – something I'd almost chickened out on. But Ramsey went in on me, reminding me how I'd been all over him the day before about the obstacle course, and the ziplining. So I went, as planned, and loved it. Touched and fed the sharks, had lunch, got to talk to new people. When we got in the car to leave, our driver had recommended a trip all the way into central Bali, to visit the holy spring at the Dalem Pingit Sebatu Temple. I didn't *want* to spend two hours in the car just to get there, but again, Ramsey insisted.

And it was amazing.

There was a little bit of a hike to get there, but once we made it, it was worth it. We were both mindful of being respectful of the local Hindu religion, but I only knew God by one name... and to my surprise, I felt him there, in that water, like it was cleansing to me. We stayed longer than we probably should, and then changed into dry clothes again for the drive back.

It was there, in the backseat, that I found myself very grateful that Ramsey had been with me. Not that we hadn't had a great time the day before – we did, despite his complaints. But today was notable because of those two experiences I wouldn't have had without him pushing. Because of him, I now had those memories to treasure.

Back at the hotel, we changed into swimming clothes and headed to the beach for the first time since we arrived. We found a cabana, ordered drinks, and settled in, soaking up the sounds of the ocean and basking in the sun.

"You having a good time?" Ramsey asked, drawing my attention away from gazing out at the water.

I nodded. "I'm having a *great* time. What about you?"

"Grudgingly."

I laughed. "Why grudgingly?"

"Because I'm still salty about yesterday," he said, taking a long swig from the Hennessey and Coke in his hand. "Would you have still wanted to be my friend if I'd gotten stuck on the obstacle course somewhere?"

"Are you kidding? I would've come to save you." I reached up, lowering my sunglasses a bit to look at him over the top. "I accept payment in the form of sexual favors, for future reference."

He scoffed. "So I would've added to my debt? No thanks. I still owe a lot more dick to pay for this whole thing, since you won't let me reimburse you."

"You don't *owe* me anything, but I'll take whatever you're willing to give. But... hey... I hope you don't feel weird about not

178

paying for this. Seriously – it was already paid for, and going to waste. And besides, you paid for your plane ticket."

"Right, because grown men are *supposed* to pay their way in the world. I may not have A-list actor money, but I do okay enough that I could pay you for this trip, Wil."

I rolled my eyes. "Oh my God, please. You were a pro football player, and I know for a fact that you have Tariq Evans managing your money. Do *not* act like that."

"I'm not acting like anything, but I'm saying... I was on a rookie contract, as a running back. Four years, five million dollars. It wasn't like today, where they're giving rookies twenty million out the gate. That's why they were so pissed when I left – they wanted to hurry and sign me to another shitty contract, and that didn't work out for them."

Wow.

"I had no idea they'd undercut you like that. You were like, their *star*."

He scoffed. "I know. But that's how it goes, when you're a poor kid from the hood, desperate just to get your mother somewhere safe, you know? It didn't even occur to me to negotiate – that I *could* negotiate. And again, big contracts weren't such a norm for a running back in those days. The Kings, however, know how to treat a man," he laughed.

"Well, I'll drink to that," I said, holding up my own fruity cocktail for us to clink glasses. "But, to backtrack a little – please don't feel weird about me having paid for this trip, okay? I just appreciate you coming with me. There's no way I would've had as good a time by myself."

He chuckled. "You don't enjoy your own company?"

"No, I'm not saying that. I've taken trips alone before, and had a great time, I just... I don't think I'm in the right space, not right now. Having you here is..."

"A good distraction?"

"I was going to say a nice change," I corrected him. "But... I guess you could say that too."

He shrugged, then took another long sip from his glass. "I don't mind it, Champ. I have thoroughly enjoyed being your entertainment so far."

"You know that's not all you are to me, right?"

I *really* didn't mean to say that out loud.

Since our initial conversation about giving our friendship room to shift, I'd tried to be careful about how I expressed myself to him – a source of frustration, honestly, since I'd never had to do that before.

But I was trying to be fair to him, trying not to set up an expectation I couldn't really fill. Ramsey was a really, *really* good man – one who deserved an actual, fulfilling relationship if that's what he wanted. As it stood right now, I was standing in someone else's way, under the guise of being his "friend", while I gained all the benefits of him being my man. What I didn't want to happen was me... stringing him along, making him believe that things were going deeper than they were.

Even though... they *were* going deeper.

I just didn't want to talk about it.

If I avoided thinking about it too hard, perhaps I could ignore that, especially now that we were intimate, I was maybe falling for a man at the same time I was getting over the one before him. Honestly speaking, I wasn't sure it was fair to either of us, but that wasn't pleasant to think about.

I preferred to focus on the joy of the moment – the teasing grin on Ramsey's face as he raised an eyebrow in disbelief, the amusement in his eyes, the fact that he was sexy, golden-brown perfection lounging beside me with a glass of dark liquor in his hand, wearing nothing but swim trunks. I'd said he wasn't a distraction, but I don't know... he'd certainly done a good job keeping my mind off of everything except being here with him.

"Tell me anything," he said, his words bringing me back to the fact that we were having a conversation. "You know you don't have to front, right? Brought me along to use me for my body, just tell the truth girl."

I laughed. "Oh, whatever. We haven't even had sex since we got here."

"That's because you've had us moving around the whole time, seeing everything. Not complaining, just saying."

"Well, you are in luck Mr. Bishop, because I am all out of "see everything" energy. I need a couple of days of just... being laid up drinking, having lazy sex."

The way he met my gaze was damn near scary, considering the fact that I was wearing sunnies, but he still seemed to be looking me right in the eyes. "Why are we down here then, when we have a whole private pool and villa to ourselves?"

"That is a great question."

It didn't take us long to get back up to the resort from the beach, but we were stopped on the way by a couple of people who recognized us from the show, and were on vacation as well. Ramsey took it in stride, taking a moment to stop and chat, but it made me antsy. Nobody pulled out a smartphone, thank God, but the whole thing freaked me out – I was on vacation to get away from everything and everybody, and being recognized just felt... like a violation.

But that was silly, and I knew it, so I didn't say anything, just thanked my lucky stars that we hadn't felt moved to do anything inappropriate out on the beach. My anxious feeling lasted until we were back in the privacy of our villa, set apart from everything, and were out in our amazing little personal infinity pool, sharing a bottle of wine.

Ramsey leaned against the edge of the pool, and I leaned against him, trading wine-laced kisses after we'd both had several glasses, and opened a second bottle. I was buzzed, but it wasn't just the wine, it was *him*. Every time I was around him now, I felt... tingly, and ready, just waiting for him to touch me, or taste me, or *take* me – a feeling I'd long lost with Darius.

"I see you really are feeling lusty, huh?" Ramsey asked, as he squeezed my ass under the heated water.

I nodded, grinning as he turned us the other way, so that it was my back against the wall instead of his. "I told you... this is what you bring out of me."

I whimpered as he dropped his mouth to my neck, sucking and biting me there. Even under the water, I could feel him getting harder as his kisses grew deeper, and then started to trail down the line of my bikini top. I closed my eyes, tipping my head back as his fingers went to the back of my neck, skillfully untying the strings.

When I opened my eyes again, it was to watch him. He'd moved us to a more shallow part of the pool, and I sipped from the last glass of our second bottle of wine as he lifted and squeezed my breasts, then dipped his head to suck one of my nipples into his mouth. He sucked hard, and it was so good that I felt the pull all the way down in my toes. That, plus the wine, made me lose my balance enough to slip a bit, but Ramsey caught me around the waist, keeping me up.

"Let's take this inside."

We didn't even close the doors. They were glass anyway, so what was the point? We were wet from the pool, so after he snatched apart the strings on my bikini bottom, he propped me up on the wide table nestled behind the couch, and plunged into me right there, so deep and so hard to our hips knocked together. But he felt so good that I didn't care.

I draped my arms over his shoulder, planting my hands at the back of his neck to pull him in. As he kissed me, he swallowed my appreciative moans, and maneuvered his hands between me and the table so he could grip my ass as he stroked. I threaded my legs around his, using the leverage to meet his motions, something that seemed to prompt him to go deeper, and faster, neither of us caring that we were rocking that little table harder than we probably should.

"You feel so damn *good*," I purred in his ear, dropping my hands to his ass cheeks. I dug my fingernails in at the same time I sank my teeth, just slightly, into his neck. That made him growl, and grab my ankles, raising my legs and then pushing them back. Because of the height of the table, he was plunging into me at a downward angle that left me wide open for him. I wanted to scream, but he caught my lip between his teeth, nibbling before he sucked it into his mouth as he filled me up, over, and over.

When my mouth was free – because he'd dipped his head to nibble and suck and lick my nipples into hard, sensitive peaks - I used it to scream and moan my pleasure, and beg him for… I don't know what. There was nothing more he could possibly be doing, because *this* was perfection.

Or so I thought.

"You sound so fucking *sexy*," he growled at me, propping my leg up over his shoulder, somehow getting *even deeper* as he wrapped one of his big hands around my neck. "This is good for you?" he asked, as he plunged again, but didn't pull back, simply circling his hips instead, knowing that he was pressing right against that spot that was going to make me come unglued.

"Yes," I breathed, swallowing hard against the light pressure of his hand.

He pressed his lips to mine for a soft kiss as he somehow pushed deeper. "Yeah?"

182

I nodded, half-moan/half-whimpering another "*yesss*" just before he pulled back, and started moving again. A few seconds later, the tingle in my core turned into full-blown tremors, and he let my leg down long enough for me to lock them around his waist, holding on, digging my fingernails into his shoulders as he stroked me until I came, with a scream that the whole resort probably heard. And Ramsey wasn't much quieter – plunging into me a growl that probably put any nearby animals on high alert.

Afterwards, we drug ourselves to the bathroom to shower, and then tumbled into the bed, tipsy and sleepy and spent. I snuggled in close to his nude body and got comfortable, closing my eyes, and letting myself be lulled to slumber by Ramsey's steady breaths as he fell asleep.

A perfect end to a perfect day.

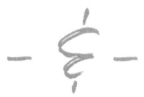

The next day, we did the cooking academy tour through the resort. Early that morning, they took us into the village, to the fish market, and then back to the resort kitchen where we were walked through a meal that we shared for lunch.

After that, we made our way to the spa, using the vouchers that came with my package to get facials and massages and pedicures and pretty much everything we could. Back in the room, we napped, and talked, and napped, and laughed, and napped a little more.

That evening, we had dinner in our room again, since we'd ended up waking up in time to catch dinner in the resort restaurant the night before.

"So who is your next interview with?" Ramsey asked, then ate a spoonful of the tiramisu we were sharing.

"Trent Bailey. They liked what I did with the rookie interview, so they're letting me talk to one of their stars. In his *home*, at that," I added, and Ramsey nodded.

"That's what's up. You know, this new show is a good look for you. Even though you're the interviewer, and your subject is the focus... I don't know. It's like your personality shines a little more."

I sat back, chewing at my bottom lip. "You think so?"

"Yeah, I do. And I've seen and heard the chatter about it, you know? You're well received, which you *know* is never guaranteed."

I laughed. "Right. I'm just glad to have something my father didn't have to buy me into," I quipped. "I might have to come back out here and jump off of one of these cliffs if I find out Daddy made a big donation to the Kings."

Ramsey shook his head. "You don't *know* that Jack "paid" for you to be on *From the Sidelines*, come on. It could have just been... a token of gratefulness, after the fact. Don't assume the worst before you talk to him – unless you've already talked to him."

"Nah," I denied. "I haven't, not *really*. I hinted at it, but he was so upset about the way all of that went down, and talking about lawyers and breach of contract and all of that, and I was just... ready to be past it. So I asked him to drop it, which means I can't really bring it up to him."

"Does it matter anymore anyway?"

I took a sip from my water, looking out at the darkened ocean as I considered that. We were out in the open air dining room again, and the sun had sank into the horizon a long time ago, leaving the firelight of the torches to set the ambiance. After a few moments had passed, I shrugged.

"I honestly don't know. It's like... I want to confront it just so that I can say – please don't do this again. But on the other hand, I'd really like to be able to trust that he thinks enough of me now, that I've proven myself enough that he wouldn't see a need to, you know?"

"That's assuming it was about that in the first place."

I rolled my eyes. "If you know Jack Cunningham like *I* know Jack Cunningham, you know that if he saw an opportunity to give his one and only baby girl a leg up... he took it. And I can't fault him for that. But you know what sticks to me most about that conversation with Connie and Sarita? I'm not even mad about being pushed out of my job anymore – I'm mad at the implication that I'm only somebody because of who my parents are. It's... frustrating."

"I get it," he nodded. The firelight reflected back at me in his eyes as he held my gaze. "But... you know that your upbringing isn't something to reject, right? You have two *good* parents, who've afforded you a life where you haven't gone without anything you needed. In college, you could focus just on athletics, not wondering where your next meal might come from if you missed dinner in the cafeteria. No worries about if your *mother* was eating. When you left the sport, you had your family to fall back on, etc, etc. Don't be so quick to downplay it, Champ. You're lucky."

"I know that," I agreed. "And I hope I don't come across as spoiled, or ungrateful, it's just… I don't want to be under a shadow, you know? I'm proud of my parents, grateful for everything they've provided for me, but… I'm a grown woman, with accomplishments of my own, that I worked *damn* hard for. But every time I'm the subject of an interview, it always goes back to Jack and Carla. There's always this undertone that something was given to me. Even Darius did it sometimes, and it drove me nuts. It's like… I just want to do enough, *be* enough, that I reach a point where people look at me and see… *me*. Just me. Just Wil."

Across the table, Ramsey smiled. "When I look at you, that's all I see."

As soon as he said that to me, I was *so* glad that it was – hopefully – too dark for him to see me blush. Ramsey had always been that guy with an encouraging word, but for some reason, it felt a little different now. And I didn't help that… I knew he wasn't just saying it. He *meant* it.

This man is trying to make me fall in love.

"Thank you for that," was the response I chose, trying to keep the emotion I felt out of my voice. But my face was hot now, and so were… other places. I needed to change the subject.

"So how are you holding up?" I asked, knowing he would know what I was talking about. "I've read that it never *really* gets easier, but… is it *any* easier now?"

He cleared his throat, then picked up his wine glass, draining the rest of the contents. "I… don't know, actually. I went to the gravesite, for the first time since the funeral. Told her about signing the contract with the Kings. Managed to stay upright, so I guess that's progress."

I nodded. "Yeah, I would say so. How did you feel afterward?"

"Like I missed the shit out of my mother, and would give anything for her to be at my first game," he told me, like he'd thought about it a lot. He probably *had* thought about it a lot – was probably trying *not* to think about it, which made me feel really shitty for bringing it up.

He picked up the half-finished bottle of wine and poured himself another glass. Before he could put the bottle back down on the table, I was in front of him, and then in his lap, snugging close.

For a second, he hesitated, but then he wrapped his arms around me as I buried my face in his neck. "I'm sorry for making you think about that," I whispered. I saw, rather than felt him shake his head.

"Nothing to be sorry about, Champ. Just like you… it's something I can't seem to get away from. So I guess… I don't know, maybe we just have to learn to take it in stride. Embrace it. Or hell… just start telling people to leave you the fuck alone about it," he laughed, which I was glad to see.

"You *know* we can't just tell people to leave us alone about something."

He scoffed. "Speak for yourself. You must have forgotten what my interviews used to look like. I never give them anything but football."

"But what if I interviewed you?" I asked. "You know you won't be able to pull that with me."

He smiled. "I guess I could give *you* the goods, *Wil in the Field*," he teased. "Exclusive access."

"Oooh, talk dirty to me why don't you?"

Pulling me closer to him – even though I was already as close as we could get – he laughed. "That turns the reporter in you on, huh?"

I nodded. "You know it."

After a few seconds of silence passed, I looked up, meeting his eyes. They were still full of firelight, and… full of something else too, that made me feel just as warm and tingly as his words had, a few minutes ago. I sighed as he brought his lips to mine – contentedly. Being with him like this, in his arms, in paradise, filled me with a kind of happiness I couldn't even describe.

So I didn't try, at least not with words.

I straddled his lap, and pulled him free from his shorts, and sank down onto him, taking full advantage of the fact that the only panties I'd packed were for *outside* of the resort. He tugged the straps of my dress down, freeing my breasts to the tropical warmth of the night air before he covered them with his hands, and squeezed. Lowering my lips to his, I kissed him deep, matching the swipes of my tongue with the movements of my hips as I rode him freely, without a single care.

For now, and for the next two days, as far I was concerned, we were the only two people in the world that mattered.

Ten

Wil

- And what do you see for yourself beyond football? Five, ten, fifteen years from now, what will you have added to the Bailey legacy?

I smiled to myself as I typed another question for my upcoming interview with Trent Bailey, the Kings' star quarterback, then got up to fix myself a glass of water. This was only my second full day back home from Bali, and I was still rehydrating from a whole week of disconnecting from everything except relaxation - and, well, Ramsey.

Lots, and *lots* of Ramsey.

More of him than I probably should have indulged in, considering that I was supposedly taking time to heal, and cleanse myself of Darius. And I *was* thinking about Darius less and less - which was a good thing, after a break up - except instead of focusing on self-examination, I was more focused on examining... *Ramsey.*

He just made it so damn easy though.

As I stood in the kitchen sipping my water, memories of our time together over the past week flooded me again, heating me from head to toe. We'd gotten to know each other very, *very* well while being out in paradise alone, especially over those days where we'd foregone the adventure seeking, opting instead to spend our time naked, in varying stages of inebriation, talking to, touching, or tasting each other.

It was *perfection*.

Or the closest thing I'd experienced in a really long time.

The level of intimacy I felt with Ramsey - of *all* people - was mind-blowing to me. Our relationship had shifted so easily into a new normal that it made me question exactly how deep my feelings for Darius had been at all. If I could switch gears so fast, so *hard*... how much devotion could I have felt for him?

Hell... maybe marrying a cheater wouldn't have been my only mistake. Maybe... it would have been marrying a man who wasn't *the one* in the first place.

So are you considering Ramsey "the one" now?

I quickly pushed that thought from my mind.

For me, for now, *I* was "the one" - the only one my heart should belong to, after having it stomped on in such a dramatic fashion, for the world to see, by a man who I was maybe only still with because I'd been with him so long that I didn't have another frame of reference.

But that was easier said than done, when Ramsey was so... *Ramsey.*

"Who will you be in ten years?" he'd asked me, our last morning in Bali. It was a question that had been playing in my mind since then – and ended up on my list of standard interview questions now. We had a flight to catch, but we'd packed the night before, only leaving out the bare essentials so that we could spend as much time as possible doing what we were doing - being naked in bed. The question hurt me, because... I didn't have an answer. The Darius thing, plus having the show snatched from under me, had me all discombobulated.

Ten years from now, at almost forty, I wasn't even supposed to be Wil Cunningham anymore. I was supposed to be Wil Hayward, have at least a couple of kids, and a second home somewhere sultry and beachy and warm. I would be a well-known name in sports news, as recognizable as any of my male counterparts.

Now, that all seemed... distant.

I didn't want to say that to Ramsey though. Didn't want to look weak, didn't want to have him giving me a pep talk, like it seemed he was always doing for me. But I told him anyway, because that was just

190

the effect he had on me. I was too comfortable with him to not give him a truthful answer.

He didn't pep talk me though. He just listened, and then explained how he felt where I was coming from, with his unexpected return to the NFL. As I laid there, looking in his eyes as he spoke about being grateful for the opportunity to keep the promise to his mother, and his fears about being the same quality player he was before, and hoping to be a real asset to the team, I felt so... *connected.* No, our paths weren't exactly the same, but there was a sense of synergy there that was hard to explain. He wasn't listing out his own problems so mine didn't seem so bad - he was relating to me. Spilling his heart and mind in a way that was beyond refreshing.

He was beyond refreshing.

My thoughts were interrupted by the sound of my doorbell, prompting me to glance at the time. It was past ten at night, and the only person I could think of who might drop by unannounced so late was Ramsey, but it couldn't be him. He'd started training camp with the rookies - he was in the "dorms" with them, under a curfew and subject to bed checks to make sure he was where he was supposed to be. It had to be someone else.

My guess was right - when I peered through my peephole, Chloe McKenna and Cole Richardson were on the other side, both wearing concerned expressions. Knowing both of their connections to Ramsey - his PR and his team liaison - worry had my fingers shaking as I hastily undid the locks and opened the door.

"Wil, how are you?" Cole gushed, as soon I stepped aside for them to come in. "Are you okay? Naima said you aren't answering your phone, and she's getting ready to come over here herself. She's worried sick about you!"

Beside her, Chloe shook her head, all business as she headed right for my kitchen counter to take her laptop from her bag. "Tell Naima to stay put - we don't need any added chaos. Unless Wil wants her here. Do you want her here, Wil? Just say the word, and we'll make it happen."

"I'm sorry - what the hell is going on?" I asked, frowning in confusion. "Why would I need Naima here? What are *you* doing here?" I asked, pointing between the two of them.

"My apologies," Chloe chimed in first, extending a hand to me. "Chloe McKenna, Ramsey's publicist and image manager."

I accepted her hand, but shook my head. "No, I know who you are, I just… I don't understand why you're *here.*"

Chloe and Cole looked at each other, as if they were puzzled, and then Cole's eyes went wide. "Waiiit… you… you don't know yet, do you?"

My frown deepened. "Don't know *what?*" I asked, which prompted them to exchange another glance, and then Cole grabbed me by the hands, pulling me to the couch in my living room. "Okay… you're going to want to sit down."

She was right to have me sit down. Just as she'd guessed, I needed extremely firm grounding to hear that this evening, while I'd been doing my interview prep for Trent Bailey, letting my phone stay on "do not disturb" so I could maintain my focus, once again the internet was running rampant with my name.

Only this time, I wasn't a woman scorned - I was a woman scandalized, with picture evidence of my trip to Bali with Ramsey.

If it were just footage of us walking around, having dinner, on the beach, etc, that wouldn't be so bad. Of course it would feed the long-standing rumors of Ramsey and I having a "thing", but still easy enough to explain away, or talk around.

There was no way to talk around my head thrown back, leg up on his shoulder, mouth open in ecstasy as he screwed me - with the door open - on top of that little table behind the couch in our villa in Bali.

Apparently, two bottles of wine had made me very flexible.

Luckily enough for me, whoever had invaded our privacy hadn't been able to get in close or get a very good angle. Somehow, I'd been granted enough grace that because of the curtains, none of the pictures had any overt nudity beyond a bit of side boob, but it was *very* obvious what we were doing.

Which, what we were doing shouldn't have really been a problem, right? We were two single people - we weren't hurting anybody.

Only, that wasn't the story the media was running with. The story was that this trip was part of a long-term affair, that Ramsey and I had been romantically involved since before my broken engagement, and even before *his* too.

They were saying *I* was the reason he and Lena McBride were no longer together, that *I* had driven Darius into the arms of another woman, by being this heartless, man-stealing, gold-digging whore with an innocent face. Apparently, I only wanted to get serious with Ramsey now because I was jobless, and he had a place on the team. It was all "confirmed" by an "anonymous" source who'd "worked closely with us in the past".

Connie and Sarita's fingerprints couldn't be any more obvious all over this, at least not to me. There was no way I could prove such a thing though, and even if I could, what would the recourse be?

"Ramsey is very, very concerned about making sure you come out on top in this - *that* is why we're here," Chloe explained, after giving me the lay of the land. "Because of Nicole's position with the team, she was able to get to him, and that was the message he wanted relayed, as well as his frustration that he's not able to physically be here for you."

"He's really worried about you," Cole added. "I pushed the rules a little to let him use my phone to call, but… no answer. He wants to know that you're okay."

I scoffed. "I mean… I don't know what I am right now, honestly. This is… I just feel numb. And sick to my stomach. And a little like throwing myself off a cliff. But no, tell him I'm okay. I'm fine. I'm *totally* fine, why wouldn't I be?"

"You don't have to pretend to be fine." Chloe's tone was very matter-of-fact as she typed something out on her cell phone. "In fact, I encourage you not to. I'm very good at my job, Wil, and I assure you that for whomever is behind this "exposure", it will *not* be going as they intended. I want the paparazzi to see you with bloodshot eyes, I want you to look destroyed by this, even if you aren't. I'm tired of the world using a woman's sexual autonomy as a way to vilify her, and if it's alright with you, Wil, I want to pursue legal action. Criminal charges."

I shook my head. "I… I really can't even wrap my head around this right now. Any of it. I don't *want* attention, don't want to be an example. I want this out of people's memories, and off their screens. I don't want to be lied on, or have pictures of me having sex - or, for that matter, being the poor dummy that got cheated on by Sugar & Spice's "sexiest man alive" as what people think of when they hear my name. None of my personal life - I want them to focus on my work."

"Well, I hate to be the bearer of bad news, but you forfeited that when you became a household name. Now that your star is shining brighter - for better or worse - the narrative has to be guided. Just as I've told clients in the past, you're going to have to give the public *something*. It's up to you - well, *us* - what that something is going to be."

"Us?" My eyebrow raised. "You don't work for me, you work for Ramsey."

"And because you two are involved, your image reflects on his. My job is making sure his public perception is positive - being portrayed as a chump does nothing for him. It's in his best interest that this is fixed."

I rolled my eyes. "Oh, poor Ramsey, being portrayed as a "chump", while I get the whore of Babylon treatment. How awful for him."

"This is the way of our world, love," Chloe said, in a clearly sympathetic tone. "I don't make the rules, I just do my very best to make them work for us. I heard you mention several things you wanted here - images scrubbed from the internet, and off of people's minds. To not be slandered. And to have people focusing on your work, and not the scandal. Okay."

"Okay?"

Chloe nodded. "Yes." She'd been scribbling furiously in a notepad as we talked, but now she stopped, using her pen to emphasize things on the page as she read them off, then supplemented each with an explanation. "Pictures gone - not possible. In this age of the internet, those pictures are saved in too many smartphones, posted on too many gossip blogs, etc, to ever be gone. I already have my IT guy working on getting them off the larger sites as a formality, but it's honestly futile. The way we tackle this is by changing the narrative around your relationship with Ramsey, which gives the pictures a different connotation. Right now, it looks like an illicit affair. So, to fight that, we frame you two as friends discovering love, while comforting each other through grief."

"But that's not—"

"Doesn't matter. We paint it this way, and at least half the people keeping the vitriol going switch gears, which drives the story we want to tell. It won't convince everyone, but when people's opinions are divided, the story doesn't last as long - gets it off of people's minds. It works, I promise you."

194

"I can attest to that," Cole chimed in, reminding me that she was even there. "I know you remember how everything blew up around me and Jordan after the Super Bowl. Chloe was the one who came up with that whole *"Love on the Highlight Reel"* thing, that had people calling us "relationship goals". Did I *want* to give the media anything about me and Jordan, about our past? Of course not. But giving that little bit was enough to get the world off of *my* back. Because the woman is always the villain, of course."

"Of course," Chloe agreed. "Listen, Wil, I understand that this is not ideal. But, it's the most favorable result we can aim for right now. And besides that, focusing on the triumph of your newfound love takes away from this idea of you as a victim of your ex, as someone to be pitied. So, it works twofold."

I scoffed. "You keep throwing around this *"love"* word, and I just… it's freaking me out, to be honest. Ramsey and I are nowhere near discussing something like that, and I—"

"Ramsey has actually already given his approval of the language," Chloe told me, smirking. "Had exactly *zero* reservations about it. So perhaps you're closer to discussing it than you think. But, it's here nor there – the public doesn't care. Either you went to Bali together because you were sneaking around, or you went because you're in love and wanted to get away together. Maybe if you were known for having short, public flings, there would be other scenarios, but for *you*… these are the options. Keep in mind that the story we give the media doesn't have to change things between you and Ramsey. There's the spotlight… and there's your *real life.*"

"I get that, I do. It's just…" I pushed out a sigh, and dropped my head into my hands. "This is *so much* to think about, while the whole world is watching what was supposed to be a private moment between me and my friend. All I want is to be respected as a journalist. How does this make me look?!"

"Well-fucked," Cole said, then quickly clamped a hand over her mouth. "Oh God – I did *not* mean to say that out loud. Sorry." Her expression was remorseful, but shifted into a bit of a smirk. "But… seriously though…drama aside… *yasssss, girl!*" she reached to squeeze my hand, looking so genuinely happy for me that I couldn't help a little grin from coming to my face.

"If Nicole is *done*," Chloe spoke in a firm tone, but I could tell she was barely holding a neutral expression herself. "How it makes you look – *if* we get in front of this – is like a woman rediscovering the pleasures in life, after several hard knocks. And as far as wanting people to focus on your work, that's as easy as getting it in front of them. Who is your next interview?"

Cole answered for me. "Trent Bailey. His schedule was so busy that we're squeezing it in this week, before he and the other veterans start training camp."

"Excellent!" Chloe seemed excited about that. "The interview will be a great way to remind people that you are *not,* in fact, jobless, and that you're a badass at what you do. And Trent Bailey is a *huge* name, which helps tremendously."

"I agree," Cole said, nodding. "And right after him, let's get you lined up with Jordan, to keep that momentum going. It shows that the Kings have full confidence in you – which we *do* – and by the time the hype from the interviews dies down, some socialite will have done something, and everyone will have moved on."

"And while all of that is happening, my team *will* find out who took the pictures, and how they got into the hands they got into. This all blew up way too fast to just be some random person posting the pictures. There's money behind this, and I intend to figure it out. From there, you can decide what, if anything, you want to do."

I nodded. "Okay."

"So…?" Chloe asked, eyebrow raised. "Am I moving forward with this, or are you still feeling skittish? The sooner we get started, the better."

I swallowed hard, then nodded again. "Um… do what you need to do, I guess. Whatever you think is best. I just want this all to go away."

She gave me another sympathetic smile. "Soon enough. For now, I want you to focus on getting some rest. You *need* to unplug. Uninstall your social media apps. Do *not* look at the notifications. Do *not* search your name, or Ramsey's name. Go be with your family, and your friends. You're going to get through this, and you're going to be perfectly fine."

I wanted to believe her.

After she and Cole left, I told myself I'd follow her directions. I'd promised her that I would. But as soon as I got to my phone, and saw the comments ranging from ugly, to disgusting, to outright violent, I just felt… sick. That's when the tears started, but I couldn't

196

make myself look away, digging deeper and deeper down the rabbit hole of commentary that *everybody* seemed to have, everyday people and celebrities alike.

What struck me most though were the women – not the ones with nasty opinions, or even the small, but loud contingency that were cheering me on.

It was the ones who claimed to have had Ramsey before me. Women whose names I'd never heard, had never seen, had never caught a mention of on the rare occasion that he'd mentioned a date. Obviously I knew he wasn't sexless, but aside from his dead relationship with Lena, the idea of him with other women never *really* crossed my mind.

Welcome to the other side of dick too bomb.

It wasn't like there were *tons* of them – only a couple who were bold and wanted a little attention, apparently – and they weren't even being disrespectful to me, not exactly. But the last thing I wanted, with everything else, was "**@kellibabiii: I see @RB_TheHammer still has that hip action. That wild look in your eyes is familiar as hell @SwiftWilly congrats girl lol! Used to be me.**" retweeted and in my personal notifications twenty-six thousands times. Or, "**@MillyFromPhilly: damn @RB_TheHammer brings back memories. Call me.**"

Nevermind that he needed to choose more discreet women for his sexual escapades – how recent were these women? Since we'd started sleeping together? Were there more? Was there someone else *now*?

That was the thought that finally drove me to turn off my phone, after a quick call to Naima, and then my parents, to assure them that I was okay. I was too upset, and too embarrassed for the call to my parents to be very long, but the reassurance they gave me in those few moments was enough to calm me.

A little.

A bottle of wine took care of the rest.

This definitely wasn't the smartest thing I'd ever done.

But I wasn't so invested in making a "smart" decision that I didn't know what the *right* decision was, and even though there was about a ninety-five percent chance I'd get my ass handed to me by the team, sneaking out of the dorm facility after bed check was a "right" decision.

If I knew Wil like I thought I did, she was probably going crazy.

My own cell had been confiscated, but between Cole, Chloe, and my childish-ass young teammates, I had a pretty good grasp of what was going on, and it wasn't pretty. Not just because of the rumors and lies, but because I'd seen those pictures, and I *knew* Wil… this wasn't the kind of thing she could sit with and be okay about, not this soon. Neither Cole nor Chloe had come back to me with a report that made me feel any less uneasy about Wil's mental state, so I took matters into my own hands.

I showed up at her door.

I hesitated a bit before I pushed the bell – it was damn near two in the morning, and in a perfect world, she'd be peacefully asleep. I pressed the glowing orange button anyway, because the likelihood of that was low, and she confirmed my suspicion a few moments later, when she opened the door with puffy, swollen eyes.

"Ramsey… what are you doing here? We clown rookies when they get in trouble for not following the rules of training camp. What are you doing out past curfew?"

I frowned at the way she leaned in the doorframe, with a thick, fluffy robe pulled tight around her, obviously not intending to let me in. "I came to check on you, Champ. Chloe said you seemed… out of sorts."

Wil scoffed. "Out of sorts? Hm. That's one way to put it."

"Okay, so, let's talk about it."

"What is there to talk about?"

"How about I come in and tell you?"

She pushed out a sigh like I was asking for a big ass sacrifice, then stepped aside to let me in. As soon as the door was locked behind me, she turned, arms crossed, and stared me down. Everything she was feeling was on her face – the hurt, the shame, and for some reason… anger, seemingly directed at me.

198

"Hey… talk to me," I said, stepping toward her to wrap her in my arms, but she eased back, holding up her hands to keep me away. I frowned. "Yo… what's up with you?"

"What's up with me, is that I have no interest in being embarrassed again. I went through it with Darius, having another woman telling me about what was supposed to be *mine*. I'm not going to do that again."

I narrowed my eyes. "What are you talking about, Wil?"

"I'm talking about Kelli, and Milly, and now Shauna, all on twitter, in my mentions, talking to me about your dick. Kelli and Milly, fine, they spoke about you like it was in the past, but the Shauna chick? You can't tell me she's not recent!"

My frown deepened. "Wil, me being here right now, to see you, is jeopardizing my career, and you want to talk to me about some chicks on twitter?"

"So you're not denying that it was recent?" She propped her hands on her hips. "How recent? Since the show ended? Since you and I got involved? Since you got the call from the Kings?"

"I could've fucked her *yesterday* and it wouldn't matter, because *you* were the one who was all on this "not ready for anything serious", "let's just be friends" shit!"

She jerked her head back, eyes wide, and instantly glossy about something I knew I shouldn't have said. "Well how about *this* – I'm off *all* of this shit, and you can get the fuck out of my home, how about that?" she spat, then turned to stomp down the hall, with me right behind her.

"*Hey*," I said, grabbing her by the hand and pulling her to face me. "That's not how this is about to work. How about we back up and you tell me what the *actual* problem is?"

She snatched away from me. "Apparently, it's that I dared to need a little bit of time before getting serious with someone else after an eight year relationship!"

"Nobody has a problem with that, Wil."

"Then why the hell did it come out of your mouth?!" she snapped, glaring at me.

"Because I'm pointing out that it's not fair for you to pull this jealous shit on me about some casual flings that were months ago, when you aren't even trying to be serious! You don't get to claim ownership if your ass isn't… claiming ownership."

She scoffed. "Oh please, Ramsey. You weren't complaining about whether or not possession was determined yet when you were knee deep in my pussy in Bali, getting all *kinds* of "man" privileges without the title."

"Right, and I wasn't in your goddamn face about who you might or might not be fucking either!"

"Okay, cool, so since *you* "could've fucked her yesterday and it wouldn't matter", I guess I have those same liberties then. *Cool.* Terrence Grant was giving me the eye when I was at the Kings' offices the other day, maybe I'll give him a call."

"*The hell you will*," I growled, surprising both of us, but fuck it. "That's some more shit we *aren't* about to do."

"Oh, because *you* decided?!"

"You're goddamned right because *I* decided. If you think I'm with that sharing shit, you've lost your damn mind. I know you're upset about the pictures and all of that, but what the hell is wrong with you?!"

"If refusing to let you have me out here looking stupid is wrong, then a helluva lot, asshole," she said, through gritted teeth, obviously trying not to let emotion overtake her words. "If you're going to be screwing other people, just fucking *tell me*, so I can opt out of this shit before I... Ramsey, *please*," she half-said, half-sobbed, as she lost her battle with the tears she was trying to hold back. "Chloe McKenna wants to tell people we're in love, that you're supposed to be my Prince Charming, but I *swear* I'd rather people think I'm evil, a homewrecker, whatever, than to push *this* story only for you to make a damned fool of me."

Shit.

I hated seeing her like this, and I instantly felt bad for pushing this particular button with her. It may have seemed over the top to me, but her betrayal was still relatively fresh, and with this scandal happening at the same time – that negatively affected her more than me – her nerves had to be raw.

Over and over – growing up, and even now – I saw the men around me skirt around commitment, not wanting to be "locked down" to one woman. They did shit that fed insecurity, bred an atmosphere of competition, out of what I'd long ago clocked as immaturity. My cousin – my *brother* – Reggie... God knows he'd done some things that made him not the first person I'd look to as an example in plenty of categories. But one thing I'd observed, and absorbed, in the way he treated Chloe – he *never* let another woman believe she might have a chance at Chloe's spot. He *never* made Chloe believe another woman had a chance at her spot.

"Nobody but you, Champ," I said, recalling that lesson as I shook my head. "*Nobody* but you. I wouldn't be friends with somebody I planned to embarrass. Wouldn't fucking… zipline in a foreign country a week after signing an NFL contract for somebody I had any intention of playing like she was stupid. I wouldn't be in your living room, right now, when my ass is supposed to be across town in bed, if making a fool of you was even an option in my mind. *Nobody* but you. I need you to understand that."

I waited for her to respond, and when she didn't, looking down at her bright yellow painted toes instead, I grabbed her hand again. This time, she didn't resist, not even when I pulled her up to my chest, then used my free hand to tilt her chin up, making her look at me.

"*No one except you,*" I told her again, adamantly, wanting to make sure my words got through. Still though, she said nothing, and instead of repeating myself anymore, I tried a different language – I kissed her. And I tried my best to pour enough feeling into it that it would dissolve the insecurity that dealing with the clown had left behind. As soon as she moaned into my mouth, my hands went under her robe, under the hem of her tee to touch her bare skin and pull her closer, against the hardness I didn't even bother trying to help around her.

"Ramsey," she whispered, pulling back just enough to look at me. "You know we can't. You're already out of bounds, and you have practice in the morning, and—"

"Nah." I shook my head, then slid a hand between her thighs, pushing a first, then second finger into her. "I need to prove this point real quick."

She gasped as I pressed a thumb to her clit, working it in circles as I stroked her with my fingers. "Sex won't prove your point, Ramsey," she panted.

"Maybe not," I muttered against her ear, then kissed a trail along her jaw, up to her mouth. "But making you come might get me back on your good side, right?"

That made her laugh, so close that I felt her lips curve up against mine. Pushing my fingers a little deeper turned that laugh into a moan as her knees gave out a little, causing her to lean into me for support.

Relief sank my shoulders as she buried her face into my neck, holding on to my arms. "Stop, so I can talk," she whispered to me, and I did, waiting for her to speak. When she looked up at me, there were tears in her eyes. "You're not on my bad side, Ramsey. I'm... *scared*. The story Chloe wants to tell... it's too close to the truth."

"Then maybe it's not a story. Maybe it *is*... the truth."

She shook her head. "Ramsey, don't play with me."

"Wil, you *know* I don't play that type of game. Not ever. Especially not with you. If you need to explicitly hear me say I want you to myself, here it is - *I want you to myself.* Maybe it's a bad idea, maybe neither of us is ready, but shit... we're here now. And I don't think either of us is confused about what's happening. I mean, I'm not. Are you?"

"No."

I shrugged. "Well then... you stop freaking out about whatever was said on twitter, which Chloe probably told you already anyway... and we let her take care of this. And, by the way, since we ended up taking a sharp left – I'm sorry this shit is happening. I don't like you talking down on yourself, so having all this going on... I'm *hot* about it. For *your* sake. I don't give a shit what they're saying about me."

"I know you don't," she whispered, bringing her hands up to my face. "I know."

I took the softness of her voice as my cue to pick up where I'd left off earlier. She was still wet, still so warm, still so... welcoming. She gasped, then buried her face in my neck again as I stroked her into that orgasm, then picked her up, carrying her down the hall to her room.

I'd just have to drink a red bull or something before practice.

I took a deep breath before I rang the doorbell. The Baileys were expecting me, but... still. After the way this week had started, I was on edge, and wasn't really sure what to expect.

I put that aside though, choosing to ring the bell anyway – as if I had a real choice. If Chloe's plan was going to work, I *needed* to do this interview. And more importantly, if I had any interest in preserving whatever credibility I had left… it had to happen.

I offered a polite smile when the door swung open, trying not to appear surprised that Jade herself – Trent's wife – had been the one to answer the door. Immediately, my brain went wild – *what if she thinks I'm here to pull some sort of crap with Trent? I'm already working on negative points if I have the woman of the house on the defensive with my personal shit* – but Jade returned my smile, and welcomed me inside.

She and Trent had a beautiful home, which wasn't surprising at all, if I judged from *her* appearance. Jade wasn't just attractive – she was *polished* – even in simple, designer lounge attire that accented the perfect roundness of her pregnant belly. The sight set off a pang of something that wasn't exactly jealousy, but… it wasn't *not* jealousy either. From my outside perspective, Jade had a lot of things to be envious of, but that baby bump – something I'd spent years wanting – made my throat hurt a little.

She placed a protective hand over her belly and I tore my gaze away, plastering a smile on my face and hoping I didn't look insane. I quickly realized it was just a subconscious thing for her – as quickly as she'd placed it there, she moved it away as she led me down the hall, making small talk as we approached the gorgeously decorated living room, where we would be doing the interview.

I wasn't surprised at all to see Cole there – she'd already told me she would be – and I was glad to see her and Trent laughing like old friends. I hoped that her presence – and her vouching for me – would put the him at ease, if there was any discomfort in his mind about this whole thing. There was *no* way he – or anyone else in the sports world, for that matter, hadn't heard.

Before he left the other night, to sneak back into the training facility, Ramsey had done his best to try to convince me Trent would be cool. After all, Trent had faced scandals of his own, in the not-so-distant past, so he knew how that privacy violation felt.

I understood that, I really did. And when Trent greeted me, he seemed perfectly cool, just as Ramsey said.

But still.

Because of the feeling I wanted for this interview, I didn't bring along a camera person, or any crew. It was just me, setting up a couple of cameras and mics. Creative editing would pull it all together later. All I needed was the words.

So I didn't waste time.

I got right to it, with Jade and Cole hovering close by as I asked Trent ice-breaking questions about his love of dancing, listening while he told me about his dearly departed Uncle Shank and his battle with AIDS, which led into a – rather lovely – few moments spent speaking in very high regard of his uncle's wife, his Aunt April. I had to bite the inside of my lip to keep myself from squirming with excitement – this was something I'd never heard him talk about in depth in any interviews, which made it journalistic gold. He wasn't answering a question anymore – he was just *talking* to me, with no regard for the cameras, which was the goal. Still, I made a note that for this segment, at least, I needed to let him review this to make sure he was comfortable with all of this being viewed publicly.

Because we were on the subject of family – something that, again, Trent didn't talk about very much, at least in any interview I'd read or seen – I went to my mental checklist of questions and asked about his parents, and their influence on the man he was today.

The whole mood in the room changed.

Trent shifted in his place on the couch, lifting a hand to rub the back of his neck, in clear discomfort.

Shit.

I'd tried to research, but had hit a dead end in publicly available information out there about his parents. I didn't realize asking about them would be stepping into a minefield.

"Next question," Jade called sharply, from the doorway. Trent and I turned to her at the same time, to find her with folded arms. He got sympathetic eyes – I got a look of warning, which I was experienced enough to heed. If I got on *her* bad side, I knew this whole thing would go down the tubes quickly, which was the opposite of what I needed.

"Of course," I said, nodding. "We can move on. Let's shift focus. When you came to the Kings, you were something of a breakout star. Talented, handsome, charismatic – you had that magic combination that creates the "It factor" a player needs to dominate professional sports, and you were well on your way to becoming one of our biggest stars… and you jeopardized that. Ended up in prison. What lessons do you feel you learned from that experience? Would you give up that knowledge in exchange for your time back?"

"Okay, you know what?" Jade interjected as she stalked into the living room, before Trent could answer. "I wasn't going to say anything about this interview, because at the wedding you seemed cool, but I see now it was just an act. You've had it out for Trent – don't think we didn't see your comments about him on that little show you got kicked off of, and now you come into our home asking questions that he's already answered for people like you, over and over, already. Who the hell are you to question him about his past?"

"Jade," Cole said, putting a comforting hand on Jade's shoulder, at the same time Trent did too. "Wil doesn't mean any harm."

"I really don't," I added, hoping I wasn't making things worse as I wracked my brain for what I'd said in the past that had caused offense. She turned to me wearing a bit of a scowl, and something about that jogged my memory. "To answer your question – who the hell am I to question him? – I'm a *fan*. A huge Trent Bailey fan, from the first day I saw him on my father's big screen TV and said "*Damn, he's fine, who is that*?!" and my daddy almost blew a gasket about me cursing in front of him."

I kept my tone light, hoping she wouldn't take my comment about Trent's attractiveness the wrong way, and to my relief, she smirked, so I continued.

"Jade, I care about every interview I do, and every player I talk to. It's always my goal to be fair, and nuanced, to give the viewer, or listener, a look into the heart of a real person, not just a replica of the same questions and answers they've done over and over. But sometimes that does mean putting the elephant in the room out there, and not skating around it. I promise you, if we can continue, we'll have an end product that gives a real glimpse into the man you love. Yes, his flaws, but his triumphs as well. And, being transparent about the flaws only makes the triumphs shine that much brighter."

The scowl on Jade's face relaxed a bit, but then she hardened again. "And why exactly should we trust you, other than Cole's word, after you went in on him on national TV?"

"Because that should let you know just how passionate I am. Again – I'm a Trent Bailey fan." I directed myself to him when I added, "And that's why I was so disappointed when you went to prison. I'm not going to try to make it sound sweet now – yes, I went in, just like I would *still* on any young player who made the same sort of mistake. Because I want to see *us* thriving, and a professional football career isn't a chance that many get, so to see it thrown away… I was *mad*. But I was also proud as hell when you came back, and turned it around, and I know you saw *that* too. I sat and filmed a New York local show in rival Connecticut Kings gear for half the season, between you and Jordan Johnson, because I was rooting for you."

"Oooh," Cole inserted. "I remember that. You had folks on twitter hot for days that first time you wore a Bailey jersey on the air."

"And I wore my Kings gear *anyway*," I laughed.

"Well, listen," Trent spoke up, stepping forward. "I'm convinced, and I'm ready to answer whatever you got for me. And Jade is cool too… right?" he asked his wife, wrapping his huge frame around her petite one to say something in her ear.

Whatever he said, she wasn't very pleased by, but she relaxed enough to let me know the interview was going forward. Internally, I breathed a sigh of relief, but that still wasn't quite the vibe I wanted to have for the duration.

"Jade… would you be interested in being part of the interview?" I asked, as new inspiration struck me. I was already formulating new questions in my head as Trent basically answered for her, by pulling her down onto the couch beside him.

I took my own seat, and smiled at the two of them, knowing – if my intuition was correct – exactly where to start to get us going in a positive direction.

"So, Jade – your wedding was absolutely beautiful, and you were a stunning bride. Tell me what it's like to be newlyweds."

She and Trent exchanged a look, and then smiled, like they knew a secret we didn't – exactly how a newly married couple should look, in my mind – and then Jade sat forward and began to speak.

Two hours later – about an hour after Jade left us to move on to something else – I walked out of the Bailey residence with footage from what I thought could very well be one of the best segments I'd ever done. We'd managed to strike a balance where Trent – and sometimes Jade – were very open, without giving more of them than anyone needed. I couldn't wait to get home and re-watch the footage, but as soon as I got into my car after tossing my equipment bag on the passenger seat, I dug out my phone to call Ramsey.

And then immediately got sad, because… I *couldn't* call Ramsey.

He'd managed to avoid any repercussions for sneaking out, but now that they were really into the swing of training camp, he couldn't have any distractions. If there was an emergency, of course there was a way I could reach him. As excited as I was though, this was *not* an emergency.

I'd just have to tell him later.

Just thinking about him made my heart race now. Not that it was much different than I'd felt in Bali, but once again something had shifted. We hadn't really said the words, but we were basically together now.

As he'd said, ready or not… here we were.

Eleven

"They overplayed their hand."

"Sure as hell did. The very definition of doing too much."

"I mean, some of us already saw right through their attempts to slander this woman, but for those who didn't – this should make it perfectly clear."

"I mean, it's trash, is what it is. Everyone knew that Wil and Ramsey's departure from their show on WAWG was too abrupt to not be messy, but neither of them has spoken negatively – not publicly at least – about the network or their executives. Clearly, they aren't being granted the same courtesy by the Petty Betties in charge over there, because why is that station constantly playing gossip about those folks like they're goddamned Spillin' That Hot Tea?"

"If you ask me, it's the same thing that a ton of folks do. Something goes down, and in an effort to get people on their side, they badmouth the other person first – that way, the rebuttal just seems like their point being proven. You can't approach it, because the other person has made it seem like you're going to lie, or you're being messy, etc etc. You can't clear your name because even that has already been painted to look like a problem."

"And too often, that bullshit works, but not this time honey, **hey!***"*

*"That's right baby, Arnez and Arizona are **not** here for the play-play. WAWG – specifically Sarita Price and Connie Blaylock, you're clearly pressed because those white folks pulled out of the deal to buy your little network when your flop ass viewership dropped last month."*

*"But implying that the amazing interview Wil released was somehow proof that she's doing Trent Bailey **and** his wife? Please! We hope y'all stretched before you made that reach!"*

*"Hello! There wasn't a lick of sexual chemistry in that interview video except between Trent and Jade Bailey, and **that** was hot enough to heat up the screen. I mean, come on – as messed up as it was that their privacy was invaded, we **all** saw those pictures of Ramsey Bishop giving Wil the business on that lil' table. She's getting all the dick she can handle. I'm sure."*

*"**Bitch. Listen.** Round of applause for ol' Wilhelmina, okay? Cause that Ramsey is a fine muhfucka – can you blame her for backing that ass up?"*

"Not around here we don't! After the way her ex dogged her for that lil funny looking white girl, Wil deserves. If you're listening – girl, you betta work! Get your life!"

"Yaaaas honey! Based on my extensive research on the topic, Ramsey Bishop is the dick you deserve girl, congratulations!"

"Extensive research? Really Arizona?!"

*"Oh yes, really! I have credible sources and all. I'll give you **that** tea later."*

*"Looking forward to it bitch. But anyway – back to trash ass WAWG – you tried it. When even the two supposedly scorned exes gave statements that an affair between Wil and Ramsey were **not** the cause of their breakup, you **know** you tried it!"*

"Tried the absolute fuck out of it. And for what reason?"

"Pettiness. You know everybody thinks that shit is cute these days."

"Until somebody delivers hands via NextDayAir."

"Never fails."

"Mmmmhmmm. But in any case, just to recap – nobody believes that shit, and I hope Wamsey sues the redbottoms off your feet for lying."

*"Wamsey? Ew, **no**. Wilsey. Wamsey sounds…"*

"Cute as fuck, hater."

"I was going to say childish."

"Ya mama."

I chuckled as Arnez and Arizona continued their signature banter. Their show was blaring from the speaker on my cell phone, which was still in the bathroom, where I'd placed it on the counter to listen while I showered. I was listening because I always listened, because I always – as they said – "got my life". They were funny, and smart, and pretty socially conscious, so I enjoyed listening to their takes on whatever random topic they brought up on the show.

I certainly hadn't expected to hear my name, but it was a pleasant surprise to hear the show of support. After another week of fresh slander, I needed it.

Chloe had brushed the new allegations off as nothing. She'd said "whoever" was behind it was overdoing it with the accusations about me and the Baileys, and she was right – nobody believed it. That, however, didn't make it any less frustrating, especially since I hadn't done anything to warrant what they were attempting to do.

I was *pissed.*

But, still. So far, Chloe's plan had worked. Instead of being tagged in ugly posts about being a gold-digging homewrecker, people were now scraping up every picture of Ramsey and I they could find, tagging us as #relationshipgoals, #friendshipgoals, and a slew of incredibly corny quotes about your best friend becoming the love of your life. In fact, most of the "negative" things I was still seeing were of a similar vein, except the captions under the pictures said stuff like, *"this is why you never trust your man's "play sister""*, *"this is why my nigga can't have "friends" that look like this"*, etc. And I mean...I felt that.

Ramsey and I were innocent friends, until we weren't.

In any case, the last two weeks had been leaps and bounds better than that first day, especially since releasing my interview with Trent and Jade. Finding out that they were happy with the end result – and thought the affair rumors were ridiculous – gave me a burst of good energy I desperately needed.

Getting to Naima's to hang out with her and Ashley was going to give me another one.

I hoped I wasn't getting on their nerves though. Even once Ramsey and I started getting hot and heavy, I made sure it didn't interfere with me kicking it with my favorite cousin –slash-best friend just as much as I always did. I'd never been the girl to drop her friends for a man, and didn't want to start now. But, with Ramsey being basically on lock-down at rookie camp, I feared I was doing the opposite. Between Naima, my parents, and phone calls with Soriyah down in the Bahamas, I was always up under somebody if I wasn't working, to keep me distracted from the swirling news stories.

Where I was usually splitting time five ways – with myself, with Ramsey, with Naima, Soriyah, or my parents – now it was just three, and somebody was bound to get tired of my ass sooner than later.

Hopefully, that day wasn't going to be today.

I'd just walked into my closet to pick out something to wear when Arnez and Arizona gave their outro, and then my phone went silent.

Can't have that.

I tossed the two dresses I was deciding between on my bed, then went to the bathroom to grab my phone and start some music. No sooner than I'd pressed play did my doorbell ring, and I groaned. *Of course* somebody was coming by before I had any clothes on.

I grabbed my robe from the hook in the bathroom and tied it tightly around me as I headed to the door. Whoever it was practically laying on the bell, which agitated me, and I was ready to curse out whoever was on the other side until I peeked through the peephole.

"Ramsey, what are you doing here?" I asked as I pulled the door open, feeling a slight sense of déjà vu from when he'd shown up in the middle of the night a few weeks ago. This time though, I hadn't been stewing with ridiculous anger over him having a sex life before me, and I was excited as hell to see him.

"Two day break before pro camp," he said, sweeping me up into his arms as soon as the door was closed. "I hope you don't have plans today."

I quickly got an answer for why he said that – less than a minute after I answered the door, we were naked in my bedroom, and he was ripping open a condom with his teeth.

And then a second condom.

And then a third.

By the time he *finally* went limp, it was hours past when I was supposed to be at Naima's, and my phone had chimed with a text in

212

her specialized tone, but no phone call – a clear sign that I was, indeed, getting on her damn nerves.

From my place beside him on the bed, I looked over at Ramsey in the daylight shining through the window, smiling at his closed eyes and the slow rise and fall of his chest. Even if he was getting plenty of sleep, I knew he had to be physically exhausted. The workouts he usually did were tough, sure, but they were nothing compared to the conditioning he needed to be in shape for the NFL. As he slept, I examined his nude body, noting the changes that were already apparent in just two weeks. Layers of fat cut and replaced by thicker muscle, wider biceps, more defined abs.

I was still admiring when my phone *did* ring, and I scrambled out of bed to grab it and shut it off before it woke him up. Snatching it up from the bathroom counter, I silenced it first, then took notice of the name and number on the screen. I took a deep breath, and then let it keep ringing as I grabbed a tee shirt and yoga pants to put on. I snuck past Ramsey as he rolled over onto his stomach, muffling the soft snores that had been filling the room.

Out on my back patio, I pulled my phone out to return the call I'd missed.

"Wil! I'm *so* glad you called me right back," my realtor gushed, from the other end of the line. "We got an offer on the house – adorable couple with kids and a dog, need a place as soon as possible, since one of them is starting a new job."

I forced cheerfulness into my voice – not that I was sad about the house, I just would rather not deal with it at all – to respond, "Oh, great. How much?" She told me a number that was just under asking price. So close, in fact, that I responded, "I accept," before I recalled that it wasn't solely up to me.

"I already know you want to ask, what did Mr. Hayward say," she started, in a knowing tone. "Well, since he was the one unsatisfied with the last two offers, I went to him first this time. He accepted as well. So… congratulations Ms. Cunningham, you just sold your house."

I expected to feel much more comforted than I actually did. I was glad to have it over with of course – it was the last thing connecting me to Darius. But more than relief, what coursed through me was… sorrow. I never expected an adventure we took on together, in love, to end up like this. As much as selling the house empowered me to move on, it reminded me that I – *we* – had failed.

It wasn't a good feeling, at all.

I arranged a time to come in to sign my paperwork, and then leaned against the deck railing as I stared across the yard, at nothing. I don't know how long I stayed out there, but when I felt Ramsey's arms come around me from behind, it was a welcome shift in energy.

"What's wrong?" he asked. He hadn't even seen my face, but he knew.

I laid my hands over his, urging him to hold me tighter. "The house sold. I have to go sign the paperwork tomorrow."

"You need me to come with you?"

"No. I've got it."

"You sure?"

"Yeah."

When he turned me to face him, I didn't even bother trying to shutter the emotion in my eyes, because I knew I didn't have to. It had occurred to me, in Bali, that this was a testament to the man Ramsey was – giving me room to finish mourning, letting me work through my heartbreak at my own pace, without being an asshole about it.

"You want to talk about it?" he asked, and I shook my head.

"Not particularly."

"Okay. Can I say something though?"

My eyebrow lifted. "About the house sale I just said I didn't want to talk about?"

"Nope."

"Okay, then what?"

A grin spread over his face as his hands slid down my waist, to my butt. "Your ass looks good as hell in these pants. I need you to take them off."

"Oh my *God*," I giggled, squirming in his arms as he pulled me into his chest. "It's only been a few weeks, and you're acting *so* sex-starved."

He chuckled into my neck as he grabbed the waistband of my pants, trying to tug them down. "Your fault. If it wasn't so good, I'd be able to stay out of you."

"You make it sound like a struggle," I teased, ducking out of his arms and back into the house before he could successfully get my pants down outside. That didn't deter him though – he easily corralled

214

me back to the bedroom, making quick work of removing my clothes and putting on a condom before he plunged into me again.

"It *is* a struggle," he grunted against my lips, as I hooked both legs around his waist. "I don't think you understand how damn good you feel."

With my eyelids squeezed shut, I shook my head. "No. I don't think *you* do."

His movements stilled. "Open your eyes."

When I did, he was looking – *staring* – at me in a way he often did, as if everything good in the world had originated from me. And then just as quickly, it shifted to pure lust as he lowered his mouth to my neck, then my breasts. The feeling of his teeth, then tongue, on my nipples made me squeeze my eyes shut again as a gasp of pleasure fell from my lips.

"Hey!" he said, with more bass than I was expecting. "I told you to open your eyes."

Oh.

So I opened them, and he met my gaze again as he pushed into me, deeper than before, scrutinizing my reaction as he filled me up, then murmured "*Good girl*" to me. My mouth opened, but I didn't – couldn't – make a sound other than a high-pitched whine as he burrowed further. When he pulled back, then dove in again, my eyelids fluttered, but I stayed the course, earning myself a smirk before he shook his head, drawing his bottom lip between his teeth as he watched me.

"See?" he asked, making me whimper as he started with a steady rhythm to his stroke. "The faces, the sounds you make… this is why I always want to be inside of you." He finished that statement with his mouth right against my ear, in a tone that sent a shiver up my spine. He put a hand between my legs, coating his fingers in my arousal before he moved them back to my clit, rubbing me there in circles that felt so good it was impossible to keep my eyes open.

"*Ramsey*," I managed to sound out, in a breathless whimper that made him groan.

"Yeah, Champ?"

He stopped moving to give me his attention, and I lifted my hands to cup his face. "You can't keep saying these kinds of things… doing me like this… unless you're prepared for me to never leave you alone. Waiting in your bushes and shit."

"I don't have any bushes, baby," he grinned.

I lifted my shoulders. "Then… in your shower. In your cabinets."

"Silly ass," he chuckled, then dropped his lips down to mine. "Glad to hear you're satisfied with my performance."

I smiled back at him. "Very… I'm confident that you have a long future ahead of you here."

RAMSEY

"Welcome back to the land of the free."

I was happy as hell to be able to toast to that with Reggie and Clay, raising my glass of bourbon to bump theirs before taking a sip. This was actually Reggie's third full day as a free man, but I'd been in training camp the day he was released, and then as far into Wil as I could get on the second day, which was part of my break. So today, even though it was Thursday, and random as hell, we celebrated.

Besides, he'd been occupied with his more immediate family – His mother, and Chloe and the kids – those first two days anyway.

Tomorrow morning, I'd be reporting to pro camp with the rest of the team, for more conditioning and practice to get us ready to start on a good note, by dominating in the preseason games. Tonight though, I was having a *real* drink with Reggie – something I'd never had the opportunity to do, since he got locked up when I was still underage.

I considered it Clay's fault that it was happening in a goddamned piano bar though, of all places. All because his latest client was Logan Lewis – the special guest on the keys tonight – and Clayton had made what I knew was a half-hearted vow to come to the next show he did in Connecticut. He probably wasn't really expecting it to happen soon, since Logan was gearing up for a tour with a neo-soul artist named Dani. But a promise was a promise, so here we were at Onyx, which wasn't half bad – especially to Clayton.

We were among a limited amount of men who weren't there with a woman, which apparently made us hot commodities. Clayton was reveling in it, but my heart and Reggie's were both elsewhere, so we were chilling. The place had a good vibe, good food, good music, which made it enough for me to have a good time without risking what I already had.

"So how does it feel, man?" Clay asked Reggie, when he finally wrapped up his flirting session with our pencil-skirted server. "The world is a lot different than it was twelve years ago, huh?" This was their first time meeting, but they'd heard enough about each other through me that they easily fell into a friendly energy.

Reggie shook his head. "That's a damn understatement. All this... smartphone shit, social media. My daughter has been talking my ear off about "Twitter", taking "usies" with me, using some crazy stuff that it made it look like I had goddamn flowers on my head. I missed *two* terms of a Black president, only to come out to a fucking orange one."

Clayton and I laughed.

"Alexis texted me," I told him, referring to he and Chloe's sixteen-year-old daughter. "Said the first thing you wanted to do when Aunt P drove them up there to pick you up was stop and get a grinder."

"Fucked my stomach up too," he chuckled. "It was good as a motherfucker though. I had my sandwich, chopped it up with them, then took mama's car down to the barbershop, got my shit cleaned up *right*. I had to, man."

"I see you bruh," I said, playfully swiping at his fresh haircut. "You're looking good, man," I told him, honestly. Gone was the harrowed look in his eyes from the last time I'd drove out to Danbury to visit him – which was better than when he was at Allenwood. Already, his light was coming back, and I was glad to see it. "Don't tell me you got locked up and turned into a pretty boy on me, gotta get a fresh cut soon as you get out."

He sucked his teeth. "Nigga, you're sitting there in a floral shirt and matching socks, calling somebody pretty," he called. "But nah... I had to be right before I saw Chloe."

I nodded. "I feel you... how did that go?"

Before he answered, he took a long swig from his drink, then shrugged. "As well as I could expect."

"She still pissed?"

He let out a dry laugh. "Unfortunately. Who would've thought the woman would hold a twelve year grudge?"

"I would," I chuckled. "We're talking Chloe here. She held you down though. Made sure the kids were good, kept them around Aunt P, made sure you had what you needed in there."

Reggie shook his head. "Not denying any of that, Ram. And not complaining, either. She gave me better than I deserved, all this time – and a warmer welcome than I anticipated, after not showing her face the whole damn time I was in there."

Clay let out a low whistle. "Damn, man. The whole time?"

"Whole time. Again though… not complaining. My dues are paid now, and I'm looking ahead."

"Smart man," Clayton said, and I nodded.

"I'll drink to that."

We actually drank to it several times, before I had to leave Reggie and Clay talking so I could swing by the men's room. On the way out of the little foyer that led to the restrooms, even though I was looking ahead of me, I somehow still ended up colliding with someone – a petite, pleasant-smelling, female someone – and I instinctively reached out, putting my hands on her forearms to steady her.

"Excuse me," I apologized, and stepped back, already heading back to my table. "I didn't see you."

"Of course you didn't," she spoke back, in a too-familiar voice that made me actually look at her. "The whole "fake bump" thing was by design, Ramsey. Checking your gentleman reflexes, and I see you still have them."

I scoffed, crossing my arms over my chest as I surveyed Lena in person, for the first time in months. As always, she was impeccably dressed, in a fitted red floral dress that hung off her shoulders, the rich color making her dark skin pop. I'd be lying if I said she didn't look good – she looked good as *hell*. But the memory of our last in-person conversation – Valentine's Day, to be exact, when she'd shown up at my door in a Cupid costume – still left a bitter taste in my mouth. I hadn't been moved then, and I wasn't moved now.

But that didn't stop a mischievous grin from spreading over Lena's face as she stepped closer to me, stopping just on the right side of *too* close. "*You* have been a very busy man, and a *very* naughty boy, Mr. Bishop. Congratulations on the new gig."

"Thank you, Ms. McBride."

She pressed her teeth into her perfectly-bright-red painted bottom lip. "You're very welcome. I, uhh... saw those pictures from your vacation. Wil Cunningham, huh? I never would've thought."

I lifted an eyebrow, knowing I shouldn't feed this beast, but curiosity got the best of me. "Why is that?"

Lena shrugged. "I don't know, I just imagined that, if you weren't with *me*... you'd get with someone with a little more edge. And that's no shade to Wil, honestly, she just seems, very *wholesome*. But you *do* have a way of bringing things out of people, don't you Ramsey?" When I didn't respond, her smile widened. "Oh come on. You don't have to play shy with me, Ram. We've known each other since we were twenty-year-olds. I *know* you like to get *juuust* a little rough, all sexy and demanding. And she probably eats that shit up, doesn't she?" Lena stopped, and giggled. "I know you're too much of a gentleman to answer that, but still... good for her. She's a beautiful girl, and she seems sweet."

"What are you getting at, Lena?" I asked, narrowing my eyes.

She laughed. "Nothing, Ramsey. But I should probably be *getting* back to my date."

Lena started to walk off, but I grabbed her wrist, hauling her back into the relative privacy of the foyer. "Nah, I *know* you, and I know how you operate. So let me make something clear – Wil is *not* your competition. There *is no* competition, because me and you... we're done. Completely."

"Duh," she snapped, rolling her eyes as she pulled away. "You know I don't handle rejection well, Ramsey. I heard you loud and clear when you put me out of your place on Valentine's Day. In top notch lingerie, might I add."

"Then *what* is your agenda right now?"

"*None*. Seriously. I saw you, made an excuse to say hello, and now I've done that. I *know* you don't think I'm pining over you? Not going to lie – I still think we would've been great, but Lena McBride doesn't *pine* – she gets engaged to last year's NBA MVP just before news of his one-hundred-fifty-million *guaranteed* contract goes public," she said, holding up her hand to show me the damn-near obscene diamond on her finger.

My face screwed up, immediately. "Marcus Ingraham? How the hell did you...?"

"Great timing, impeccable planning, and these," she said, groping her breasts. "I did my research – Marcus likes titties, I have titties. Marcus likes money, *I have money.* Marcus likes fame, I have fame. And after next year, Dr. Lena Ingraham-McBride – I like that order better than the other way around – will be a household name."

Yeah.

There it was.

She'd already done all she could on her own to reach whatever it was she was looking for. The woman was a doctor – actually a good one, who would probably be a great one, with experience. She came from a whole family of them, with enough money to make their reality show happen and all of that. What she never could seem to get was the celebrity factor she wanted, which was where I had come in – she'd been planning the shit out for a while. And apparently, since I wasn't down with that, Marcus was her ticket to get there.

And really, he was a bigger name than me anyway.

"Don't look so disappointed Ramsey," she laughed a little. "Marcus is a really good guy, and I actually like him. *Almost* as much as I liked you."

I shook my head. "And that's enough for you? *Liking him?*"

"Hell yes," she exclaimed, looking at me like I'd lost it. "I'm certainly not looking to fall in love. Ramsey, come on," she stepped closer, lowering her voice. "I've watched my mother cry too many tears over my whore of a father to trust any of you with something like my heart. Since I was a teenager, my plan has been to find somebody I can tolerate enough to build this social capital with, while I do my own thing, and he does his. Love doesn't get my juices flowing, Ramsey... but status and money... they give me butterflies. And I am *happy.*"

Honestly... I believed her. Now that I was on the outside looking in – and had grown up some myself – I could see that in her, where I couldn't before. But still...

"It would have been nice to know that *before* we got involved."

She sucked in a deep breath, and actually had the decency to look remorseful. "You're right. And I'm sorry. Seriously."

I chuckled. "Yeah, I know. You wouldn't have said it if you didn't mean it."

"Damn right. I guess you *do* know me pretty well, huh?"

"Damn right. But… I have to admit being surprised as hell that you – low key – defended Wil, by telling the press she wasn't involved in us breaking up."

Lena propped her hands on her hips. "Wow, Ramsey, what kind of bitch do you think I am? I mean, I *am* one, admittedly, but I'm a fair one. I know the two of you were just friends when we were together. And besides –I couldn't have the world thinking another woman took my man from me. The fact that it helped Wil was just… gravy."

"Uh-uh," I said, wagging a finger. "I mean… maybe that's part of it, but something about that doesn't quite fit. It's more than that. Spill it."

She sucked her teeth. "Ugh. Fine. *Maybe* I really like her for you. There was a picture of the two of you randomly out in New York, and the way you looked at her… it was almost the way you used to look at me. Only… amplified. And she looks at you the same way. The way you probably *wanted* me to look at you. And I mean… you deserve somebody that looks at you like that, and vice versa, and I really hate you right now, for making me admit this corny, *sappy* shit, that I don't even believe in. Bye. See you around."

Lena turned and sashayed off, stopping a few feet away to turn and blow a kiss in my direction. I shook my head, then headed back to the table to find Reggie and Clayton rolling about something as the server delivered a fresh round of drinks.

"The fuck y'all laughing about so hard?" I asked, as I dropped into my seat.

"The fuck you *been*?" Reggie asked. "Dropping the kids off at the pool in this nice ass establishment?"

I laughed. "Hell nah. I… ran into Lena."

Both guys instantly went quiet as hell, and exchanged a look, which kinda pissed me off, because they didn't even know each other like that to be exchanging *looks* and shit.

"What?" I asked, breaking the silence before I reached for one of the freshly delivered drinks, to take a swig.

Reggie shrugged. "Nothing… just… shorty had your head a little messed up, so I'm wondering if you're good."

I stopped with my glass halfway up to my mouth to consider the question, and… "Actually… yeah. I am."

Even though unwanted feelings had lingered, I'd been officially, no take-backs, no flags on the play, *done* with Lena since Valentine's Day. Before that, even though we were broken up, I'd toyed with the idea of us getting back together. Maybe I was just seeking a companion for comfort because of what I was watching my mother go through. After she passed, maybe I was seeking a distraction from my grief. But whatever it was that had me going against all my common sense, intuition, and mother's advice, to consider getting back with Lena disappeared when, three months after I buried my mother, she showed up half naked on my doorstep for sex and wedding plans.

I'd cancelled our engagement while my mother was in the worst part of her battle with cancer, because Lena's selfish ass was trying to put cake samples in my face and asking me to choose between 38 different shades of white for tablescapes. She thought I was just too preoccupied with my mother to focus on the wedding, but in reality, I was disgusted by her selfishness, and wanted nothing to do with her. She – wrongly, and way too soon – thought that after my mother passed, we'd be right back on.

Talk about tunnel vision.

Over these last few weeks though, ever since Bali, even though I'd spent a little time messed up about realizing how big a mistake I'd almost made… Lena was the furthest thing from my mind.

"Yeah man… ol' Ramsey here is on something new. Wil's fine ass," Clay said, tempering his normally inappropriate remarks about her, now that she and I were involved.

Reggie gave a deep nod. "That's right! The whole yard was hyped up about that shit – Wil is…" he whistled. "That's quite a woman."

"Wait until you see her *friend*," Clay insisted, whipping out his phone. I chuckled as he pulled up pictures of Soriyah, happy to let the conversation go there instead of staying on me, especially when my own phone buzzed in my pocket. They were too distracted to clown me about the grin that overtook my mouth when I saw that is was a message from Wil.

"I know you're out with your boys, and I hate to be "that girl", but… you're gonna come see me before you report to pro camp, right? – The Champ"

"If that's what you want, you know I'll make it happen."

222

I shook my head at myself as soon as I sent that text – it hadn't taken nearly enough time for Wil to have me so completely wrapped around her finger that I'd bend over backwards to make her happy.

But I wasn't interested in changing a damn thing.

Twelve

Wil

August 2017

I need to go on a damn diet.

It wasn't even negative self-talk this time – it was just the damn truth. I tried – and failed – one more time to button my favorite pair of jeans, but it wasn't happening unless I wanted to walk into the Connecticut Kings box looking like a can of Pillsbury.

I did not.

Nor was I interested in potentially fainting because all my organs were compressed in weird ways, in my pursuit of squeezing into a damn pair of jeans. I dropped onto the end of my bed and laid back, spreading my arms out in defeat.

The last month and a half had finally caught up to me.

Ever since Ramsey reported to training camp – and I ended up in the middle of a sex-scandal – I'd been eating every feeling I had, when I actually had an appetite. My accidental intermittent fasting had probably ruined my metabolism, and the fact that I hadn't set foot in a gym or on a track definitely hadn't helped either. I was paying for it.

Luckily for me, it was summer, and I had a closet full of cute dresses.

Ramsey *loved* me in dresses.

And with the way pre-season had been going so far, I didn't feel a shred of hesitation about dressing solely to please him. If nothing else, his woman could look good, and if this game went like the rest… the sight of me might be a needed win.

It wasn't that Ramsey had played *badly*, not at all. He just hadn't been… great. Those were words that would never come out of my mouth, if I could help it, but there were plenty of people saying it for me. One of the harsher critics had referred to his performance as "disappointingly average".

I desperately wished I didn't agree.

But I knew what it was – nerves, plain and simple. Ramsey got out there on the field, in front of a roaring crowd, for the first time in years, and did *exactly* what he was supposed to do. Nothing more. Nothing less. For a rookie, that probably would have been fine. But he was goddamned *Ramsey Bishop*.

We all wanted to see magic happen. But making that magic required risks, and for some reason, Ramsey's head just wasn't there yet.

I wished I knew what it would take to get him there.

Instead of dwelling on it though, I just sent up a prayer that today would be the day those jitters cleared, and he was able to play at the level we all knew he could. Shifting my head to see the clock, my eyes widened when I saw the time. I needed to be moving.

As soon as I sprang up to my feet, intending to push the too-small jeans down my hips, my head started spinning, like I'd gotten up too fast. I tried to turn and put my hands on the bed for balance, but ended up tripping on one of the pairs of shoes I'd pulled from the closet in my quest to find something to wear to the game.

The next thing I knew, I was twisting and falling backward. My hand shot out, closing around my bedspread, which I thought would save me.

It did not.

What it did, was slide off the bed and land right on top me as the back of my head bounced off the floor. Tears sprang to my eyes as dull pain blossomed through my skull.

Had to have the damn hardwood floors, huh genius?

Flipping the covers off my face, I groaned as I sat up, with stars swimming in front of my eyes.

"*Shit*," I muttered, hesitantly pulling myself up from the floor, then lifting my hand to touch the tender spot that would surely be a knot later. "*This day is starting on a great note.*"

Instead of waiting for it to get worse, I took a couple of anti-inflammatories and then finished getting ready, so I could make it out of the door on time. I brought my laptop with me, to take my own notes during the game, to use for future interviews.

By the time I made it to the team box, my head was pounding so hard that it was making me sick to my stomach, and I hoped no one would try to talk to me. Obviously, that didn't happen. It seemed like everybody and their mother wanted a word with me, about an interview, or something I'd said on the show, or my relationship with Ramsey.

Luckily, Ramsey's cousin, Reginald, who I'd been introduced to a couple of weeks ago, seemed to notice the distress in my eyes and pulled me away, tucking me into a seat on the other side of him and Ramsey's niece and nephews, basically out of reach from the crowd.

"*Thank you*," I whispered, and he grinned, extending his fist in my direction.

"You're welcome," he said, as I bumped my fist against his. "You were looking a little wild in the eyes, like you were just about ready to cut somebody."

I laughed a little, then winced in pain. "I just don't feel that great. Knocked myself in the head getting ready."

He frowned. "You good? Ram know you hurt yourself?"

"No, and please let's keep it that way," I pleaded, holding out my hand as I saw him already going for his cell phone. "I'm fine, and Ramsey doesn't need any distractions. I'm good."

"You sure?"

"Yes, I'm sure, Ramsey number two," I teased, and he shook his head.

"My bad – the chivalry is in our blood I guess," he laughed, then turned to look at something one of his sons was showing him. As

I watched him interact with his kids – with *Chloe's* kids, which had blown my mind – the story Ramsey had told me about him played in my mind. As well-known as Chloe was, her having children wasn't common knowledge, and a whole-ass husband in federal prison, that *no one* had known about?

Nobody could say she wasn't good at her job, because she'd crafted the hell out of her *own* image.

My eyes were drawn to the large screens first, and then the field, as the game started. I took a deep breath, reminding myself that no matter what, this was just preseason – the perfect time to get rid of nervousness, and work out the kinks before the games that were vital started. There was no need for concern – Ramsey was going to get out there and play like he had in years past. He was going to *dominate.*

Only... not so much.

The frustration in the box was palpable as the game unfolded before us. On more than one play, we watched Ramsey take a snap, and then hesitate a second too long before deciding where to move, seconds that cost us valuable yards in offense. Or didn't keep good control on the ball. Or didn't completely follow through on a play. And so on and so forth. Once again – not blatantly *bad*, just... not that good.

Certainly not the Cinderella story football fans had been hoping for.

We didn't lose the game, fortunately, which meant there wouldn't be a ton of close focus on Ramsey's performance in the game. It wasn't going to be ignored though – something made clear when, before I'd even headed out of the box to try to catch him coming out of the locker room, he was stopped by a reporter.

As I watched from the TV screen, the look in his eyes cut me deep.

"Ramsey Bishop... how are you feeling about today's game?" the reporter asked – a weak question, and Ramsey knew it, but would be respectful.

"I'm feeling about how anyone would," Ramsey shrugged – the kind of answer reporters hated. Good. "Obviously, I'm happy that my teammates pulled off a win, but I'm looking forward to being more of an asset next time."

The reported nodded, pushing the mic closer to Ramsey's face. "So you aren't pleased with your performance today?"

228

Ramsey smirked, with zero amusement, considering his words before he answered. "I have the ability for a better performance than what I gave today."

"What do you think needs to happen for us to see that? What are your plans to deliver in the next game?"

His shoulders went up again, and he shook his head. "Hard work. Practice. Getting my head in the game. I have teammates with whole families to tend to, and they still manage to get out there and do what needs to be done on the field. I don't have any excuses. I'm going to buckle down, and focus on improvement."

"Thank you, Ramsey. And congratulations on the win."

Ramsey's eyebrow twitched, and I watched the muscles in his jaw tighten before he nodded. "Yeah. Thanks."

He stalked off toward the locker room and I let out a breath I hadn't realized I was holding. The back of my head was still aching, but I ignored it in favor of rushing down the locker rooms as quickly as I could, working through the throngs of people leaving the stadium and standing around talking, so I could get to him.

I knew he had to talk to other reporters first, so I hung back. Once the players were dressed, the locker room started to clear out. Jordan spotted me, and then Trent, and they came up to talk to me, which gave Ramsey's family a chance to get to him first – which was probably best anyway.

By the time I actually got to Ramsey, the locker room was almost empty. At first, neither of us said anything, but then I extended my arms, and he shook his head as he stepped into them, returning the gesture to wrap me into a hug.

"Reggie said you hit your head," he murmured into my ear, bringing a hand up to gently cup the back of my head. Even that slight touch was tender, making me cringe in pain, and he pulled back, eyes narrowed in concern.

"It's *nothing*," I insisted. "I just had a little accident, being clumsy. I'm fine."

"What's a "little" accident?" he asked, unconvinced.

"I tripped over some shoes, and… kinda twisted around, I guess. Fell backward, bumped my head. That's all."

"From standing?!" The explanation that I thought would ease his mind only seemed to worry him more, and I made a mental note to never, ever tell Reggie anything again. "Come on," Ramsey said, grabbing my hand. "Let's get medical to take a quick look for you."

"Oh my God, it is *not* that serious!"

"Unless it *is*. You could have a concussion."

I rolled my eyes. "A concussion? Ramsey, *please*."

"Wil, *please*. Your head still hurts, right? Do you feel dizzy? Sick to your stomach? Tired? Irritable?"

Ugh.

I felt all of that, but didn't say anything. However, my silence seemed to be answer enough. A few minutes later, I was seated in front of one of the team doctors, alone, since Ramsey had gotten pulled away by his coach for an impromptu meeting. I answered the doctor's questions as best I could, while sitting there wishing the whole extra ordeal would be over. I did the tests they wanted, counted backwards, all of that, and as *soon* as they told me I could leave, I got out of there, and went to find Ramsey.

"So... what did they say?" I asked him, after a silent trip to the car, where he'd seemed deep in thought. I'd found him in the hallway, on his way back to get me, and since he hadn't driven himself to the stadium this morning, he sent his security to ride behind us, while he and I rode together.

My question seemed to snap him back to the present, and he shook his head. "They said what I expected. That if I didn't get my shit together, they were going to downgrade me to a... "more appropriate" level."

As soon as I heard that, I knew he didn't need anything extra on his plate. *Nothing* else to worry about. So when he followed up my question with a question of his own – "What did the doctor say?" I shrugged.

"I'm completely healthy," I told him – the truth. "Just a little bruise, and a knot on the back of my head. They want me to rest."

He nodded. "Good. We'll make sure that happens."

After that, I left him alone, as my phone lit up with a message from Cole, about setting up my next interview. I tended to that, and let Ramsey retreat into his head, which was what he needed. *Not* being worried about me.

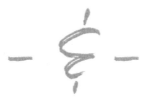

I shouldn't have responded to Cole's message.

If I hadn't, I wouldn't have been fighting a headache as, a day after preseason ended, I set up cameras to record my next interview.

With Ramsey.

Her reasoning was that Ramsey needed the boost in image, and Chloe agreed. Chloe had pushed for it to be available before regular season started, which wasn't much time, with the Kings having their first game in about a week. That meant we had to get this done, so I could get it edited, and released.

But football was the *last* thing I wanted to talk to Ramsey about.

I pushed – well, tried to push – my personal feelings aside as I sat down with him to talk about what *everybody* was talking about. His lackluster presentation in the preseason games.

The last game was a little better – enough to keep him from being downgraded, but still not great. This wasn't something that would make it to the ears of the public, but he was essentially on probation, and no part of me wanted to be the one to press him about it, to ask any tough questions.

But he'd blown up – A Ramsey blow up, which was louder in feeling than actual words, but made an impact – at a reporter after the last game, and he needed this. Needed to be accountable, needed to show he could answer tough questions. Needed to show the world that he *was* up to this.

And if I could help with that in any way… I certainly wasn't about to leave him hanging.

So we sat down for the interview. Just me and him, at his place in New York, because I knew that was the energy that would make him most comfortable.

"Where is the Ramsey Bishop we saw before you left the NFL?" I asked, not pulling any punches with my first question. "Why aren't you playing with the decisiveness and superiority that you used to?"

"*Damn*," he said, laughing as he stretched his arms across the back of the couch. It was a tough question, but his body language was open, laid back. And he looked good in that blue and white tee shirt that I'd wanted to tell him was too busy to wear on camera, but... again... he looked good. "You're just going to come out swinging like that, huh?"

I nodded. "Yes. A wise sports reporter once told me, "Nobody is watching to hear the player's favorite color. Get to what the people want to know.""

He grinned, knowing I was referring to him. He'd made me *so mad* when he told me that, three years ago. Even though I was pissed off, I took that lesson to heart, because he was right. "A wise one, huh?"

"Very. And... this is what the people want to know. What the hell is going on?"

His smile faded, but not because he was bothered by the question. As usual, he was considering his words, and I was waiting on the edge of my seat to hear them. He and I had talked throughout preseason, sure, but this was something I didn't know how to approach on a personal level with him, and he hadn't sought me out to talk about it either. Maybe now I'd hear an answer.

"Well... I've thought about that a lot, over this whole preseason period. And I've been asking myself that question – dude, what the hell is going on with you? So I had to sit with it, and take it back to... when I played at first, what was it that gave me my energy? What was my reason for working so hard, training so hard, giving it my all when I got out there? And I love football, don't get me wrong, but when I asked myself those questions, and really dug out that answer... it was my mother. At first, it was so I could finally give her the life she deserved. Then it was just to keep making her proud. Then... it was to give her some light in her days, while she was fighting for her life. When I left the game... that hurt. But I was doing what I needed to do, to make sure she was good, because she *always* did that for me. I promised her I would go back to the game when I could, and I've done that. But now that she's gone... I'm still trying to figure out my energy, you know? Still looking for that *why* that made me a confident player, and... just hoping that I find it."

For several seconds after he stopped speaking, I sat there in stunned silence. I don't know what answer I was expecting – or even

232

that I was expecting *anything*. But I hadn't known he was going to say *that*.

I took a deep breath, swallowing a lump of emotion as I planted my feet on the floor, keeping myself in my chair instead of giving into the urge to fling myself into his arms and hug him. His voice had been even, and his eyes were clear, but... I could just *tell*. That hadn't been an easy conclusion for him to come to, and it hadn't been an easy truth to speak.

But I was supposed to be professional right now. I would have to save up all my comforting for later.

I cleared my throat. "So, it sounds like your family is very important to you."

"*Very*," he said, nodding. "My aunt, and my cousin who's like a brother, so I call his kids my niece and nephews. All of our extended family, all of that. Those are the people who kept me alive, kept me going. Family is... everything."

"Any plans to start your own soon?"

I didn't even know where that question came from, and it seemed to surprise Ramsey too. He actually blushed about it – something he surely wouldn't have done with another interviewer. Honestly, he probably wouldn't have answered something so personal from someone else, but... this was *me*. Which was precisely what made it such an awkward thing to ask.

"Ah... soon? No. I mean, yeah, I'm getting older, and it's something to think about, but I *just* got back into the game. I need to take some time without distraction to work out what I'm doing on the field. These young guys that want my spot? They have all the time in the world to review tapes, and practice, and get faster and stronger. I can't go up against that with a family to take care of, not at my current level. Maybe once people mention "elite" with my name again, I can plan for that. *Maybe*. But no... not soon."

I blinked, hard. "Completely understandable. So, you aren't moved by the birth of your teammate, Trent Bailey's baby girl? It was the same day as the last preseason game, right?"

He grinned. "Yes. And while she is an absolutely adorable little girl, I have to keep in mind what's best for my career, and a baby isn't that. But maybe they'll let me babysit some time," he chuckled, and I forced myself to laugh with him.

"Right, um... okay, so let's switch focus," I said, ignoring the way my stomach was currently flipping inside out. "Um..." I pushed out a deep breath, and Ramsey narrowed his eyes.

"Hey... are you okay? You're not still having those headaches are you?"

I waved him off. "No. *No*. I'm fine, just... a little flustered. I'm a little warm, but I'm okay."

"Do you need some water or something?"

"I'm fine."

I was *not* fine.

I was nowhere near fine, hearing him say that a baby wasn't part of his ideal future, at least not "soon". But listening to him, it didn't sound like it was high on his priorities, *period* – something I'd never even considered. I wanted children – had spent a good part of my adult life feeling desperate about it – but it hadn't occurred to me that... maybe Ramsey *didn't*.

"Alright, so... the way that you came about joining the Kings, it was a little unconventional. A viral video at minicamp, running into the team owner at a wedding, getting called in for a workout, losing your position as a news anchor, and then getting the call that you were wanted on the team. Why don't you tell us that story?"

I finished with a smile, but Ramsey didn't smile back. Instead, he raised an eyebrow.

"Well... you kinda just told it yourself, Wil."

I frowned for a moment, and then processed his words, sitting back and closing my eyes when I realized he was right. I shook my head, and then pulled myself up from my chair, going to the cameras one by one to turn them off.

"I'm sorry, I... I need a break."

I didn't give Ramsey a chance to respond before I turned to walk out of the room, getting even more flustered than I already was when I realized I didn't really have anywhere to go. I was in *his* condo, which was spacious, but open. If I wanted privacy, I was going to have to go into one of his bedrooms, or the bathroom or something, when all I *really* wanted to do was get away.

"Wil," he said, his tone soothing as he approached me from behind. "What's going on, Champ?" As soon as he touched me – putting his arms around my waist to close me in – I burst into the tears I'd hoped to be able to hold back. His voice was heavy with alarm as he turned me to face him, asking what was wrong. I was sobbing too hard to do anything except shake my head, but he wasn't accepting that. He cupped my face in his hands, making me look at him. "Wil, *tell me what is wrong.*"

"I'm pregnant," I blurted, and it was as if my words sucked all the air out of the room.

His lips parted, and moved, but nothing came out for a few seconds, until finally… "*What?*"

"I said I'm *pregnant.*" I pulled out of his grasp – easily, because he wasn't holding me very tight anymore anyway. "I'm pregnant, and you… don't want a baby."

He shook his head. "I… when did you find out?"

"Two days ago," I said, swiping tears from my face. "When I hit my head, you had me talk to the team doctor, remember? Well, he didn't think I had a concussion, but from everything I explained to him, he joked that maybe I was pregnant. As soon as he said it, it made me uneasy. But then I realized that I hadn't had my period, but I'd been so wrapped up in everything else I hadn't noticed. So I took a test. And it was positive, but it was the day before your game, and I… I didn't want to give you anything extra to think about."

Absently, he nodded. "Yeah, but… how did this happen?"

My face scrunched up. "What do you mean, how did it happen? We had unprotected sex, Ramsey, that's how it happened."

"Yeah, but the few times we have, I pulled out."

"Not in Bali," I reminded him, simply. And from the look on his face, there was no need for elaboration – he remembered.

A fresh round of nausea rocked my stomach as he raised his hands to his face, and pushed out a sigh. "Okay. Okay. So… do you want to keep it?"

My eyes almost bugged out of my head. "Of course I want to *keep* it! Why would you even ask me that?! After everything I've been through, I'm praying I *get* to keep it. Are you fucking crazy?!"

"It's just a goddamn question," he shot back. "Last I checked, I can't carry a baby, so I thought it would be wise to figure out if it was something you even wanted to do!"

"*Yes,*" I snapped. "I *want* to have this baby!"

"Then we're having a baby."

I scoffed, shaking my head. "You say that like it's so simple. Like this isn't terrifying!"

"People have babies all the time, Wil. Don't be dramatic about it."

My nostrils flared as a siren went off somewhere in my brain, and I saw red. But just before I gave into the urge to try my best to physically tear him into shreds for that insensitive comment, my last working molecule of sensibility kicked in, and I remembered.

He doesn't know, Wil.

That's why he could make light of the miracle of a healthy pregnancy, why he could even form his lips to ask me if I "wanted" to keep this baby. I'd never shared with him the sob-induced headaches, the doctor's appointments, the tests, the ovulation kits, the absolute terror I'd felt seeing the evidence in my underwear that my body was rejecting what I'd prayed would be a full-term pregnancy.

"Ramsey…," I started, with an eerie calm that I had to pull my deepest depths. "I spent the last years of my last relationship hoping, praying, *begging* for my body to give me a baby. Before that? I lost *two* different pregnancies, both of which were unexpected, but wanted, very much. I never got answers for why. Never could get an explanation as to why pregnancy eluded me. But then… here you come. We go to Bali, and you're so damn charming, and sexy, and make me so damn comfortable, and stress-free, and bring so much peace, that I guess… you created the conditions that my body was looking for. I'm pregnant. God willing, I will be that way for a whole forty weeks, and I will tell you *now*… you don't have to be a part of it. You don't want to have a baby? *Don't.* But I will."

"Now which one of us *fucking crazy*?" he asked, stepping into my face with an expression so intense I took a step back, but he grabbed me, hauling me against his chest. "If your ass thinks you're about to have *my* child by yourself, I promise you I'm not the crazy one."

"But you *just* said—"

"Man, *fuck* what I said! Erase that bullshit," he growled. "Wil," he said, his tone suddenly desperate as he cupped my face in his hands again. "A hypothetical baby is one thing. My best friend carrying my child though? A baby with *you*… that's something else entirely, Champ."

My heart slammed to the front of my chest. "Ramsey… seriously?" I breathed.

236

"Seriously," he answered, and then his mouth was on mine, and I was so full I was sure I was going to burst. I started sobbing again, and between that, and him kissing me, I could barely catch a breath, but that was okay. I felt so high on happiness I wasn't even sure I *needed* to breathe. In that moment, it honestly seemed like pure joy was enough to sustain me.

Suddenly, he swept me up into his arms and started down the hall, and I laughed. "Wait, what are you doing?" I asked.

He stopped moving to look at me like I'd lost it. "Uh, I'm about to make love to the mother of my child – what do you *think* I'm doing?"

"What about the interview?"

He sucked his teeth, then finished his trek to his room, where he lowered me to the bed, then crawled on top of me. "We'll get back to it later. Gotta scratch most of it anyway."

RAMSEY

This was it.

First game of the regular season, and I was sitting in the locker room, surrounded by teammates who were loud, hyped, ready to play.

My head was across the country, with the mother of my child.

I'd left her sick – sick as *hell*, actually – and in the care of her own mother, who assured me Wil would be fine. In the week since she'd told me she was pregnant, her symptoms had virtually exploded, and I now understood that "morning sickness" was a misnomer. Wil was sick *all the time.*

Her mother, Carla, had given me a reassuring pat on the back as she sent me out the door on Wil's orders, to make sure I got on the plane with the team. "It'll pass," she promised. "This is part of the process. Sickness is a good sign, believe it or not – her body reacting to the pregnancy hormones, which means... still pregnant."

They knew better than I did, so... I got on the plane.

But still – neither my mind nor my heart were going to be out on that field unless I got it together, and I needed both if I was going to turn my shit around the way I'd promised the team, and the fans, that I

237

would. I had one game, *this game*, to get it together, or one of those hungry ass rookies would be in my spot, and I couldn't even be mad about it.

I just didn't want the shit to happen.

Looking around the locker room, my eyes landed on Trent and Jordan, who were laughing about something. I grabbed my helmet from the bench beside me and hopped up, walking over to where they were.

"Jordan… let me holler at Trent for a second, bruh," I said, and they both looked at me with questioning eyes before Jordan nodded.

"Yeah… you good?" he asked, and I nodded, even though I was sure my face probably told a different story, judging from Trent motioning for me to follow him to a quieter spot, while Jordan moved on to join the growing excitement from our other team members.

We could hear them on the other side of the lockers, but Trent was focused. "You look like you're about to puke, nigga," he said. "What's up with you?"

I chuckled. "Man… don't even really know where to start, but… I know you and Jade, you just had your baby girl."

Immediately, a smile broke over his face. "Yeah."

"Right. So… dude, how do you keep your head in the game when you know… you're thinking about your wife, thinking about baby girl, and Kyree too. Your *family*. Like… how do you stay focused?"

Trent frowned. "I feel like there's something you aren't saying right now."

I scrubbed a hand over my face, and then pushed out a sigh before I glanced around to make sure nobody was lurking before I told him something I hadn't told *anyone* – not even Reggie or Clayton yet, because Wil was so insistent on keeping it quiet until she got through her first trimester.

"Wil is pregnant."

Instantly, Trent's eyes went wide. "Yo… you *serious*?!"

"Yeah."

"You got Wil Cunningham, goddamn America's Olympic Sweetheart, knocked up? *No wonder* your ass was grinning so hard in that interview," he said, cracking up so hard that he clutched his stomach.

238

"Nigga, *relax*," I hissed, fighting the urge to start laughing myself, just because it was contagious.

"My bad, Ramsey," he said, straightening up, but still chuckling. "I guess we should've known though, after those pictures – that looked like some very "we finna make a baby" shit y'all was doing down in Bora Bora."

"Bali."

He shrugged. "Same difference. But nah, in seriousness – congratulations, man. Wil is a good girl – she's a good look for you, man."

"Thank you, but… it'll be an even better look if I can keep my ass on this team. But I can't even think about a goddamn football when she's back at home, sick and shit. That's why I'm asking you – cause you're on your job, *every week*. How do you do it?"

Trent nodded. "Aiight, so… I saw your interview, right? My lady had me watch it with her while she was up feeding the baby, and you had her all misty and shit, talking about how your mother was your "*why*" on the field. Well… Jade, Kyree, baby girl… those are my "*whys*". I love the game, passionate about it, all that, but there ain't *nothing* like going out here to do this shit for my family, and set them up for life. I wasn't born with a silver spoon in my mouth, man, and I know you didn't grow up with shit either, I've heard your story. You know what that shit feels like – and I know you don't ever want your lady, or your seed, to experience that. So real talk… Ramsey, you gotta stop bullshitting. I've seen your tape nigga – Just like you used to get out there and run the ball like your mama's life depended on it, you gotta replace that with Wil, and your unborn child. You ain't gotta keep looking for your *why*. It's looking *you* right in the face."

I needed that.

I didn't know I needed it until I got it, but as soon as I absorbed those words, it made perfect sense. I didn't even verbally respond – I nodded – but honestly, words weren't needed.

Action was.

So that's what the fuck I did.

I went out there and ran the ball, and ran niggas over, and ran the plays not like *my* life depended on it, but like Wil's did, and like the life she was cultivating *needed* me to get my shit together. If this was how I was providing for them, how I was making my name, the legacy I was leaving behind for my kid… I couldn't half –ass it.

I was gonna do the shit like I *meant* it.

I walked off the field with more tackles than I'd cared to keep track of, 109 rushing yards and two touchdowns to add to my stats.

Back in the locker room, Trent caught my attention just before a reporter approached me, and tipped up his chin. I returned the gesture, grateful for the wisdom he'd given me – words I'd taken out onto the field, and dominated.

I got through the post-game interviews as quickly as I could, wanting nothing more to get to my phone and check on Wil. As soon as I picked it up though, a text from her was already on the screen, and I grinned so wide it made my cheeks hurt.

"Well damn. If I'd known a baby was all you needed to remind the world why they called you Sledgehammer, I would've paid a little more attention to my body. ;) Great game. Congratulations. – The Champ"

Thirteen

Wil

September 2017

"So, you know this baby is going to be like, some type of super-baby, right?"

I looked up from the pregnancy magazine I was pretending to read to raise an eyebrow at Naima, seated beside me. "Uh... what?"

"Come on, don't tell me you haven't thought about that. Between you and Ramsey – and goodness, your *parents* – this is going to be one strong, fast baby. You *sure* you want to breastfeed?"

I couldn't even form words to respond to that, so I just laughed. I knew Naima's current silliness was for my benefit – her way of trying to cheer me up. She further confirmed that when she reached over, grabbing and squeezing my hand.

"He'll be here for the next one," she said, as if she'd read my mind. And she was right – most likely, Ramsey *would* be the person by my side at the next prenatal appointment. But this was the *first* one. Although Naima was one of my favorite people in the world, the *only* reason she was here, instead of Ramsey, was because of an away game and a delayed flight.

"Is your phone fully charged?" I asked her. "And here's mine. Make sure you get everything on video, I don't want him to miss anything."

"I know, Wil."

"And make sure your finger isn't covering the mic, so he can hear."

"Wil. I know."

"And make sure—I'm doing a lot right now, aren't I?"

Naima laughed. "You are, but I'm going to let you have your moment, since I know you're on edge."

I frowned. "Me? On edge? I'm not on edge. I'm breezy," I said, then immediately flinched as the door to the waiting room swung open. I damn near fell out of my chair craning my neck to see who was coming in, and didn't relax until I saw that it was just another doctor in the practice, who barely looked up before continuing past us to get to the offices.

"*Sooo* breezy," Naima teased, shaking her head.

"Well, can you blame me?" I asked. "Can you imagine the headline if the wrong person walks in here, snapping pictures of me at the OB?"

"You're the one who insisted on doing it this way, like you're not having a baller's baby. Don't you celebrities get private home visits for this?"

I scoffed. "I requested a private time slot, at a pretty exclusive doctor. That's the best I can do. I'm not *that* kind of celebrity yet."

"And yet, you consistently get followed now."

"Only because of those damn pictures."

Ugh.

Before that, sure, people knew me, but not like… *knew* me. I wasn't doing red carpets, eating at celebrity hot spots to be seen, etc. I was just Wil, the former Olympian turned journalist, and if someone randomly recognized me, fine.

Not so much anymore.

The release of those pictures had made me more recognizable, and it didn't help that pictures of me out and about ended up on fashion blogs, dissecting my clothes, on hair blogs wondering what

242

products I used, etc – all in addition to the whole "relationship goal" thing, which wasn't showing signs of slowing down.

On the bright side, my viewership and social media growth for "*Wil in the Field*" were both doing great. So... maybe I couldn't complain too much.

"Hey," Naima said, in a mischievous tone that let me know something crazy was about to come out of her mouth. "What if *that* was the day you got pregnant? Like, that exact session. Everybody has maternity pictures. You have *conception* pictures."

"I cannot *stand your ass!*" I howled at her, then clapped a hand over my mouth, trying not to laugh, or maybe cry. "Why would you say that!?"

She shrugged. "I'm just saying, the two of you *looked* like you were trying to make a baby. Your goddamn foot was on his shoulder! Like, you may as well have hung an "insert sperm here" sign off your clit, you know, so it would be in the perfect spot right above the opening."

"What is *wrong with you* Mimi!?" I shrieked as she sat back, looking immensely proud of herself. If cheering me up / keeping me occupied was her goal, she was definitely doing a good job at it.

Well... the best she could.

The truth was, even if Ramsey were here, instead of on a plane, I would still be a nervous wreck. Or, trying *not* to be a nervous wreck, even though my mind was running through all kinds of nightmare scenarios.

What if something was wrong?

What if there was no heartbeat?

What if the test had been a false positive, and my pregnancy symptoms were just in my head?

I wasn't really sure how I would react to any of those – I was just hoping it wouldn't be necessary. When Ramsey had called me earlier, letting me know he wouldn't be back on time to make the appointment with me, he'd taken the time to calm me down, and then prayed with me, which gave me a little more peace than I'd had before.

Voices from down the hall where the exam rooms were caught my attention, and Naima and I both sat up a little straighter. I was a little early for my appointment, but it was still after normal hours – I expected to be the only one here, and the receptionist hadn't given any warning, even though the whole office was well-apprised of my special situation.

A little feeling of dread swelled in my chest as the voices grew louder, meaning they were coming closer. It was two women – two pairs of heels click-clacking against the polished floor. As soon as they came around the corner, laughing, I realized why I'd felt so uneasy.

One of the women was Dr. Violet Cho, who'd come highly recommended by Ashley. The name had thrown me off a little, since I was in the market for a Black woman doctor, but after a scolding reminder that race and nationality weren't the same thing, Ashley eased my mind with the addendum that Dr. Cho was her sorority sister.

The other woman was Lena.

Horror-movie music played in the back of my mind as Lena and Dr. Cho looked up, noticing Naima and I in the waiting area. Both women smiled, but Lena's presence sent my agitation level through the roof. What the *hell* was she doing here?

"I don't have to guess which of you is my patient," Dr. Cho grinned, as Naima and I stood up. "I recognize this face from TV, and you're even more beautiful in person, Wil," she said, pulling me into an unexpectedly warm hug. "Maybe your pregnancy will convince Ashley and Naima to come and experience the miracle of science?"

Naima's eyes went big. "Oh, *no* thank you," she laughed, then accepted a hug of her own. "I think we'll leave that to the real grown ups around here."

"Oh please," Dr. Cho laughed. "Wil, Naima, this is my colleague, Dr. Lena McBride. I'm sorry to have kept you waiting, but she needed a consult for one of her patients."

"Yes, my apologies," Lena said, in that smoky-sweet voice that men seemed to go wild for, as she extended a hand to me, and then Naima. "I start talking about bodies and get a little too enthusiastic. I've met Wil before, but not you Naima. It's a pleasure."

"You've met Wil?" Dr. Cho asked, and Lena smirked.

"Yes, back when I was dating Ramsey Bishop, the two of them were working together."

Dr. Cho's light brown skin flushed red as she nodded awkwardly, catching the obvious elephant in the room now that it was right on her toes. "Oh, yes. That makes sense."

Lena looked from her back to me, her sleek ponytail bobbing behind her as she moved her head. "And now... *wow*. Women usually only come to the lovely Dr. Cho for one reason, so I hope I'm not premature in offering my congratulations. I remember Ramsey talking about wanting kids," she sighed. "I had to let him know it wasn't happening with me. But anyway... he didn't mention this when I ran into him a few weeks ago."

"You talked to Ramsey?" I asked, in a sharper tone than I intended.

Lena's eyebrow cocked up. "Yes, but please don't let that raise your blood pressure. You must not have seen last night's episode of the show." She held up her left hand, showing us a blindingly large ring, that was undoubtedly real. "Finally announced my engagement to the world."

"I've never seen your show," I lied, and Lena's smirk grew into a grin.

"Of course you haven't. But besides that... Ramsey is quite enamored with you. Even if I *was* the type to chase other people's men, he made it quite clear that he isn't available for catching. Congratulations on *that* too. Much better than corny ass Darius Hayward, *ugh*," she said, with a look of disgust that I felt in my chest. "That man did you a favor, because no. Anyway – thanks for the advice, Vi. I'll follow up with you later. Ladies," she said, addressing herself to me and Naima, "nice running into you. And don't worry Wil. Secret's safe with me."

With a wink, she was off down the hall, leaving the scent of Tom Ford perfume in her wake. That was my first time ever *really* interacting with her, and... it felt weird that I somehow... didn't hate her.

That can't be right.

"You work... closely, with her?" I asked Dr. Cho. Maybe in another situation, I wouldn't have been bold enough to speak up about it, but this was something pretty damned important. Before I really knew Ramsey, I'd hate-watched Lena for several seasons, and didn't trust her, at all.

Dr. Cho nodded. "Yes, I've known Dr. McBride for many years. Why?"

"Oh, it's just... I don't know how comfortable I am with that, after seeing her on her show. It doesn't exactly leave a good impression, and if you work closely with her..."

The doctor's eyebrows went up, before she nodded. "I believe I understand. But, I've never seen a single episode of the show – I didn't want the magic of television to color my perception of someone I know personally to be funny, smart, and a very good young doctor. But, Dr. McBride isn't an obstetrician, and she belongs to a different practice, so if your concern is about her having access to any of your personal records, anything like that, I assure you that won't be the case. Ethics are important, to both of us. You have nothing to be concerned about."

It wasn't like I was going to leave the appointment anyway. I was just uncomfortable with the idea of my man's ex being close colleagues with the woman who was supposed to be helping bring my baby healthily into the world. But Ashley had raved about this woman, and so had the reviews I'd seen of her online. She was knowledgeable, she was discreet, and she dealt with high-risk pregnancies. Even though my pregnancy hadn't been classified as such, it made me feel better knowing it was something she could handle.

I would just have to push my concerns about Lena to the side.

Five minutes later, Lena was the last thing on my mind.

Dr. Cho listened intently as I detailed my years of trying and failing to get pregnant, the two miscarriages, and my fears now. She took blood, and did a pelvic exam, gave me a whole spiel about raw meat, and soft cheese, and being careful about where I traveled. All things that were familiar – too familiar – and did nothing to lower my anxiety.

And then… the ultrasound.

Naima brushed off my insistence on recording with both cell phones so that one of her hands was free to hold mine, and I was grateful. My stomach twisted in knots as Dr. Cho inserted the ultrasound wand, and a few seconds later, my uterus was in black and white on the screen in front of me.

Inside that gray mass was a black one, and inside that black one was… a baby. Of course, right now, it looked like a gummy bear with a really big head, but… it was a baby.

"Let's get some sound going here, shall we?" Dr. Cho asked, and a few seconds later, the room filled a loud, whooshing sort of noise. She made a slight adjustment to the position of the wand, and then there it was… the strong, steady thump of the heartbeat.

I was greatly unprepared for the apparently new technology that put a soundwave image on the screen, tracking the heartbeat. As soon as it started up, something in me... snapped. I put my hands over my face, and broke into sobs that I couldn't articulate a reason for.

Luckily, Naima and Dr. Cho let me have that moment.

It lasted maybe a minute or so, and then I was okay. Just okay.

"Wil, it looks to me like you're about nine weeks into the gestational period. Does that sound right to you?"

I cleared my throat, and nodded. "Yes. Exactly right."

"Very good. Everything looks okay here, and we have a nice strong heartbeat for nine weeks, about 182 beats per minute, which is a good number. I don't see anything here to be concerned about, but I want you to not be afraid to call me, okay? Don't be worried you're bugging me, or anything like that. If something feels wrong, go with your gut, but again... I think you're well on your way to a healthy pregnancy."

A bit after that, she left for me to get dressed. Naima must have noticed that I wasn't saying enough – or very much at all – because she caught me by the shoulders to look me in the eyes.

"Willy... are you okay?" she asked. "How are you feeling? I thought you would be... I don't know. More excited about this."

I pushed out a sigh. "I really am happy, it's just... Mimi, you know I love you a lot, right?"

"Uh... right..." she said, raising an eyebrow. "But...?"

"But... all this did was make me even more scared, honestly. Now that I've seen it, heard the heartbeat... I can't deal. All I can think about is "what if?", and I really, *really* want Ramsey here," I said, just before I broke into a fresh round of sobs.

"Aww, sweetie..."

I was *so* grateful to Naima for the way she wrapped me into a hug, rubbing my back as I cried. Dr. Cho came back in to give me a little tote bag full of information, prenatal vitamins, and printouts from the ultrasound, and as soon as I'd pulled myself together enough to leave, we got out of there.

I was ready to get home, and curl up in my bed.

RAMSEY

I tried not to read too much into the fact that she wasn't answering her phone. But I'd been waiting to hear about the doctor's appointment for the whole flight, wanting to know every detail, good or bad. So once I was finally alone, just me and my security, the first thing I did was make that phone call.

And then at least ten more, because she wasn't answering.

I bounced on the balls of my feet, impatient, waiting for her to open her front door, if she was home. Not answering calls meant showing up to her place, and if she didn't answer here, I was going to her parents, then her cousin, but *somebody* was going to point me in the right direction.

Turns out I didn't have to go anywhere.

Her cousin, Naima, opened the door.

"Ramsey, hey! How was your flight?" she asked, totally casual as she stepped aside for me to come in.

"It was cool. Where is Wil? She's not answering her phone…"

"Sleeping," Naima explained, gesturing upstairs, where the bedrooms were. "It's been a bit of an emotional day for her."

My eyes went wide. "What? What happened? Is everything okay?"

Naima shook her head. "I'm not going into any details or anything, I'll let her tell you all of that, but the baby is fine."

I pushed out a heavy sigh of relief, and Naima smiled.

"Now that you're here, I'm going to head out. I just didn't want her to be alone, and if I'd told my aunt and uncle she was having a rough time, they would have turned it into a big deal. So I figured it was best to just wait on you."

"Thank you," I told her, and she nodded.

"You're welcome. Not a problem at all." She had her purse and cell phone in her hands, but instead of saying goodbye, or moving to leave, she hesitated, giving me this strange look for a few awkward seconds before she spoke again. "Actually… there's something I've been wanting to say to you."

"Should I be scared?"

248

"*No*," she laughed. "It's just... thank *you*," she started, a statement that lifted my eyebrows. "Wil is... that's my heart, you know? Like a sister to me. And seeing your relationship grow from honest-to-God friends to more than that... I like what it's done for her. I watched her whole relationship unfold with Darius, and it's crazy to me how different this looks. In a good way. I know it's probably a little hard to see it, with everything that's been going on, but you've really brought out this light in her, that I don't think I've ever seen before. And I appreciate it."

I shook my head. "Thank you for that, but I can't take credit. Wil has been a great friend, supportive, a good listener, a motivator, a muse... all of that. Without her being who she is, I don't know that I'd be able to be that person for her, so... that's all her."

Naima's lips parted a little, and then she narrowed her eyes. "See?" she said, wagging a finger in my direction. "This is the kind of thing – *you* – are the kind of man that makes it make sense that women even like men at all," she laughed. "Many of your brethren are wild garbage, but *you*, my brother... You're alright."

I frowned, feigning offense. "Just alright? Damn, it's like that Mimi?"

"Who told you that you could call me Mimi?" she asked, propping her hands on her hips.

I lifted my hands. "My bad. *Naima.*"

"Oh bye, I'm playing with you fool," she giggled, then laughed harder when I pulled her into a hug. "I know I don't have to tell you to take care of my girl, but... take care of my girl."

With two fingers, I gave her a little salute. "That's absolutely the plan."

She headed out, and I headed upstairs, finding Wil in the middle of her bed, curled into a ball underneath the covers. Instead of immediately waking her, I jumped in the shower, then grabbed a pair of my basketball shorts from a previous visit from her clean laundry.

Carefully, I lifted the covers back, smiling when I saw that she'd fallen asleep with her hand pressed to her stomach. I crawled in with her, getting close enough to see her peaceful face, then as lightly as I could, ran a finger from her forehead to the tip of her nose.

She frowned a little, shifting position before she settled again. I repeated my same action, and this time she mumbled something under her breath before her eyelids parted. For a moment, she squinted at me, probably still half-asleep. I could tell the exact moment awareness and recognition hit her, with widened eyes and a smile I felt all the way in the depths of my chest.

"Hey," she whispered, scooting closer to me. "You made it back."

I cupped the back of her head, bringing her in to kiss her forehead. "Yeah. Heard you've had a rough day."

"A little bit. Better now that you're here."

I grinned.

Damn this woman knows how to make me feel good.

"Ditto, Champ. Tell me how the appointment went?"

"Grab that bag," she said, pointing to her dresser. I climbed out to get it and then came back as she sat up, motioning for me to hand it to her.

As I sat down beside her, mimicking her position with the headboard against my back, she dug into the bag, then handed me several thin, glossy pages. She turned them right side up in my hands, and then pointed at the photo.

"This is our baby."

Wow.

I hadn't expected it to look so... *real*. I listened intently, seeing it immediately as she pointed out what would become arms and legs. "It looks like a gummy bear with a big ass head," I chuckled, and her whole demeanor shifted as she turned her head to stare at me, instead of the pictures. "I'm sure it's going to grow into it though," I added, trying to clean it up. But then another smile took over her face, and she shook her head.

"No, I see it too," she said, her eyes shining as she looked at me. "Oooh, here!" She reached beside her, for her cell phone, then frowned at the screen. "Oh damn," she murmured, then glanced up, looking sheepish. "It's on silent. I didn't know you'd been trying to call, sorry."

I waved her off. "It's fine. I know you're okay now, which is what mattered. What were you going to show me?"

"This." She tapped the screen a few times on her phone, and then handed it to me as a video began to play on the screen. She reached around me to turn the volume up, filling the room with a trippy thumping sound.

My eyebrows went up. "Is that... that's the heartbeat, right?"

She nodded. "Yeah. That's the heartbeat."

I couldn't help smiling as I continued listening, but then a different sound – the sound of Wil sobbing – permeated through the phone, and real-life Wil quickly snatched the phone away, to shut it off.

"Hold up," I said, trying to get it back from her. "What was that?"

"Nothing," she insisted, tucking the phone behind her. "I just... got a little emotional. Hearing the heartbeat, and actually *seeing* it, after having tried so long before. It was moving. I really wished you were there."

"Ah, babe." I pulled her into my arms, and she snuggled in close. "I really wish I could've been."

"It's okay. You had a game, you can't help that. It's not your fault your flight got delayed coming back. Gotta do what you gotta do."

I know she meant for those words to be comforting, but instead, they hit me with a disconcerting sense of déjà vu, reminding me way too much of when my mother would say the same thing when I missed a doctor's appointment with her. And maybe that's why missing Wil's appointment bothered me so much – it was too reminiscent of the reason's I'd left football in the first damned place.

"What's wrong?" Wil asked, making me realize that my uneasiness must have been showing on my face.

Quickly, I schooled my expression into something neutral, but the damage was done. Even when I responded with "Nothing", Wil's expression was still uncertain.

"Are you sure? You're not having second thoughts are you? Because—"

"*No*," I said, grabbing her hand. "I am *not* having second thoughts. Just... hoping that I don't let you down. Hoping that I'm *not* letting you down."

She scoffed. "I'm not even sure you're capable of such of thing," she said, sitting up, and then moving to straddle my lap.

"I'm glad to hear you have that kind of faith in me," I told her, resting my hands on her hips as she draped her arms over my shoulders.

"Only because you've earned it." She leaned in, pressing a soft kiss to my lips before she sat back. "We're due in April. I'm nine weeks along right now."

My eyebrows lifted. "Damn, really?"

"Yep. It doesn't even seem like Bali was that long ago, does it?"

"Not at all," I said, shaking my head. "Bali was amazing though."

"Wasn't it?" She moaned a little as she leaned in again, this time resting her head on my shoulder. "Had to be, if we went down there and made a baby."

I laughed. "Yeah, I would imagine so."

For a while after that, we just sat in comfortable silence before she lifted her head to look at me.

"Hey, so…" she started, then hesitated for a second. "My parents want us to come to their house. For like a cookout thing."

I frowned. "Okay… but why do you sound nervous about it?"

"Because… what was actually said was, "Bring that nigga over here, since he suddenly forgot the address. I need to talk to him." Or… something like that."

"Oh, damn."

She nodded. "Right, damn."

I chuckled a little. "Okay, well… I guess I can't really refuse an invitation like that. When are we supposed to go?"

"This week. Since you guys have a home game. Yeah – he checked the schedule."

"He must really have something on his mind," I laughed. "But that's cool, set it up. I'm sure it's a *what are your intentions with my daughter*" kind of thing, which I can handle."

She raised an eyebrow. "You sound *mighty* confident about that… like you know what your intentions are."

"Do you really want to have that conversation, Champ?" I asked teasingly, already knowing the answer. "Because we can *definitely* have that conversation."

"No, I'm good," she laughed. "Keep it. I'm perfectly content to let you and Jackie Cunningham have your sexist conversation among *yourselves.*"

"Oh, it's like that?"

"It's absolutely like that," she said, giggling. But then she cupped a hand over her mouth, and suddenly launched herself out of my lap, bolting to the bathroom. She closed the door behind her, but I cringed as the sound of her retching carried into the bedroom anyway.

At the bathroom door, I knocked and then waited for her to respond. A few seconds later, the toilet flushed, and then the door swung open. The look on her face before she went to the sink and turned it on made my chest hurt.

"I'm sorry you're feeling bad, babe," I said, stepping up to rub her back as she rinsed her mouth out.

Once she was done, she shook her head as she turned to face me. "Don't be. I will *gladly* pay this price to have our baby."

"Damn." I wrapped my arms around her waist, pushing her back against the vanity. "If you weren't already pregnant..."

She smirked. "Yeah, but... we could definitely practice for next time... *after* you go grab me some wings or something. I'm starving."

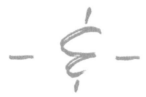

"Come on back here to the grill."

I followed Jack out of the back door, leaving Wil in the kitchen with her mother in favor of facing whatever it was he wanted to talk to me about head on. I'd been expecting this conversation since the whole picture scandal, and had been dreading it since the discovery of Wil's pregnancy.

Wil's parents liked me – I was sure about that. And on more occasion than one, especially after she and Darius broke up, they hadn't made it a secret that they would like to see us together. But with that said... it was a little different now, with me being the man the whole world quite possibly saw getting their daughter pregnant.

Their reception of me lately had been cordial, sure, but not quite as warm as usual. And though I'd been legitimately busy for the last two and a half months, it was time to stop putting it off.

The conversation was going to have to happen sooner or later.

"What you know about that, young man?" Jack asked me, lifting the cover on the grill to show off two slabs of ribs on one level, and countless chicken wings on the other.

I whistled. "Man, looking good. *Smelling* good too," I told him, and nodded.

"You going to be able to eat? Or do they have you on a restricted diet?"

I grinned. "Protein is always on the menu, so I don't see a problem."

"There you go," he said, clapping me on the shoulder. "That needs a few more minutes though. Come on out here, let me show you around Carla's garden."

Although I wouldn't have been surprised if he'd taken me around the deck to show me a shallow grave he'd dug for me, as an attempted intimidation tactic, he did lead me to a large, neatly cultivated garden. Stopping in front of several huge tomato plants, he turned to me, crossing his arms.

"So... gonna be a father, huh?"

Squinting my eyes against the glare of the late summer sun, I nodded. "God willing."

"That's always the determining factor there, isn't it?" he asked, then turned his gaze out toward the garden. "Learn from it. Grow closer to him. Even when it hurts, it always comes down to that. That's a valuable lesson to remember – especially when it comes to the people you love. You want to protect, and shield, and intervene... even when you're supposed to be letting them do their learning, their growing, their hurting."

I mimicked his stance, turning out to the garden. "Is that what happened with the show?" I asked, remembering something that, even though she hadn't mentioned it in a while, Wil had been bothered by. "You wanted to protect her from the chance of failure, or rejection?"

"I sure as hell did. Wouldn't take it back either. That not-so-little-anymore girl is my heart. My legacy. Anything I *could* do to give her a leg up, I absolutely did. That's what these white folks do for their kids, that's what I did for mine. You tell me what you would've done?"

"Wil isn't my child," I chuckled.

"But she's going to be having *your* child, and that should mean something to you. For eighteen years and beyond, I have nurtured,

254

loved, protected, and that won't ever change. But someone is going to have to do the providing, the supporting, the taking care of, the writing the TV network a check to make a point. I need to know if you're going to do that, son."

I pushed out a deep breath, and cross my arms. "All due respect, sir... Wil is a grown woman. She can take care of herself." I glanced over to find him giving me a hard stare, and I met his gaze as I continued. "Wil isn't particularly interested in having a check written on her behalf. She can write her own checks. Create her own opportunities, to pay her own bills. Do I plan to support my family? *Absolutely*. But it would be foolish of me to think that holds any weight with her, romantically."

"You said all of that, and still haven't answered my question. What would you have done?"

"I wouldn't have written a check," I answered, firmly. "And that's not knocking the fact that you did. I'm just saying... you and I have different roles in Wil's life. You did what you felt was right, to help your daughter. I would have done something different."

He nodded. "And what exactly would that something have been?"

"Supporting her efforts to pitch her show. Listening to her pitch, giving her feedback, helping her craft it. Gassing her up, making her believe there wasn't a damn thing she couldn't do. Keeping her distracted while she waited to hear back, holding her while she cried if the answer was no. Motivating her not to let that "no" be the end. Dragging her out of bed to try the next thing, to build her *own* thing if that's what she had to do. Investing in her directly. *Not* going behind her back, infantilizing her and giving anybody room to say she hadn't worked for it. And... I mean... I don't know that I *could* write a check big enough," I chuckled. "But if she *did* want that... *then* I would make that happen."

For a long moment, the only sound was the chittering of a pair of squirrels playing in a nearby tree. But then Jack nodded, raising an arm to hook around my shoulder as he led me back up to the deck.

"Grab those tongs, young blood. Let's get this meat off the grill, and then I'm going to take you out to the garage. Carla's mad, but I got me a little micro-brewery out there. These bearded hipsters with their "man buns" and plaid shirts ain't got *nothing* on Jackhammer's Ale."

I chuckled, and grabbed the tongs, listening as he told me about his beer. Even once we were done unloading the grill, and he was opening a refrigerator in the garage to hand me a home-brewed beer, the conversation didn't swing back to where it was before.

But the fact that he didn't seem to have a need to say anything more about it… said everything.

Wil

"Your daddy isn't going to do anything to that boy," my mother called across the counter as I watched him and Ramsey walk off the deck, and disappear from view. Yeah, I heard what she was saying, but hearing and believing were a little different from each other. I'd said I was fine with whatever they needed to talk about, but honestly I was a little worried.

Ramsey was a pretty laid back guy, but he was nobody's pushover. He wasn't even a little afraid to get… firm, if necessary. And my father was the kind of man it may be necessary to get firm with. But if those two butted heads…

"Bring your behind away from that window and come stir this lemonade," my mother scolded. I couldn't see them anymore without going outside anyway, so I did as she asked. On the other side of the counter, she was putting together the salad that would finish off our meal.

"Stress isn't good for the baby," she warned, and I tried not to roll my eyes. *They* were the ones who invited us over here for this ominous ass dinner, and now she wanted to tell me not to stress about it?

"Well, it's hard to help when two men nicknamed "Hammer" may or may not be fighting to the death over your "honor" in the backyard," I said, picking up the peeled lemon slices and dropping them into the dispenser of fresh lemonade.

My mother laughed. "I already told Jack to act like he has some sense. He just wants to make sure everything is on the up and up, since you two snuck this relationship past us like a couple of teenagers."

256

"We weren't *sneaking*. I mean… not from you guys, at least. And it's not as if we were doing anything much different than what we'd done the whole time we were friends before."

My mother looked up from slicing a cucumber, staring pointedly at the place where, in a few months, I would hopefully have a baby bump. "You were obviously doing *something* different, girl." I blushed, reflexively placing my hands on my stomach, and she chuckled. "No sense in trying to be shamed about it now. You're an adult. Having sex usually comes with the territory."

"Yeah, but still."

"Still what?" She slid the finished cucumber into the bowl with the other vegetables, to toss. "You think your mama hasn't lived long enough to *not* be scandalized by you sleeping around with your "friend"? Or better yet – do you think I haven't been rooting for this outcome in the first place?"

My eyes widened. "Mama! I thought you liked Darius!"

"Oh, I did, honey. He was a perfectly fine young man… until he wasn't anymore. But he was always just that – *fine*. Ramsey, on the other hand – that's a *man*. Reminds me of your father."

I took a seat at the counter, wiping my lemon scented fingers off with a towel before I propped my chin in my hands. "So… there was a point when you didn't think Darius was the one either?"

"I think that it was something that was for *you* to decide."

I snorted. "And we see how that turned out. Just the first thing in a long trail of everything going wrong, for *everybody* to see. Can you imagine what the press is going to do with this pregnancy news? It hasn't even been six months since the wedding that wasn't, and I've been fired, had a sex picture scandal, and now a pregnancy."

My mother shook her head. "I could knock you upside the head, girl. Do you really look at your life and only see the things that aren't as you planned, instead of the things that are as you *wanted*? You wanted your own show – you have it. You wanted a man that *really* loved you – you have it. You wanted a baby – you're *going* to have it. You are blessed, my dear. Focus on that."

I stayed quiet for a moment to absorb her words, watching as she used a pair of tongs to mix the salad.

"You really think he loves me, mama?" I asked, and when she looked up, eyes narrowed, mouth set in a frown – the classic "have you lost your mind" expression – I raised my hands, speaking quickly to clarify. "I mean, I *know* that he cares about me, a lot. That's clear, I'm not blind, it's just… the way this thing happened between us, isn't conventional. I just don't want it to be a thing where pressure from the media, or pressure from the news of my pregnancy, pushes us too far, too fast. I don't ever want to feel like an obligation to him."

My mother smirked. "Well, it's too late for that, sweetheart. But from what I've seen with Ramsey, I don't think it's something you should stress yourself with. Nor do I think that feelings have a time limit. I mean, there was no meter I had to press to start when I met your father," she chuckled, putting the salad bowl down to come and sit beside me at the counter. "And I want you to remember, it's not as if the two of you are starting from scratch – you've been friends for years, which is a beautiful foundation to start a relationship on. The idea that you've "rushed" things between you two is unfounded, in my opinion. If anything, the fact that you were with Darius delayed the inevitable."

"You think so?"

"Yeah, I do. Once you got past your little tantrum about having to work with him, I've always seen… this *light* in you, whenever he was around. And it's only grown brighter now that the two of you are in love. *Pregnancy* isn't the only thing making you glow."

"But we're not…" I stopped, and let out a sigh.

My mother laughed, putting a hand on my knee. "You can't even tell that lie, can you? That you don't love him."

"I don't *know*."

"I think you do," she countered. "And it's okay, nobody is pressuring you – I don't think?"

I shook my head. "No. Neither of us have said those words."

"When it's time, you will. Saying the words is about the least potent expression of it anyway. Of course we want to hear it too, but *always* remember – let his actions speak louder than his words. A man can *say* anything, but his actions tell the real story."

Yeah.

So far, Ramsey's actions had painted a narrative so enthralling it made my teeth hurt just thinking about it.

"*And*," she added, squeezing my knee. "Don't ever think that ignoring or denying your feelings makes them go away. If you love him… sweetheart, you just *do*. There's nothing wrong with it. And

258

nothing wrong with *you* for feeling that way. You could've left Darius last *week*, and that would still be true. Okay?"

I nodded. "Okay. Thank you mama," I said, then wrapped my arms around her waist. I let out a deep, gratified moan as she returned the gesture, giving me a hug that filled a little void that *only* a hug from her could fill.

"You're welcome baby," she said, glancing back toward the window that looked out to the backyard. We could see Ramsey and my father heading back up to the patio, and my mother stood. "Okay, enough of that. They're probably about to get the meat off the grill, and then your daddy is going to make Ramsey drink one of those nasty beers he's been working on. Come on upstairs. Let me show you my spoils from the trip to the Ase Garb store that he doesn't know about yet."

Fourteen

RAMSEY

October 2017

"There we go! Finally, damn."

I fought the urge to say something slick to the photographer in response to his – unwarranted – enthusiasm over me finally giving him "something he could use." Instead, I focused on Wil, who'd just snuck into the back of the room, and was trying to remain unseen behind the crew members.

But I'd felt, rather than seen her coming.

That's where we were, I guess, it terms of how close we'd become. I knew exactly why she was there, too, and it definitely wasn't just moral support. She'd woken up craving Sucre Noir for lunch today, and I couldn't make it, because of my interview and photoshoot with Sugar&Spice magazine at one of their satellite offices. But she'd never gone by herself, even when we were friends – she considered it "our" thing. So if I had to guess, she'd grabbed something light earlier, to hold herself over until I was done. But now, she was ready to *eat*.

It was time for me to go.

Rashad, the photographer, must've spotted her too, because he grinned. "Damn, you should've brought your lady with you if that's what it took to get a genuine smile on your face brother," he said, still snapping away.

I tucked the football in my hands under my arm, then ran a hand over my waves as I grinned through the *little* hint of embarrassment from those words. I didn't *think* my smile looked fake, but shit – I was tired. We'd lost at home last week, and the coaches had been all over our asses about it as we prepared to go into the next game. Not to mention, I'd be getting on yet another plane in a few days, to *get* to that game.

So yeah, my mood wasn't great.

But Wil's presence always had the power to change that.

A few shots later, we were done. I shook hands with the photographer and small crew, and then went to where Wil was perched in a chair she'd hustled from somewhere.

"Mr. Bishop," she purred, as she stood. "You are looking *very* good."

I shrugged. "I guess. It's plain though. White shirt, black tie."

"It's *classic*," she corrected, grabbing the ends of my undone bowtie. "Every occasion doesn't call for your flair for fashion. Everybody knows you can dress."

"*Outdress* most of these niggas," I teased, dropping the football on a nearby table to pull her into my arms. She bit her lip, only releasing it in time for my mouth to meet hers for a kiss – other people in the room be damned.

While I had no qualms about publicly displaying my affection, I quelled the urge to touch her stomach like I wanted. After what happened with those pictures, we agreed – we weren't saying anything about pregnancy until we absolutely *had* to, and Chloe was on board with it as well. She was just about thirteen weeks along now, and wasn't showing yet, especially not to public eyes. Even once she did start to show – it was getting cooler now, and she was already starting to dress in light, loose sweaters that would change to thick ones soon enough, which would camouflage for a little while longer.

We were keeping this for ourselves, as long as we could.

"You ready to eat?" I asked, and she gave me a deep nod. "Yes. *Please.*"

Chuckling, I took a step back. "Okay. Let me change real quick, and then we can go. I'll be right back."

I made it as quick as I could, not even stopping to read the message that popped up on my screen from Chloe. If it were vitally important, she would have called instead of sending a text. Getting the mother of my child fed seemed more urgent in the moment.

The photoshoot area had cleared out by the time I returned – the only people there were Wil, and my security guard Dre, who I'd left with her. Before we went public with this pregnancy, I *would* talk her into security for herself.

For now though, I just took the time to admire her for a moment. The last few weeks of this first trimester had been rough, but it was obvious she was feeling good today. She'd done an interview earlier in the morning with a girl's high school track squad in Bridgeport, and we were getting ready to eat at one of her favorite places.

I didn't have to ask – she was having a good day.

At the moment, her face was buried in her cell phone, so much that she didn't even look up from whatever video she had playing when I approached.

"What's up, you ready to go?" I asked, looping an arm around her shoulders.

She looked up, shaking her head. "Did you see this text from Chloe?"

"Nah," I said, feeling a little alarmed now, knowing that she'd sent something to Wil too. "Everything okay?"

Her face was impassive as she tapped the screen, starting the video from the beginning. "See for yourself."

"Bitch."

"Biiiiitch."

"Biiiiiiiiiiiiiitch!!!"

All of those were said with different inflections, and I knew from my experience with the black women in my life that the back and forth on the screen had just delivered a whole introduction to the conversation.

"I don't know if they're hearing it here first Arnez, but baby, we got the scoop on today."

"Biiiiitch!"

"Actual, factual, credible, not fake news sources have confirmed – formerly iconic, struggling television network WAWG, which ran into the ground by petty management and greedy execs has been purchased, through the joint efforts of the Whitfield and Drake families – our very own Black royalty."

"Bitch."

"According to reports, they are already making major changes – job postings went up for an entirely new executive board, and checks have been put in the mail to pay out the remaining contracts for any shows that will no longer be produced by the network, such as From the Sidelines, which suffered a catastrophic drop in ratings after the exit of the former hosts."

"Bitch. Bitch, bitch, bitch, bitch bitch."

"When asked, recently divorced Nashira Haley commented that she and her good friend, Nubia Perry were excitedly working together on the new vision for the network, which they hope will restore it to it's former glory, and restore their reputation for putting black excellence at the forefront. She mentioned a model search show from Nubia, a "fashion on a budget" show from popular vlogger Bianca Bailey, home improvement and DIY from Raisa Martin, a cooking show from Charlie and Nixon Graham, and they're hoping to snag recently-departed Wil Cunningham to bring her sports expertise back to the small screen."

"Hallelujahhhhhhh!" the Arnez character shouted, standing up, and throwing his hands in the air as he tossed his head back. *"Gloraaaay, hallelujah, I say won't he do it!!!"*

"Will you sit your silly ass down boy! Anyway – that's not all the tea."

"Ohhhhh, shanannnanana glory!"

"A little birdie told us that the purchase was made at a steep discount, due to impending legal action against two of the network execs by Wil Cunningham and Ramsey Bishop. Apparently, they took a price cut in favor of getting paid sooner, so they could cut those checks right to their lawyers."

"And I don't feel even a little bit bad – you can find the released email chain in the story we broke just two weeks ago, after it was revealed that they would escape criminal conviction over a technicality. Because there was "technically" no actual nudity in the

photos they conspired with a local vagabond to obtain, after a fan tweeted about seeing Wil and Ramsey while on vacation in Bali, a judge ruled that criminal action would be overkill, but a civil case could move forward."

"We don't have the exact number, but reportedly, Wil and Ramsey are seeking an amount in the "high multi-millions" in damages. It's a damn shame that someone else has to buy the network, to get it away from the family of the people who built it before they damage it beyond repair – but hell, at least our girl will get paid."

"No wonder she's been looking especially good around town lately."

"Good dick and a paycheck will do it for you honey."

"Wow," I said, as Wil took the phone from me, silencing the video. "I… wasn't expecting that. Like, at all."

When Chloe's IT guy had uncovered the emails confirming that Connie and Sarita were behind the leaked photos, I'd been good with that, and Wil had too. She wasn't into making a big deal – which would revive the story – so were content with simply suing the fuck out of them.

Having the network purchased from under them, and hearing that they were fired… that was just a nice extra.

"So… you gonna leave your show and go back to TV?" I asked, and Wil reared her head back like I was crazy.

"Hell yes," she exclaimed. "I mean, if they actually ask, you know? And, if I get to produce it myself. Make my own decisions about guests, and direction, all of that. It would be amazing. And did you *hear* that lineup? Oooh, I know Nashira Drake works with Warm Hues Theatre… I wonder if she would do something about getting *quality* theatre broadcasts on TV, to make them more accessible. That would be *so* amazing!"

I listened to her go on and on as we made our way to the restaurant, long after my interest in the topic waned. Even once she had her food, she was talking between bites – not about the prospect of what it meant for her, but excitement about the restoration of the network, and what it might mean for *other* people.

The idea of this making people happy… made *her* happy.

And as she kept going, one thought repeated in my mind.

My child couldn't be coming from a better mother.

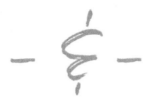

"I don't know why you dragged me up here with you," Reggie complained, peering up and down the street, keeping look out like we were on the block.

Old habits die hard, I guess.

"Moral support, nigga," I told him, then pressed the doorbell and stepped back, waiting for an answer.

I still had a key, but I'd never felt *that* comfortable to just walk, unannounced, into my mother's home. That's what it still was, to me, and probably always would be. Even though she was gone, her spirit still permeated this place, from the carefully collected pillows on the porch swing, to the neatly landscaped flowerbeds in front of the house.

The *still* neatly landscaped flowerbeds.

He was keeping the place up like she would've wanted.

I appreciated that.

I braced myself when the door swung open, unsure of how I'd be received. I hadn't called or anything, just showed up on a notable day, not knowing if I was interrupting plans or anything.

"Ramsey? Is everything okay?" Desmond asked, wearing a concerned expression as he stepped into the doorframe.

For a second, I wondered why he was asking me that, but then I remembered that we'd spoken maybe once since my mother passed, even though it had been almost a year. I would deserve it if he did, but… I hoped he wasn't holding it against me.

Truth was… it was hard to look at him, because he reminded me so much of *her*. I'd learned to deal with it when it came to my aunt, because she wasn't playing any games about seeing me at least once or twice a week anyway. With Desmond, it was easy to stay away. For one, being in the home I'd purchased for my mother was something I wasn't interested in. Period. Maybe much, much later, I would be, but for now – even today – hell no.

Second, Desmond and my mother had met and connected later in life, so it wasn't as if we'd been around each other often, until she was at her sickest. He and I got along fine, never had any issues, but we weren't… close like that. Disconnecting to avoid the pain of my memories was low hassle.

But it wasn't cool.

Even if me staying away was relieving to him for the same reason it was relieving to me, I should still make the effort. He called to check on me at least once a month, even if I didn't answer, and had made sure to congratulate me on going to the Kings. My response to that voice mail had been to send him passes – box seats to every home game the Kings played, for him and two guests.

I hadn't called back.

But here I was on his doorstep, early as hell in the morning, with Reggie and his prison muscles looking like he was my security.

"No," I told him. "Everything is fine. It's just… I know it's your birthday today… right?"

He nodded. "Yes."

"Yeah. Well… I don't know if you have plans or anything, but… I was gonna see if you wanted to go grab some breakfast or something. On me, obviously."

Desmond smiled, and nodded. "That would be great. But… who is "we"?" he asked, looking pointedly at Reggie.

"Oh, my bad. Desmond, this is Reggie –Aunt Phylicia's son."

Reggie stepped forward, extending his hand, and Desmond returned the gesture.

"Good to meet you in the sunlight, young man. Debbie spoke *very* highly of you. Talked about how you acted as Ramsey's big brother, kept him on the straight and narrow. She was incredibly fond of you."

"Heard good things about you as well," Reggie answered.

"I'll tell you guys what," Desmond said. "Instead of going out, why don't I whip up something here? I've got all the ingredients, and you've been promising almost three years to let me fix you some of my world-famous hashbrowns."

"I like hashbrowns," Reggie spoke up, and I gave him a look. He knew goddamned well that going into this house to sit down and chill wasn't the plan, but now that he'd said something, Desmond took it and ran, as if it were settled.

And I mean… I guess it was.

I glared at the back of Reggie's head as I strolled through my mother's house for the first time since she passed away. The chances that I was going to break down and crawl into a corner somewhere to cry were admittedly low, but still... I just didn't feel right.

I didn't feel comforted by the feeling of *her* throughout the house. The pictures he still had up, the furniture she'd picked that was still there, my grandmother's ceramic dishes still on display behind glass-front cabinets... the shit didn't make me feel closer to her. It pissed me off, that she wasn't still here. It was fucked up, but... I kept it to myself, sitting down at the counter beside Reggie as Desmond started pulling out ingredients.

"So... I see you've got yourself a lady friend," he said as he pulled out a cutting board and knife to start chopping vegetables. "The young lady you were working with, Wilhelmina."

"Just "Wil", but yeah." Manners wouldn't let me stay seated to watch, and my subtle shove to Reggie's shoulder wouldn't let him stay seated either. At my request, Desmond got another knife, and Reggie and I went to work helping cut veggies while he scrambled sausage in a skillet.

"You two serious? Planning to get married?"

My hands slowed over the onion I was chopping. "No, not yet. We haven't really talked about it. But she's uh... she's pregnant."

Desmond whistled. "Even more reason to put a ring on that woman's finger, while you have the chance. I'm telling you... don't make the same mistake I did."

I put the knife down completely. "Which was?"

"Hold on a second."

He took the skillet he was using off of the heat, then left the kitchen. When he came back, he put a tiny velvet box on the counter in front of me.

It was going to stay closed if he was expecting *me* to open that thing.

"At first, I kept putting it off because I wanted to be sure," he started, gripping the edge of the counter. His head was up, but he wasn't looking at me, or Reggie. When I followed his gaze across the open kitchen, into the living room, and realized he was looking at a wall of family pictures, I turned my gaze back to the pile of vegetables.

"Then I got sure, and I put it off because I wanted to be sure *she* would be sure. And then we got there, and she got sick again, and I didn't want to put something else on her mind. And then, I wanted us

268

to be able to celebrate properly. I just *knew*... she was going to get better, or at least... have a good day. But it wasn't happening. She was getting worse, and worse, and... then she gave up. And *that's* when I asked, because I thought maybe..." he stopped to clear his throat, and I closed my eyes, wanting badly to escape this story, but at the same time, wanting to give him the respect of listening.

"I thought it would change her mind."

I shook my head, and opened my eyes. She'd never told me about this – this was outside of my scope, as her son – but still, I knew how this particular part went. "It didn't change her mind."

"It did not." He pushed out a sigh, then released his hold on the counter to return the skillet of scrambled sausage to the heating element. "And I have been regretting the fact that I waited since then. Now I'm not suggesting you run out and buy a ring, but..." he stopped, letting out another breath. "Ramsey, I'm not your father, and I came into your mother's life a little on the late side to take on a role like that, or attempt to be that type of figure to you. But if you don't take this old man's advice on *anything* else, listen to me on this – when you *know*? *Act.* Don't let that woman spend a single day not knowing what she meant to you, because... you never know when it's going to be one day too late. And trust me – that's not the type of thing you want haunting you."

"Damn." I'd forgotten Reggie was there, but now I looked up and across the counter, to find his chin cupped in his hand, attention rapt on Desmond. "My bad for cursing, but... that's real. I was already married to my lady when I got locked up, but... she'd been begging me to stop doing what I was doing, especially once she was pregnant a second time. I wouldn't listen though. It was always one more day, one more day, even though I knew she looked at it like I was disrespecting her, and putting the family at risk, but she... she didn't get that *that* was the only way I'd ever taken care of her, taken care of them. She just didn't want me locked up, or hurt, didn't want somebody to hurt one of the kids to get to me." Reg stopped for a second, running his tongue over his lips. "I never said this to anybody, but... she was gonna leave. Right after you graduated high school... maybe the day after. She packed up bags for her and the kids, and told me I had to make a choice. And I made the right one – I chose her. Chose my family. And then... feds raided the house the next day."

"Too late," Desmond said, and Reg nodded.

"Yep. Too late."

I didn't say anything as they continued talking, but I absorbed it all. No, I wasn't feeling any need to rush out and buy Wil a ring based on this conversation, but just like I'd taken lessons from Reggie in the past, I was listening.

When they finally moved to another topic, I joined them, but it never left the back of my mind. By the time me and Reg left, and climbed back in my truck to head off, the course of action was firmly cemented in my head.

I wasn't ready to take my relationship with Wil there quite yet, but when I *was* ready? I wouldn't hesitate.

Wil

I tugged the brim of my baseball cap even lower as I rounded the end of the grocery aisle to go to the next, bobbing my head to the music in my ears as I went along. It was the middle of the night, but I was wide awake, putting a little wind in my hips as Bruno Mars sang about sex by the fire at night.

I wanted hot Cheetos and ice cream, and maybe a few peaches, and definitely a can of Pringles. And maybe a candy bar. And a case of sparkling water. And some cookies. And since Ramsey was off in San Francisco for a game, I had to retrieve it all myself.

Which was fine, I guess.

I tucked my hands into the front pockets of my hoodie as I stood in front of the freezer doors, scrutinizing the flavors from the outside before I subjected myself to the cold. Late October was cold enough here already.

I settled on a pint of pistachio-flavored gelato, then headed toward the checkout, stopping at a big glass donut display in the middle of the store. Donuts were one of the few things *not* on my mental list, but that didn't mean I wasn't about to have one. I was pulling a piece of wax paper from the dispenser to grab it when I heard my name.

270

Immediately, I swallowed a groan.

I'd hoped that the late hour – and baseball hat, and hoodie – would shield me from running into anyone that might recognized my face. And maybe, if someone *did* recognize me, they would notice that I clearly didn't want to be bothered. But that didn't seem to be the case.

Whoever it was said it again, and this time it registered to me that it was a man. A strange man, calling my name, in the middle of the night at the grocery store… suddenly Ramsey trying to convince me I needed security didn't seem quite so dramatic.

Pulling my earbuds out, I slowly turned around, bracing myself to have to smile for a picture or autograph – and hoping it stopped at just that. But when I turned around, the sight that greeted me wasn't a fan at all.

It was Darius.

Standing beside Jessica.

No.

Holding Jessica's hand. Fingers intertwined, and seeming to grow tighter as my gaze lingered there. But I brought it back to his face, running my tongue over my dry lips.

"Hello, Darius."

"Hey, Wil," Jessica said, inserting herself – something she was obviously an expert at doing. I paid her exactly the amount of my attention she deserved – none – and put the wax paper I'd grabbed in the trash so that I could grab the handle of my cart, and move along.

I didn't need the donut anyway.

"Wil, wait up," Darius asked, but I didn't because fuck them. I'd been having a good night, editing my latest interview, and going over my pitch to the new WAWG network, so that I would be ready whenever, if ever, they called.

Instead of catching the hint though, he jogged ahead of me, catching the side of my basket to essentially *make* me stop.

"What the hell do you want, Darius?" I asked, annoyed. I got especially annoyed when his eyes went to my basket, surveying the contents instead of answering my question.

"This is an interesting combination. Cookies and hot Cheetos?"

"I'm babysitting," I lied, and his eyebrows went up, looking around me for the children I *obviously* wasn't watching.

A second later, those eyebrows dropped, in understanding, and he stepped closer – too close, all in my personal space. "Wil... you're...?"

"I swear to God, if my business gets out, I will make you regret the day you laid eyes on me," I warned, finger in his face. "And you are *way* too close to me right now."

Raising his hands, Darius took a few steps back, and I could see Jessica glaring suspiciously at him from a couple of feet away.

"I don't care what you do anymore," I told him. "But your little girlfriend has already proved she can't hold water – I suggest you not tell her this. I followed my mother's advice about you, and didn't do anything petty for revenge –"

"Closet full of chocolate covered shoes."

"Didn't do anything *else* petty, fine," I conceded. "But God knows you deserved more. In any case, my *point is* – I left you the hell alone. If I hear a single whisper of a rumor about this before I reveal it myself, my *own* way – I will *never* leave you alone. Ramsey will never leave you alone. My parents. My family. My friends. Hell, I bet I could even get the team owner on board – he *loves* Ramsey. I will make *sure* you suffer. Keep your mouth shut."

He shook his head. "I'm not going to say anything. I wouldn't. Not when I know how much you... how much you wanted... *this*," he said, with a distinct thickness to his voice that let me know he was right on the verge of tearing up. "Wow. How far—can I ask that? How far along you are?"

I swallowed hard. "Um... sixteen weeks."

"That's further than—"

"Yeah."

"Congratulations," he said, with a little smile that actually seemed genuine, if a little sad. "Do you know if it's a boy, or a girl?"

I shook my head. "No. We decided it'll be a surprise. We'll find out at our baby shower."

He cleared his throat. "We. So... you and Ramsey... that's really not just a PR thing?"

"No," I said, letting out a dry laugh. "It's not. Go figure, you know? That it took finding out that you were a cheating liar to finally get pregnant, by somebody who *actually* gives a shit."

"Wil, you know that's not—"

272

"Maybe not, Darius, but what does it matter? Why are we doing this right now?" I asked, frowning. "Why are you even in Connecticut at all? You know what? No, don't answer that. But on the off chance you run into me again? Keep walking."

"Wil—"

"*Keep walking.*" I put my hands back on my basket and walked away, relieved that he didn't follow me this time. As soon as I was out of their line of sight, I took out my phone and navigated to Chloe's name in my contact list, hesitating when I glanced at the top corner of the screen and saw the time.

Shit.

Instead of calling, I sent a text, and debated on sending Ramsey one too, but decided against it. Ramsey was liable to charter a private jet back to Connecticut to kick Darius' ass for daring to speak to me at all, so telling him about this conversation probably wasn't a good idea.

Just like the fact that he still hadn't mentioned running into Lena – sometimes, it wasn't even worth getting your partner upset if you knew *you* were in the clear. Still, it was risky – I'd been a little pissed hearing about the run-in after the fact, even though he'd done nothing wrong.

So maybe I'd tell him tomorrow.

Definitely not tonight.

Honestly, more pressing on my mind now was what I *didn't* feel in the aftermath of that conversation with Darius. I'd managed to avoid him when I went to sign the final paperwork on the sale of the house, and hadn't had to see him in person at all since that day at the house. Occasionally, I saw him on commercials for his show, and in the last few weeks, in ads for a high-end men's fragrance after I'd been searching for a gift for Ramsey online. At first, it was disconcerting to be on social media and randomly see his face, but I'd quickly come to feel… nothing.

And that was the case tonight, too.

To be clear, it was still *fuck him*, and her too, for what the two of them had done. It wasn't okay, there weren't any excuses for it, and I could live forever without interacting with either of them again.

But I didn't feel… *destroyed,* like I had before. I barely felt angry, and only a little bit disgusted. In fact, my strongest reaction was to the possibility of my pregnancy being revealed to the world before I was ready for it, not the fact that I'd been faced with the man whose betrayal had me flat on my face six or seven months ago.

Whenever it was.

Too much had changed since then for me to dwell on it.

That realization made me smile.

I didn't really care anymore.

Okay… so maybe I still cared some, evidenced by the fact that I'd actually been a little moved over his emotional reaction to my pregnancy, but I wasn't rushing out of the store to go cry in my car, and that *meant* something. I was cool. I was relaxed. All I *really* cared about was whether or not my ice cream had started to melt dealing with that fool.

It was *such* a yummy feeling.

So yummy that I practically skipped to the checkout lane, and then to the car with my bags. I locked myself inside, and then pulled my emergency spoon from my purse to dig into my ice cream early. While I was sitting there, my phone chimed, and I dug it out of my purse to check who it was. When I read the name on the screen, I smiled.

"Hopefully you're sleeping peacefully right now, but it's just past eleven here, and you just popped in my mind. Naked. You're fine as hell, girl. – R. Bishop."

I giggled, then stuck another spoonful of ice cream in my mouth before I texted back. *"I'm actually wide awake, eating pistachio ice cream. Tell me more about how fine as hell I am."*

"Nah, can't have you getting a big head. What are you doing up? – R. Bishop."

"Was editing. Ran to the store for snacks. Sitting in the car now."

"Did you at least have Dre go with you? He didn't travel with me, and I purposely set it up so he'd be available to you. – R. Bishop."

"You already know the answer to that."

"Get home. Call me when you pull up. – R. Bishop."

For reasons I couldn't seem to pinpoint, though I'd given it a ton of thought, it didn't really bother me when Ramsey got bossy. Actually… it kinda turned me on, but these days, so did most everything else. Instead of arguing, I put my ice cream down and

274

obliged him, calling as soon I pulled my car into the garage at the back of the townhouse.

"Are you happy now?" I asked, as I settled into my bed, snacks at the ready beside me. Now that I was home, video-editing didn't seem nearly as appealing as my pillows and comforter.

"Now that you're safe inside your apartment, instead of out in the middle of the night? Yes, I am." Ramsey's warm chuckle crackled through the phone, making me close my eyes. "Must you be so damn stressful?"

I fake-gasped. "Me?! Stressful?! No idea where you got that from." I reached over to flip on the lamp, then put the phone on speaker and opened my camera app, snapping a picture that I sent to him. "See? Look at that innocent face."

The phone was quiet for a second, while he opened the picture I texted him, and I bit down on my lip to keep myself from laughing as I thought about what he would soon see. I'd swapped my baseball cap for a peacock print headscarf, and my hoodie and sweat pants – and the underwear underneath – for nothing but a Connecticut Kings tee shirt. A moment later, he laughed.

"This is adorable, Champ," he said. "You look comfortable as hell. Eyes all sleepy."

"I *am* comfortable as hell. Now that I'm actually in the bed, I am *not* wide awake anymore."

"Yeah, it's damn near three in the morning there, so I can imagine. I'm not going to keep you, just needed to hear you get in safely."

I smiled. "Your diligence is appreciated. And I saw that work you put in at the game tonight. 96 yards. Not bad."

"Could've been better."

"Oh whatever," I laughed. "Hate on yourself on your own time – *I'm* proud. You helped secure that win, let me celebrate you fool."

He chuckled. "Fine, *fine*. Hey… before I let you go… did your belly pop anymore?"

That question sent immediate warmth through me, as I remembered how excited he'd gotten upon waking up two mornings ago to realized that I'd finally "popped"

"No," I said, hating that I had to disappoint him. "It's still just a little…*boop*. You want a picture?"

"Would you?" he asked, and my face damn near split open from grinning so hard.

"Yeah, of course."

I extricated myself from the bed and went into the bathroom to stand in front of the mirror. Turning to the side, I pulled my shirt up to just below my breasts, and I snapped a picture of my reflection.

"Done," I said, hitting the "send" button before I flipped out the light, and went back to the bed.

"Got it," he answered a moment later, then went quiet again for a second. "I don't know... it looks a little more pronounced to me."

"Nah, I ate a pint of ice cream on the way home. That's all that is," I laughed.

For a moment, he laughed too, and then... "Wait a minute... you aren't wearing any panties in this picture."

"Oh, would you look at the time? Gotta go," I sang, then pulled the phone away from my ear, giggling as I ended the call.

"You ain't right. – R. Bishop." was the text I got a moment later, making me laugh again.

"Or am I ALWAYS right?" I shot back, a response I was sure made him smile.

"This question seems like a setup. Good night, Champ. – R. Bishop"

"So the answer is yes then? Good night to you too."

Fifteen

Wil

November 2017

Where in the world did the last few weeks go?

I found myself wondering that more and more often lately, and the feeling was only intensified by the arrival of a notification from the pregnancy app on my phone.

At 18weeks, your baby is about the size of a sweet potato.

How cute!

You may start to notice an increase in food cravings – May?! – *especially for specific, and sometimes strange, things. Outside of your cravings, make healthy choices so you don't feel guilty about that candy bar, or extra slice of pizza.*

I was supposed to feel guilty about it?

You may or may not be "showing" much if this is your first pregnancy, or if you started your pregnancy at a high level of fitness. Every woman is different, but don't worry – the signature "baby bump" is coming your way soon!

My hand went to my barely-there baby bump as soon as I read those words. I didn't fall in *either* of those categories, but any further "popping" of my belly was certainly taking it's sweet time. As Darius had reminded me in the store a few weeks ago, I'd never made it beyond week 13, so all of this was new to me. Sometimes, I still had to fight the overwhelming fear of waking up without a baby, but this app, as silly as it seemed, was one of the things that helped ground me.

I nodded to myself as I read the list of symptoms I "may" be feeling right now.

Restlessness, swollen hands/feet, cramps, backaches, trouble sleeping.

A panicked call to Dr. Cho just a few nights ago had led to me taking the advice to sleep on my side instead of my back, to accommodate my uterus, which seemed to be expanding inside, just not outward.

"It's a common thing," she'd assured me. *"You're experiencing a perfectly healthy pregnancy."*

Dr. Cho was *definitely* on the unwritten, *"Bitch, calm down"* list I had to mentally tap into sometimes.

You're almost halfway through your pregnancy, which means one of your most important prenatal appointments is coming. You'll have to give blood, and you'll probably have the advanced ultrasound where your provider will measure your amniotic fluid levels, check the location of your placenta, and make sure your baby's growth, development, and heart rate are all on track. Don't be scared! This is an important step to make sure you're prepared for everything your baby might need.

*If you haven't been thinking about your birth plan, now is the time to start! You'll want a chance to change your mind, and change it back, and plan accordingly **before** you go into labor.*

That was another thing. I *was* already thinking about that, among other things. I'd drastically underestimated just how busy Ramsey would be, especially now that he'd been performing at a high enough level to start taking meetings about potential endorsements. Add *that* to constant practices, meetings with the coaches, meeting with his manager, meetings with Chloe, flights, and then the actual *games*. And at some point, the man had to sleep, and tend to the other people he knew too. Even though he rarely slept at the apartment the

278

team had set up for him here in Connecticut, opting instead to stay at the townhouse with me, I felt like I didn't have... *enough* of him.

Perils of dating a professional athlete.

And, hell, speaking of those living arrangements, we were going to have to do something. I had no real desire to live in New York, but in terms of space and security, Ramsey's condo in Harlem was more practical than the townhouse. If it came down to it, of course I'd live there, but the truth was, I wanted us to find a place that was *ours.* Together.

Because that ended up going *so* well for me last time.

I wasn't "supposed" to be at the nesting period quite yet, but my urge to start creating a space for this baby was strong. However, the niggling feeling to not get too far ahead of myself was equally strong – if not *stronger.* So I didn't inundate Ramsey, or my friends, or my mother, with details of the elephant themed yellow, gray, and aqua nursery I was building in my head. I kept it to myself, often abandoning actual work to dive into the far reaches of the internet, fawning and gasping over DIY projects I would never actually do.

And *none* of that was considering the fact that I was busy as hell myself.

It turned out that the mention of the new WAWG coming to me about a show wasn't just a rumor. When they called, I answered, and was on the verge of signing a new contract for what was essentially an expansion of what I was already doing on my own. Same name, pretty much the same format, just with better cameras and a bigger budget, and the chance to add "producer" and "show runner" credentials to my growing resume.

While I *didn't* like that Chloe had advised me to disclose my pregnancy to them, in the first meeting. There were laws that protected women against pregnancy discrimination, but they weren't strong enough, it was hard to prove, and quite honestly, the people in charge just did whatever the hell they wanted, and paid the fine later. But Chloe assured me it wouldn't be like that – that not only would the informational be kept confidential, but it would be a positive character point for me, in the eyes of people who were working in the best interest of their investment. Disclosing my pregnancy said that I was honest, vs how *not* saying anything, knowing I was expected to work, could be seen as sneaky.

As it turned out, she was right – they appreciated me being upfront about it. They actually offered solutions like using women who were rising stars in the sports news world, and even some female athletes, as guest hosts in my post-birth absence.

It felt like a blessing.

But, as blessings go, it wasn't something I could just sit with, passively. There was work involved with developing the show, not to mention the fact that I couldn't let the current iteration of it just fall apart.

And then, there was my *own* social life.

I still had friends and family to maintain relationships with, but now, as part of the "Ramsey "Sledgehammer" Bishop" package, a new world was presented to me. I'd already loosely known Jordan to be Ramsey's friend, but now that they were on the same team – and Ramsey and I were together – his presence was becoming more of a staple, and so was Trent Bailey's. With the two of them came their partners. Even though Cole and I had already started to grow closer through our Naima connection, it was still new to be invited out together, or to be invited to the Bailey's home for dinner, to sit out on their back porch and talk, on a *social* level.

But at least those relationships were easy breezy.

Tonight's dinner?

Not so much.

I was supposed to be getting ready to have dinner at Eli Richardson's home. Instead, I was standing at my bathroom counter in nothing but a towel, reading pregnancy app notifications. I was... procrastinating.

But, we couldn't be late, not for the owner of the team. Looking in the mirror, I smoothed my eyebrows with my fingers, then scrunched my face, trying to decide if my features were spreading yet. I didn't even know if it was supposed to happen this soon, or if it would happen at all, but I was constantly looking for the ways that pregnancy was changing my body.

Dropping my towel, I examined my breasts first, running my fingers over the nearly imperceptible wine-colored veins that had appeared as they swelled in size. Lower, starting at my ribs, I could just, *juuust* barely see a line starting there too, and followed it with my fingers. Down my stomach, over my belly button, slightly wider as it led down to my pubic bone. I only knew it was there because I was looking for it, having seen it on other pregnant bellies before.

I'd *longed* for this line. It wasn't fully formed yet, but it would, maybe in a few more weeks, getting darker and darker. Things like that excited me, but still.

Don't get too excited.

I cupped my stomach on both sides, caressing the beginnings of my baby bump. As I stood there, I felt a shift in the air behind me. Looking up at the mirror, I met Ramsey's gaze through his reflection, standing in the open bathroom door.

"What are you doing?" he asked, stepping forward to wrap me in his arms. He was already dressed, mostly – he only needed shoes, belt, tie, and jacket, and to finish buttoning his shirt.

I closed my eyes as his lips, then teeth, met the back of my neck. "Just… looking," I told him, as his hands moved to rest on my belly. "I'm almost ready. I'm finished with my hair and makeup, just need to put my dress on."

"For what though?" he asked, drawing a moan from my lips as one of his hands slid down, pushing between my legs. I was already wet – was *always* wet, these days – and he groaned against my ear as his middle finger slipped into me, easily. His palm blanketed the rest of that hyper-responsive area in heat. He was only moving that one finger, exploring a place he already knew well, but just the skin-to-skin sensation was enough to have me throbbing.

"*Ramsey*," I whimpered, as his other hand came up to cup one of my breasts in a gentle squeeze as his thumb brushed my nipple – so sensitive now that even such simple contact sent goosebumps racing over my skin. "We can't be late for this dinner."

"Mmm. Guess you'd better come fast then, Champ."

I gasped as he ground the heel of his hand against my clit, creating a delicious friction that almost made me do exactly that. His teeth sinking into my neck distracted me though, enough that I rocked against his hand, trying to recreate the feeling he'd interrupted.

He laughed at me, withdrawing his touch to scoop me into his bulky arms, carrying me to the bed. He spread me out, propping me on a couple of pillows so I wouldn't be laying flat, and then stripped – I got my chance to laugh at him in the way he carefully laid out his clothes across the chair in the corner so he wouldn't have to iron again.

There was nothing funny about his mouth on me though.

Teasing, barely there touches of his tongue to my nipples, an act that filled me with a pleasurable sort of rage. An act that had me flooding, and fuming, at the same time.

"Ramsey, *please.*"

"*Shhhh.*"

He quieted me with a hand caressing my face, his thumb resting against my lips as he closed his mouth over one of my nipples. A gentle, perfect suck, and then a long, lazy drag of his tongue that was so good it made my stomach contract, and cave inward. He did it again, on the other side, and I brought my hands to his head, keeping him there.

Well… trying.

There was zero effort to him taking his lips further south, trailing kisses along the line I'd caressed just minutes ago. There was no rush to it, either. Slow, deliberate, loving kisses, especially once he reached the subtle curve of my bump, made even smaller by me being on my back.

It wasn't all sweetness though – his eyes were hooded with lust as he pushed his fingers into me again, staring past my little bump to look me right in the face as he ran his tongue between my lower lips. My head fell back when he stretched my legs wide, breaking eye contact to bury his face between my legs. His hands went under me, gripping my ass cheeks as he lifted me up for better, deeper access, circling his tongue in places that still made me blush, but also… made me *scream.*

His name, nickname, field position, all of it fell from my lips with abandon, because it felt just that damn good. Something about the hormones coursing through me made every touch more electric, every sensation more vivid, everything just… *better.* Which was saying a lot, because the sex had always been amazing, but this was *different.*

My throat was raw, legs weak, core throbbing with the aftershocks of orgasm by the time he lowered me, then moved to position himself between my legs. I kept my eyes closed, anxiously awaiting the sweet pressure of him inside of me, but it didn't come.

He hooked one of my legs over his arm then wrapped his free hand around his dick. My halfway-sitting-up position gave me a perfect view of what he was doing – only adding to the pleasure that coursed through me as he rubbed it over my clit, teasing me again.

"Ramse—*mmm!*"

Before I could even say anything, he'd dipped his thumb into me and then put it my mouth to quiet me – so fast that he *had* to have been planning to do it as soon as I tried to speak. He smirked as I scowled at him, but a moment later I was moaning around his thumb as he finally sank into me.

He only managed a few strokes before he flipped us over, pulling me on top of him. As soon as I was firmly grounded, his hands went to my hips. He guided me as I rode him, then moved those hands to my breasts. I pushed everything out of my head, except how good it felt to be filled like this, how hot his hands were, the skill of his fingers as they worked my nipples, worked *me* into a frenzy.

I closed my eyes, rolling my hips as I moved up and down, reveling in the tension building in his thighs, the tightness of his shoulders as I gripped them for leverage.

"*So fucking **good**,*" he growled, burying his fingers in my hair to pull my face down to his. He ruined my hair and my makeup at the same time as our lips crashed together, but I couldn't bring myself to care. His tongue pushed into my mouth, caressing and exploring as he moved his hips, meeting my movements with upward strokes of his own. We were so close together that his pelvis ground against mine, creating the friction that sent me galloping into an orgasm so strong that for a few seconds, I couldn't see or hear.

He was still moving as my senses filtered back to me, his strokes forcing my climax to go on, and on, and on, rolling over me in waves until he finally slammed into me one last time, with a ragged groan.

We laid there like that for several minutes, sweating and panting and trying to fall into a natural breathing pattern again. And... we did. With him still inside of me, still hard, my inhales and exhales slowly... synced with his. His hands came up, wrapping around me and resting against my back. My head was against his chest, and the strong, steady thump of his heartbeat was so soothing that I closed my eyes, not caring that we had somewhere we were supposed to be.

This was... peace.

December 2017

I felt like I was walking on eggshells – completely foreign territory for me, when dealing with Ramsey. I'd known it was coming, and had called myself being mentally prepared. But he'd been cool all last week. We'd done our big appointment for the baby two weeks ago, got great results back from all the testing, with a positive report about the baby's health. He was still on board with not finding out the sex, even though it was written down in an envelope that I would give to Naima and Soriyah, who were planning my shower.

He was *happy.*

But today… he wasn't.

He had a plane to get on, in just a few hours. He'd been offered the time off, but insisted he wanted to go. It was an important game. The Kings were contenders for the championship game, and he wanted to be there. I didn't know where his head would be for tomorrow's game in St. Louis, but it wasn't with me now, and it *definitely* wouldn't be on the field, not at this rate.

It would be with his mother.

I hated for him to be like this. He hadn't accepted my offer of anything to eat, had been ignoring his phone all morning. It wasn't even in the bedroom, where he was. He'd left it in the kitchen hours ago, when he got up for a glass of water that was still sitting on the bedside table, untouched.

He'd declined my offer to bring it to him.

On the other side of the counter, it lit up again, moving across the granite surface as it lit up with a call. This time, I got up and peeked at the screen, smiling a little when I saw Clayton's name. I loved that his friends and family were all reaching out to him, even if he wasn't receptive right now.

It was what they *should* do, on the anniversary of his mother's birth, and death.

Clayton's attempted call ended, and the phone went back to it's normal screen. For a second, my eyes narrowed, but then I smiled as I realized that the image on his "lock screen" was one of him and me,

284

one I'd snapped before we headed out to that twenty week appointment. I was stretched out across him while he lounged on the couch, holding the phone above me.

I *loved* that picture of us, and apparently so did he. Social media had loved it too – I'd actually posted it across my accounts, getting a little kick out of the fact that to me, I was *obviously* pregnant in the shot. But it was still a secret.

Not for much longer though.

I only had a few more weeks, if I was lucky, that I could hide underneath bulky sweaters. Our little gummy bear was slowly but surely shifting my belly outward, past what we could pass off as simple "happy weight". Soon, the world would know I was having a baby.

As if it could read my mind, I flinched as I felt a little jab to the inside of my belly.

I'd already experienced – and cried my eyes out about – the "flutters" of a moving baby, for the first time. That was weeks ago, and since then, the movements were becoming more and more steady, but baby had been shy about moving for anybody except me, growing still whenever anybody else touched my stomach.

But as I looked down at my belly, I watched as, very subtly, he or she… stretched out or something, and then flipped, moving so vigorously that I actually *saw* my belly moving. When it stayed lopsided, I hopped up from my place at the counter, rushing upstairs to the bedroom.

Ramsey was in bed with his eyes closed, but he wasn't asleep. His eyes popped open when I practically dived on top of him, grabbing his hands to put them on my stomach.

"Wil, what in the world—"

"Just…*shh*," I urged, smiling at him. He looked so drained, so wounded, so… not himself. Silently, I prayed, asking God to give him peace to get through today, and the day after that, and the next one. Ramsey's expression shifted from confusion to annoyance, but I held his hands, urging him to just wait.

A moment later, I felt that familiar thump again. And then again. And again. And then Ramsey's eyes went wide as my stomach shifted under his hands, like the baby was changing position again.

"*Holy shit*," he whispered, staring between me and my belly with a look of wonderment that brought the tears I'd been fighting all day to my eyes. "That's… that's the baby?"

I nodded, smiling at him as I took my hands off his to wipe my face. "Yeah."

"That was…*holy shit*," he chuckled, giving me a grin – a beautiful sight I hadn't experienced all day. "That was amaz— there it is again! That's what that is, right? That thumping?"

"Yeah," I laughed, wiping away a fresh stream of tears as I tried to hold it together. "I don't know why it's so active today."

His big hands caressed my stomach. "I don't either. But God knows I needed this."

He said that just above whisper, so low that I wasn't sure the words were meant for me. But it struck me so much that I lowered my hands, placing them on top of his again. "Maybe that's why. *Because* you need it."

He kept his gaze trained on my stomach, and didn't say anything. I started to leave it alone, but then something else occurred to me.

"Do you remember telling me that your mother wanted me and you together, so I could have her grandbabies?"

Then, Ramsey looked up, staring at me like he *hadn't* remembered, until just then. But he nodded. "Yeah."

"So if you think about it, that means this baby is… a physical manifestation of her dreams for you. These movements, on today of all days… her and God working together to remind you." I took my hands from his to cup his face. "She hasn't left you, baby. She's right here." I moved to touch his chest, over his heart. "And right *here*," I added, touching my belly. "In the history, and bloodline of our child. She's still here."

For a second, he just stared at me. But then he sat up, wrapping his arms around me so tight it almost hurt, but it was nothing I couldn't take. I returned his embrace, closing my eyes as he rested his head in the swell of my breasts. The moisture that slowly soaked my shirt brought tears to my eyes too, but I forced myself not to burst into sobs. This wasn't my moment – it was his. If he felt safe enough, secure enough, to have it with me… I was going to let him.

After several minutes had passed, he looked up. There weren't any tears in his eyes, but they were red, and I just… *knew.* He was still feeling raw.

"Thank you for those words, Champ. I needed that," he said, and I smiled.

I opened my mouth to say *you're welcome*, but what came out instead was, "I love you."

His eyes didn't go wide. No raised brow, nothing except a subtle brightening of his expression as he pushed forth a grin. Because he wasn't surprised. My quiet admission was simply a statement of a truth we both already knew.

He grabbed my chin, pulling my mouth to place a gentle kiss on my lips.

"I love you too."

RAMSEY

January 2018

"You're *killing* me here, Ramsey. Seriously. Me and your money. We're dead. Done for. Finito."

I chuckled into the line as I peeked up the stairs, making sure Wil was still occupied, trying on all 32 – or so it seemed – pairs of maternity jeans she owned.

"Tariq, stop being dramatic. I'm an ideal client, bruh."

He scoffed. "You *used* to be ideal. Now we're paying for baby doctors, Clayton called me about your budget for a house, and now you want to know if you can spend *how much*?"

"It's not cars and gold chains, damn," I laughed. "Cut me some slack."

"Cut *me* some slack," he countered, with amusement in his tone. "You know I'm just giving you a hard time… mostly. Your wealth *is* still in recovery from the costs for your mother's care. You're *okay*. I just want you to be mindful. You sure you can't wait until that SuperBowl bonus check comes through?"

I shook my head. "That's not even guaranteed yet, haven't finished playoffs. And even if it was… money is already spent. "

"Don't remind me. Please don't call me *after* you've written the check next time," Tariq complained, and it was easy for me to visualize him shaking his head. Tariq Evans was usually laid back – when it wasn't about the money of the athletes he worked with. He'd been my financial advisor for not-nearly long enough. I didn't have the sense to have somebody managing things for me at first, but I was glad to have learned that lesson, and gotten Tariq working on it for me before it was too late.

"Got it," I told him. "But I gotta let you go, so we can head out. I want to make it there before everyone else does."

"Okay, man. And good luck today. Let me know how it goes. And keep your checkbook in your damn pocket, please."

I laughed as we got off the phone, and then went upstairs to grab Wil, who I found pulling a thick sweater-dress over her head.

"What happened?" I asked. "You gave up on the jeans?"

She nodded. "I gave *all* the way up on the jeans. They are apparently *not* in the plans for me, not today. I'm ready now though," she said, fluffing out her hair. "Did I hear you on the phone?"

"Yeah, that was Tariq."

She raised an eyebrow. "Your finance guy? Is everything okay? It wasn't about today, is it? Because I told you I could—"

"Will you hush, woman?" She tried her best to hold a scowl, but it melted as soon as I pulled her close, slipping my hands under her dress to caress her stomach. At six months pregnant, her belly was well pronounced – so much that it was damn near impossible to camouflage. Because of it, she'd been stuck in the house the last few weeks, even going to the length of conducting an interview via Skype, which really wasn't ideal for her.

After today though, she wouldn't have to hide.

"I hope you aren't trying to start anything," she said, in a low, seductive voice as my fingertips brushed the lacy edge of whatever panties she was wearing.

288

I put my mouth to her ear. "Why you always think I'm *starting something.*"

"Because you are."

"Or maybe you're just always *wanting* something, how 'bout that?" I teased, cupping her belly again. "I'm just seeing if the baby is awake, get your mind out of the gutter."

"Only because we really do have somewhere to be."

She slipped away from me, sitting down on the edge of the bed to put on her shoes, and I just watched her. She was *so* chill lately – not really stressing about the baby, not worried about paparazzi, none of that. I knew she was busy a lot, which kept her going too much to worry about outside shit, but something about her whole vibe, since the pregnancy, was just different.

Happiness.

Something nudged the back of my mind, implanting that word. And maybe that's what it was – she was just, *finally,* back to happy again, which was the natural set point of the woman I'd long considered my friend. It radiated off of her, even her appearance. Her eyes were brighter, smile was bigger. And even the changes the pregnancy had brought to her body, I hadn't heard her complain, not even once. She'd expressed frustration about the fit of her clothes, but it was always *this is too small* not *I'm too big.* She'd embraced it, and… I was glad.

Pregnancy was sexy as hell on Wil.

Her teasing about *always starting something* was based on the truth. I'd already had a hard time keeping my hands off her, and it was only amplified now. Luckily for me, her appetite seemed to match mine, and she was always down. Today though… we couldn't act on those urges.

At least not until later.

For now, we had to get up to my place in Harlem. We walked inside, and were alone for maybe five minutes before the doorbell chimed, and it seemed like it didn't *stop* chiming for the next hour as we let in stylists and makeup artists and a hair stylist, and photographer and crew, and whoever else decided to show up, apparently. It was early for a maternity shoot, but this was important to Wil, and after what she'd been through to have this baby, there was nothing that would make me deny her the opportunity to announce her pregnancy in style.

Besides – if she decided she wanted to do another one later… we were doing another one later.

For now though, I hung back as they got shots that were just of her – surrounded by multicolor rose petals in my oversized tub, in a regal gown in front of the big windows. Then, there were ones of me and her, with her belly exposed in one of my button-ups as we relaxed in bed. And *then*, what I considered the "fun" shots – both of us in "Bishop" jerseys, in front of a solid black backdrop. I was seated in a throne – that I didn't know or care where the photographer had found, but the shit was *fresh* – with my helmet hanging off the side. Wil was in my lap, still done up all glamorous, but with stripes of eye black at the top of her cheeks, just because we were corny, and I didn't care, cause my lady was happy.

Her belly was exposed, and she was wearing a crown that suited her nicely. Through the miracle of some kind of cosmetic glue, her baby bump was wearing a little crown too – gender neutral, since we didn't know yet.

Chloe was at the ready, with instructions for the photographer – once he got this shot, it needed to go to her social media team immediately. We'd already approved the caption she wanted to use when it was posted to mine and Wil's social media accounts.

"Watch the Throne."

Wil was absolutely giddy when we finally got the thumbs up. It was a weight off her back that we'd no longer have to hide the pregnancy from the world.

She jumped up off my lap, making the camera crew laughed as she danced to the music that was pumping in the background, looking absolutely silly with that crown stuck to her stomach.

"Come here," I told her, not standing up. Instead, I pushed myself out of my seat and down to the floor, on one knee in front of her. She'd glanced away, her attention grabbed by the sight of her father on the other side of the room. While she was distracted, I snagged the black velvet box I'd tucked behind me in the chair.

"Ramsey… what is going on?" she asked, as the rest of our family and friends came into view, after sneaking in while we were doing the other shot. When she looked back to find me on one knee, her hands flew up to her mouth.

I hope to God I'm not about to embarrass myself.

"Wil… I love you. You know that right?"

Her eyes filled with tears as she nodded. "Yes. I love you too."

"Well... a very wise man told me that when I knew... I shouldn't hesitate. This is me not hesitating," I said, opening the box to show her the 4 carat, cushion-cut diamond, set into an etched rose gold ring that had Tariq ready to cry earlier in the morning when he found out I'd pulled the trigger on it. "Wil, I'm not... a wealthy man. There are certain things I can't give you right now, but I can promise you – neither you nor our child will ever lack anything you need. I love the way you carry yourself, your passion for your career. I love that you love sports, and you're big on family, and you're an *amazing* friend. I know for the last few months we've been more than that, but the friend that you've been, through my loss, and through getting back on the team, your genuine happiness for me, and the support you've shown... I could go on and on, honestly. But I'll get to the point. I want you to be my wife, Champ. Will you marry me?"

"*Yes,*" she blubbered immediately. "*Hell yes!*"

Her hands were shaking as I pulled the ring from the box to slide on her finger, then stood to pull her into my arms. Well, after I gently peeled that crown off her stomach.

As I kissed her, it really was like we were the only people there. I knew there were at least thirty camera phones on us, but all I wanted to do was love on the woman who'd just agreed to be my wife.

And apparently, she was thinking the same thing.

She was pressing herself into me more and more, her hands moving under my jersey to slide her fingers along my abs. My dick was responding enthusiastically to her little moans, and to her hands, and the heat of her body, and I pulled back from the kiss enough to announce, completely seriously, that, "Aiight, it's time for y'all to go home. Everybody. Get out. We'll see y'all later."

My statement was met with laughs, but Clayton and Soriyah were the ones who seemed to understand that I was serious. I pulled Wil back to the bedroom as they corralled everyone to leave, but stopped for a second, going back to confer with Clayton. Soriyah had flown in for this, as a surprise to Wil, and I didn't want her to feel slighted. Clayton said he would take care of it, making dinner arrangements for all of us, for a little later in the night, and making sure Soriyah got back to Connecticut okay.

When I went back to the room, I found Wil standing in the middle of the floor. One hand curved around her stomach, the other held up to the light, examining her new engagement ring with a look of pure joy.

"So you like it huh?" I asked, startling her a little.

She pressed her hand to her chest, and nodded. "Yes. I *love* it. I love *you*," she repeated, reaching up to pull her crown off as lust darkened her eyes.

"Nah," I said, catching her by the wrist. "You can keep that on."

Sixteen

Wil

February 2018

It felt like my "last hurrah".

Sure, there wasn't really a ton to do in friggin' *Minnesota* of all places, at least that couldn't be done in Connecticut or New York. But somehow, even in below freezing weather, this trip felt perfect.

The Kings were playing in the SuperBowl… what more could I ask for?

At 29 weeks pregnant, I was rapidly approaching the point where I wouldn't be able to travel anymore. Ramsey had been talking about getting on a plane to somewhere sunny, somewhere that would transport us back to the feeling we'd had in Bali, the day after the game, no matter the outcome.

It sounded amazing.

But nearly everywhere sunny had travel warnings for Zika virus for pregnant women. And though there were ways to protect myself, and lower the already low chances of something going wrong,

I was so protective of this pregnancy that I just couldn't settle into the idea. For his part, Ramsey gave me *zero* friction about it. There were other places to see, and other things to do.

Like winning the SuperBowl.

I'd promised the man a whole damned sheet of banana stickers, so he had *plenty* of motivation to go out on the field and do his part. While he was practicing and all of that, me, Soriyah, Clayton, and Naima, had been all over Minnesota. Ramsey – and Ashley, as part of the training team – had been there since the Monday before the game. The other four of us came a few days later.

Ashley had been able to join us every day, but Ramsey had only come once, opting to keep his head focused on the game. I didn't feel slighted by that – for three years on air together, Ramsey and I had talked about these things, the difference in players that spent the week partying, and those that spent the week anchoring themselves on the field. I hadn't even wondered which type of player Ramsey would be – *I knew.*

Having fun on his behalf had always been the plan, and we'd done it. Sight seeing, the Saint Paul Winter Carnival, all of that. Clayton didn't, in the least, mind being the only guy in our group – he actually seemed to thrive, being surrounded by "baddies", even though one of us was pregnant with his best friend's child, and two of us were only interested in each other. That left the only person to give him any returned interest was Soriyah, who I expected was the *real* reason Clayton had been so eager to "escort" us to Minneapolis, and to stick around.

He'd been a little too giddy when, at dinner after Ramsey's proposal, Soriyah had dropped the news that she was spending the next few months in the United States. She had a niece here, who'd been making waves in high school track, just with Soriyah's long-distance advice. Now, the opportunity had come to take things further, and Soriyah wanted to be more hands on with her.

And Clayton wanted to be more hands on with Soriyah.

He'd never even met her before the proposal, but the few days we were here, he hadn't left her side except to help me from a chair or into the car occasionally. Even now, in our box at SuperBowl, he was in her ear, flirting. I glanced over to where they were, and smiled to myself.

294

Clayton, with his smooth, dark chocolate skin and panty-dissolving grin was halfway out of his seat, leaning toward Soriyah. Even if that wasn't my friend, I would think she was gorgeous. Cinnamon complexion, an enviable head of thick dark brown natural hair, and big, almond shaped green eyes – a constant source of conversation when I was around her family. At least one person always told the story of her opening her eyes for the first time as a baby, and a collective shout going up around the room, wondering where in the world *those* had come from.

But Clayton was enthralled, and Soriyah was eating it up. I damn near felt bad for the man. I know he thought probably thought he was charming the hell out of Ri, but I knew better.

It was happening the other way around.

That's why I didn't feel bad when I stood up, grabbing her hand to get her attention. "I need to use the ladies room. Come with me," I said, and she shot a smile at Clayton that was apologetic, but turned mischievous as soon as she was facing me.

"Come on," she beckoned, and we headed to the semi-private restroom – elegantly maintained, with three stalls. After she checked that they were empty, she locked the door. I took the middle stall, swinging the door closed as she checked her face in the mirror.

"I'm feeling a little bamboozled, Wilhelmina. Why did you not tell me about this Clayton Reed character? I've known for months that I was coming, but if I'd known about him, I maybe would have done a few more squats," she complained in her melodic Caribbean accent, as if she weren't known for her perfect ass.

She'd come to a meeting at WAWG with me just last week, and after running into Braxton Drake himself, had been asked about a daily morning fitness show. Sure, Soriyah was still a very notable name – she'd beasted the Olympics in 2016, while I was sitting behind a desk reporting on them – so the offer wasn't *solely* based on her... assets. But we'd simply been walking down the hall, me with my pregnant waddle and sciatica, her in skinny jeans and high-heeled booties, when we'd heard the familiar "*Aye!*" of a man who saw something he liked.

Imagine our surprise to turn around and find ourselves facing two of the new network owners – Braxton, and his sister Nashira, who seemed exhausted with her brother's antics.

"Because Clayton is… Clayton," I called through the door, as I finished my task. "He's not exactly the *hey, so my man has this friend I think would be great for you*" type."

I opened the door to the stall to find Soriyah's eyebrows up, and her perfectly turned up nose looking *extra* haughty. "And *why* not? If you think I'm not touching a champagne flute to that man's dick to toast the Kings' win tonight, you don't know me at all."

I laughed at her craziness as I washed my hands. "Oh no, I've been expecting to hear about that since the two of you sat next to each other on the plane. I'm actually shocked it hasn't happened yet – he was *all* over you Friday night."

Soriyah grinned. That was the one night Ramsey had come out with us, and we'd managed to figure out where the black people in Minneapolis hung out. The presence of half of the Kings' starting roster had the crowd at the lounge excited – so excited that I was relieved at the well-secured VIP area where we stayed most of the night. Ramsey didn't do any drinking – in solidarity with me, and out of respect for the shape he would need to be in on Sunday – but the rest of our little crew had no such hangups.

Song, after song, after song, even after Ramsey and his teammates left to turn in early, Clayton and Soriyah were up under each other. The DJ did a whole little reggaeton section, and I thought Clayton was going to lose his mind behind the way Soriyah whined on him, undoubtedly creating a situation in his pants. But shortly after that, she'd gotten away from him, mischief all over her face as she insisted it was too late for me to be out.

He didn't see it coming yet, but there was no way she was going to leave him with his pride.

Soriyah picked up one of the thick disposable hand towels from the tray on the sink and handed it to me. "Just because I planned to screw him from the time I laid eyes on him does *not* mean he shouldn't still work for it."

"Very true," I laughed. "So long as you remember to put a saddle on that horse."

"Of course," she readily agreed. "Wouldn't want to be in your state six months from now, pregnant and engaged, because you know I won't be able to get rid of him. A man like Clayton! Could you imagine?"

296

I knew her words were harmless – she was *unquestionably* happy for me, excited about the baby, loved Ramsey, all of that. But… her words played on an insecurity I'd been struggling with, ever since the proposal. Absently, I scratched at my hand, fingering the diamond that accented the rose gold band. Such a beautiful, perfect ring, that I loved, and was proud to wear… mostly. It was just that…

"Do you think I did this too fast?" I asked, my first time expressing it out loud to Ri. I hadn't even said anything to my mother and she'd been all over me, based on the conversation we'd had at her house, warning me not to overthink the "too fast" thing. But, *seriously*. "In two months, it'll be April again. What was supposed to be my one year anniversary, with Darius. And don't get me wrong, I'm way past tripping on that. I'm not sad about it, I *love* my life right now. I just… of course people have been saying ugly things, it comes with the territory of being in the public eye. But it's been said a lot that Ramsey only proposed because I was pregnant."

"That's bullshit."

I scoffed. "Oh, I *know* that, because I *know* Ramsey. He wants me to be his wife, that's without question, in my mind. And I want him to be my husband. With every part of me, I feel like *he* is my one, my destiny, but I can't help wondering… if I weren't pregnant, would I have said yes? Not even a year after this other thing ended, if I weren't carrying a Bishop in my belly, would I have said *yes*… or would I have pepper sprayed his ass, because this is *crazy*."

"Why does it matter?" Soriyah said, waving me off. "Wait. Back up. I don't mean to sound as if I think your concern isn't valid, or that you shouldn't spend time in self-examination, thinking through the course of your action, but… it *doesn't* matter. I know you're just talking to me, getting it out of your head. But that's exactly where *this* should stay – *out*. These hypothetical scenarios aren't good for much of anything outside of causing unnecessary stress. Are you about to give the ring back, call the engagement off?"

"What?" I took a step back, protectively covering my ring. "*Hell no!*"

"Then who gives a shit what you would've said if you weren't pregnant? You were *very* pregnant. And you said yes. Because that man out there running people over in the name of this silly violent sport is the love of your life. So what is your purpose, girl?"

"My *purpose* is making sure that I'm doing this for the right reasons. I was so upset about how it seemed like life just wouldn't stop kicking me in the ass. Publicly cheated on and humiliated, conned out of my job, privacy violated, unexpected pregnancy. But then my mother helped me shift my perspective. I accepted everything, focused on the positive that came from it all... I'm well on my way to the career I wanted, I'm finally going to have a baby, and I am *all the way* in love. And I just *wonder* if so eagerly accepting such a fast proposal – just seven months after we became more than friends – is my way of trying... hurry up and get to where I thought I'd be. Career. Husband. Baby."

Soriyah's eyes narrowed, and then she chuckled. "O-kay. Let me see if I have this right. This man proposed to you – asked you to be his wife – and you are wondering if you are taking advantage by saying yes."

I planted my hands against my lower back, trying to give a little support, since I'd put it through paces this week, with all the running around we'd done. "Yes."

"And this sounds reasonable, to your ears? This has to be another of these American things, having so few *real* problems that you have to invent some, so you are not bored. My God, Wil. The Jamaicans, they have this saying that American tourists love to spout in the Bahamas, for some reason. *It's irie, mon.* It's all good. Relax."

"You know you didn't have to go in on me like that just now, right?"

"I think maybe I did. Are you good now?"

I sucked my teeth. "Aside from feeling stupid now, yeah I guess."

"Don't be mad at me Willy," she sang, looping her arm through mine as we left the bathroom for our private box. "It's just, you're mostly back to Little Miss Sunshine, and I can't have you slipping back. Embrace these good things happening for you."

We must have lost track of time in the bathroom, because we came back to the box just in time to see the Kings down by four, with only enough time left in the game for a single play. When we stepped out, they were ahead, which a good amount of time left in the game. Dread rocked my stomach as I watched them line up, trying to figure out the impossible – what they were about to do.

298

This time last year, the Kings were under similar conditions, and they had walked away from the field defeated. My eyes went over to Cole, who was up on her feet with the other execs, hands clutched in front of her chest. Last season, Jordan hadn't *walked* off the field at all.

My attention returned to the game as the players broke away, into an "I" formation. As Jordan moved into position at Trent's direction, my heart dropped.

No. No!

They were at the goddamn one-yard line, and Ramsey had been a beast on the field all day! Why the hell would they risk a pass? I watched, helpless, as the red-clad Kansas City players descended on Jordan, already having read the scene, and ready to disrupt the play attempt that would cost them the "champion" name.

A sudden, collective gasp went up around the room, and I realized my mistake as my eyes scanned the field. I'd been so busy watching Jordan – by design – that I hadn't noticed the ball getting handed off to Ramsey.

But I *absolutely* noticed as first one foot, then the other stepped into the endzone, with the ball tucked securely under his arm. Me, the rest of the box, and what seemed like the whole stadium went up at the same time. It was so loud that I could barely hear *myself* screaming about the fact that Ramsey – *my Ramsey* – had been the one to make the game-winning play.

I couldn't even see him anymore – he was buried in the middle of a crush of his teammates, and the field was filling up with people, fast. Half our box was gone, barely thirty seconds after the game was over, wanting to make it to the field for congratulations. When I glanced around and didn't see Cole, I assumed she was already on her way down there. Even the baby excited apparently, making me flinch as it pushed down into my pelvis, creating a lingering pressure that made me feel a little sick.

But that was okay.

We'd won.

He'd won.

"Let's meet him in the locker room," Naima urged, hooking an arm around my waist. I didn't even know I was crying until she wiped my face.

Happy tears.

We were *all* giddy though, shaking hands and fist bumping and hugging like *we* had been the ones on the field. Ashley was down with the team, helping treat the in-game injuries, so it was just me, Soriyah, Clayton, and Naima. Soriyah and Clayton led the way, with me and Naima behind them. We'd just gotten past the doorway to the box when a sudden wave of dizziness hit me, followed shortly by a feeling like my stomach was turning inside out.

I cringed, reflexively cupping my belly, and Naima's arm tightened around me.

"Hey," she said, concerned. "You good?"

I nodded, even though I was honestly feeling fuzzy. "Yeah. I think… maybe I just got a little too excited. And it was so loud, all the noise. I'm okay."

"No, I think we should sit down for a minute," Clayton said, having stopped and turned around when he noticed what was happening. "Let you get your bearings."

"I'm good," I insisted, shaking my head. "My man just won the damn Super Bowl – I *need* too see—*ahhhh*," I hissed, involuntarily bending at the waist as something like a cramp ripped through my pelvis. I reached in front me, trying to find support, and Clayton and Soriyah rushed to give it, one on each side, helping a struggling Naima to keep me upright.

"What is it?" Naima's voice was pleading in my ear as I closed my eyes. "Tell us what's going on."

My eyelids felt heavy, tongue seemed glued to the roof of my mouth as I struggled through the steady, excruciating discomfort to explain.

"*P-pain,*" I wheezed, digging my fingers into Clayton's arm. "Like cramps."

"*Shit,*" Soriyah cursed. "Wil. *Wil.* Look at me. Open your eyes, and look at me. Listen," she said, when I finally did.

"You *cannot* have this baby right now."

RAMSEY

"Ramsey Bishop," the reporter started, yelling over the sounds of screaming fans. There was blue and gold confetti covering everything, stuck to my face, stuck to her face, but I wasn't bothered. *Nothing* could bother me right now. "The whole country wants to know – exactly how amazing do you feel right now?"

I laughed at the question. "I... honestly can't even put it into words. Can't begin to describe it."

"Totally understandable. This was a tough game for both teams tonight, with no major leads for either side of the field. It seemed as every single point out there was a battle this time, but your stats prove that you more than carried your weight. Twenty-three carries for 117 yards before that last, game-winning play. How did you pull this off?"

I shook my head. "I can't possibly take that credit, Kendra. Trent took that hit in the third quarter, and still came back to the field ready to put this thing to bed. Jordan lived up to that "The Flash" nickname with ever play. This whole team, honestly – we came out here to make our fans, family, and friends proud today, and we delivered on that. These guys embraced me as a last-minute addition to their team, making me feel welcome, and I'm just glad I was able to play in a way that contributes to the Connecticut Kings name in a positive way."

"Is that a reference to some of the negative talk around your preseason performance?"

"It is."

Kendra Fulton, who'd been my colleague for years as a journalist, smiled. "This was quite a way to put a muzzle on your naysayers, some of whom thought you should have stuck to talking about football rather than playing it. In an exclusive interview with Wil Cunningham, you spoke about feeling that you'd lost your hunger for the game after the unfortunate passing of your lovely mother. Many felt that you should have remained retired if you couldn't find the passion to play at your pre-retirement levels, but you've *obviously* regained your mojo. Where does it come from?"

301

"My fiancé. My child. My mother's memory. This team. Pre-season was a long six months ago, Kendra. A lot has changed."

"Obviously," she grinned. "Thanks for talking with me Ramsey, and again, congratulations! I'm sure your friends and family are waiting to celebrate with you."

I gave Kendra a nod, then headed through the crush of people shouting, dancing, and whatever else. Anybody who tried to stop and talk to me got a hand toss or a nod – I wasn't trying to be rude. I was trying to get to my lady.

There was no way she was going out to the field amongst all those people, especially after she'd been complaining about a backache since that morning. If I knew Wil, she and the rest of the crew were waiting in or near the locker rooms, so that was where I headed. Or *was* headed, until I heard my name and one of the physical therapists – and Naima's girlfriend – Ashley came rushing up to me, out of breath.

"There you are!" she said, grabbing me by the arm to pull me in the opposite direction, but I planted my feet.

"Hey, what's going on?" I asked, tugging her in front of me so I could see her face. "Where are you taking me."

She glanced around first, plastering a smile on her face as a group of my teammates passed us, slapping me on the back. Then, she leaned in, to quietly tell me, "Naima was blowing up my phone, frantic. They had to take Wil to the hospital."

"For *what*?" I growled, suddenly understanding her urgency. And from the look on her face – like she barely wanted to tell me – I knew it had to be serious.

"They think she's in premature labor, but this was a few minutes ago, and they were pulling up to the hospital then. Maybe they know more now."

My eyes bugged out. "A few minutes ago?! How long is a few minutes? Why didn't somebody tell me as soon as it happened!?"

"I'm telling you *now*! Whatever happened, it was right after the game, and I've been trying to get to you, through all those people on the field, and then I get there, and you're gone."

"Right," I nodded, then swiped a hand over my head. "Sorry for snapping at you—"

"You're good, I get it," she assured me, then grabbed my arm again. "Now, come on. Your security is waiting to get you to the hospital."

My heart was racing as I rushed through the doors of Hennepin County Medical Center, not caring even a little about the stares I was getting in my muddy, grass-stained uniform. A call to Clayton from the car had confirmed a fear I didn't even know I had – premature labor.

Wil was only 29 weeks pregnant.

But this hospital could handle it, I was assured, as soon I shoved open the doors to the birth center. I was stopped outside of Wil's room by a nurse – a tiny woman I really wanted to shove out of the way for blocking my access to the only person I cared to see. At Clayton and Soriyah's insistence, I chilled, comforting myself with the fact that at least Naima was in there with her while… whatever was happening, happened. At least she wasn't alone.

After several restless minutes, I took myself into a corner for a quiet moment of prayer, supplementing the pleading I'd already done in the car. Dre brought up a bag for me, and I gave in to the pressure to use an empty room to shower and change into clean clothes.

The door to Wil's room opened right as I was stepping back into the waiting room.

"Is Ramsey here?" the doctor asked, holding the door open. I practically sprinted up to her, and she smiled. "Come on in."

Naima stepped out as I came in, and I tried to take heart in the fact that the situation didn't seem to be an emergency anymore. But Wil… she looked so helpless laying there, with an oxygen mask clipped to her face and IVs connected to her arm.

"So we had a little scare, didn't we?" Dr. Page according to the pin on her lapel, asked. "To update you, Ramsey, Ms. Cunningham went into spontaneous premature labor today, but because we need your little one to cook for at least a few more weeks, we intervened to stop it. The drug we're using is actually an anti-hypertensive, but what it does for pregnant women is keep your uterus from contracting, which is what we have here. Your cervix has opened a little, but not enough that I'm worried about you. As soon as you get home though, I want you to go see your regular doctor."

My shoulders sank in relief. "So she's going home, still pregnant?"

"Yes," Dr. Page smiled. "We'll keep you here for today," she said, touching Wil's leg, "But I'm confident that we've gotten you on a strong enough pause to get home. And we ran tests that look for a specific protein in your vaginal secretions that would clue us in or whether or not this baby was coming, an FFN test. Your results were negative, so... you can breathe. And actually," she glanced at monitors – one tracking Wil's vital signs, the other tracking the baby's – "you really *can* breathe. You and baby are stable enough that you can take that oxygen mask off now."

Wil did so immediately, unceremoniously tossing the thing away from her. "Do you know why this happened? It's because I've been doing too much this week, isn't it? Flying out here, and shopping, and festivals, and the club, and... Ramsey, I'm *so* sorry," she sobbed, seemingly out of nowhere, covering her face with her hands.

My first move was to grab her hand as I stepped closer, gently pulling her upper half toward me so I could wrap my arms around her. "Wil, come on. You *know* I'm not blaming you for this, right?"

"Good," Dr. Page said, as she grabbed Wil's other hand. "Because none of that sounds like any sort of abnormal activity. Contrary to popular belief, pregnant women don't necessarily have to "take it easy" just because they're pregnant. Some of my patients hike, and run marathons, all sorts of things. You did *not* go into premature labor because you were having fun."

"Then *why?*" Wil sniffled, trying to calm herself down.

"You aren't going to like this answer, but we may honestly never know. We're still waiting on test results, but it could be something as simple as a urinary tract infection that wasn't even causing symptoms, or it could be a cervical flaw, an irritable uterus. Or it could have just *happened*, because the human body is complex, and sometimes baffling. We'll get you an answer to that if we can, but the important thing to know is that you, and your baby, are both healthy."

I pushed out a sigh. "That's what I needed to hear."

304

"What if it doesn't work?" Wil asked, squeezing my fingers. "The drugs, to stop the labor. What if ten minutes from now I'm having contractions again?"

"If that happens, we'll try something else. If *that* doesn't work... we'll attempt to slow the labor long enough to administer corticosteroids to help your baby's lungs develop as much as we can, and then we will do the safest possible delivery. This hospital has a level four NICU, and some amazing doctors and nurses. You and your baby will be in excellent hands."

After a few more questions, the doctor left, and it was just me and Wil in the room. I started to speak, but then the door opened again, and the nurse that had kept me from coming in before eased in.

"I was just coming to see if you two needed anything? Pillows, blankets, anything to make you more comfortable?"

I looked to Wil, who shook her head, and then turned back to the nurse. "No, not right now, but thank you."

"Hungry or anything?" the nurse persisted. "Mommy can only have ice chips for now, but we were all around the nurse's station wondering if... the Super Bowl champion needed anything?"

I was smiling before I could help it, and Wil rolled her eyes as I laughed. "No, but thank you, seriously."

"You sure? Not even just the hospital food, one of us can run up the street and grab you something. There are three of us who are *huge* Kings fans. That *touchdown?*" she stepped forward with her fist extended, and I returned the gesture, bumping it with mine. "You let us know if you all need anything," she said, patting my shoulder as she bustled out, obviously giddy.

I was glad she hadn't made that encounter a single second longer, because Wil's expression was... displeased. I scooted the chair I'd dropped into even closer, and tried to engage her.

"Hey... you know JJ told me the nurses were like that with him last year, down in Texas. Remember, he went to the hospital after the Super Bowl too."

She scoffed. "Yeah, but at least that was for his own injury, after they lost. He probably *wanted* to be lowkey. His team wasn't off celebrating without him because his pregnant fiancé landed herself in the hospital. Hell – he wasn't even saddled with a fiancé at all."

"But he is now," I told her, grinning. "You must not have been paying attention to the TV."

The one in her room was on now, with the sound off, replaying the video footage of Jordan proposing to Cole on the field after the game, something I hadn't even realized was happening at the time. Dre had told me about it in the car on the way, attempting to give me a distraction. I was doing the same thing with the information now, and was glad when the distress on Wil's face gave way to a smile.

"No, I didn't realize," she murmured. "I was… a little busy."

I nodded. "Yeah. But, just so we're clear, there's nowhere I'd rather be right now. I can party any time. The Kings are the official champions, until next year. There will be *plenty* of time for celebration."

"Yeah, but you should've been able to have *this* time," she said, laying back on her pillows. "You've worked hard for this."

"I've worked hard for *this*," I corrected her, laying a hand on her belly. "There is nothing in this world more important to me than the knowledge that two of you are okay."

She sighed. "Yeah, and look at what *I* do, running around this city like I'm not six months pregnant."

"Stop it. She *just* said this didn't happen because you did something wrong."

"And what the *fuck* do they know?!" she snapped. "They always spout that bullshit, *we don't know, sometimes things just happen*. I lose two babies, they can't give me a goddamn answer, can't get pregnant, can't get an answer for *that* either. Why the hell should I believe them now?"

"Because God doesn't break promises, Wil," I told her, simply. "You remember that day I felt the baby move, you told me that it was a manifestation of my mother's dreams for me. Her and God, working in tandem. You remember that?"

She grudgingly nodded. "Yes."

"Okay then. I *know* you don't think that was only for me? Like there wasn't a blessing for you in the equation. That your pain was invisible or something. He *sees* you. Maybe neither of us prays like we should, or attends service like we should, but I promise you that doesn't mean we're exempt from what he has for us. Those things you said to me that day… you believe that?"

"Yes, absolutely."

"Then it's not about believing them. It's about believing *him*. If he said that you and this child are my destiny, nothing is taking that away. Okay?"

Wil sniffled again, and I reached up to wipe tears from her cheeks as she nodded. "Okay."

"You good now?"

"No," she shook her head, but managed to laugh. "I will be though. I want to talk about you. You made the play that *won the SuperBowl*. And put me into labor, according to Ri."

"Ah, damn," I laughed. "That's what we're doing?"

She nodded. "That's what *they* are doing. Her and Clayton cracked jokes and flirted the whole ride to the hospital. Their antics were actually a nice distraction."

"Do I need to get them back in here?"

"No," she murmured. "I'm tired, but maybe later. I know you're tired too, but can you just sit with me, a little longer?"

Her eyes were already closing, probably a combination of exhaustion from the day, and whatever was churning through those IVs. I leaned in, pressing a kiss to her forehead.

"You didn't even have to ask."

I must've been as tired as she was, because I dozed off, waking up maybe an hour later to a lot of noise in the hall, a loud "*shhhhh!!!*" and then a disproportionately soft knock at the door. Frowning, I got up to open it, only to end up immediately yanked out. I balled my fists up as I snatched away, ready to throw hands.

But then I realized I was surrounded by my teammates.

"Get in here nigga!" somebody said, and somebody else put a hat on my head – probably the same one the rest of them were wearing, declaring us the latest NFL champions. Eli Richardson himself held out the heavy trophy to me, urging me to take it onto my hands as cell phones went up around me.

"The nurses are fans, but they told us to make it quick," Eli laughed, as I clutched the trophy to my chest. "You did the right thing, coming to see about your family, but you earned this moment, son. We wanted to make sure you got it."

I burst out laughing at some wise ass started blasting audio of the screaming crowd from his phone, and somebody tossed up a handful of confetti. In no time, the nurses were all over us – it was still a maternity ward – kicking people out.

I tucked the trophy under one arm, shifting so that I could shake Eli's hand. What I'd told Wil was the truth – there was nothing more important than making sure she and the baby were okay, but I realized now… I'd *needed* this moment.

"Thank you for believing in me," I told him, nodding.

"Thank *you* for not letting this team down."

Wil

March 2018

"This is the day. This is the day. This is day," I sang in front of the mirror, doing a very, *very* gentle two-step to music that only existed in my head. Ramsey laughed as he slid his feet into his shoes, then stood to approach me.

"Damn, baby. You don't seem excited at *all*," he teased, kissing the side of my neck before he continued to the dresser, where his tie was.

I giggled. "How could I *not* be?! We're gonna find out if we're having a boy or girl today, which makes closing on the house next week *that* much more exciting!"

"Why?"

"*Because!* Then, I can spend these last 5 weeks before my due date decorating the nursery. I can't wait to start picking things out."

Ramsey frowned. "Wait… I thought you had everything all picked out? Yellow, gray, and turquoise, gender neutral. No pink princess clothes for a baby girl, no big trucks for a baby boy, fighting gender norms and all that?"

308

I waved him off. "Oh screw that. After all the stress I've been through with this little gummy bear, we're wearing *all* the frills, *all* the dinosaurs, *all* until he or she is old enough to say, "pink is really not my color", okay?"

He threw his head back and laughed as he finished with his tie, a gorgeous silk paisley one I'd bought him, and had been thrilled he actually liked. It was a blend of light neutrals, tan and gray and white, and I'd chosen a dress for today – baby shower day – that vaguely matched. We were a few days out from spring, but the gauzy watercolor print, in gray and white, was perfect for today. Once we found out which gender, I'd get a sash around my waist in the color that matched the décor Soriyah and Naima had come up with – either teal or coral.

"I'm glad to hear you say that," he told me, stopping to watch me put the last touches on my hair. "Not going to lie – I've been remembering how adorable Alexis was as a baby, when Chloe would put all those big ass flower headbands and stuff on her, and sweating a little bit."

I stopped, and turned to look at him. "Sweating? For what?"

"Thinking about how ugly our fight was going to be when I came home with a bin full of hairbows if this baby is a girl. You were gonna let my baby be fashionable, goddamnit."

A snort of laughter came out of me before I could help it, and the next thing I knew, I was laughing so hard I was crying – because Ramsey was serious as hell, even though he was laughing too.

Eventually, he took me in his arms, and I leaned on him for support, glad to take some of the pressure off my aching feet. I'd been dealing with low back pain for the last two days as well, and after standing for so long to get ready, it felt good to brace against him.

"*Mmmm,*" I groaned, as low pain started in my belly.

"You okay?" he asked, and I nodded.

"Yeah. Probably just Braxton-Hicks again," I said, rolling my eyes as I referred to the false labor contractions that had sent us rushing to the hospital again just last week.

We'd been three times since getting back from Minneapolis. Once, I'd had to have my labor stopped again, but the other two times were true false alarms. Based on how I was feeling, this was another of those false alarms.

If it wasn't, Soriyah was going to kill me. She'd put a ton of effort into this shower, and according to her words before she'd left this morning after having breakfast with us, it was going to be amazing.

"We can sit down for a minute," Ramsey offered. "Nobody's going to be mad if we're a little late."

I thought about it for a moment, then nodded. "Actually, yeah. Maybe just for a minute."

We'd only take a couple of steps before I stopped, frozen in place.

"What's wrong?" Ramsey asked, holding on to my arms. "Is it another cramp?"

I shook my head. "No," I whined as my face grew hot with embarrassment. "I… I think I just… I peed on myself."

"What?!" Ramsey took a half step back, looking me over. "I don't see any—"

"Not like a *lot*," I hissed. "But I definitely just soaked my panties, ugh. I didn't even feel like I *needed* to pee."

But, on the other hand, since the baby had decided its favorite place was resting low on my pelvis, head on my bladder, feet in my back, it wasn't as if I had a great handle on what I was feeling down there anyway.

I took another step, toward the bathroom this time, to wash up and change, but I felt the same thing as before – a subtle gush of liquid.

Shit.

I squeezed my thighs together as I pulled away from Ramsey, awkwardly attempting to "rush" to the bathroom that way. But every time I moved, there was more and more, and I realized I was *really* about to find out if this man loved me today.

If he could take literally *watching* me piss myself, he could take anything.

"Wil!" he called out.

"I know, it's disgusting. I can't help it!" I cried.

But when I looked back at him, it wasn't disgust on his face – it was confusion, and concern. I followed his line of sight to the floor, where I realized why. It wasn't really visible on the hardwood in the bedroom, but against the marble of the bathroom, you could tell.

I wasn't having an incontinence issue. Whatever was currently dripping down my legs was... *pink*. But that meant...

"Shit."

"Shit?" Ramsey asked. "Why shit? Talk to me, what's happening?!"

"*Shit*, because that is amniotic fluid. My *water*, Ramsey. It's broken."

He lifted his hands to head, eyes wide. "Oh. *Shit*. This... is not how it happens in movies."

"No shit, Ramsey. We gotta—"

"Yes! Yeah, right! I'll grab your bag, and we'll go, and call Dr. Cho on the way. You can text everybody else on the way."

"Okay."

He nodded. "Okay. I'll grab the bag and stuff."

He darted out of the room, and was gone for one, then two, then five minutes, as I grabbed a few towels, tucking one between my legs before I gingerly moved to throw the others on the floor, to soak up my "accident".

Finally, he came rushing back in the room, out of breath.

"What took you so long?" I asked, and he shook his head before letting out a dry laugh.

"Well," he said, wrapping an arm around my waist, "... I was on the way to the hospital, and then I realized... you probably need the pregnant woman, fool."

I burst out laughing, cupping a hand over my mouth to try to make myself stop when the action sent a fresh gush of water rushing out. My laughter was easily killed ten seconds later, when a pain that made every other pain I'd ever felt seem... mild.

"Holy *shit*, when did you get this strong?!" Ramsey asked as I dug my fingers into his arm, trying to offset the pain. It lasted for what seemed like almost a minute before it let up, and I was finally able to breathe.

"Ramsey... this is it," I wheezed. "For real this time."

He grinned. "We're about to have a baby?"

"Yeah. We're about to have a baby."

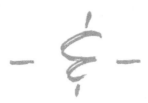

"Thank you."

I looked up from the baby attached to my breast – asleep, but I didn't have the heart to pull away – to meet Ramsey's gaze. He was as shirtless as I was, having passed the baby to me after their "skin to skin" moment.

The NICU nurses had encouraged that.

Ramsey had actually been the one to do the feeding – my milk hadn't come in yet, and neither had baby's mouth control, to breastfeed properly. But the nurses had still encouraged us to try, just to get both of us used to it, so that's what I'd been doing after every feeding, since yesterday.

We had time, though. Even though it was a late preterm birth, it was *still* preterm. They said maybe a two week stay, but I was hoping it wouldn't be quite that long.

"For what?" I asked Ramsey, biting my lip to keep from grinning at the obvious adoration in his eyes.

He chuckled a little, like the answer was obvious, then reached forward, peeling back the blanket a little bit to peek inside. Then, he leaned in, pressing a soft kiss to my lips. "For my son, Champ. That's what."

I gave up on trying to hold it – I openly smiled, scooting a little so that he could sit beside me on the tiny loveseat. "You're welcome, but... no. Thank *you.*"

"For what?"

RJ finally pulled back on his own, perfect little lips moving feverishly for a second before he slipped back into sleep. "For being a man I could proudly name him after."

We had other names picked out. Names that were so obviously wrong now that I couldn't even bring them to mind. As soon as I laid eyes on his little face, it was obvious that he was supposed to be named after his father.

Once we arrived at the hospital, things went fast. *Crazy* fast. Less than two hours after I got to the hospital, I was pushing, no time to administer an epidural, with my water already broken, and cervix dilating so fast.

Afterwards, I sobbed over the fact that RJ had to be rushed off to the NICU to get a full exam, to make sure he was okay. I'd gotten to hold his little wet, screaming self for maybe a minute before they whisked him away. With tears in his eyes, Ramsey had stood over the bed and met my gaze as he grabbed my hands.

"I didn't think I could love you more, and then you did this. Like a Champ."

After that, I was mostly okay.

And *now*, I was all the way okay. Better than that, in fact. I shifted my position so that I was leaning into Ramsey, and he wrapped his arms around both of us.

Nothing could top this.

When I'd been given my April due date, a part of me felt like it was my chance to create a new memory for that month, so I wouldn't find myself wallowing in the shadow of what was supposed to be my wedding date. Now, I realized how little that mattered when I had everything I wanted. Maybe the day would pass without me noticing it at all, and… maybe I *would* feel a little down. But ultimately, everything about my life was better than it would have been if those plans had gone forth.

I'd *never* been happier for an interception.

I closed my eyes, relaxing into the comfort of Ramsey's arms. I had to relish it while I could, because the nurses would be coming in soon to check on RJ, and make sure he was maintaining his temperature and vitals, which would keep him out of the NICU. But for now, this was perfect. Even with everything thrown my way over the last year… I felt like I'd won.

I tilted my head back at Ramsey and grinned, laughing when he smiled back.

"What?" he asked, and my smile grew a little wider.

"Touchdown."

- the end -

Christina C. Jones is a modern romance novelist who has penned more than 25 books. She has earned a reputation as a storyteller who seamlessly weaves the complexities of modern life into captivating tales of black romance.
Prior to her work as a full-time writer, Christina successfully ran Visual Luxe, a digital creative design studio. Coupling a burning passion for writing and the drive to hone her craft, Christina made the transition to writing full-time in 2014.

Christina has attracted a community of enthusiastic readers across the globe who continue to read and share her sweet, sexy, and sometimes scandalous stories.
Most recently, two of Christina's book series have been optioned for film and television projects and are currently in development.

Other titles by Christina Jones
Love and Other Things
Haunted (paranormal)
Mine Tonight (erotica)
Hints of Spice (Highlight Reel spinoff)
The Truth – His Side, Her Side, And the Truth About Falling In Love
Friends & Lovers:
Finding Forever
Chasing Commitment
Strictly Professional:
Strictly Professional
Unfinished Business
Serendipitous Love:
A Crazy Little Thing Called Love
Didn't Mean To Love You
Fall In Love Again

Made in the USA
Monee, IL
17 December 2020